W9-AGK-328

Good

DATE DUE

DE 16 '97			
JA 09 '98			
JA 27 '98			
MR 12 '98			
3/28			
AP 15 '98			
MY 06 '98			
MY 17 '98			
JU 2'98			

DEMCO

To my Parents,
Charles and Elizabeth Coulter

FIELD OF DISHONOR

Henrietta stood on the damp grass as the mist
dissolved in the light of dawn. In her hand she held a
razor-sharp rapier, swishing it in the air before her
to test its weight.

Across the expanse of field that separated her and
her foe, she saw the powerful figure of Lord Jason
Cavender standing erect, rapier in hand and a smile
mocking what he believed to be the hotheaded
stripling who dared challenge him.

This was the moment that Henrietta had been
waiting for. The crowning triumph of her
masquerade as a man. Her moment of truth.

Would she die at the hands of the most dangerous
duelist in England?

Or could she bring herself to plunge her sword into
this man who already had used a different kind of
weapon to penetrate her heart . . . ?

LORD HARRY'S FOLLY

Lord Harry's Folly

by
Catherine Coulter

SEVERN
SH
HOUSE

This title first published in Great Britain 1992 by
SEVERN HOUSE PUBLISHERS LTD of
35 Manor Road, Wallington, Surrey SM6 0BW
This first hardcover edition published in the USA 1993 by
SEVERN HOUSE PUBLISHERS INC of
475 Fifth Avenue, New York, NY 10017
by arrangement with New American Library,
a division of Penguin Books USA Inc.

British Library Cataloguing in Publication Data
Coulter, Catherine
    Lord Harry's Folly
    I. Title
    813.54 [F]

    ISBN 0-7278-4391-5

Printed and bound in Great Britain by
Dotesios Limited, Trowbridge, Wiltshire

1

"Lord Harry! Lord Harry! Are you yet attired? Your friends grow impatient!" Pottson pressed his ear to the closed door to hear the reply, for he could not enter unless given permission.

Lord Harry twitched the snowy cravat into a creditable semblance of a style affected by Lord Alvaney. "I am ready, Pottson, you may come in."

Although of a certainty Mr. Scuddimore and Sir Harry Brandon were comfortably seated near the fireplace in the small parlour down the hall, Pottson gazed back to assure himself of this fact before entering Lord Harry's bedroom.

He stood on the threshhold and critically eyed Lord Harry's appearance, as was his habit and duty. " 'Tis quite an accomplished dandy you've become," he said with a humourless grin after inspecting Lord Harry's shining black hessians, fawn breeches and Weston coat of superfine buff. "And just what would that creation be called?" He sniffed, his eyes flitting from the white starched cravat about Lord Harry's neck to the half dozen mangled failures discarded on the dresser top.

"I call it Lord Alvaney's Fall, Pottson. I have been practicing for hours at home. I don't think I've done too badly. I drew a quick sketch of his lordship's cravat at White's one afternoon. Hopefully, the gentleman in question did not notice. And I've changed the style sufficiently so that he should not recognize it as his own." Lord Harry followed Pottson's disgruntled gaze to the hopelessly rumpled cravats he had thrown aside and grinned ruefully. "Not more than six or eight cravats *manqué*. I have heard it said that the Beau rarely achieved perfection before his twelfth try!"

"Well, that don't make it any less work cleaning up after you." Pottson shook his grizzled grey head. "At least you don't go trying to ape those tight knit pantaloons the gentlemen wear. You still have the good sense for that, I hope." Pottson's grumbling and admonishments had grown markedly less severe with repetition.

Lord Harry gave a hearty laugh, perhaps a trifle high in pitch for a gentleman grown, but certainly passable for a

1

young buck of nineteen or twenty. "I am not such a fool! Of course, Scuddy and Sir Harry are forever twitting me about my abominably fitting breeches. They think me still a rustic in my tastes. 'Tis just as well."

There was a loud knock on the bedroom door and both Lord Harry and Pottson whirled about in consternation. "Ho, Harry," came an aggrieved voice, "we are already late for the first act. Dawdle much longer, you young fop, and we will come in and drag you out!"

"Go about your business, Harry! I shall be ready in a trice."

Pottson groaned aloud and mopped his forehead with a discarded cravat, but only after he was certain that he heard retreating footsteps from the bedroom door. " 'Tis an old man you're making of me, Lord Harry. My heart nearly bounded into my throat!"

Lord Harry grinned and patted Pottson on the arm. "You're already a twitchety old man! Come on, now, we've come through unscathed so far. Trust me to carry it off. For God's sake, Pottson, hide that wretched gown!"

After one final look in the mirror to ensure that the buff coat and the fawn breeches did not show off the wearer's figure, Lord Harry proffered a mock bow to the ruminating Pottson. "Do stop fussing so! I shall try not to be too late tonight." After a brief pause, Lord Harry added significantly, "Lord Cavander is returned just recently to London." Lord Harry's voice grew chill. "It's been eight months that he was away, Pottson. Undoubtedly, he was loath to leave Italy and the plump arms of willing Italian ladies, who assisted his grace to assuage his grief for his dead wife. Certainly since his return to London, he has wasted no time. I, myself, have seen him in the company of a beautiful new mistress. 'Tis even possible that he and his lovely new ladybird will be at Drury Lane tonight."

This bit of information produced another groan from Pottson.

Lord Harry's mouth drew upward into a twisted grin and he clapped his distressed valet on the shoulder. "There can be no going back now, Pottson. Finally, the plot thickens. Remember what Damien used to say: 'Many a battle was lost because the generals were scurrying the other way!' I shall soon have the first close look at our enemy."

"Take care," Pottson entreated, knowing there was little more he could say in the face of the cold determination that glittered from Lord Harry's eyes.

2

Lord Harry waved a negligent hand and sauntered from the room with a swagger of a young gentleman bent on an evening's pleasure.

It was not many minutes after Lord Harry had entered the hired hackney with Sir Harry and Mr. Scuddimore that his mood of gay insouciance dimmed, his thoughts returning to Lord Cavander.

"Never seen you so sunk into silence before, Lord Harry," Mr. Scuddimore said, as the silence grew overlong. "What the devil ails you?"

Lord Harry looked up to see his chubby friend regarding him closely in the dim carriage light. "Not a thing, I assure you, Scuddy, not a thing. I was just thinking about the first time I was come to London—not above four months ago, you know. Unlike you and Harry here, I am not yet jaded by all the marvels."

Sir Harry Brandon tapped his cane on Lord Harry's knee. "'Tis not at all the thing in any case, old fellow. Scuddy's perfectly right there. Don't want to get the reputation of being a dead bore! You'd be dashed to the rocks in a fortnight! Shows you're a rustic, you know." He sat back against the soft swabs and took in his friend's appearance, his blue eyes narrowing with distaste.

"Really, Lord Harry, you must allow us to go with you to Weston's. Pottson's a good valet, but it's naught he can do if you don't give him the proper-fitting clothes to work with. I am shocked that any of Weston's fellows would make a coat that hangs off the shoulders in such a way."

Mr. Scuddimore, who was not attending to Sir Harry's admonishments on fashion, laughed suddenly.

Sir Harry, offended by his friend's mirth, declared, "Damned good advice, Scuddy. Lord Harry here—"

Mr. Scuddimore succumbed once again to a throaty giggle. "No offense, Harry, it's just that I still can't get used to you being a plain Harry and Harry being a *Lord* Harry! Damned amusing, I think."

Sir Harry said in the tone of one instructing a slow, yet good-natured child, "Scuddy, I've told you several times how it must be. I am a mere baronet and Lord Harry here is the son of a baron, or a Scottish laird—something outlandish like that! In any case, the both of us can't be Harrys—damned confusing that would be! Since Lord Harry is of higher rank, it's only right that he be the 'lord' and I simply a 'Harry.' I know you ain't a strong one in your mental works, Scuddy,

3

but I swear, if you bring this up one more time, I'll proclaim you a worse bore than Lord Harry at his most rustic!"

Mr. Scuddimore shook his head, aggrieved. "I ain't a nodcock, Harry."

"He's right, Harry, you know," Lord Harry said with a wide grin, displaying even white teeth. " 'Tis rather strange. But see here, Scuddy, we simply must contrive. 'Twas a good notion on Harry's part, I daresay. And I for one, do not mind in the least *lording* it over both of you!"

"Most proper solution," Sir Harry agreed, pointedly ignoring Lord Harry's sally. He eyed Mr. Scuddimore with as much distaste as he had Lord Harry a few minutes before. "Lord, I hope my reputation don't suffer being seen with the likes of both of you! Here is Lord Harry with baggy breeches and coat, and you, Scuddy, *you* are simply too heavy to be sporting yellow knitted pantaloons! Damned if I know why I put up with the both of you!"

Lord Harry patted Sir Harry's arm consolingly. "We will walk ten paces behind you, Harry, if you wish it. The way the women do in India or Arabia, or some such place."

Mr. Scuddimore scoffed, "Bad thought, Lord Harry. Imagine us behaving like women! Don't like the sound of it at all, I can tell you!"

Lord Harry turned away and grinned ruefully into the darkened carriage.

"Now, Scuddy," Sir Harry said severely, "Lord Harry was only bamming you. Ten paces behind, indeed! You must learn to see the point, old fellow!"

Lord Harry interposed, seeing Scuddy frown not in anger, but rather in confusion. "Tell you what Scuddy and I will do, Harry. If we happen to see the Honourable Miss Isabella Bentworth at the play tonight, then we will pace back ten steps."

Sir Harry Brandon shifted uncomfortably against the carriage swabs. Although he was the first to acclaim the lovely Miss Isabella to be a diamond of the first water, he did not think that as a sophisticated man of the world his deeper feelings concerning the lady should be so obvious. He blanched at the thought of his friends pushing him to come up to scratch with the lady, and sought to disabuse them. "Now see here, Lord Harry—"

"Yes, Harry?" his friend mocked.

"Oh, very well," Sir Harry conceded with ill grace, "you win! I won't say another word about your wretchedly fitting

4

clothes if you and Scuddy will keep mum about Miss Bentworth."

"But why should we, Harry? You do not plan to make the young lady an offer?"

Sir Harry said desperately, "Dash it all! I'm but twenty-four years old! Far too young to be leg-shackled! Even to Miss Bentworth." He murmured a silent plea of forgiveness to Miss Isabella. If only she were still in the schoolroom, say fourteen or fifteen years old, instead of a marriageable age, ripe to be plucked from the marriage mart! Even his very self-assured brother-in-law, the Earl of March, had not met and married Harry's sister, Kate, until he was twenty-eight! And Kate, very rightly, was but eighteen.

He looked up from his ruminations to see mischief brewing in Lord Harry's expressive blue eyes. He said frankly, "I'll tell you why you must keep quiet, both of you. Word like that gets around and before you know it, some poor fellow is the butt of wagers at the clubs! The next step is an announcement in the *Gazette*! Happened to Lord Davenport several times. Poor fellow just managed to shear off in the nick of time!"

Mr. Scuddimore hastened to add his guinea's worth of knowledge on the topic. "Same thing happened some time back, I remember. There were several gentlemen in the running. Lord Cavander . . . the Marquis of Oberlon," he added at the sudden peculiar look in Lord Harry's eyes, "won a vast sum from Sir William Filey—vast sum! He married the lady, you know, quite routed the opposition, he did!"

Lord Harry sat suddenly forward in the carriage. "Were there other gentlemen involved in the wager, Scuddy?"

Mr. Scuddimore pursed his lips and narrowed his eyes in concentration. "Yes, damned if there wasn't another gentleman," he said finally. "A dashing military man as I recall. Always in his regimentals—quite turned all the ladies' heads, he did."

"Do you remember his name, Scuddy?" Lord Harry asked.

Mr. Scuddimore cudgled his brains, then suddenly brightened. "The fellow's name was Rolland—yes, that's it— Captain Damien Rolland! Lord Cavander never collected the lost wager from him—Rolland up and left England, later got himself killed at Waterloo, if I remember correctly. In fact, some wagging tongues put it about that Rolland sheared away, put himself out of the running before the lady made up her mind. One day he was pursuing after her, then the next—gone without a word to anyone!"

Lord Harry went suddenly pale, but since the interior of the carriage was in dark shadows, Sir Harry and Mr. Scuddimore did not notice. Lord Harry asked in a voice of casual interest, "Do you recall the lady's name, Scuddy?"

Mr. Scuddimore shook his head and shot a hopeful glance at Sir Harry.

Sir Harry shrugged. "Sorry, Scuddy, it was before my time, you know. Over in Spain at the time."

Lord Harry prompted gently, "Did the lady's name happen to be Springville?"

Mr. Scuddimore nodded vigorously. "Yes, that's it— Springville. Elizabeth Springville. Lovely little filly, she was. Dead now, really quite a pity."

"Ho!" Sir Harry interrupted, quite uninterested in any story whose characters he did not know. "Here we are at last." He leaned his fair head out of the carriage window. "Deuced crush tonight, and being late don't help," he added, glancing balefully at Lord Harry.

Lord Harry bit back further questions. Since all of Mr. Scuddimore's attention was focused upon extricating his ample person from the carriage, and Harry did not wish to be bothered by ancient history, it would simply have to wait. It was enough for now that Lord Harry had discovered there had been a wager, and that Lord Cavander and Damien had been a part of it.

Lord Harry forced a pleasant smile to his lips as the three friends wended their way into Drury Lane Theatre, his eyes searching the throng of playgoers for Lord Cavander, Marquis of Oberlon.

"Fie on you, your grace!" the lady chided to the gentleman in question in a caressing voice. "You give me this lovely ruby necklace and then hold me prisoner. Would you not like someone other than you and my maid to behold its beauty?"

The lady's brown eyes sparkled with anticipation at the thought of the many envious glances she would enjoy. 'Twould serve those simpering young misses and their stiff-lipped hypocritical mamas right to see her, Melissande Challier, more richly jeweled than they! Let them put their noses in the air, as if she were not fit to be near them! Her escort would be one of the most eligible peers of the realm, and her gown and jewels unparalleled.

Lord Cavander touched his fingers lightly to the ruby necklace, an expensive bauble he had procured in Italy. He had bought it on a whim, and having no one else upon which to bestow it, had most willingly given it to Melissande. It was a welcoming present, he had told her. Welcoming him home from Italy and welcoming her to his protection. Since the exquisite necklace was the only item of apparel that the lady was wearing, his fingers soon strayed to her soft rounded shoulders and full white breasts. Actually, he admitted to himself, he was quite sated, Melissande having most superbly seen to his pleasure. But he was tired, tired of the seemingly endless stream of agents, advocates and tenants who had occupied his waking hours since his return from abroad. He would have preferred to spend the evening quietly with Melissande, perhaps allowing himself to emerge from her charmingly furnished apartment on the morrow, not a tired, but an exhausted man. But he saw the gleam of excitement in her dazzling brown eyes, and knew without her telling him that she wished above things to dazzle the gentlemen and ladies at Vauxhall Gardens this evening.

He lazily propped himself up on one elbow, gazed appreciatively once more at her voluptuous body, and then smiled. She was exquisitely beautiful and she did not yet bore him. He did not mind in the least giving her what she wished.

Although Melissande could place herself in the efficient hands of her maid, Ginny, Lord Cavander had to see to himself, a small mirror in the adjoining dressing room his only assurance that he would not put his epitaph as the Nonpareil among Corinthians in jeopardy this evening.

Ginny was carefully tugging a long curl of rich auburn ever so gently into place on Melissande's shoulder when Lord Cavander returned to the bedroom. Melissande rose and smiled at him with the confidence of a lady who knows herself to be the elixir of pleasure and beauty. She touched her fingers to the ruby necklace that lay nestled in the hollow of her throat. "You approve, your grace?" she asked softly.

"I am a man of undisputed taste, Melissande," he drawled slightly. "Shall we go, my dear?"

She blinked several times in an effort to understand his meaning, and gave up the attempt when she observed his lips curl with impatience. She replied playfully, laying her hand upon his sleeve, "You are a great wit, your grace! Yes, I am ready to leave."

Ginny paused a moment from straightening her mistress's brushes when she heard Melissande say with great relish to her lover as they left the room, "How I hope that Lady Planchey will be in attendance this evening! Why the effrontery of her snippity ladyship to believe that you could be interested

7

in her whey-faced daughter!" Although Melissande was very much aware that wives and mistresses were poles apart in a gentleman's mind, she knew, with sublime confidence in her own charms, that even the loveliest of débutantes would receive no more than a disinterested glance from Lord Canvander while she, Melissande, was in his company.

Miss Henrietta Rolland yawned prodigiously the next morning, and forced her eyes open when she heard Millie "hurrumph" again by her bedside. "Come, Miss Hetty," Millie repeated, "your father will no doubt miss you if you do not join him for luncheon."

"Yes, you are right, Millie," Hetty said with a langourous stretch and a sigh. "Lord, but I am tired!"

"Well, 'tis no more than you can expect if you persist in staying out until the chimney sweep begins his work," Millie said matter of factly, no censure in her voice.

While Hetty bathed from the porcelain basin atop the marble commode, Millie, with practiced efficiency, told her mistress of the previous evening's events. "You should know that your father was engaged with Sir Richard Latham, Mr. Alwyn Settlemore and Sir Lucius Bentham. These gentlemen arrived at about eight o'clock. They drank sherry in the drawing room until half past eight, discussing politics all the while, then left for Sir Mortimer Melberry's house. Of course, your father did not think to say goodnight to you, so we had no worry there. Grimpston informed me that Sir Archibald returned just after midnight with two of the gentlemen, drank more sherry, and held more political discussions until just after two in the morning. Sir Archibald rose at his usual time of nine o'clock and repaired to the study after breakfast. And," Millie finished, glancing at the clock on the mantel piece, "if you do not hurry, miss, you will quite ruin his schedule!"

"That would indeed be fatal!" Hetty grinned ruefully. "We must never interfere with his schedule!"

Millie quickly brushed out her mistress's short blonde curls, threaded a white ribbon through the hollows and fastened it at the nape of her neck. "There," she announced, stepping back to survey her handiwork, "no one could accuse you of not looking the perfect young lady of fashion. Now, go, Miss Hetty, I just heard the clock chime twelve!"

Hetty sped down the carpeted stairs into the small entrance hall. "Good morning, Grimpston," she said, tugging at a curl that was tickling her cheek.

8

"Good morning, Miss Hetty," the butler replied, his eyes lighting up.

Hetty sped past him down a small corridor that led to the dining room. She turned and waved a friendly hand before disappearing through the open door. She stopped short and smiled. Her father, Sir Archibald Rolland, esteemed member of the House of Lords, Tory by birth, economic persuasion and passionate conviction, sat at the head of the long table, his head buried behind the *Gazette*.

Mrs. Miller, the Rolland housekeeper, stood at his elbow, a look of patient resignation on her face, waiting to discover his preference of soups. It was a sacred rule among the servants that Sir Archibald was never to be interrupted in his ritual reading of the newspaper. She looked heavenward and Hetty could almost hear her silent sighs.

"Good day, Father," Hetty said brightly, and walked to her father's side.

"Father," she repeated, as his silver head did not emerge from his newspaper.

"Damned idiots," he muttered to himself, "why can they not understand the simplest of economics? Their constant, radical inveigling against the Corn Laws makes me wonder if they share an entire brain amongst the lot of them!" He jerked his head up. "Eh? Oh, Hetty! My dear child! I trust you slept well?"

"Excellently, Father," she replied, and dropped a kiss on his smooth forehead. "And you, my dear?"

"Like a top, my dear, like a top! If it were not for these infernal, cursed Whigs! I'd like to send the lot of them spinning!" He chuckled at his own joke and Hetty smiled, somewhat surprised that her father could joke about the Whigs, the bane of his political existence.

"Sir Archibald, may I now serve the soup? Would you prefer the turtle or the potato, my lord?" Mrs. Miller's thin, rather pallid face was perfectly matched with her patient voice.

"I say, Mrs. Miller," Sir Archibald said, giving a start. "You really ought not creep up on one like that! The turtle soup will be fine, Mrs. Miller. Cook does quite nicely with the turtle. Not at all the thing with the potato soup, though. Come, dish it up! We must not dawdle all afternoon."

Hetty thought wryly to herself that her father's condemnation of the potato soup had naught to do with Cook's inability, but rather with the circumstance that potatoes had the disadvantage of being a vegetable. And that, she decided, grinning to herself, reminded him of the Corn Laws. Not wishing to sound like a reprehensible Whig, no matter how farfetched her vegetable comparison, Hetty hastily concurred with the turtle soup.

As Mrs. Miller suffered from arthritis in her knee joints, Hetty, as was her habit, dismissed the housekeeper. "Thank you, Mrs. Miller. We shall be fine now."

"Very well, Miss Hetty," Mrs. Miller said gratefully. After standing ten minutes by Sir Archibald's chair, unnoticed, she wanted nothing more than to take the weight off her aching legs. She dipped a stiff curtsy and left father and daughter to their luncheon.

As Hetty spooned a mouthful of turtle soup to her lips, she thought about her activities for the afternoon. Sir Harry Brandon had insisted that they ride to Cowslip Hollow to see a local mill. She made a *moue*, for she had no particular liking for prizefights. Yet, not to show a modicum of enthusiasm for one of the most popular of the gentleman's sports would surely not hold her in good stead with her companions. At least, later, they would ride in Hyde Park. In all likelihood, Lord Cavander would be among the glittering *ton* that made their daily appearance during those fashionable hours of four to six in the afternoon. She smiled wryly, her turtle soup for the moment forgotten. How very grateful she was that Mr. Scuddimore did not possess the most awesome of intellects. He had offered her the use of a hack without the slightest hesitation, and more importantly, without questioning her rather lame story that her father needed her own bay mare for stud purposes.

"Studding, eh? Laudable solution! I say, England has need of more bay horses," he had agreed enthusiastically.

Hetty looked up to see her father smiling at her in that vague way of his. He surprised her by saying, "I trust poor Drusilla's sick sister has not disaccommodated you, my dear child. Your first trip to London and all that—I would not wish you to be bored."

She stifled a giggle. Poor Drusilla Worthington had left London a good four months ago. Seemingly, Sir Archibald had not been struck by her former chaperone's absence until this moment. She reached out and clasped her father's hand warmly. "Dear sir, I assure you that I am never bored. I have made many friends and am never at a loss for something interesting to do. In fact, after luncheon, I am promised to meet friends and go to . . . Richmond Park to walk through the maze."

Sir Archibald beamed his relief. He was delighted that Hetty had settled so quickly into London life. In truth, he wanted her to enjoy all the routs, balls and whatever else young ladies were supposed to enjoy, but the thought of chaperoning his daughter to such insipid social affairs made him blanch. Hetty was such a good daughter, not at all bothersome, never demanding this or that from him. She never overspent the generous allowance he made available for her and ran his house with silent, uncomplaining efficiency. He made Hetty blink in an effort to understand his mood when he said sadly, "How very much like your lovely mother you are, my dear child. Never importuned me for a thing, did the wonderful woman." He heaved a heavy sigh and turned his attention back to a wafer thin slice of ham.

"Why . . . why, thank you, Father," she said, trying not to gasp. She was about as much like her deceased mother as Mr. Scuddimore was like her father! Poor Mother! Even as a small child, Hetty could remember Lady Beatrice complaining bitterly of her husband's neglect, of his blind preoccupation with all that "political rubbish." When she contracted a chill and died swiftly of an inflammation of the lung, it required a stirring eulogy by the curate to make Sir Archibald aware that an important member of his family had passed to the hereafter. He grieved for her perfunctorily, focusing his beautiful, vague eyes on Hetty and patting her on the head in recognition of their mutual sorrow for the better part of two weeks. But then, suddenly, there was an election. Perceval became Prime Minister, and as a result, the Whigs began to wield such political power that Sir Archibald sought to throw himself immediately into the fray. He patted Hetty on the head for a final time and set off to London to launch a counteroffensive. Hetty went back to her prim governess with the natural dread of a lively child condemned to sewing samplers in a cheerless schoolroom. And then Damien had arrived to rescue her. Wounded in a skirmish on the Peninsula, he was packed to the country to recuperate. How quickly he had realized that the country offered very little in the way of amusement! He had turned to her, recognized her deep loneliness and instantly taken her under his wing. Miss Mills, Hetty's governess, was charmed to her very soul by Damien's cavalier treatment of her, and so raised no great fuss. Thus it was that Hetty had found herself riding to the hunt, shooting at bottles with Damien's dueling pistol, and quickly becoming the most skilled ten-year-old piquet player in England.

Hetty felt a lump rise in her throat. Although she did not

in the least resent her father's vague dismissal of her mother's demise, she could not help but think Sir Archibald oddly selfish when he had shown no more emotion at his son's death. She wondered with a tinge of bitterness if her father would even remember Damien if it were not for the large portrait of him that hung in the drawing room over the mantelpiece. Lady Beatrice, unfortunately, had never achieved a like immortality through the artist's brush.

Hetty was pulled away from her thoughts by the sudden sound of her father's impassioned voice. "Of course, as *true* Englishmen, we would never consider the application of such vile methods as those employed by those more radical members of parliament! Yes, gentleman, I speak of the incitement to riot, the unconscionable exploitation of the workers by the more irresponsible members of our company. Nay, I would not wish to indict the whole of the opposition—"

"Bravo, Father!" Hetty applauded, having realized that Sir Archibald was rehearsing a speech for the House of Lords. "You speak this afternoon?"

"Eh?" Sir Archibald jumped at his daughter's interruption, the words of his next sentence waiting impatiently on his tongue. "Oh, excuse me, my dear, I did not realize that you were still about."

"Yes, Father," she replied hastily, seeing the glow of preoccupation shadowing his bright blue eyes, "but I was just on the point of leaving. Is there anything I may do for you, sir?"

"Do for me? Such a good, considerate girl you are, Henrietta. No, my dear, it is off to make a speech this afternoon for me. If you are dining in, my child, do not have Cook hold dinner. Sir Mortimer and I will be discussing whether or not we should journey to Manchester, to determine if large scale insurrection is in any way a possibility. I will, of course, inform you if I am to leave London."

"Thank you, Father." Hetty rose and lightly kissed her father's cheek, then quietly walked from the dining room. As she closed the door behind her, she heard her father's resonant voice rise to an impassioned crescendo.

2

Later that same day at Rose Briar Manor in Herefordshire, Lady Louisa Rolland pursed her lips and tapped her fingers in thoughtful concentration. "I say, Jack," she said finally to her husband, who was busily occupied with cleaning his guns, "this is all very odd, you know. I've a letter from Drusilla Worthington, that mousy little dab of a woman who is supposed to be chaperoning Hetty in London. She is full of apologies that she had to leave the dear child suddenly to attend to her sick sister in Kent."

"Sounds proper," Sir John grunted, not at all interested in Drusilla or her sick sister.

"What is odd, Jack," Lady Louisa explained patiently, "is that she left nearly four months ago. In fact, but four weeks after Hetty arrived in London! Neither Hetty nor Sir Archibald have mentioned it in their letters!"

Sir John looked up, a look of patent disbelief on his square, handsome face. "Surely you're mistaken, old girl! Quite impossible, in fact!"

"I assure you it is true," Lady Louisa said.

"But I've never known my father to write a letter to anyone. Something smoky there, Lou."

Lady Louisa shook her head in exasperation. "No, Jack, I did not mean that! I merely used Sir Archibald's name in a manner of speaking. You know very well that Hetty is the only one who ever writes. And she," the lady continued, her brow puckered in a frown, "has not mentioned one word of it."

"Now, Lou, you're not thinking about playing Miss Propriety, are you? Can't say I blame Hetty a bit for not telling us. The Worthington woman was probably a damned nuisance!"

"Damned nuisance or not, my love, Hetty is but eighteen years of age. Even though she's in mourning for Damien and won't be attending Almack's or any of the large *ton* parties, it concerns me that she is not attended by anyone. You know that the veriest whisper or hint of anything at all not *comme il faut*, can quite ruin a young lady's chances."

"Chances of what?" Sir John interrupted with a decided

glint in his dark eyes. "Do you mean that poor Hetty might have to forego the pleasure of having some elegant, worthless fop asking for her hand in marriage? Really now, Lou, Hetty's got a sound head on her shoulders. And I'll wager she hasn't even stirred much from the house these last four months, much less offended any of your great ladies!" He added thoughtfully, "Maybe it would be better for her to offend the proprieties. At least we would know that she's not still prostrated by Damien's death."

"My point exactly," Lady Louisa declared, channeling her argument to match her husband's new observations. "The poor child should have someone with her. You know that Sir Archibald might as well be on the moon, for all the attention and comfort he provides her!"

"You said yourself, Lou," her husband said, most unfairly harking back to her own point, "that Hetty hasn't mentioned a word about the Worthington woman leaving. Shows you, doesn't it, that Hetty is perfectly content not to have anyone with her." He grinned and put down the now sparkling clean pistol. "Got you there, old girl," he said, and pulled her to her feet. "No need to worry about Hetty. We will be going to London next month anyway, you know. You can make yourself content that your sister-in-law is feeling just the thing for a few days, before we continue on to—" Sir John's voice trailed mysteriously off.

"Oh, Jack!" the lady cried, flinging her arms about his broad shoulders, "do you really mean it? You have arranged it? We are really going to Paris?"

"Don't strangle me, my dear," he replied fondly, dropping a kiss on the chestnut curl that lay provocatively over her left ear. "Of course I mean it. Will you be satisfied to spend a few days with Hetty then?"

"Yes, of course I shall. Only—"

"Only what, my dear?"

Lady Louisa sighed. "I only hope that Hetty will not get herself into any scrapes in the meantime. You know how she and Damien were always larking about!"

Sir John said softly, his dark eyes hooded, "Damien is dead now. When we saw Hetty at the funeral, the poor girl was so griefstricken that she barely spoke a word. No, I do not think that we have to worry about Hetty larking about, as you put it."

"I miss Damien too, Jack," Lady Louisa said hesitantly, knowing that her husband's grief was as real as Hetty's. "He died a hero for England, Jack. We must remember that."

14

"A grievous loss, no matter England," Sir John said heavily. He managed to shake off his memories and tweaked one of Lady Louisa's bouncing curls. "Come, my love, let us see if Little John has driven Nurse to distraction!"

3

Less than a week before Miss Drusilla Worthington had been matter of factly summoned from Sir Archibald's townhouse on Grosvenor Square to attend her sick sister, Lady Elmire Chandliss, in the far reaches of Kent, she had sat quietly in the drawing room across from her charge, Miss Henrietta Rolland. As several attempts at conversation had met with only abstracted replies, she applied her needle more vigorously to the flounce she was mending, hoping that her display of useful activity would encourage Hetty to resume setting stitches in the tambour frame that lay unnoticed in her lap.

She gazed up several minutes later to observe with a tiny sigh that her laudable intention had met with dismal failure. Her charge's eyes were focused upon the brightly dancing flames in the fireplace, and yet, Hetty seemed not even aware of the fire, much less the rest of her surroundings. Lady Louisa had told her that Henrietta was much affected by her brother Damien's death at Waterloo, but still, that was four long months ago. She, herself, had been with Henrietta for three weeks, but all her unflagging efforts to suggest diversions and amusements seemed not to penetrate the shell of grief that enveloped her charge.

Miss Worthington's eyes clouded as she gazed at Hetty. All that unremitting black the girl persisted in wearing! What a pretty picture she would present if she but attended to Miss Worthington's repeated, gentle suggestions. True, perhaps she was a trifle tall for society's current whims, but still regal in that straight, proud way she carried herself. Miss Worthington thought of Sir Archibald, and a decided glint appeared in her normally unassuming grey eyes. Probably off at some political gathering, all his mental energies focused upon his one passion. It seemed that there was scarce a moment in the day when he was aware of the presence of his daughter, much less of Miss Worthington's tireless efforts to provide a normal atmosphere in his home.

If the truth were told, Miss Worthington felt like a floundering fish in a fisherman's net. It was not that Henrietta was unkind to her or made her feel unwelcome in any way. But the only visitors to be seen were Sir Archibald's political cronies, severely dressed gentlemen that made Miss Worthington feel woefully inadequate and most discomfited. To make matters worse, if Henrietta was not sitting quietly in front of the fireplace, simply staring off at nothing in particular as she was now, she would take long walks by herself, an activity that made Miss Worthington tremble with trepidation. When she had very tactfully pointed out that a young lady walking about by herself was not at all the thing, Henrietta had merely cocked her head to one side and appeared to look straight through Miss Worthington. "You need not worry that I am ogled by all the young bucks, Miss Worthington," she had said earnestly, "all these heavy black veils keep them at their distance, I assure you."

Miss Worthington had blanched at her charge's use of the cant term "ogle," yet she had felt unable to the task of reprimanding Hetty. Such hints that she had ventured upon occasion to drop into her charge's ear had been greeted by indifferent shrugs or vague nods.

She saw that Henrietta's hands were knotting and unknotting a handkerchief in her lap. She sighed and put down her needle. "Hetty, dear child, but look outside. The fog is lifting and I do believe that the sun will be out soon. Would you like to accompany me to the Pantheon Bazaar? You have not visited there, you know."

Hetty raised dark blue eyes, which looked suspiciously red about the rims, and slowly shook her head. "No, thank you, Miss Worthington. If you would like to go, I shall be happy to ring for John coachman."

Miss Worthington felt the familiar naggings of defeat. "No, Hetty, I am quite content to finish my mending," she said, with scarce a tremor to show her disappointment. They sat in silence until the afternoon sun began its descent into the distance. Miss Worthington rose to light a branch of candles. A knock sounded on the drawing room door, and as Henrietta did not stir, Miss Worthington called, "Enter."

Grimpston, the Rolland butler, and in Miss Worthington's opinion, a man of great efficiency and tact, appeared in the doorway. "Miss Henrietta," he began. As his mistress did not turn, he cleared his throat to gain her attention.

Hetty glanced up disinterestedly. "Yes, Grimpston?"

"There is a person here asking to see Sir Archibald, Miss Hetty."

"Sir Archibald is not here at the moment, as you know, Grimpston."

Grimpston continued in his gentle voice, " 'Tis a man named Pottson, Miss Hetty. He informs me that he was batman to Master Damien."

"Damien's batman, you say, Grimpston?" Miss Worthington watched her hitherto listless charge rise hurriedly from her chair. "Ask this man, Pottson, to attend me in the back parlour. I shall be there directly."

"Yes, Miss Hetty." Grimpston smiled slightly at the surprised look on Miss Worthington's face, quite pleased with himself at the reaction he had achieved. He returned to the entrance hall and said to the diminutive grey-haired man who stood still clutching a crumpled wool hat between his hands, "Miss Henrietta Rolland will see you. If you will follow me."

Pottson was certain that he'd made a mistake in coming when he was ushered into the presence of a tall young lady who stood watching him come toward her, an unreadable expression in her eyes. Drat the butler anyway, he thought. What he had to say was for Master Damien's father's ears— not for a gentle young lady! He found himself gazing at her curiously, for unlike his late master, Miss Henrietta was very fair, with short curling blonde hair framing her face. Yet, the eyes were the same—a deep blue and wide, set beneath distinctively arched brows. There was a dreaming quality about such eyes, Pottson thought. Kind of a curious blend of amusement and compassion.

"Miss Rolland," he ventured, stepping forward. His fingers mangled his hat to an unrecognizable lump of wool.

"Yes, I am Henrietta Rolland. You were Damien's batman." She moved gracefully forward and clasped the startled Pottson's hands in hers. The hat fell unnoticed to the floor.

"Yes, ma'am," he managed to say, blinking rapidly at the young lady who stood several inches above him. "I had intended to see Sir Archibald, but the butler insisted that I was to see you instead."

How very like dear Grimpston, Hetty thought, and how very perceptive of him. She drew a deep breath and smiled warmly. "Yes, I am the one for you to see. Do sit down, Pottson, I believe we have much to discuss." Hetty did not spare a moment's thought about the pain the batman's words must inevitably bring her, laying raw her grief. She knew only that she had to know what had happened to Damien during those long months after he had suddenly left London.

Pottson confined his small person to the edge of a chair. Saying what he had come to say would have been bad enough with Sir Archibald. But Master Damien's younger sis-

18

ter! Scratching old wounds, that was all he was doing. The thought had kept him away these summer months since Master Damien's death.

"I only came because of the letter!" he blurted out, throwing caution to the wind.

"Letter," Hetty repeated, frowning. "What letter are you talking about, Pottson?"

"You see, ma'am, me and Master Damien were together for nine months, traveling from Spain to Italy, carrying dispatches to the generals and such as that. Master Damien was always a right proper gentleman, ma'am, yet never too starchy in the collar, if you know what I mean."

Hetty knew exactly what he meant, and resolutely swallowed the lump in her throat.

"Always ready for a good joke was Master Damien, never seeming to worry much about what the next day would bring. Several of those dispatches he carried, well, I can tell you, ma'am, they weren't about the weather! I thought a lot of him, I did." Pottson paused a moment, fearful that he was offending Master Damien's sister by speaking so familiarly about her brother.

"Yes, yes," she prompted with a wave of the hand. "Please continue, Pottson."

"Well, ma'am, sometimes it seemed to me that all wasn't right with Master Damien. Just when I'd expect him to be charting the route for some important document he had to deliver, I'd find him instead sitting alone in his room, not even a candle lit, brooding like, you know. I didn't mean to be forward or anything, ma'am, but I'd ask him if there was anything bothering him. He'd just smile at me, a kind of sad smile.

"Just before Waterloo, back in the early days of June, he got his orders to attend the Prince of Orange in Brussels, a safe spot, I told him, seeing as how we all knew it was coming to a bloody battle and all. Next thing I knew, he was assigned under a General Drakeson, a very different kettle of fish, I remember him telling me, from being on the Prince's staff. I was with him when he got orders to lead a frontal cavalry charge, right in the thick of the fighting. He wouldn't let me come with him, ma'am, just patted me on the shoulders, that sad smile on his face. I'll never forget what he said. 'Well, Pottson, I must believe that my charmed existence is about to come to an end. It looks, old fellow, as if I'm to be the sacrificial goat.' I never saw him again, ma'am."

Pottson saw that the young lady's face was as white as her

gown was black. Her hands were trembling in her lap, but she did not move, nor cry, as he was dreading. "What about the letter, Pottson?" she asked finally, only a slight catch in her voice.

"Well, I got to wondering about what Master Damien said before he left, ma'am. When I was preparing his personal things to be sent back to your family, I found a letter folded up and tucked inside the lining of his valise. I read it, ma'am. I'm sorry, but I couldn't help myself."

"Let me see the letter, Pottson." Hetty unfolded the single sheet of paper and slowly read its contents. She gazed up, past Pottson, then lowered her head and read the letter yet another time:

> MY DEAREST LOVE—
>
> I cannot believe that you have been torn from my arms. Oh, Damien, if only we'd had time to be together, if only I had some hope that you could return to me. You must see now that I have no choice. I do not know what Lord Cavander will do now, but you must understand that my own fate is no longer in my hands.
>
> May God damn him for what he has done. I will love you forever, my darling. Adieu—
>
> YOUR DEAREST ELIZABETH

Hetty straightened and carefully folded the letter. "You did quite right, Pottson, to bring the letter to me. Yes, you have done quite right."

Even though Miss Worthington considered it a trifle odd for her charge to spend nearly an hour in the company of a servant, she gave it only cursory thought. The next morning, she found herself in a sudden whirl of activity. The quiet young lady who had sat so very many long hours staring into the fireplace, who had taken long walks, seemed to be no longer in existence. It was Henrietta who suggested over breakfast that they visit the Pantheon Bazaar. At last, Miss Worthington thought, her patient efforts had reaped their rewards. She had succeeded in redirecting Henrietta's thoughts. Being a Christian woman, she also admitted to herself that the timely visit by the late Captain Damien Rolland's batman must have, in some small way, assisted Henrietta to recover her spirits. She most willingly assisted her charge to exchange the black gowns for soft grey ones and pack them, black veils and all, in an attic trunk.

When she received her sister's plea a few days later to attend her in Kent, her lips tightening in recognition of the barely veiled command, she gazed up at an innocently smiling Henrietta. Miss Worthington was torn, not knowing precisely where her duty lay. Although Henrietta very prettily begged her to remain, she did hasten to say that she, of all people, well understood one's feelings toward one's own dear family. Miss Worthington wasn't at all certain just what her feelings were toward her domineering sister, but from long years of habit, she knew that Elmire was not to be denied. Thus, she departed London two days later with the happy conviction that she had performed her duty by Henrietta. She never realized that Henrietta was fairly itching for her to be gone.

But three days after Miss Worthington's departure, Lord Harry Monteith made his first appearance in London.

"Thompson Street will suit us just fine, Pottson. 'Tis but a short distance from St. James, so we need not worry about the expense of hackneys. How much did you say the furnished rooms would cost by the quarter?"

Pottson grunted a price that he secretly hoped would put an end once and for all to Miss Hetty's mad scheme. He was doomed to disappointment, for Miss Hetty beamed at him. He supposed that he really shouldn't be surprised at anything Miss Hetty proposed now, though he had thought himself entered into Bedlam, when, but three days before, she had summoned him back to Grosvenor Square and poured her idea into his ear. He looked up as she said, "You have done excellently, Pottson!" She clapped him on the shoulder, delighted. "Of course, we must now see to my clothes, and, to be sure, set aside enough money to secure my *entrée* into the fashionable world. Damien saw to my education in piquet and faro. I vow that with any luck at all at the gaming tables, we will live in a most sumptuous manner."

"But, Miss Hetty," Pottson essayed once again, " 'tis a crazy, wild scheme! You just ain't a man," he added bluntly, his eyes critically surveying Miss Rolland's feminine figure.

She merely laughed. "I have ideas on *that* score, Pottson. I have made out a list of my measurements and colors of breeches, waistcoats and coats that I would like. The gentlemen's current whim toward those tight knitted pantaloons are, unfortunately, out of the question. I have no desire to tempt fate, I assure you!"

"But Miss Hetty," Pottson cried, finally hitting the kernel of the corn, "just say that we can make you look like one of

21

those fashionable young bucks. You still must approach the Marquis of Oberlon, and, from what I hear, he's a powerful gentleman and an acclaimed sportsman. You tell me that you will have your revenge on him for your brother—but how, Miss Hetty? How?"

Hetty did not answer her new valet directly. Her eyes clouded with poignant memory. "Besides teaching me gaming, Pottson, Damien also saw to it that I was a crack shot. As to fencing, I admit to needing lessons. I have been making discreet inquiries myself, you know, and will begin fencing lessons with a Signore Bertioli very shortly. If you will know, Pottson, I rather fancy pistols for the marquis."

Pottson groaned. The mere thought of a gently nurtured young lady even talking of gentlemen's weapons! " 'Tis not right, Miss Hetty! A young lady aping gentlemen's ways! 'Tis simply against the laws of nature!"

Hetty said sharply, " 'Tis men who so conveniently proclaimed these so-called laws of nature! Come now, Pottson, it is far too late for you to be carrying on with these nonsensical arguments any longer! My mind is quite made up. Either you help me, or I shall simply find someone else." She spoke with more confidence than she felt, and was mightily relieved when Pottson, who was looking like a man floundering in deep waters, wiped the appalled look from his face, and nodded in resignation.

"I'd like you to tell me one thing, Miss Hetty. Master Damien, like I told you, was always a proper gentleman, treating ladies just as he ought. Why would he teach his own sister such unladylike activities?"

Hetty laughed. "He was bored, Pottson. Perhaps too, he felt a trifle sorry for me, for Mother had just died and Sir Archibald had returned to London to carry on his never-ending battle against the Whigs. He was recovering from a wound, as I recall. He said, I would have you know, that I was an apt pupil."

Pottson shook his head, defeated. He was on the point of leaving when it occurred to him that yet another obstacle was to be overcome. "I can't be dressing you, Miss Hetty. And more than that, you can't be sneaking back here to Sir Archibald's house looking like a gentleman!"

"An excellent point, my dear Pottson," Hetty concurred with a smile. "Do you doubt my wits so much to think I would not already have seen to that problem? When next you come, I shall introduce you to my maid, Millie. You can both preach doom to me, if you like. But I warn you, I have quite secured her cooperation, so it will do you no good to plot against me."

Pottson sighed gently in resignation. His hand was on the doorknob to the drawing room door when he realized he had no ready blunt.

"I'll need some guineas for the rooms, Miss Hetty, not to mention a credit for the tailor."

"Thank you for reminding me, Pottson. I shall see to it now. It is providential that my mother left me a competence in my own right. We shall use my quarterly allowance until circumstances or my ill-luck at the gaming tables forces me to dip into the principal. One other thing, Pottson, do not forget that my new name is Harry Monteith."

Pottson paused a moment and scratched his sparse grey head. "Where'd you get such a name, Miss Hetty?"

"From an old atlas of world explorers. I really don't remember what the man discovered," she added mendaciously. Actually, Hetty knew that hundreds of years ago, a Baron Monteith had set himself against the de Medicis, vowing revenge for the poisoning death of his sire. It had seemed like the biblical David and Goliath struggle, and Hetty's casting herself in the role of the avenging Monteith had quite stirred her imagination. The only note that jarred her fantasy was the fact that she could not discover what ever became of the baron.

"Come, my lord! Your wrist is flaccid! An iron wrist, my lord, you must have an iron wrist!" Signore Bertioli stepped back from Lord Monteith and leaned lightly on the handle of his foil. Not one bead of perspiration was evident on his forehead, and his bushy black brows drew closely together at the heaving, sweating young gentleman. How very intense and eager the young lord was, so unlike the vast majority of his other pupils—young dandies who sought to exhibit good form and style, the practice required to become truly proficient in the art an abhorrent thought to most of them. He softened his tone. "It is strength you lack, my lord."

Hetty wondered if she would survive her first lesson, for her heart was pounding so severely that she feared it must burst. She managed to gasp out between heaving breaths, "Yes, Signore, I fear what you say is true. But there must be something I can do." At least, her main fear that Signore Bertioli would realize that he was instructing a female had not come to pass.

Signore Bertioli drew back, surprised at the seriousness in

23

the lad's voice. "You know, my lord," he said after a moment, "strength need not be everything. You have grace and agility. Perhaps with much work, my lord, I can teach you some of the more . . . unusual techniques. It would hold you in good stead, if," he paused pointedly, "you are willing to apply yourself."

Damn, Hetty thought, rubbing her arms, he was right about her endurance and her flaccid wrist. She focused upon his last words. "You mentioned unusual techniques, Signore?" Hope reared itself and she gazed at the olive-skinned master with such intensity that he turned suddenly away from her.

"Sit down, my lord," he said, sweeping a face guard from a chair.

Hetty nodded gratefully and sank down, wiping her white full sleeve across her sweating brow.

"You are new to London, my lord?"

"Yes, Signore, I arrived just this past week. You wonder at my lack of skill. I come from the far north of England, where, unfortunately, there were naught but cows and girls to fence with. My apologies for being such an inept pupil, Signore."

There was much earnestness in the young gentleman's unabashed candor. And yet, he thought, even if Lord Monteith never became a credit to the noble art of fencing, it made no great difference, at least in England. With dueling outlawed for some years now, fencing had become a showy sport for Englishmen, just as playing the harp was for the young English ladies. An accomplishment, nothing more. He fanned his hands and said with a chuckle, "Cows and girls, you say, my lord? 'Tis a pity to be sure. You have courage, my lord. But I must say, there can be no duels for you as yet."

To his surprise, Lord Monteith suddenly squared his shoulders and sat board straight, his mouth drawing into a thin line. "You say I have courage, Signore. I will tell you that I am willing to do anything. You spoke of unusual techniques. You must teach me, Signore."

Ah, the young gentleman does not take my words as a frivolous joke, Signore Bertioli thought. He paused and cocked his thin, intense face to one side. "You press yourself, young sir, far beyond the limits of most of the young gentlemen who come to me. It is certainly not to ready yourself for war. You English, after all, have finally dispatched that pig Corsican to his island hell. And even if it were for war, young sir, the art of the foil becomes outmoded, just as the

24

bow and arrow. Were I not in England, my lord, I would think that you prepare to execute a *vendetta*."

"*Vendetta*, Signore?"

"Yes, young sir. A *Vendetta* is a sworn act of revenge. In my country, a *vendetta* can carry from father to son for many generations. Many times, the cause for revenge is lost over the years. Yet the desire for revenge upon one's enemies remains, as if it were born into the soul itself."

"Your Italian word, *vendetta*, I like it much," Hetty replied pensively.

Signore Bertioli said wryly, "If you carry such an idea for revenge, my lord, I would suggest the pistol. You have a keen eye, and to kill a man with the little ball requires no more strength than your cows or girls have."

"You must know, Signore, that in England, in a duel of honour, the one who wishes the revenge cannot select the weapon. I am an excellent shot, Signore, but it is not enough. I have not much longer. You must teach me so that my *vendetta* is not simply an empty wish."

Signore Bertioli gazed down into the young set face. But a boy the lord was, a mere boy, with smooth cheeks and many years of life before him. He felt sudden fear for Lord Monteith. If he was truly in earnest about a duel of honour, Signore Bertioli seriously doubted his ability to endure in the face of a more powerfully built opponent. He said quietly, "Yes, I will teach you. We will contrive. If you are rested, my lord, there is much more for you to learn today."

"Thank you, Signore," Hetty said simply, and rose with new energy to her feet. "Yes, I am rested."

"*En garde*, then, young sir!" Signore Bertioli slashed his foil through the silent air, its gleaming steel soon connecting with Lord Harry's blade.

At each clash, the impact sent quivers of pain up Hetty's arm. She gritted her teeth, silently repeating her catechism of hate against the Marquis of Oberlon, to keep her mind from the pain. *I shall send you to hell, your grace, just as you sent Damien to his death. As your blood flows from your body, I shall tell you who I am and why you are dying. I shall bring you to your knees, you despicable bastard!*

4

"I say, Lord Harry, you're not looking at all the thing tonight. Down pin you are!" Scuddy leaned his yellow and green striped elbows on the cardtable to peer more closely into Hetty's exhausted face.

Hetty's arm was so sore that Pottson had had to take great care when assisting her into her coat. She said lightly, "Signore Bertioli is a stern taskmaster, Scuddy, as I've often told you. He very nearly unmanned me today with the pace he set. I've taken lessons with him for nearly as long a time as I've known the both of you, yet I still leave him feeling like my right arm is a useless, dangling stick of wood."

"Any hope for you, Lord Harry?" Sir Harry asked with a wide grin. "I'm surprised that with your magnificent physical presence there would be any problem at all!"

"Signore Bertioli assured me that I could have sliced you to pieces two months ago, Harry!" Hetty retorted.

Sir Harry said slyly, "Well, I pray you are not too tired for what I have planned for tonight. Time to test your northern mettle, old boy."

"My northern mettle? Talk about testing mettle, Harry— you should look to yourself, for I have already fleeced you of five guineas! You are really an abominable piquet player, my friend."

"Lord Harry's got you there, Harry," Scuddy chimed in. "Ever since I've known you, you've always told me what an accomplished player *you* were. Lord Harry's beaten you regularly. Met your match, you have!"

"I don't recall having sought *your* opinion, Scuddy! Besides having rust in your upper works, you're becoming a rattle-pate. Becoming fit to gossip with the ladies, you are."

Hetty sat back in her chair, amused by their squabbling. She twirled a delicate crystal goblet of wine between her fingers, only halfheartedly attending to their good-natured bickering. The four months she had been Lord Harry Monteith seemed an eternity to her, the demands of being a young gentleman exhausting, sometimes dangerous, but always exhilarating. How very lucky she had been that Sir Harry Bran-

26

don and Mr. Scuddimore had so quickly and unreservedly taken her under their collective wing. Her thoughts went back to that first evening, four months ago, when she had emerged from Thompson Street as Lord Harry Monteith. Her deep fear had been that the first gentleman she would meet would look at her, stare with open curiosity, then look horrified. She had pomaded down her normally fluffy blonde curls and tied the queue securely with a black ribbon. Her cravat had caused her to gulp with fresh anxiety, for to any experienced masculine eye, it was indeed an abomination. Notwithstanding, she had sallied forth, all her thoughts firmly focused on swaggering like a young gentleman, her slim hips resisting every urge to sway. She had tried to nonchalantly swing her black malacca cane in her hand, as if she had not a care in the world, and had made her way to Drury Lane, her heart pounding most uncomfortably against her ribs.

She would never forget her first evening at the theatre, the title of the garish play, *The Milkmaid's Dilemma*, and the freak accident that had brought her together with Harry and Scuddy. A very rowdy play it was, following about a seductive milkmaid who, in the most maddening manner, refused to be bedded by her ardent young man. The hero had been just about to succeed in his amorous endeavors when the milkmaid's cow—a very real bovine specimen—became suddenly irked with the proceedings, mooed loudly, kicked over the milk can, and after gazing balefully at the uproarious audience, took violent exception. But a moment later, the cow lumbered off the stage, down into the pit, with frantic stagehands, a harried director and the tousled heroine chasing behind her. The laughter suddenly turned to panic and Hetty found herself being pommeled and pushed roughly this way and that by the now stampeding audience.

"Out of me way, m'lad!" a burly man growled behind her, buffeting her on the shoulder. She would have gone sprawling to the ground had not a strong hand grabbed her arm and pulled her upright and back from the aisle.

"I say, old fellow," a laughing voice said, "really must keep out of the way of the rabble, you know! Hope that damned cow kicks in a few of their heads!"

Hetty looked up into twinkling blue eyes, set in a quite handsome face. "I thank you, sir," she said. " 'Tis my first visit to the theatre and I'm afraid that I did not act wisely. Does this sort of thing go on very often?"

The young gentleman grinned. "Well, if it ain't a cow to liven up the rabble, it's always something else. They threw rotten apples last week. Ho! They've finally got the poor beast in tow!" A sudden look of surprise crossed the young gentleman's face. "First time to Drury Lane, you say?"

Hetty nodded. "Yes, I have just arrived in London—from the North. It is all rather . . . interesting, I think."

"Don't mean to tell me you're a rustic! Well, I'll be damned! Hey, Scuddy, pay attention, old boy!"

Hetty looked past her rescuer at a heavyset, cherubic faced young man who had an open frankness about him that made her lips curl into an instant smile. No guile in him at all.

"Well, what's your name, old boy? 'Tis only fair that you tell me since I pulled you out of the way of the rabble."

"Monteith," Hetty replied. "Lord Harry Monteith."

The cherubic faced young man blinked. "Damned coincidence! His name is Harry too—Sir Harry Brandon. Me, well, you can call me Scuddy," he offered kindly and extended a plump hand.

Hetty obligingly pumped his hand, praying that the touch of her soft white hands would not betray her.

Sir Harry poked Scuddy in the ribs. "His name's actually Mr. Thayerton Scuddimore, but we don't like to hang the poor fellow with that mouthful, so Scuddy it is."

"It is a pleasure . . . Scuddy," Hetty said. So far, so good, she thought to herself. Both Harry and Scuddy appeared bluff and good-natured. She could not help but wonder just how they would have introduced themselves had they known she was a female.

Sir Harry turned to gaze at the now empty stage. "Well, it looks as though our milkmaid ain't going to tumble in the hay after all, at least tonight. Scuddy and I were going to White's for a late supper. If you would like to come along—"

Hetty looked down in embarrassment. "You see," she said slowly, "because I am so new in London and have no friends here, I am not a member."

"Scuddy and I are," Sir Harry said obligingly. "You may come along as our guest. No harm done there."

Hetty could still recall how in that moment, she had silently thanked the recalcitrant cow for throwing her willy-nilly into Harry and Scuddy's company.

"I say, Lord Harry, I've asked you the same question three times. Stop your woolgathering, ain't at all polite, you know."

Hetty blinked away her memories and brought her attention back to the present. "I was just thinking about the cow at Drury Lane," she said by way of apology.

Scuddy laughed and thumped the table with the palm of

his hand. "Damned funny sight! First time we met you, eh, Lord Harry? Damn, it seems longer than what—four months ago?"

"Well, it was four months ago," Sir Harry cut in. "I do wish you would stop prosing about the time, else it will be close to dawn before I can tell you what I've got planned for the evening."

Hetty gulped, well recognizing the pronounced rakish gleam in Harry's eyes, that, were it emanating from any other gentleman, would have been decidedly lecherous. Her palms were beginning to sweat as she forced herself to ask, "Tell us, Harry, what is this plan of yours?"

"A visit to Lady Buxtell's house on Millsom Street. It's been a damned long time since I've been there. About time to make another call."

Palms sweatier still, Hetty thought only to spar for time. "Lady Buxtell? A friend of yours, Harry?"

Scuddy gave a chuckle and tapped Hetty on the arm. "Lord no, Lord Harry! She ain't his friend—much less a lady—it's her girls Harry's interested in!"

Hetty knew of a certainty that feigning further ignorance would not hold her in good stead. It had been with something of a shock that she had discovered that gentlemen's conversations frequently settled in a most direct way upon the assets or lack thereof of various young ladies of their acquaintance. It was to their credit, Hetty supposed ruefully, that young ladies of quality were excluded from such ribald comparisons. But the bodily charms of females of a different class were bandied about in quite another manner. Up until now, Hetty believed that she had performed in a quite unexceptionable manner, aping their rakish remarks and behaving in as lusty a way as her friends.

She bit her lip, wondering just what the devil she was going to do now. She endeavored to achieve an air of insouciance, and shrugged her shoulders. "Really, Harry, a brothel! I, myself, prefer to partake of goods that are not so blatantly damaged."

"Mighty high in the instep you are, Lord Harry! I tell you, it's a very select house, not at all in the common way." Sir Harry turned eagerly to Mr. Scuddimore. "Come, Scuddy, you ain't said a word about the matter. I know for a fact you haven't had a girl since you tossed your father's serving maid!"

Scuddy sputtered into his glass of port, and shot Sir Harry an aggrieved glance. "No need to shout it to the world,

29

Harry! If you will know, I'm not too plump in the pocket, it being midway through the quarter, you know. M'father wouldn't take it too kindly if I outran the carpenter again!"

"Damnation, Scuddy, this one visit ain't going to send you down the River Styx! And as for you, Lord Harry, I begin to wonder if you've ever even been to a house of pleasure! Just what is it you chaps do in the North Country?"

"Chaps in the North Country do much the same as you do, I suspect," Hetty retorted, searching about frantically for some plausible excuse to extricate herself from Harry's plans. "Actually, we tend to marry before we become old men. Solves a lot of problems, you know."

It was Scuddy who turned upon her, his eyes filled with disbelief. "Damned silly notion! M'father is forever telling me that marriage has nothing to do with pleasure. Don't want to be an old-fashioned stick, old boy."

"Scuddy's quite right, Lord Harry. A man's got to have his pleasure. Well, what do you say, chaps? I'm off to Lady Buxtell's. Do you have red blood in your veins or are you all talk and excuses?"

Scuddy painstakingly calculated the remainder of his allowance until the first of the quarter, brightened and said, "I'm with you, Harry." He downed the rest of his port and turned an owlish stare at Hetty.

In that moment, Hetty knew that she could not refuse, for to do so might plant suspicious seeds in her friends' minds that Lord Harry Monteith really wasn't the lusty young man they believed him to be.

With a show of bravado, she tossed down her wine, as Scuddy had done, thumped her glass on the table and rose with a swagger. "Well, my lads, the night grows late. Lead on, Harry. I, for one, am ready to sample Lady Buxtell's wares!" She turned and allowed a hovering footman to assist her into her cloak.

There was a miffed frown on Sir Harry's smooth brow. Why *he* should be leading his friends, not Lord Harry! After all, it was his suggestion. He clapped Scuddy on the shoulder. "Well, don't just sit there, old fellow, it's off for a night's pleasure!"

Once outside White's, Sir Harry recovered his good humour and a wide grin of anticipation lighted his face.

As for Hetty, she cudgeled her brain as block after block melted away beneath her boots, bringing her nearer and nearer to Millsom Street. Somewhere, she thought, there must be some humour to this ridiculous situation.

She was momentarily surprised at the somber picture Lady Buxtell's establishment presented to the passerby. It was a huge, three-story brick structure that dominated a street corner, its façade of Georgian columns unpretentious to the point of austerity. No more than a modicum of candlelight shined through its front windows, and for an instant, Hetty thought that Harry had made a most welcome mistake in his address. This wish was soon dashed when Harry stepped smartly up the stone steps and loudly sounded the heavy brass knocker. Only deep silence followed the echoing knock, and again, Hetty allowed herself the hope that Lady Buxtell was not receiving gentlemen this evening.

A slight grating sound reached her ears, and she had the uncomfortable notion that they were being observed. It was some more moments before the heavy oak door was eased smoothly open, and a tall, cadaverous-looking man, replete with severe black garb, stood silently before them. His gaunt face was devoid of expression, yet his small dark eyes assessed them quickly and thoroughly. As the man's eyes rested briefly upon her, Hetty felt her heart thump erratically. She had the uncanny sensation that somehow he knew her to be an imposter. She pictured in that instant her humiliating exposure as a female, saw the shock and condemnation on Harry's and Scuddy's faces. But then the man stepped back, offered a negligent bow, and motioned for them to enter. How strange, she thought, that I am relieved to be allowed to enter a brothel! Another black clothed man divested them of their canes and cloaks. Hetty would have sworn that the rheumy old eyes leered as he silently pointed them down a long, narrow hall toward the back of the house.

"Most discreet," Hetty muttered to Harry, trying to keep condemnation from her voice. She wondered with a curl of her lip if the Marquis of Oberlon would be in attendance tonight. Stupid thought, she chided herself an instant later, his grace kept his mistresses privately. She doubted if the marquis had relinquished such pleasures even during his brief marriage to Elizabeth Springville.

Her own precarious circumstances quickly banished the marquis from her thoughts. As Sir Harry confidently directed them into a spacious drawing room, he asked her slyly, "Well, what do you think, Lord Harry? More elegant than you expected, eh?"

On first glance, Hetty was inclined to agree. The long rectangular room was richly appointed with heavy crimson velvet hangings in marked contrast to delicately wrought clusters

31

of chairs and sofas fashioned in the gold and white style of the late Louis. At least half a dozen black-clad footmen moved unobtrusively about the room, quantities of drink held on large silver trays. A more penetrating glance informed Hetty that the occupants of the room were a far cry from the habituées of Almack's. There were many more ladies than gentlemen present, and though they were garbed in keeping with the elegance of the room, more white bosom than Hetty ever considered possible was daringly exposed. She noticed with plummeting confidence that although conversation appeared lively and high giggling laughter was a commonplace amongst the *ladies*, the gentlemen still managed to caress and stroke any unclothed limb that was near to them. She felt frightened and embarrassed to the tips of her toes at the spectacle before her, and at the same time, biting anger for the gentlemen who so abused her sex. She managed to control her voice and reply to Harry's inquiry. "A most tasteful brothel, Harry. Yes, most tasteful."

"Gawd, ain't *she* ever a beauty," Mr. Scuddimore whispered in awe, his widened eyes fastened upon an ethereal-looking girl whose shining hair lay long and thick and black as polished ebony down her slender back. Her melting brown eyes were curiously slanted at the corners, giving her an exotic, striking appearance.

"Ah, I can see that you are taken with Lilly, young sir. She has come to us just recently from a faraway land called China. Most charming, is she not?"

Mr. Scuddimore jumped and reddened, unaware that his remark had been overheard. He turned, just as had Sir Harry and Lord Harry, to gaze into the light green eyes of a tall, willowy built woman, who, unlike the rest of the females in the vast room, was dressed in a blue velvet gown that revealed not one patch of bosom. The smile on her reddened lips was one of amused condescension. Hetty realized that she was the *madam*, the woman who procured and sold the bodies of these other women. Anger boiled up in Hetty's breast and without thought to her precarious position, she looked the woman up and down, and said with haughty insolence, "How interesting that you must needs search to the ends of the world to procure *ladies* for your etsablishment ... or perhaps *calling* is a more apt description."

Sir Harry shot a look of confused surprise at Hetty, and she forced herself to swallow her anger. She shrugged her shoulders and allowed her eyes to gaze with lazy interest about the room.

"I am Sir Harry Brandon, Lady Buxtell. Perhaps you remember me. 'Twas not above a month ago that I was last here."

Lady Angelique Buxtell, Martine DuBois by birth, cloaked her anger at the uncalled for rudeness of Sir Harry's friend, and forced a polite mask of recognition and welcome to her painted face. Actually, she had no memory of him at all, but he appeared eager to please and somewhat embarrassed by his friend's churlishness. Thus, she nodded her dark brown curls, only slightly brightened by the dye jar, and stretched her hand to Sir Harry. "Of course, Sir Harry, I remember you well," she lied smoothly. "I see that you have brought two friends. If you will follow me, gentlemen, I will see to your wants. Perhaps some champagne, cards or pleasant conversation with one of my lovely girls?"

Mr. Scuddimore, having gathered his scattered wits back together, replied with unabashed directness to Lady Buxtell's suggestion. "Didn't come here for cards, ma'am. Already lost too much blunt to Lord Harry here."

Ah, so the rude young man is a lord, Lady Buxtell thought, instantly revising her opinion of Hetty and forgiving her her insolence. Lords were, after all, the making of her success. It would not do at all to offend one of them. "Well, in that case, gentlemen," she said, focusing a bright smile on Hetty, "champagne and conversation it shall be."

Lady Buxtell ushered them to a plentifully laden sideboard at the far end of the room and poured each of them a glass of sparkling champagne. "To your evening's pleasure, my lords," she said with practiced gaiety, motioning toward the girl, Lilly, as she spoke.

Sir Harry leaned over to Hetty and whispered, "See, I told you Lady Buxtell's was far above the common touch. There's Lord Alvaney next to the fireplace and over there is Sir John Walterton."

Hetty interrupted, "Yes, and the gentleman already far into his cups is Lord Darcy Pendleton. Bedamned!" she swore suddenly. "Sir William Filey! How I pity the poor girl who must see to his wants."

Hatty despised Sir William Filey, for he was debauched, cunning and ruthless. That a good part of her hatred of him was heavily mixed with fear, she freely admitted. At White's, several months before, he had made a mocking remark about the inordinate smoothness of her cheeks. That very evening, she had made an obvious show of departing from Sir Harry and Scuddy, leaving no doubt that she was off to enjoy a man's pleasures. She had contrived whenever possible to avoid Sir William's company, fearful that he would see through her disguise. When Scuddy had told her and Harry about the wager, her condemnation of him had been complete.

"Lord Harry, for God's sake, stop staring at Sir William! Wouldn't do to offend him, I assure you."

Hetty turned her eyes back to Sir Harry. "You are right, of course, Harry. It is just that he *offends* me." Her thoughts returned quite readily to her own predicament. She realized that she was not behaving as a normal gentleman would. After all, the only reason a man would come to Lady Buxtell's establishment was to gratify his appetites. Thus, she stood without a word as the diminutive Lilly bore off a suddenly tongue-tied Scuddy. She found her eyes again wandering to where Sir William Filey sat, one of his hands resting possessively over the full breast of a voluptuous raven-haired girl. In that instant, as if he was aware of being observed, Sir William swiveled about, his dark eyes meeting Hetty's over the rim of his glass. He gazed at her in a way that made Hetty feel as though she were standing naked on display, and then, lazily, lifted his glass in her direction in a mock toast. Knowing that her cheeks were flaming, Hetty quickly nodded and turned back to Sir Harry. It was with a mixture of dismay and relief that she saw Sir Harry's attention was no longer even partially focused upon her.

"I'll leave you now to your own devices, old boy," Sir Harry said absently, winked broadly, and strode purposefully off in the direction of a long-legged blonde, whose features were remarkably like his own.

Hetty felt as if she were frozen in her boots. She knew that she had to do something, at least act interested in one of the girls. She watched as Sir John Walterton led a giggling, flushed girl from the room and toward a wide circling staircase that began its ascent just outside the door of the drawing room. She felt a cold, numbing fear wash over her.

She forced herself to attend to those females in the room who appeared as yet unattached by any of the gentlemen. It was only the second time her eyes swept over the occupants that she chanced to notice a slightly built redheaded girl who stood partially hidden by a red velvet hanging. Even across the room, Hetty sensed the almost imperceptible darting of nervousness in the girl's vivid green eyes. She made her way slowly toward the girl, halting only to procure two glasses of champagne from a footman's tray. As she neared, she was

34

aware that the girl had seen her approach, and started guiltily. Dear God, Hetty thought angrily, she appeared to be younger than Hetty herself was. She looked to be no more than sixteen!

She heard her own voice say calmly, "Hello, my name is Lord Harry Monteith. Would you care to join me for a glass of champagne?"

"Yes, yes, of course," the girl replied quickly, too quickly, Hetty thought as she handed her the glass. She watched the girl's eyes dart past her. She turned her head slightly and saw that Lady Buxtell's sharp eyes had narrowed to mean slits as they rested on the girl. Hetty took a step sideways, effectively blocking Lady Buxtell's view.

"What is your name?" Hetty asked gently.

"Mavreen, my lord."

"You seem very young to be here, Mavreen."

"Oh no, my lord! Why I am not at all young. I shall soon be eighteen!"

You are a pitiful liar, Mavreen, Hetty thought to herself. She saw that Mavreen's hand was trembling slightly, the champagne sloshing near to the rim of the glass.

Hetty suddenly felt a ray of hope as she gazed down upon the girl's pale face. Mavreen was as yet quite inexperienced at her trade, of that Hetty was certain. At least, she prayed for this certainty, since it was quite likely that her future as a gentleman rested upon this assumption.

Mavreen started nervously at the touch of his lordship's hand on her bare arm. "Please forgive me, my lord, would you care to be seated?"

As Hetty seated herself beside Mavreen, she had the sudden fleeting picture of herself in the girl's situation, her livelihood dependent upon pleasing gentlemen. For a moment, she hated herself for aping the sex that took such despicable advantage of females who had the misfortune not to be well born. As Hetty did not have a philosopher's luxury to dwell upon this particular injustice, she turned abruptly to Mavreen and said in a no-nonsense voice, "You need not lie to me, Mavreen. You cannot be more than sixteen, I know. Come, tell me the truth."

Mavreen jumped. Normally, gentlemen were not the least interested in her age, or, for that matter, any thought she might have in her head. She tried to assess his lordship's intentions, but her lack of experience did not provide her any clues. She said hesitantly, "I am sorry, my lord, but you are correct. I am just turned sixteen but three months ago." She saw the young lord's jaw tighten and hastened to reassure him as best she was able. "Even though I am young, my lord, you must not believe that I am not adept at whatever you would wish of me." Mavreen saw a look of sadness pass over the young gentleman's face, and was at once alarmed and confused. She wished she could set down her glass, for her hand would not cease its trembling.

"How long have you been in this establishment, Mavreen?"

"Two weeks, my lord," Mavreen whispered, still at sea as to his lordship's intentions.

Hetty was momentarily diverted at the sight of Scuddy, firmly in the grasp of the raven-haired Lilly, headed purposefully toward the staircase. Damn, *her* friend was going to make love with a girl about whom he knew absolutely nothing—a stranger! And there was Harry, his arm languidly circling the blonde girl's shoulders, his fingers inching toward her full breasts. Hetty felt a deep revulsion at her own body.

"Have I displeased you, my lord?" Mavreen ventured in a flurry, her eyes inadvertently flying to where Lady Buxtell stood in conversation with a newly arrived gentleman.

"No, *you* do not displease me, Mavreen," Hetty said, her voice harsh. She lifted the girl's hand and patted it. "You tell me you have been in this place but two weeks. Why did you come here, child?"

"My Uncle Bob was killed, fighting with Wellington at Waterloo," Mavreen blurted out, her grief, still raw, forcing her to honesty. "My lord, please forgive me, I should have not spoken so!" she cried, knowing that she had been woefully impertinent.

"Mavreen, I trust that Lord Monteith is receiving all that he wishes." Hetty jerked about to see Lady Buxtell hovering at her side, the significance of her observation unmistakably clear.

Hetty replied smoothly, a touch of arrogance in her voice, "I was just telling Mavreen that the room is close. I dislike all this noise. If you will excuse us, Mavreen is going to take me for a stroll." She rose, her back turned insolently to Lady Buxtell, and assisted Mavreen to her feet. "Come, Mavreen," she said softly, "I do not like it here."

Lady Buxtell clamped her lips over an acid reply at being so preemptorily dismissed by the haughty Lord Monteith. She watched dispassionately as the couple slowly made their way across the room and disappeared from her view up the staircase. She was not at all a stupid woman and found herself wondering at what she sensed was the young lord's ill-concealed distaste for her famous establishment. As no ready answer popped into her mind, she shrugged her shoulders indifferently and let her thoughts veer to a more pressing problem, namely, to her new kid slippers that were cruelly pinching her toes. She glanced up at the clock and saw, with some irritation, that it was nearly one o'clock in the morning. Many of the fancy gentlemen were still dawdling about, evidently content to fondle her girls and pour her expensive champagne down their gullets.

"You are bothered about something, my dear Angelique?"

Lady Buxtell swiftly planted a complacent smile on her lips and said to Sir William Filey, "Nothing in particular, my lord. It appears though that the gentlemen are more fond of drink tonight than the pleasures my lovely girls offer." Sir William gave her pause. Although he was always silkily polite to her in that slightly mocking manner of his, she knew there was a deep streak of cruelty in him. Even though it was never directed at her, she was afraid of him.

He laughed softly and she found herself shivering at the sound. "Do not worry, Angelique, I shall myself lead the gentlemen upstairs where they belong." He proffered her a mocking bow, turned, and said over his shoulder, "My thanks for the young French girl, Marie. A tidy morsel, my dear, exactly to my tastes. So young and so very untouched! I congratulate you, Angelique, upon your means of procurement!"

Lady Buxtell momentarily forgot about her pinching slippers, and offered a silent prayer that the foolish, whining Marie had learned her lessons well. Not, of course, that she begrudged the time she had spent with the girl, cursing and threatening her each time she seemed to rebel against the description of what Sir William would require of her. If nothing else, Sir William was most generous when he was pleased. She looked after Sir William as he made his way back to Marie. Despite the habitual sneer that marred the line of his full mouth, he was a handsome man, not above forty. He showed to advantage in his tight knitted pantaloons and his coats had no need of buckram padding. She had heard that by the time he had reached thirty-five, he had already buried two wives. She thought about these two faceless ladies and decided it was probably fortunate for them that they had passed to the hereafter. A night spent in Sir William's bed was not an experience that any of her girls relished. Just imagine how those prudish, simpering innocent young ladies had reacted to his demands! Well, it was none of her affair. She did wonder, though, about the rumor that had recently come to her ears. It seemed that Sir William was hanging out for another wife—a very rich one, in all probability. Lady Buxtell shrugged her thin shoulders and took a glass of champagne from a passing footman.

Hetty, in the meanwhile, followed closely after Mavreen, with what she prayed was a convincing display of eagerness. They passed down a long, thickly carpeted corridor, Mavreen finally drawing to a halt in front of a closed door. Hetty pushed the knob and preceded Mavreen into a small room furnished almost entirely in dark blue velvet. Exotic pictures displaying in the most provocative detail various positions of lovemaking caught her fascinated gaze, and it was with an effort that Hetty forced a telltale blush to remain under her skin where it belonged. Her eyes rested on the four-poster bed in the center of the room, and she felt her heart jump into her throat. At that moment, Mavreen leaned heavily against Hetty and threw her arms about her shoulders. Hetty quickly thrust her away, an instinctive reaction, for she could not trust her tighly laced chemise to completely flatten her breasts. A look of dismay and consternation settled upon Mavreen's face. Hetty thought quickly, knowing that at the very least, she must not give Mavreen any reason to think that she did not appreciate her woman's charms. She took the girl's hands in her own and lifted them to her lips, slowly kissing each slender white finger. "You are exquisite, Mavreen," she murmured in what she hoped was a convincingly husky voice. She forced her eyes to sweep over the girl's gently sloping shoulders, and then down to the fullness of her breasts.

"Oh, thank you, my lord," Mavreen said, her voice breathless and filled with relief. She dared not think what would have happened to her if she failed to please Lord Monteith. "Would you like me to . . . disrobe now?"

Hetty pretended to ponder Mavreen's question. Lord, the last thing she wanted was to have a naked girl standing in front of her! She tried to determine exactly what a man would say and do. As the answer was an obvious one, she was forced to charter new ground. She replied casually, "No, I think not now, Mavreen. Actually, I would know more about you, and why you are afraid of Lady Buxtell."

Mavreen's green eyes flew to the young lord's face. God, she thought wildly, he must be one of her spies! "She is really a . . . kind mistress, my lord, I assure you. She most kindly took me in when I would have starved in the streets."

38

"You are a pathetic liar, my dear. You are terrified of her. You may trust me, you know."

"I—I do not know what you mean, my lord," she essayed lamely. She saw a gleam of anger narrow Lord Monteith's dark blue eyes.

"Has she asked you to do unspeakable things, Mavreen?" Hetty asked, trusting to her instincts.

A blush of shame covered the girl's cheeks, and Hetty continued with sudden hope, "You are not yet convinced you are a trollop, are you, Mavreen?"

"No!" Mavreen whipped back her head, her face as pale as her heaving breasts. Her voice broke on a low sob. "I—I was a virgin, my lord. It is true that she pulled me from the street, but 'twas not my fault that I was there. After word came that my Uncle Bob was dead, the creditors came to our milliner shop and all but threw me out! I had no money and no family I could go to. She told me that I was most lucky, that I was to be . . . deflowered by a handsome lord. It was Sir William Filey." It was as though she felt again his lordship's mauling hands on her body, demanding of her humiliating and painful acts. She choked down a sob and gazed helplessly up at Lord Monteith.

"And what of the other men, Mavreen?"

Mavreen's jaw worked frantically. The thought of the score of faceless men, only their callous, uncaring desire stark in her mind, made her shoulders hunch forward in despair. "Nay, my lord," she pleaded, "please do not ask me. I shall do as you ask. You must not tell Lady Buxtell that I have been so ungrateful!"

Though a haze of unshed tears, Mavreen realized that she had disgraced herself. Lady Buxtell would be informed that she was unworthy of her protection. She would starve in the streets, alone, friendless. She jerked her hand free of Lord Monteith's and covered her face. She sank to her knees and began to sob softly, helplessly.

Hetty stared down at the crumpled girl, pity making her tremble. Sudden anger exploded through her. That this girl—no more than a child—should be forced to suffer such indignity, such humiliation!

Hetty became suddenly brisk. "Come, Mavreen, enough tears. 'Twill solve naught." She pulled a handkerchief from her waistcoat pocket.

"Here, dry your tears. I believe that you and I have much to talk about."

"You—you are not going to tell Lady Buxtell?" Mavreen raised her tear-swollen face, her voice bewildered.

"No, of course not!" Hetty curled her lips scornfully. "I would hang the old harridan from Tyburn if I could! But it is you who are the important one. We must figure out what to do with you."

5

Grey streaks of dawn were lighting the black sky as Pottson ushered Miss Hetty through the servants' entrance into Millie's efficient hands. He had remonstrated only briefly with her, for the angry blaze in her blue eyes had stilled his tongue.

He sighed and shook his head as he turned from Sir Archibald's townhouse in Grosvenor Square to make his way back to Thompson Street. This latest exploit of Miss Hetty's was making his grey hair frizzle. Imagine Miss Hetty—a young, gently reared lady—in a brothel!

He lowered his head into the howling February wind, so tired from his long night of waiting for Miss Hetty that his legs trembled with fatigue. He thought longingly of his bed and sighed again. Not many hours of rest awaited him at Thompson Street.

"Well, you've not got long to sleep, Miss Hetty," Millie said matter of factly, as she tucked her exhausted mistress into her bed. "Sir Archibald and his holy schedule, you know. I will awaken you just before luncheon."

"Thank you, Millie," Hetty said with a tired little smile. By the time Millie had quietly closed the bedroom door, Hetty was drifting into a deep sleep.

To Millie's surprise and relief, near to eleven o'clock that morning Sir Archibald informed the housekeeper, who then informed Millie, that he would be lunching with Sir Mortimer Melberry. Such an unheard of change in Sir Archibald's schedule left the servants stunned. "But you can set your watch by Sir Archibald," Grimpston muttered, bewildered.

" 'Tis not what I am used to," Mrs. Miller, the housekeeper, told Millie over a cup of hot tea in the kitchen.

"Well, I for one," Millie continued her own line of thinking, "would never think of talking against his lordship, but, 'tis a sad thing that Sir Archibald doesn't even think to send a message to Miss Hetty! I tell you, Florence, if his lordship cared as much for his own flesh and blood as he did for those dratted Tories, then perhaps Miss Hetty would not—" Millie stopped her dialogue abruptly and quickly downed a gulp of

41

tea. She had very nearly let slip a secret that only she knew in this house.

To Millie's relief, Mrs. Miller did not seem to notice her sudden lapse. Indeed, Mrs. Miller's thoughts were far away from Miss Hetty and Sir Archibald. The pain in her joints had grown suddenly sharper. She rose stiffly to search out Grimpston. Perhaps he would unlock the cabinet so that she could add a drop or two of medicinal sherry to her tea.

Hetty awoke in a panic. She knew instantly that it was long past noon. Her eyes frantically sought out the ormolu clock on the mantelpiece. Half past four in the afternoon! Where the devil was Millie? She dashed out of her warm bed and pulled vigorously on the bell cord.

Millie entered her room a few minutes later, a faint smile puckering out her thin cheeks. "No need to fret, Miss Hetty. Sir Archibald did not lunch at home today."

" 'Tis impossible!" Hetty declared, grabbing at her shift.

Millie continued patiently, "He informed Mrs. Miller that he was lunching with Sir Mortimer Melberry. In fact, Grimpston overheard Sir Archibald muttering about some elections and how he must keep a very close eye on the Whigs. I cannot believe that he will be back for dinner."

Hetty dropped her shift and said in an awed voice, "Dear heavens, Millie, these elections must be something quite out of the commonplace to send Father out of the house before noon! I daresay I shall discover what is afoot tomorrow—over luncheon, of course."

"No doubt," Millie replied, holding back the heavy covers on the bed. "Back into bed with you, Miss Hetty. No racketting about for you this evening. I have told Cook to send a tray later to your room."

"Such a martinet you are, Millie! Since that is exactly what I intended to do, you will get no arguments from me."

After Millie quietly closed herself from the room, Hetty snuggled down into the warm covers—not to sleep again, but to think. It seemed fantastic to her, now that she was once again the protected young lady of quality, that she could ever have been embroiled in such a sordid affair. She raised thankful eyes upward that she had managed to come through with her identity as Lord Harry Monteith in no question.

She found herself becoming angry once again as she thought about Mavreen's plight before she had intervened. How many other young girls were in a like situation—forced to sell their bodies so that they would not starve? As much as she deplored the inevitable answer to her silent question, she realized that her hands were quite full enough trying to untangle just Mavreen's future. She had made firm promises to the girl, promises that she was honour-bound to fulfill.

Hetty sat up in her bed and fluffed a pillow behind her head. She had promised to settle Mavreen in some sort of position. As her knowledge of these matters was limited, the only ideas that came to mind centered around governesses and ladies' maids. She pursed her lips, deep in thought. Suddenly, she remembered Louisa, her sister-in-law. Indeed, it was inspiration!

Dear Louisa was always complaining about Little John's high spirits. Were not Louisa's letters full of how she wished for a younger person to temper his moods? Hetty smiled smugly to herself. All would be well now, for she had hit upon the perfect solution. She could not help but remember with painful clarity that she had felt not one whit of smugness the night before, when she had faced that formidable dragon, Lady Buxtell, at four o'clock in the morning. What a very different kettle of fish that had been!

There stood Lady Buxtell in the empty drawing room, undoubtedly relishing her success in dispatching all the gentlemen either upstairs with her girls or politely removing them from her establishment. Hetty had approached her with a brisk stride, a scowl of contempt on her face.

"My Lord Monteith," Lady Buxtell greeted with a brittle smile, not forgetting or forgiving his sneering rudeness upon his arrival. " 'Tis early that you are leaving us. Let me see now, you were with Mavreen—"

Hetty interrupted coldly. "Yes, I had the misfortune to be with that whining, fearful little fool! I was told, my dear Lady Buxtell, that a gentleman would not leave your house unsatisfied. I shall regret telling my friends that your establishment is sorely lacking in service, ma'am!"

Lady Buxtell's thin face grew alarmingly red and Hetty knew a moment of fear. To her surprise, Lady Buxtell's wrath fell instantly upon Mavreen's head. "Damned little tart!" she growled viciously. "I picked her out of the gutter, I did. Gave her the best of everything! I should have known when Sir William did not approve of her that the little wretch would cause me nothing but trouble. I shall have her thrown back in the street where she belongs!"

" 'Tis no more than she deserves!" Hetty agreed with great conviction.

Lady Buxtell drew to a sudden halt in her diatribe against Mavreen. She realized with some irritation that she had allowed her veneer of polished manners to slip dangerously. She turned her eyes to Lord Monteith, and said in an ingratiating manner, "Dear Lord Monteith, you must forgive my exuberance in condemning the deplorable behavior of that girl. Of course, there is no charge at all for the evening, let me assure you! Perhaps you have a fondness for redheads—impeccable taste, my lord! I shall install another such a one for your pleasure, but this time, I shall find a girl who knows her place! I would hope, my lord, that with my assurances to make amends, you will not feel it necessary to inform your friends of this incident."

"Another redhead for my pleasure, you say?"

"Oh yes, my lord."

Hetty flipped an indifferent hand. "Very well, ma'am. I shall say nothing if you promise that this one blighted specimen is out of your house this very day. I want none of my friends to make love to a sniveling, limp excuse for a female! I require more creativity in my pleasures, just as, I understand, does Sir William." Hetty realized instantly that she had scored a masterstroke with this added glaring bit of untruth. Lady Buxtell's eyes gleamed and she smiled slyly. "Yes, indeed, my lord, I quite understand you now. It will be just as you say, my lord."

Hetty bowed slightly and made as if to take her leave, then stopped and said sharply, "Well?"

Lady Buxtell, believing that she had pulled quite well through this hazardous situation, blinked in confusion. "Well, what, my lord?"

"I want to see the wench thrown out, madam. Not of course that I disbelieve that you will do what you agreed to, but—"

"This very instant, my lord!" Lady Buxtell walked briskly from the room, gritting her teeth at the irritating young lord's blatant insult.

Moments later, a well-coached, sobbing Mavreen was roughly dragged down the stairs, her arm painfully held in Lady Buxtell's long, sharp nails. "Here is the little trollop, my lord!" She turned viciously to the cowering Mavreen and boxed her ear. She cried shrilly, "Get out of here, you wretched little fool! The street is too good for the likes of you! And don't you try to come sniveling back, my girl!"

Hetty watched with her jaw clamped tightly closed for fear that she would tear into the old termagant, as Mavreen was roughly hurled through the front door into the cold night.

Hetty said evenly as Lady Buxtell turned triumphantly

back to her, "You have done just as I wished, ma'am. I shall bear you no grudge. I bid you goodnight."

Hetty caught up with Mavreen, as they had planned, at the corner of the next street. As she was a gentleman, after all, she gallantly placed her own cloak over the girl's scantily clad shoulders. "Everything will be all right now, Mavreen, you will see," she said gently.

Hetty pushed back the bedcovers with a sudden spurt of energy. She felt at once elated and quite pleased with herself. She padded over to her writing desk, lit a branch of candles, and sat down to quill and paper. She might as well inform John and Louisa of their good fortune in obtaining the services of a young person perfectly suited to Little John's temperament.

Words flowed from her quill and before she had done with her letter, she had covered two pages of flowing, heart-touching prose about Mavreen. Of course, she made no mention of Mavreen's brief professional stay at Lady Buxtell's.

Hetty rose and stretched. Both Mavreen and her letter of introduction would be dispatched from London on the morrow by dear Pottson. She only hoped that he would not let anything slip; Mavreen must always believe that her rescuer was Lord Harry Monteith. Miss Henrietta Rolland was only a dear friend who was sending Mavreen on her way to a different life.

Pottson, in the meanwhile, had finally settled the excited Mavreen into Lord Harry's bed, and bid her a more friendly goodnight than he would have considered possible only that morning. When he had first laid eyes on her, Mavreen had looked her profession—a painted little harlot. But after their shopping this afternoon, when she had shyly but proudly paraded before him, dressed in a modest dove grey muslin gown, her fiery red hair smoothed down into a bun at the nape of her neck, all the paint wiped clean from her young face, he was of the firm conviction that Miss Hetty had behaved just as she ought. Poor little mite, he thought, Mavreen deserved much better from life than being a gentleman's whore. Before he had tucked her in a fatherly manner into bed, she asked wistfully, "Mr. Pottson, will I see Lord Monteith again?"

"No, miss, he is staying with friends, not wishing to compromise you in any way by staying here."

"Do you know what will happen to me, Mr. Pottson?"

"Don't worry your head about it, miss. Lord Harry will inform me as to your future plans on the morrow."

He received his summons to call upon Miss Hetty in Grosvenor Square very early the next morning. As he sat opposite her in the small back parlour listening to her unfold her plan for Mavreen's future, he felt his respect for her grow to impressive heights. He readily applauded her solution, thinking to himself that kin of Master Damien would undoubtedly behave toward Mavreen with a great deal of kindness. Thus, it was with a light heart and a wide smile on his leathery face that he assisted Mavreen onto the mail coach that same morning.

"Now, be careful, miss, not to lose your letter of introduction to Sir John and Lady Louisa." He lifted her gloved hand and pressed five guineas into her palm. " 'Tis a gift from Lord Monteith," he said smiling. "He said, miss, that self-respect doesn't have anything to do with money . . . but it helps in many other ways."

She returned his smile, but felt a large lump rise in her throat. "Please thank his lordship, Mr. Pottson, and tell him that I shall never forget all he has done for me."

Mavreen's gratitude to Lord Harry made Pottson uneasy. He hastened to say, "Don't forget that you know only Miss Henrietta Rolland. It is she who is your benefactress. It won't do at all for you to ever mention Lord Monteith. You won't go forgetting, will you, miss?"

Mavreen sighed and shook her head. "No, Mr. Pottson, I shall not forget."

When Pottson returned to Grosvenor Square before noon to give Hetty an accounting of what had happened, he found her looking much like the cat who had swallowed the cream.

" 'Tis done, Pottson?" she asked, looking up.

"Aye. The poor little mite was so grateful, Miss Hetty. Said she'd never forget you."

"Never forget Lord Harry, you mean," Hetty corrected with a wry grin.

" 'Tis a bit of truth in what you say. But you know, Miss Hetty, it makes me quake in my boots to think of you in a brothel!"

"As a young gentleman with no mistress in keeping, it is what one does," she replied calmly. "Don't fret further about it, Pottson, for we did manage to scrape through unscathed . . . and did a good deed in the bargain! I have devised a plan that will, I trust, keep me away from such establishments in the future."

"What plan, Miss Hetty?" Pottson asked dubiously.

"I will see Sir Harry and Mr. Scuddimore later today. After I endure a recital of their exploits at Lady Buxtell's, they will undoubtedly want to know how I fared. I shall tell them that I found Mavreen to be just what I require, and have set her up as my mistress! 'Twill do marvelous things for my reputation!"

Pottson stroked his chin. "It just might serve," he admitted finally.

"You are too slow to agree, Pottson. Of course, I shall not tell them where I have installed her. That, I am convinced, will only add to my consequence as a confirmed young man of the world."

The smile of triumph slowly dwindled from Hetty's face. "You know, Pottson, Sir William Filey was at Lady Buxtell's. He is really most vile, I believe. Just the story Mavreen told me about him made my blood run cold. I cannot believe that Sir William ever intended to marry Elizabeth Springville."

She paused a moment and gazed into the fireplace. "I suppose that since Lord Cavander did marry her, his intentions, at least toward the lady, were honourable. Of course, we need have no doubts whatsoever as to Damien's intentions."

As Pottson made no comment, Hetty rose, becoming suddenly brisk. "Well, enough of our good deed, Pottson! We must get back to business. I must have lunch shortly with Sir Archibald, then there is Sir Harry and Mr. Scuddimore and a rout at Blair House this evening. As to Lord Cavander being in attendance—I will make no more predictions. The wretched man continues to unwittingly evade me."

6

Jason Charles Cavander, Marquis of Oberlon, sat comfortably in the reading room of White's, his long breeched legs stretched out toward the fire. He was reading a rather involved article in the *Gazette* which recounted in grisly detail a recent murder on Hounslow Heath, when he heard a "hummph" beside him. He gazed up to see his uncle, Lord Melberry, at his elbow. His surprise held him silent for a moment, for his staid uncle, the very cornerstone of the Tory bastion, had not to his knowledge, stepped through the portals of White's in many years.

"Good heavens, Uncle! Do not tell me that the Tories have taken to meeting in this frivolous place!"

The marquis dropped the paper on the smooth mahogany table at his side and grinned engagingly at Lord Melberry. He pumped his hand in welcome, but forebore to clap him on his gaunt shoulders.

"Well, at least you *do* read the newspaper, my boy. I don't suppose the article has aught to do with politics." Lord Melberry removed his boney hand from his nephew's strong clasp, grunted in vague disapprobation at his surroundings, and, flipping up his black coattails, sat himself down in one of White's plush leather armchairs, across from his nephew.

"Narry a bit," the marquis replied cheerfully. "What with Bonaparte no longer the bane of England's existence, I vow the only news worth reading is the gossip about the Regent." He gazed with some amusement at his uncle, wondering as he had many times before, whatever possessed his delightful, flighty aunt, Lady Corinna Melberry, to wed herself to this dour, single-mindedly political gentleman.

Lord Melberry was casting his dark eyes, set beneath incredibly bushy eyebrows, about the reading room. It had been quite a long time since he had been in White's and although the reading room was a sober enough place, he knew that most of its members were drawn just beyond the great double doors to the glittering gaming salon.

"You're looking well, nephew," he said finally, slewing his eyes back to the marquis.

"I thank you, Uncle. As you can see, though, I'm back to my old habits. I suppose," he added, a twinkle in his eyes, "that to track down the fox, one must go ahunting to his lair."

"And you don't look any the worse for all those months in Italy," Lord Melberry continued, refusing to be drawn into nonsensical speech.

"As you see, Uncle," the marquis said, his tone becoming almost perceptibly more reserved. Abruptly, he said, "I trust my aunt is well?"

"Have you ever known your aunt to be otherwise?" Lord Melberry said rather in a sour voice. It occasionally irked him that a man such as himself should be plagued with gout, while he carried the burdens of England's political affairs on his thin shoulders, whereas his wife, who never concerned herself with aught but worthless amusements, was the very picture of enduring health.

The marquis thought of his engagement with the Earl of March and Lord Alvaney—to arrange a prizefight near to London without the magistrates getting wind of it—and sought to bring his laconic uncle to the point of his visit. "I know that you must be much occupied, sir, what with the Whigs and Tories stabbing political knives in each others' backs. Come, Uncle, why would you search out such a fribble as myself? Not, of course, that I am not flattered."

"The Cavanders were always a flighty bunch," Lord Melberry said without much heat. It had been several years now since he had ceased his most pressing efforts to bring his nephew into the Tory fold. As all his blandishments had met unerringly with a smile of amused indifference, he had eventually admitted defeat. "If you must know, my boy, I am here to execute a favor for your aunt."

"Good lord! Please assure me that she has not produced another tongue-tied débutante for my inspection!"

"Hardly, Jason, since your own wife has not been dead yet a year." He wished instantly that he had not been so blunt, for he saw a strange bitter gleam in his nephew's dark eyes.

"Forgive my lack of tact, Jason." He hurried on. "No, your aunt most pressingly commissioned me to invite you to one of her soirees."

"What? My poor aunt finds that she suddenly has thirteen sitting down to dinner?"

Seeing that the marquis had recovered his good humour, Lord Melberry did not hesitate to conceal his own disgust at such a worthless gathering. "Evidently, as she was in quite a

49

taking, until, that is, she recalled your return to London. I trust you are not otherwise engaged for tonight, Jason?"

The marquis sighed inwardly, for he had consented to take Melissande to Covent Garden this evening. But then again, he quite liked his good-natured aunt and wanted to see her. "I should be delighted, sir. What time does my aunt require my presence?"

As Lord Melberry had neglected this mundane detail, he merely shook his head irritably and rose stiffly to his feet. "Come whenever you feel the need for sustenance. Now, lad, if you'll excuse me, I have much to do this afternoon." The tone of his voice left no doubt in Jason's mind that his uncle considered this commission on behalf of his beloved to be a shocking waste of his valuable time.

He rose and cordially shook his uncle's thin hand. A smile touched his lips as he watched his uncle grunt a stiff greeting to a gentleman who had the misfortune to offer a polite how d'ye do.

"He may be your uncle, your grace," Mr. Denby said a few moments later, still affronted by Lord Melberry's bad manners, "but I swear that politics does naught to a man but make him crotchety."

"Be relieved, Denby, that he is not *your* uncle," the marquis said with a wide grin and strode downstairs, deciding how many guineas he would wager with Alvaney over the new prizefighter he was backing.

While the marquis was attempting to set a wager with Alvaney, Hetty, having heard the clock strike noon, rushed toward the breakfast room to greet Sir Archibald.

"Good day, Father. I trust the Tories have the English affairs of state well in hand." Hetty kissed Sir Archibald lightly on his cheek and rested her hand on his shoulder until he reluctantly turned away from the *Gazette* and looked up at her.

How very handsome he is, she thought, admiring his still smooth forehead topped by thick silver hair, handsome and distinguished. His sparkling blue eyes must inspire trust and confidence. The fact that his eyes normally became markedly vague when he gazed upon her did not overly disturb her, for, she thought philosophically, she was of no concern to his electorate.

To Hetty's surprise, Sir Archibald's gaze did not become vague today, not did he seem preoccupied. He said exuberantly, thrusting aside his paper, "Hetty, my dear, we have got those damned Whigs by their radical collars this time! In two borough elections, *two*, mind you, our Tories ousted the incumbents by a great margin! What do you think of that!"

" 'Tis marvelous news, Father," Hetty agreed enthusiastically, preparing herself for a complete account of the brilliant strategies executed by the Tories. To her further surprise, Sir Archibald showed no disposition to favor her with the details of the triumph. Instead, he said, "Come, child, do sit down, and let us have our lunch. There is much I have yet to do this afternoon. And," he added in a conspiratorial manner, "I have a surprise for you."

Hetty was intrigued by her father's unusual behavior and managed to spoon down a modicum of soup before demanding, "Father, tell me, what is my surprise?"

"Surprise? Oh, yes. Lady Melberry has invited you to attend a musical soiree this evening. Nothing fancy, of course, just some squawking Italian soprano to give you a headache. But I fancied it would be just the thing for you. I accepted her invitation on your behalf."

Hetty felt herself go pale. She had realized that sooner or later Miss Henrietta Rolland must make her entry into London society. She had optimistically hoped it would be much later, perhaps even after she had dealt with Lord Cavander. If both Miss Henrietta Rolland and Lord Harry Monteith appeared at social gatherings, it could not be long before someone noticed the marked resemblance between them. "This evening, Father?" she asked, a slight catch in her voice.

Sir Archibald regarded his daughter over the top of his spoon. "I know, Henrietta, that you are still in mourning for your brother. But I did not think you would mind a small informal gathering. I told Lady Melberry that you were a quiet girl, with no racketty notions at all." As his daughter did not comment, he continued in a stern voice, "You stay too much at home, Henrietta. You must not be concerned that you will not comport yourself as befits your station. I will, myself, conduct you to Melberry House. I cannot stay, of course, but no matter. Lady Melberry assured me that she would personally ensure that you are seen safely home." Thus having dispatched any argument that in his view would be of concern, he returned, quite satisfied, to his lunch.

Hetty thought philosophically that there was simply no hope for it. "It is kind of Lady Melberry, Father, and I shall be delighted to attend her soiree. But just this once," she amended quickly, in the hope that her parent would consult her in the future before accepting invitations on her behalf.

After dispatching a message to Pottson through Millie to inform Sir Harry and Mr. Scuddimore that she would not be joining them at Blair House for the evening, Hetty curled up in front of the fireplace in her bedchamber. She cupped her chin in her hand and allowed thoughts of impending doom to roam through her mind. Regardless of the fact that Lord Melberry was one of Sir Archibald's cronies, this soiree was to be a social gathering, not a political one, and as such, the guests would undoubtedly include some of those gentlemen and ladies that Lord Harry Monteith had met over the past four months.

She groaned at the thought, and, clutching at straws, quickly reviewed any illness that would last no longer than twenty-four hours. As none came to mind that could possibly serve her purpose, she was close to crying with vexation when Millie entered her bedchamber with Doby, the footman, in tow, carrying a bucket of steaming hot water on each arm for her bath.

Hetty sat in her copper tub for some time in abstracted thought, when suddenly, she jerked forward with a start, aware that her bathwater was tepid at best and gooseflesh was rising on her arms. She looked over at Millie and asked with despair, "Oh, Millie, whatever shall I do? Sir Archibald knows that I am revoltingly healthy so even a convincing headache would not serve!"

"Well, you can't stay in your bath all day, that's for certain, Miss Hetty," Millie replied prosaically, holding up a large fluffy towel for Hetty to step into.

"You must know too, Millie," Hetty continued as her maid pulled a shift over her head, "that I have nothing suitable to wear. Everything has gone to Lord Harry's wardrobe. As to my old gowns, I have grown taller and they have not!"

Hetty sank down in front of her dressing table and sank her head into her hands. "I am undone," she said dramatically.

"Stuff and nonsense!" Millie retorted sharply. "You tell me that Lord Harry is cool and calm in all circumstances. I fail to see why Miss Hetty cannot be the same." She paused a moment and gazed down at the fluffy cluster of blonde curls atop her mistress's head. "You know, Miss Hetty," she said slowly, an idea taking form and substance in her mind, "Lord Harry wears a disguise, even pomades down his hair. What would you say if all the high and mighty ladies and gentlemen did not think Miss Henrietta Rolland to be a diamond of the first water?"

Hetty's head jerked out of her hands and the troubled frown was wiped from her forehead. "Millie, I do believe you are an absolute wonder!" She bounded up from the dressing table and flung her arms about her maid, squeezing her thin ribs so hard that Millie grunted for air.

"Diamond of the first water indeed! You know, I care not one whit what anyone may say about Miss Henrietta Rolland! With any luck at all, they will not even accord Miss Rolland a second glance."

Just before eight o'clock that evening, Hetty grinned a final time at the image in the mirror, trying as best she could not to double over with laughter. A large, lacy alexandrine cap of pale green covered her blonde curls, leaving only the vaguest suggestion that the head beneath the cap was indeed endowed with hair. A pair of spectacles, borrowed from Cook, sat precariously on the bridge of her nose, the narrow prisms dimming the brilliant blue of her eyes. If the cap and spectacles were not enough to convince the most tolerant that Miss Rolland had neither taste nor style, her ill-fitting gown of pea green—just one sickening shade darker than the cap—would certainly put the polish on the boots!

"Lord, Miss Hetty, a more unattractive female I have yet to see!" Millie cried between giggles.

Hetty turned from the mirror and pulled the spectacles from her nose. "Since my eyesight is as nigh perfect as my health, I had best not don Cook's glasses until after I leave Sir Archibald. I vow, Millie, that I shall be declared an ape leader before the night is over!"

Although Sir Archibald would never connect such a vulgar term as ape leader with his daughter, he did think it most odd of Henrietta to wear such an overpowering cap. Was she not a bit young for such a confection? Hetty replied with composure that such a cap was all the crack this season. Sir Archibald was a trifle daunted by this calm bit of assurance and hastened to say in that charming, vague way of his, "Well, no matter, Henrietta, you will outshine all the other young ladies. Oh, yes, child, Lord Melberry informed me this afternoon that your ears would not be offended by that squawking soprano I told you about—'tis to be a small card party and ball. Just the thing to help you learn your way about."

Hetty would have infinitely preferred the squawking soprano, for it would have meant that all attention would be diverted away from her. As John coachman assisted her into the carriage, she muttered a quiet wish that Lady Melberry's

53

soiree be a very small one, with no persons of particular consequence in attendance. Or, at least, all politicians, for they would never demean themselves by chatting away social nonsense. She sighed, knowing this would probably not be the case at all, and tightly clutched her reticule.

Hetty alighted from the carriage at the Melberry townhouse with the air of a young lady readying for an evening's pleasure. She waited a moment on the front steps until her father's carriage had bowled away down the cobblestone street. Then she carefully pulled the spectacles from her reticule and balanced them at a most awkward angle on her nose.

She took a deep breath, affected a very noticeable squint, and soundly thwacked the knocker.

The Melberry butler, Higgins, a man of discriminating taste and uncompromising propriety, answered the summons. Although his nose quivered ever so slightly in distaste at the homely looking female on the front door steps, his tone was smoothly impassive. "Yes, madam?"

An excellent beginning, Hetty thought, noticing the quivering nostrils. If I have offended the butler's sensibilities, perhaps I shall pull through this evening without a second glance from anyone. "I am Miss Henrietta Rolland," she said to the butler, forcing her voice to a high nasal twang.

"If you will please to follow me, Miss Rolland." Lord, Higgins thought, wincing, whatever will her ladyship think when she sees this fusby-faced female?

As Higgins divested Miss Rolland of her black cloak, he blanched visibly at the pea green gown. It came to him suddenly that she must be the daughter of Sir Archibald, a most distinguished man and ardent political crony of Sir Mortimer's. He was profoundly shocked. Such an ill-appearing offspring could scarce do credit to Sir Archibald's political career. No wonder his lordship scarcely ever entertained at Grosvenor Square!

Lady Corinna Melberry gazed about her overflowing drawing room, and smiled with the contentment of a successful hostess. Sir Mortimer had obligingly removed himself and the majority of the more somberly clad, serious gentlemen of his political persuasion. The few who remained were clustered austerely apart from the gaily chattering ladies and gentlemen of the *ton*. In a few moments, when she was certain that most of her guests had arrived, she would signal to the orchestra to strike up a waltz. That fast German music would rout the politicians!

54

The smile was still upon her lips when she looked up to see Higgins standing with a pained expression on his face next to a tall, abominably gowned young lady. That wretched green cap! Good heavens, she thought with a start, whoever could that be? She planted a smile on her lips and moved gracefully forward.

"Miss Henrietta Rolland, my lady," Higgins intoned noncommittally.

Sir Archibald's daughter! After another glance at Henrietta, Lady Corinna felt the arousal of her motherly instincts. She remembered that Sir Archibald's wife had died many years before, and saw his poor daughter as a neglected, orphaned waif.

"My dear Henrietta," she said brightly, "how very kind of you to come this evening. Do not tarry, child, I would introduce you to all my friends. You are new to London?" Before Hetty could form two words together, Lady Corinna had clasped her gloved hand tightly in hers and drawn her toward a knot of ladies and gentlemen.

Taken aback by her unexpectedly warm reception, Hetty finally managed to say in a tight voice, "No, ma'am, I have been in London many months. I am in mourning for my brother, you know."

"Oh, how very sorry I am," Lady Corinna hastened to say. She had forgotten about Sir Archibald's handsome son who had lost his life at Waterloo. Had this poor child been immured all these months with only the occasional company of her father to bolster her spirits? That in itself was an appalling thought, for Lady Corinna assumed that Sir Archibald, like Sir Mortimer, exuded a limitless array of parental shortcomings. She stilled her uncharitable thoughts, and with grace born of long intercourse in society, drew Hetty forward to meet a fat dowager, who was in fact, her very closest friend. "Eve, do allow me to present Miss Henrietta Rolland. She is Sir Archibald's daughter, you know. We must make her welcome in her début."

Lady Eve Langley, a quite good-natured woman who had not an unkind thought in her head, turned and smiled at Hetty. "So pleased, Miss Rolland." She saw nothing amiss with Hetty's appearance, only wondered at the cap, for only dowagers and proclaimed spinsters donned this proof of their status in society. "You must allow me to present you to my daughters, Maude and Caroline."

"I would be honoured, ma'am," Hetty replied. She had not expected such honest kindness and was at a loss to explain it.

55

She was certainly not an asset to any lady's drawing room, and yet, Lady Melberry had appeared to take her under her ample wing. She found herself wondering if, contrary to her common sense, she had sorely misjudged London society.

Hetty was hard pressed to preserve a straight face as she approached one of the young ladies in question. She had seen her at Drury Lane, simpering and smiling enticingly at all the young gentlemen. Lord Harry Monteith had appeared to be much to her taste when he had chanced to gaze up at her box.

Miss Maude Langley, a rather narrow-faced, narrow-bosomed young lady in her second season, looked most willingly away from her younger sister, who was the center of attention of several gentlemen, at the sight of a young lady who was homely enough to make Miss Maude appear a celestial angel by comparison. She smiled superiorly down from her thin, long nose. "How famous!" she cried with unwonted enthusiasm, "a new arrival in London! But surely, Miss Rolland, this cannot be your *first* season!" She eyed the green cap with glee.

Hetty restrained a smile at this blatant assault, and replied with shy tentativeness, "Yes, indeed, it is, Miss Langley. You see, I have spent many years in the country." If Miss Langley wished to think her a maiden beyond her years, Hetty would not disabuse her.

Lady Corinna noticed with some asperity that her dear friend, Lady Eve, did not even have the wherewithal to see that her daughter—a most irritating girl—was being rude to Miss Rolland. She nodded majestic dismissal at Miss Maude and drew Hetty away to meet Miss Caroline Langley. Hetty had also seen Miss Caroline at Drury Lane, and was forced to admit upon closer inspection that this sister confirmed Lord Harry Monteith's initial impressions. Miss Caroline was a beauty, her dark, flashing brown eyes set beneath perfectly arched dark brows. Her black hair, all the rage this season, was a cascade of shimmering curls, bound only by a blue velvet ribbon over her left ear. She was petite, trim of figure, her full bosom covered modestly—by order from her mama, no doubt—by the most exquisite Brussels lace. There was a slightly petulant curving about Miss Caroline's full red lips, and her lovely eyes darted restlessly about the room.

In truth, Miss Caroline was peeved and bored. She realized that it was highly unlikely that the man she had wanted so badly to see would present himself. How foolish of her to have spent so much time over her *toilette*. She hunched her shoulders. The heady experience of being sought out by every young buck had paled over the past several weeks, and she refused to consider the thought of bestowing her beauty on any of those worshiping young puppies, as society expected her to do at the end of the season. Of course, she did not wish to end up like poor Maude, still dangling on the shelf in her second season. But to wed any of the gentlemen so far presented to her made her wrinkle her lovely nose with distaste. No, she wanted to attach an older man, a man with experience, a man who would not languish at her feet composing ridiculous lines of poetry that praised her slender swan's neck. She had seen such a man, and the thought that he might be in attendance this evening had brought a delicious flush over her cheeks.

She looked up to see Lady Melberry leading one of the sorriest excuses for a female that Caroline had ever seen. She shuddered in distaste, then painted a bright smile on her oval face. After all, one should not be a sour apple, like poor Maude.

"My dear Caroline, I would like you to meet Miss Henrietta Rolland, the daughter of a very dear friend of Lord Melberry's."

"Charmed, I am sure," Caroline drawled, inclining her head slightly to Miss Rolland.

"How very lovely you are, Miss Langley!" Hetty thought she owed this enthusiastic compliment to Lord Harry, who, she decided, would have been far more outrageous in his flattery.

Miss Caroline looked again at Miss Rolland, surprise widening her eyes. She was not used to receiving such frank praise from another lady. She revised her opinion, forgot her affected drawl and smiled pertly. "You are a flatterer, I fear, Miss Rolland!"

"Oh, do not say that, I beg of you, Miss Langley," Henrietta said with obvious sincerity. "You are indeed one of the loveliest ladies I have yet seen in London."

It occurred to Miss Caroline that such frankness and candor should be encouraged. After all, she had nothing better to do at the moment, and conversing with such a homely girl as Miss Rolland might very well make her appear noble and virtuous to the dowager who had jealously proclaimed her to be a conceited Miss.

"Do come sit with me, Miss Rolland, I think I would like to know you better." Hetty nodded and trailed after Miss Caroline to a small sofa by the fireplace. If she continued to fill Miss Langley's ears with compliments, it would at least keep her from further notice by Lady Melberry's other guests.

The young ladies disposed themselves comfortably upon the sofa. "Now, Miss Rolland, you must tell me all about yourself," Miss Caroline begged sweetly.

Hetty knew very well that Miss Caroline could give two farthings about her, and so prepared to give a very limited account of herself. She had scarce time to open her mouth, when she realized that Miss Caroline's attention had riveted itself to the drawing room door. She saw her pink lips part ever so slightly and her vivid eyes sparkle with excitement. Hetty followed her gaze and felt herself stiffen.

"His grace, the Marquis of Oberlon." Higgins' voice was deeply resonant and carrying, bringing everyone's attention to the gentleman who stood with negligent ease beside him.

Hetty, who had never before seen the marquis at such close proximity, was aware that her own eyes had widened in surprise. At a distance, she had thought him swarthy and tight-lipped, had imagined his dark eyes cold and menacing. Had he displayed horns and a pitchfork tail, she would not have been overly taken aback. But now, with the narrow expanse of the room separating them, she saw that his deeply tanned face was quite pleasant to behold and that his dark eyes were warm and alight with amusement. When he laughed at one of Lady Melberry's remarks, Hetty found his smile so disarming that for an instant she forgot who he was.

Miss Caroline grabbed Hetty's hand and whispered, "Is Lord Cavander not the most dashing, handsome man you have ever seen, Miss Rolland?" Her words whipped Hetty back to a harsh reality.

Miss Caroline continued, "I feared he would not come tonight, for he is not known to present himself at such insipid affairs as this. Yet, I dared to hope. He is Lord Melberry's nephew, you know."

"No, I did not know," Hetty managed in a croaking voice. She resolutely turned her back upon Lord Cavander and nodded, stiff-lipped, for Miss Caroline to continue.

"Lord Cavander's father, like Lord Melberry, was very influential in the ministry before his death several years ago," Miss Caroline said. "Of course, my mama and Lady Melberry are the dearest of friends." She rose, her movements intensely feminine, and fastened her eyes upon Lord Cavander's face. "Do excuse me now, Miss Rolland," she tossed over her shoulder, "I really must pay more attention to our kind hostess."

58

"Not at all, Miss Langley," Hetty responded dutifully at the lady's back. Really, Miss Caroline, she thought wryly, you should not be so very obvious in your intentions. She watched Miss Langley move quickly to where Lady Melberry and Lord Cavander stood in amicable conversation. She herself sat back to watch Lord Cavander with forced objectivity. The familiar hatred welled up inside her. Here he was carefree and quite at his ease, while Damien lay dead, forgotten by all save his family. How ironic it was that she should finally be in the same room with him not as Lord Harry but as Henrietta Rolland. She thought the fates must be against her.

She continued to study him. She was forced to grudgingly admit that he was a superb guest who would swell the breast of any hostess. He mingled easily with ladies and gentlemen alike. It occurred to her that his good manners might lead him to even seek her out, and without further ado, she rose swiftly and slipped into a half-hidden position behind a curtain.

Later in the evening, when Hetty had relaxed her vigilance, she chanced to see with a sinking heart that he was approaching her. She quickly turned her shoulder and attempted painstaking conversation with the deaf old dowager next to her. She thought she saw a puzzled frown sweep over his brow at her blatant rudeness. But then, he turned easily, and was soon caught up in Caroline Langley's gay chatter.

Hetty turned suddenly at the sour, whining voice of Miss Maude Langley. "I fear my sister must learn decorum. Is it not shocking, Miss Rolland? She has been hanging on Lord Cavander's arm all evening! Of course, you must know about him!"

Hetty, who had drawn a fatalistic sigh at Miss Maude's jealous attack on her sister, now raised her eyes to the young lady's face, all attention. "No, Miss Langley, I fear I do not know about Lord Cavander, save that he is Lord Melberry's nephew and the Marquis of Oberlon. He appears to be charming to all of Lady Melberry's guests, I think."

Miss Maude arched a thick brow, darted her eyes once again in Lord Cavander's direction, and simpered in the most annoying way. "Oh, la, Miss Rolland, you are new to London!" She lowered her voice and leaned closer to Hetty. "Mama would not approve my saying so, but you must know he is a rake. But then, from all that I have heard, I suppose a gentleman who is a rake is perforce charming."

"But why is he a rake, Miss Langley?" Hetty pursued innocently.

Miss Langley lowered her voice even more and cupped her gloved hand over her mouth. "His wife died but eight or nine months ago, in childbirth, so I overheard Lady Melberry telling Mama. He left England immediately, scarce after her funeral, and traveled to Italy. His exploits with the Italian ladies were all the talk of London. Indeed, I have seen him with a new mistress; he flaunts her all about London in the most high-handed way! Have you not seen them, Miss Rolland?"

"From a distance, Miss Langley," Hetty replied perfunctorily. Elizabeth had died in childbirth! Surely Miss Langley must be mistaken, for had Elizabeth not married Lord Cavander only seven months before her death? Hetty asked cautiously, "Who was Lord Cavander's wife, Miss Langley? How sad that the poor lady died so quickly after their marriage."

Hetty watched Miss Langley's eyes narrow and her mouth turn down in a thin disapproving line. "Elizabeth Springville was her name. She and I were both in our first season last year. She was loose, Miss Rolland, and a flirt. I suppose that she was pretty enough—in a sort of blousy way—but I cannot excuse her flightiness. Lord Cavander was only one of several gentlemen dangling after her. When he suddenly married her by special license, and then removed her immediately from London to one of his estates in the West Country, there was much speculation. I will tell you, Miss Rolland, that I do not need to speculate! My mama is Lady Melberry's best friend, and *she* is, of course, Lord Cavander's aunt—well, I know for a fact, that Elizabeth was in the family way."

"It would appear to me, dear Miss Langley, that Lord Cavander behaved in a most honourable way. Surely a rake would not have married the lady."

Miss Maude looked pityingly at Hetty. "You did not let me finish, Miss Rolland. It was rumored that after he took his bride to the West Country, he left her and returned to his dissipations. Shocking, is it not? I only pray that my own sister will not fall into the same dire predicament that led poor Elizabeth to her death!"

"She is a spiteful, jealous cat, Millie, and I am not certain that I can believe all that she told me." Hetty fumbled with the buttons on her nightgown, forcing them into their proper holes before continuing. "But the fact of the matter is that Lady Langley is Lady Melberry's best friend and what with Lord Cavander being her nephew, well, it does make some sense that Miss Maude could find out that Elizabeth had been pregnant. Oh, Millie, you do not think, do you, that perhaps the child was Damien's?"

"Well, it may as be the truth, Miss Hetty. You remember that we could not understand why Elizabeth would have *no choice*, as she put it in her letter to your brother. It would appear that she wished to avoid a scandal by marrying herself off as quickly as possible. You told me yourself that her father, Old Colonel Springville, was a stiff, proper old gentleman. Probably curl up his toes were his daughter to disgrace him in such a way!"

"Poor Elizabeth! I can see it all now, Millie. She loved Damien, and though I cannot condone her behavior, or my brother's, for that matter, they must have planned to marry."

Millie was silent a moment, staring thoughtfully over the top of Hetty's head. "Do you think, Miss Hetty," she said slowly, "that Lord Cavander married Elizabeth without knowing that she was pregnant?"

Hetty nodded, her eyes sad. "Yes, she must have kept silent to protect herself. When Lord Cavander realized that she was pregnant with Damien's child, he practically deserted her, just as Miss Langley said. It is ironic, is it not, Millie? He sent Damien to his death, thus winning the lady, only to discover that *she* had used *him!* How Damien must have suffered, knowing that she carried his child, and he could do nothing about it."

"Miss Hetty, hold a moment, there is something here that simply does not allow the key to fit the lock!" Millie frowned and rubbed her fingertips against her thin ribs.

"You are thinking that Lord Cavander's actions were not altogether those of a despicable rake," Hetty said.

"Perhaps. Sounds like to me that his grace loved the girl. My ma told me that when men are smitten they will do any number of outrageous things to get what they want."

Hetty cut in harshly. "I do not care about Lord Cavander's motives, Millie. The fact remains that it was he who is responsible for Damien's death! He deserves all that I have planned for him!"

Several hours later, Millie quietly entered Hetty's bedchamber to ensure that she had indeed locked away the fine pearl necklace her mistress had worn this evening. She stood silently at her mistress's bedside, the slender candle flame darting shafts of orange light, and gazed down upon Hetty's face. Millie felt a sudden wrenching of fear. Deep in sleep, with her tousled blonde curls softly framing her small face,

61

Miss Hetty looked like an innocent, vulnerable young girl. Millie turned, the candle trembling in her hand. What chance could Miss Hetty have against such a powerful, ruthless man as Lord Cavander?

7

Lord Harry and Sir Harry Brandon stood outside the Earl of March's elegant three-story townhouse on the corner of Grosvenor Square. A blustery February wind whipped their greatcoats about their ankles and tugged at the top hats set rakishly over their carefully pomaded locks.

"I tell you, Lord Harry, if my brother-in-law backs you, we will have you a member of White's by this very evening. You can't go on missing out on all the good sport. Just be yourself and Julien will like you well enough. Already dashed him a note, telling him all about your pedigree, you know."

"Harry, are you certain? I would not wish to disaccommodate him."

"For God's sake, Lord Harry, I begin to think you a coward. My brother-in-law don't bite! After all, he and my sister, Kate, have just returned from St. Clair. Since he hasn't seen me for a good while, I expect him to be very well disposed toward me."

Sir Harry grasped Lord Harry's arm and pulled him ruthlessly up the front steps. Hetty could not be certain why she felt so uneasy about making the acquaintance of the powerful Earl of March. But the die was cast, and Harry was right, she could not draw back now. It was imperative that she become a member of White's, a regular habitué of that famous club, the club where Lord Cavander spent a good deal of his time.

But an instant after Harry rapped the large brass knocker, the door was opened by one of the most distinguished looking men Hetty had yet to see.

"Good morning, George," Sir Harry said heartily, grinning in his boyish way at the butler.

George stepped quickly aside for them to enter. "Sir Harry, what a surprise! Do come in—your friend too. Her ladyship will be mightily pleased to see you!"

"My sister well, George?"

"Quite fit, Sir Harry, quite fit." George shifted his kind gaze to Lord Harry and lifted an elegant grey brow inquiringly.

Sir Harry said with a wide grin, "This gentleman is another Harry, George—Lord Harry Monteith."

"A pleasure, my lord." George bowed and unobtrusively snapped his fingers. A footman appeared in practically the same instant, and assisted the gentlemen out of their greatcoats.

"Kate never was a slugabed, George. Is she up and about?"

George looked a trifle discomfited, Hetty thought, before he answered smoothly enough, "Yes, of course, Sir Harry. Her ladyship and lordship are in the library."

"Excellent! Come on, Lord Harry, we don't want to dawdle about all day." Hetty fell into step beside Sir Harry.

An embarrassed frown passed over George's face. He called, "Do you not wish me to announce you, Sir Harry?"

Sir Harry waved dismissal. "Don't trouble yourself, George. I know my way well enough."

The footman, Mackles, was grinning wickedly. George rounded on him. "Enough of your insolence, my lad! Off with you, his lordship wants this coat taken to Weston's this very morning!"

"Damned elegant house, ain't it?" Sir Harry asked, as they made their way down a long corridor. Hetty had no time to reply, for as they neared the library, they drew up in unison at the sound of angry voices.

"Damn it, Kate, I should thrash you to an inch of your life, then lock you in a convent! You little idiot, why did you not tell me that—"

"Don't be a fool, Julien," came an angry lady's voice clearly through the closed door. "I am not some sort of fragile little miss who will fall apart just because of a little sport! You are being altogether ridiculous!"

Sir Harry grinned ruefully at Lord Harry. "That's my sister, you know. Quite a vixen's tongue she's got in her head. Always trimming my brother-in-law's sails. Come on, let's pull them apart."

Hetty felt her unease grow and grabbed at Sir Harry's sleeve.

"Surely, Harry, it is not the time to broach the subject of my membership to his lordship!"

But Harry had already turned the knob to the library door and swung it open. Hetty stood rooted in the open doorway, blinking rapidly at the scene before her eyes.

A gentleman and lady stood facing each other across the expanse of a large oak desk. Of all things, the lady was dressed in tight knitted men's breeches and a white silk shirt.

64

In her hand was a foil. She was young, and exceedingly lovely, her dark auburn hair flowing down her back, bound only by a narrow black ribbon. The young lady suddenly turned. "Harry!" she cried, dropped her foil and rushed forward.

She threw her arms about Harry's neck and hugged him heartily. "Oh, my dear, it is so good to see you again!" She drew back, her vivid green eyes sparkling with delight. "How very smart you look, my dear! Oh—" She drew to a halt and looked past her brother into Lord Harry's embarrassed face.

"Now, Kate, don't ruin my waistcoat, old girl! This is Lord Harry, a special friend of mine. My sister, Kate."

There was no sign of discomfiture on Kate's face as she sent a dazzling smile to Lord Harry. "How very nice of you to visit, my lord. Julien, come out of your sulks! It is not just Harry, you know. You must be polite!"

Hetty observed with some degree of shock that the Earl of March did not at all take his wife's strictures in a disagreeable way. He straightened his tall frame, smiled lazily at Harry and strode forward. "It is good to see you again, Harry. Now, who is your friend here?"

"Lord Harry Monteith, Julien. You know, I wrote you about him yesterday. Dashed good fellow, and needs your backing for White's."

"I am honoured, my lord," Hetty said formally and bowed. She had the inescapable feeling that his lordship's grey eyes saw straight to her chemise. He was an extraordinarily handsome man, and as a woman, Hetty could not prevent the slight flutter in her bosom.

"Another Harry, eh," the earl said with a smile, and pumped Hetty's hand. He turned to Sir Harry. "As always, Harry," he said with an amused twinkle in his eyes, "your timing is impeccable. Your sister and I were just having a rather . . . heated discussion. It will be difficult, but if Kate agrees, we will turn the battleground back into a library."

"Oh, pooh, Julien, this is not a melodrama!" She looked imploringly toward her brother. "Harry, I am becoming quite accomplished with the foil. And now, just because I am breeding, Julien must play propriety! It is too bad of him!"

"Breeding! By jove! Wonderful news, Kate, Julien." Suddenly a look of shock passed over his fair countenance. "You are breeding, Kate, and still hopping about in boy's clothes! Good lord!"

"No help for you from that quarter, Kate," the earl said, his eyes resting upon his wife's flushed face. There was such tenderness in his gaze that Hetty felt suddenly like a chair in the middle of a crowded ballroom. "Your termagant of a sister just informed me a few minutes ago, else I would never have allowed her to indulge in such strenuous activity."

"Well, I think both of you are being quite ridiculous," Kate grumbled, as Sir Harry and the earl happily clapped each other on the shoulder. "Men! You are both acting like crowing bandy roosters, so proud of your prowess! I ask you, Lord Monteith, is it just for a woman to sit docilely about, doing nothing at all that is any fun, just because she is pregnant, while men issue all the orders and strut about?"

"It is most unfair," Hetty replied promptly, forgetting that she was a gentleman. "I have heard that exercise is very beneficial for a lady who is . . . breeding." She felt herself flush as the earl's grey eyes rested upon her, a surprised gleam in their depths.

Kate rounded on her husband with a crow of delight. "You see, Julien, not all gentlemen are so confoundedly staid and pompous! I insist that you back Lord Monteith instantly for White's!" She made a little *moue*. "How I wish that I could be a member of White's. What sport it would be!"

Hetty looked away from Harry's sister to see that the earl's eyes were still resting upon her quizzically. "A most unusual stance you take, sir. A member of White's you shall be. Perhaps your unconventional views may sway some of us more pompous, staid gentlemen."

Hetty felt the flush deepen in her cheeks. She quickly averted her face, wondering if the earl meant more than his teasing words conveyed.

"Oh, Julien, it is too good of you!" Kate threw her arms about the earl's neck and hugged him fiercely. To Hetty's surprise, the earl seemed quite delighted with his wife's exuberance. Laughing, he clasped her about her still slender waist and lifted her above him. Her long hair swirled over her shoulders and onto his face. "Let me down, you bully! We must not shock poor Lord Monteith. He is not used to your ways, my lord."

"*My* ways, madam!" the earl mocked, his white teeth gleaming. He lowered her gently, but still did not release her from the circle of his arms. "Lord Monteith will learn soon enough that I must fight for every shred of male dignity. Come, Kate, should we not offer our guests some tea or something?"

"Oh," Kate started guiltily. "Do forgive me, Lord Monteith. Harry here is nothing, but since you are here, we must mind our manners!" She moved gracefully away from the earl and tugged on the bell cord. It seemed to Hetty that George, the butler, was merely waiting for this formal cue, for but an instant later, he entered the library bearing a tray of tea and morning cakes. The earl laughed. "George helps us maintain decorum. Do sit down, Lord Monteith, and take some refreshment. I assure you that we are not always so rough and tumble!"

"I thank you, my lord," Hetty said, and eased herself into a chair next to Harry's.

"Dashed good cakes, Kate," Sir Harry pronounced, his mouth still full with his second bite.

"I will inform François that you approve, my dear. If you must know, he feels it quite beneath himself to prepare such very obvious English fare."

"François is their uppity chef," Sir Harry said by way of explanation to Hetty.

"And a most boring topic of conversation in the drawing room," the earl added, and turned to Hetty. "Harry here informs me that you hail from the North Country. I suppose you must find London ways a bit unusual."

Hetty readily assented to this fact, thankful that the earl had not asked her to be more specific about her familial antecedents. "Yes, my lord, 'tis different in many ways, but I own that I like London much. Everyone has been most kind to me."

Sir Harry chimed in. "Lord Harry ain't so much the rustic anymore either. Except for his clothes, that is."

Kate said, "How unkind, Harry. I find nothing at all wrong with Lord Monteith's clothing. It is just that you have an overfondness for yellow-striped waistcoats."

"I ain't talking about the color, Kate. He must needs wear everything sizes too large."

"A grave shortcoming," the earl said, an amused smile on his lips. "Harry tells me that you fence with Signore Bertioli."

Hetty nodded, unconsciously rubbing her arm. "I have a fondness for the sport, as does, it appear, her ladyship."

The earl pursued, "I have, myself, fenced with Bertioli upon occasion and found his techniques most stimulating. Perhaps you would care to cross foils with me, Lord Monteith."

Hetty thought the possibility quite unlikely, if she had any say in the matter. She smiled and said lightly, "I would say that her ladyship must have first claims, my lord. If her quickness of wit is any measure of her skill, you hold in her a very worthy opponent."

Kate crowed in delight. "Now, Julien, don't you dare accuse Lord Monteith of being a blatant flatterer. I vow that I quite approve the truth of what he has said."

"Perhaps it is her ladyship I should fence with," Hetty said, suppressing an inward grin. Two ladies indulging in a masculine sport!

"She's a damned brute," Sir Harry said, not mincing matters. "Nearly thrust her foil through my gullet once. Lord, Kate, but that seems ages ago!"

"True, Harry, and of no interest whatsoever to Lord Monteith. Tell me, sir, do you also shoot wafers at Manton's?"

"Now that is Lord Harry's forte," Sir Harry said proudly before Hetty could reply. "Never challenge him to a duel, Julien, for I vow he could trim your sails!"

"You exaggerate, Harry."

"Narry a bit! You must come with us to Manton's, Julien. You can see for yourself that Lord Harry is quite the expert."

"I just might do that," the earl replied easily.

Sir Harry rose from his seat, walked over to his sister and kissed her rather clumsily on the cheek. "Lord Harry and I really must be going now, Kate. Pray take care of yourself."

Kate dimpled. "Since you've gotten what you came for, Harry, 'tis obvious that you wish to be gone from your poor pregnant sister! Lord Monteith, it has been an honour to meet you. I trust that you will temper this madcap's activities."

Hetty rose and took the countess's hand in hers. "Harry is an excellent friend, my lady. He has the sunniest of tempers, I assure you."

Sir Harry turned to his brother-in-law. "Now don't forget, Julien, to take care of Lord Harry's membership this afternoon. 'Tis quite a celebration I've planned for this evening!"

"May Saint George preserve you, my lord," Kate said, rising.

"Rest assured that I shall do what I have promised. Take care, Monteith. No doubt I shall see you at White's."

"Thank you, my lord, for your kindness," Hetty said.

Sir Harry turned before leaving the library, and cast a long, darkling glance at his sister. "Well, at least you'll be out of boy's clothing before long. Just imagine—a breeched, pregnant lady!"

"Be gone with you, scamp," Kate called.

Late that same evening, as the Earl and Countess of March lay close together in their bed, Kate nuzzled her cheek against her husband's neck and whispered with mock severity, "Now, my lord, will you allow me to continue with our fencing lessons? You must admit that it is no more strenuous than our lovemaking."

The earl shifted his position so that he could gaze into his wife's vivid green eyes. "At least, little shrew, we confine our lovemaking to the bed. If you wish to draw comparisons, I vow this exercise is much closer to riding."

"What a vulgar thing to say!" the countess said, trying valiantly to suppress a giggle. She was forced to admit the truth of his concern, and sighed. "Very well, I suppose riding—in all its varied forms—must content me for a while."

"If it does not, you may be certain that I shall blame myself." He kissed her gently, then absently began twirling thick curls of rich auburn hair about his hand. "What do you think about Harry's new friend, Lord Monteith?"

The countess pondered a moment before answering slowly, "I think he is somewhat different from Harry's usual friends. He seems sober and quite mature for his years. I vow he cannot be much older than I am. You know, Julien—and do not tease me—but at first I thought him to be a rather effeminate young man, for he is quite a pretty fellow. But after listening to his calm good sense, watching him gently and good-humouredly temper Harry, I must own that I like him."

The earl laughed softly and tweaked her nose. "Nay, I would not mock your views, little one. It would seem that regardless of the fact that Lord Monteith is a pretty fellow, as you phrased it, he has already gained something of a reputation for being a young rakehell."

"No, Julien, you cannot mean it," the countess said.

"Harry was quick to inform me that Monteith has already installed a mistress here in town. The story goes that he found her in Lady Buxtell's establishment, plucked her out and set her up."

"Having a mistress cannot make him a rakehell! After all, my love, you had a string of mistresses in keeping before we met."

"Good lord, Kate, you make it sound as though I was a sultan with a harem!" The earl quickly shifted the subject, finding this one none too comfortable. "In any case, I have seen to the young man's membership at White's. I do not doubt that he and Harry have already registered Lord Monteith's name in Henry's famous book."

"It is kind of you, my love," the countess approved and promptly displayed her sentiments in an unmistakably sensuous way.

Before succumbing to his wife's alluring proposal, the earl said half to himself, "I find young Monteith most interesting. Now that he is a member at White's, I can more easily follow what I believe will be an interesting career. Now, my temptress Kate, enough of both Harrys!"

Both Harrys and Mr. Scuddimore were seated at that moment in the large dining room at White's, toasting each other from a seemingly endless supply of champagne bottles.

"Keep the best the cellar boasts of coming," Sir Harry ordered the waiter, then turned with a wide grin to Lord Harry. "Damned fine banquet, Lord Harry! But now 'tis time for another toast!"

"To the wilds of Scotland," Mr. Scuddimore offered, and clicked his glass to Lord Harry's.

Hetty obligingly sipped at her champagne. She thought of the price of this orgy of food and drink, and blanched. She knew she must not outrun the constable, just on the off-chance that Sir Archibald might inadvertently speak to his man of business. A game of piquet or faro would be just the thing to cover the cost of her celebration.

A marked leer set somewhat comically in Sir Harry's unworldly eyes. "Well, Scuddy," he said, "now that Lord Harry is officially one of us, I think it only fair that he tell us where he has hidden his little ladybird."

"Hold, Harry, I believe Scuddy is far too much the gentleman to demand such knowledge." She nearly broke into laughter at the sight of Scuddy's fallen face. "Suffice it to say that she is quite well and supremely happy." Hetty silently toasted the absent Mavreen, praying that what she said was indeed true.

"Don't suppose you will be coming with us again to Lady Buxtell's," Scuddy said over the rim of his champagne glass.

Hetty shrugged an indifferent shoulder. "Perhaps, if my little ladybird, as you call her, Harry, ceases to please me, I shall return to your sacred bordello. Variety—the spice of life, old fellow."

Harry was more than a little envious of Lord Harry's nonchalant bravado. He carefully stored away Lord Harry's words, changing them about just a bit so that they would be in his style, hopeful that at some time he could say them with the same insouciance to other gentlemen in his acquaintance.

70

Hetty rose, straightened her powder blue waistcoat and gave a mock salute to her friends. "Since you two are drinking up my assets, I can see that my only recourse lies with the luck of the cards downstairs. Now that I am an esteemed member, I can hold the faro bank. To your health, gentlemen!" She tossed down the remainder of champagne in her glass, and left Sir Harry and Mr. Scuddimore to their own devices.

As Hetty entered the elegant gaming salon, she felt a tinge of smugness mingle with her excitement at finally being an accepted member of this exalted male stronghold. She looked up at the heavy chandeliers, their twinkling prisms catching the glowing light from the candles and shimmering down upon the gentlemen's heads, and gave them a conspiratorial wink. The array of black and gold clad footmen, the trademark of White's, still impressed her with their silent efficiency. They hovered unobtrusively about the gaming tables, holding sparkling decanters on exquisite silver trays, ready for the snap of a gentleman's fingers.

She sauntered to the faro table and stood quietly at the elbow of Lord Alvaney, a very likable Corinthian who had vied with Beau Brummell but a few years ago in the arena of fashion. His wry pronouncements upon the misfortune of being in the same era as the Beau made Hetty feel that he cared not a whit about the vagaries of his fellow men. She felt no fear of a snub at standing near to him.

She had thought Lord Alvaney engrossed in the play, and was surprised when his soft voice reached her, without his even looking up. "Ah, Monteith, allow me to felicitate you. New blood and youth you bring us. I daresay that you will stir up the arid old bones rattling around at White's. You play at faro, my boy?"

"Yes, sir, I much enjoy the game," Hetty replied, easing herself into a delicate French chair next to his lordship. "Now that I am a member, sir, I can hold the bank."

Lord Alvaney smiled kindly at this ingenuous remark, and made his play. He did not guess aright, having forgotten the suits already placed to one side of the dealer, and grimaced slightly. "What a ridiculous way to lose twenty guineas," he mumbled, rubbing his hand against his rather pointed chin. "Would you care to take on Sir Robert, Monteith? Robert, attend, old fellow, I am giving you a new lamb for the fleecing."

Robert Montague, a tall, gaunt gentleman, renowned for his tact and deep sense of propriety, raised his dark brown eyes to the newcomer. "Monteith? You hale from the North Country, I understand."

Hetty knew that the gently phrased question cloaked the most vital of concerns to Sir Robert, namely whether her pedigree and prospects were sufficient for her to be considered as a future son-in-law.

"Yes, sir," she replied with the utmost deference. "My father is Baron Charles Monteith, whose major holdings lie in the lowlands of Scotland."

"Humm," Sir Robert allowed, deciding that it would not be good manners to delve further into young Monteith's exact prospects at present. There would be plenty of time to determine if young Lord Monteith was worthy of the signal honour of courting one of his three daughters.

Hetty eased herself into the seat vacated by Lord Alvaney and sat forward to cut the deck. She lost the cut, and was a trifle downcast, for she had always fancied that with Damien, being the dealer brought her luck.

Sir Robert neatly inserted the shuffled deck into the faro box, an elegant, hand-lacquered affair, so exquisite a piece that it effectively masked its purpose of preventing the dealer from any falsecarding. Sir robert shoved the bank forward and withdrew the jack of diamonds from the box. The two of hearts followed, and Hetty set her memory into motion. It was vital to remember the suit and value of each card played, and Damien had taught her any number of quaint devices to remember the order of play. She repeated to herself that the diamond Jack loved the two . . . but the queen of spades must interfere . . . and on and on, weaving a nonsensical rhyme and story with each turn of the cards.

Sir Robert noted with interest the intense concentration on Lord Monteith's face. After some five more minutes of play, he decided to offer a rather unusual wager, to test the young man's mettle. "Twenty guineas, my lord, if you can call aright the last three cards in the box."

The king lost his heart when the eight of spades clubbed the trey . . . Hetty looked up, eyes sparkling. "Yes, indeed, Sir Robert, I accept your wager. I declare the seven of hearts, the ace of spades and the four of clubs . . . in any order, of course."

The ace of spades slipped from the faro box. " 'Tis one you've gotten." Next came the seven of hearts and finally, to Hetty's incalculable delight, emerged the four of clubs.

"Well done, my lad, well done," Sir Robert said, sitting

back in his chair. "You have your wits about you. Remarkable, I think, for one so young."

"Monteith shows his prowess in other areas, I see," came a drawling, mocking voice from behind Hetty's shoulder. She turned quickly in her chair and gazed up at Sir William Filey.

"Ah? In what other areas does young Monteith show prowess, Sir William?" Sir Robert did not particularly care for Sir William Filey, but his code of civility forbade him to ignore the gentleman.

Sir William's full lips drew into a pouting sneer. "Quite a reputation Monteith is acquiring with the ladies. I, of course, use the term loosely, as the bits o' muslin in Lady Buxtell's house can scarce lay claim to it."

Hetty felt herself flush with anger. She saw Sir Robert's dark eyes widen in surprise and the lines about his mouth turn down in disapproval.

Hetty said softly, her eyes glittering and hard, "Perhaps, Sir William, the pot should not be calling the kettle black, particularly when the pot is renowned for boiling over on so many stoves."

Sir William bared his teeth in a snarl, but Hetty was drawn to a short bark of laughter behind her. She swiveled in her chair to see Lord Cavander standing negligently, an elegant Sèvres snuffbox in his hand.

Sir William ignored the interference from this new quarter and leaned down over Hetty's chair. "You've a careless tongue in your head, Monteith. I suggest you keep it behind your teeth, else you may find yourself quite mute one of these days."

Hetty felt Lord Cavander's eyes upon her. I am baiting the wrong man, she thought, but could not help herself. Above all things, she would never let the marquis believe that she was a coward. She relaxed into her chair and lifted a booted leg over the brocade arm. "I fear you mistake my harmless metaphor, Sir William. When I spoke of the pot and the kettle, I was in error. Rather, dear sir, I should have said *pot de chambre*. It is much more fitting, do you not agree?"

"You arrogant puppy!" Sir William hissed, his large hand lifting to strike. "I shall make you pay for your ill manners!"

The negligent ease of Lord Cavander disappeared in that instant, and Hetty sensed his powerful body coiling, his muscles tensing for action. "Hold, Filey," came a sharp command, slicing through the air like the hiss of a foil. "You provoked the lad, as I think Sir Robert will agree. I suggest you respond with wit rather than fists."

Sir William turned angrily on Lord Cavander. "Your grace interferes with no invitation! Monteith needs to be taught manners!"

Sir Robert rose suddenly, his gaunt frame a looming shadow commanding attention. "I must concur with his grace, Sir William. Monteith is new to London ways, just today made a member here."

Lord Cavander said with a derisive curl of his lips, "If it is a duel of honour you seek, Filey, turn your anger upon another man, not a mere boy. You know that I will most willingly oblige you."

Sir William drew back, a glimmer of fear in his eyes.

"It is your manners I find execrable, not the lad's."

Hetty felt as though someone had jerked the chair from under her. Damn Lord Cavander for coming to her aid! In what a ridiculous situation for her to finally come face to face with him. But she had gained her opportunity and had no intention of letting it slip by. She uncoiled from her chair and rose to stand between Lord Cavander and Sir William. Though her eyes were on a level with Sir William's, she was forced to tilt back her chin to look into Lord Cavander's face. She said with biting sarcasm, "I did not know that your grace was a defender of all gentlemen who have not yet reached your exalted years! I am not a callow youth who is in need of your protection. I shall fight my own fights, and find one bully much the same as another, no matter the guise!"

There was a sharp intake of breath behind her, but whether it emanated from Sir William or Sir Robert, Hetty neither knew nor cared. She thought fleetingly of Signore Bertioli and his feigned optimism at her progress with the foil. Was she at last to be put to the test?

Not a flicker of emotion registered on Lord Cavander's rugged countenance. She thought she saw a gleam of surprise in his dark eyes, but he looked down so quickly, she doubted what she saw. She found her hands balling into fists at her sides. Why did he not strike her?

With studied, almost indifferent movements, his grace flipped open the Sèvres snuffbox, and with an elegant flick of his wrist, inhaled a pinch, then breathed deeply. He brushed a fleck of snuff from his sleeve, and to Hetty's surprise, looked her full in the face and smiled gently. His voice was low, almost meditative. "It would appear, Filey, that Mon-

74

teith has no use for either of us. Your tongue is sharp, my boy, and untamed. May I suggest that you temper your fits of arrogant bravado, particularly in my presence."

Sir William sneered. "You had best heed his grace's advice. You may be certain, callow youth or no, that you will pay for your insults!" Sir William sensed that young Monteith had so thoroughly offended Lord Cavander that his Parthian shot would not draw his grace's wrath upon his own head. He glanced a final time with loathing upon the lad's flushed face, turned abruptly and strode away.

Sir Robert, his mouth prim and disapproving, bowed with the slightest dip of his thin shoulders and retired to another table. Hetty found herself alone, facing her enemy. She sensed his strength, his rippling muscles barely held in check by the exquisitely molded coat and knitted breeches. She thrust up her chin. A bullet or my foil will bring you to the ground, even though you be a giant, she told herself, her eyes flickering back to his face.

He spoke again, the gentleness of his tone somehow emphasizing the stern warning that lay behind his words. "You are young, Monteith. Although I applaud your dislike of Sir William and indeed, find myself amused at your wit in felling his vile pretensions, you must take care. I do not think you stupid, my lad, so attend me carefully. Know well your victim before you lash out with your cutting words."

"*Victim*, your grace? How oddly that word sets upon *your* shoulders! I see you in the light of the predator, and you may be certain that I will indeed know the predator before I lash out. I do heed your advice, your grace, with only the minor adjustment to your character." She saw the smooth line of his jaw harden, the twitching of a small muscle beside his mouth. He will strike me now, she thought, bracing herself. An arrogant man as he is will never tolerate such insults.

Lord Cavander slowly replaced his snuffbox into his waistcoat pocket. He gazed down at her not with the anger she expected, but with a tolerant sort of indifference. "I find you amusing, Montieth," he drawled, "but really, dear boy, a predator? It would appear to me that you have decided to number your years by willy-nilly insulting every gentleman who is unlucky enough to come into the sphere of your spiteful tongue."

Hetty struggled to find words to push him to anger. "Nay, your grace, in your case, I do not insult a *gentleman*, but rather a *nobleman!*"

In the same instant, Hetty felt her wrist clasped in an iron grip. She thought the fine bones would break under the pressure, and she shut her lips tightly as jabs of pain shot up her arm. She looked down dispassionately at her hand. His fingers were long and squared at the tips, overlapping about her slender wrist. I have succeeded, she thought, her heart thumping wildly in her chest. He jerked suddenly on her wrist, pulling her within inches of his face. He said softly, "I deplore bad manners and scenes, Monteith. You push me, purposefully. I ask myself why. Why, lad, do you do this?"

Damien's name formed on her lips, but she bit it back. He deserved no explanation, not until she had put a bullet through his black heart. As his lifeblood flowed from his body, then and only then would he know the reason for his death.

"Ho, Lord Harry! What is this? You brew some mischief with his grace? Do not tell me, Lord Cavander, that Monteith has falsecarded you at faro!"

Hetty bit her lower lip in frustration at Harry's bantering words. Her wrist was dropped, and Lord Cavander's eyes flickered but briefly to her face before he turned to Harry. There will be another time, she promised him silently, another time quite soon.

"No, Brandon, Monteith does not, to the best of my limited knowledge, resort to such subtle tactics as cheating at faro." His voice was flippant, yet Hetty felt the sharpness of his insult.

Lord Cavander bent his gaze on Mr. Scuddimore. "I trust, Scuddimore, that your parents are well? Your father has recovered from his hunting accident?"

Scuddy bowed deeply, cognizant of his grace's signal honour of speaking to him. "So kind of your grace to inquire. No problem there, your grace, my father goes along quite well now."

The marquis nodded, smiling easily. "Excellent. Brandon, give my regards to your charming sister and Julien. I shall call upon them presently. Scuddimore, my compliments to your parents."

He turned to Hetty. "Lord Harry, we shall chat again. *A bientôt.*" He flipped his hand in an indifferent salute and strolled away.

"What was that all about?" Sir Harry asked curiously, his eyes following after the marquis.

"Oh nothing, a paltry disagreement, really, Harry. 'Twas of little importance, I assure you! Tell me now, how much

76

champagne have you consumed for *my* celebration? 'Twas only twenty guineas I won at faro."

"Damned if you ain't a real sharp!" Sir Harry exclaimed, impressed. "Who was your victim?"

Hetty controlled her agitation at Sir Harry's unfortunate reference to Sir Robert as her *victim*. "I made a lucky guess on the last three cards with Sir Robert as the dealer. He offered the wager, and I had no choice but to accept."

"Twenty guineas, eh?" Sir Harry rubbed his jaw. "You know what I think, Scuddy?"

Mr. Scuddimore obligingly demanded, "No, do tell me, Harry, what do you think?"

"So that we make Lord Harry neither rich nor poor, we must consume two more bottles of Henry's best champagne!"

"Lead on, MacDuff!" Hetty laughed at his logic. "We certainly want Sir Robert's guineas to be used to good purpose."

"MacDuff who?" Scuddy demanded. "Does the fellow like champagne? Won't do to bring him along if he don't!"

8

Lord Cavander stirred a cube of sugar into his rich Spanish coffee and savored the pungent aroma before swallowing the black liquid. Although it was after nine o'clock in the morning, it promised to be another dreary winter day, and the marquis wished he could have stayed abed. A howling wind was battering noisily against the long French windows in the small breakfast room, and heavy pellets of rain blurred the triangular park just opposite his townhouse in Berkeley Square.

A damned depressing day it would be, he thought, pouring himself a second cup of coffee. Poor Spiverson! He could picture his stooped little man of business, walking hunched forward against the rain and wind, presenting himself to Lord Cavander in a dripping shiny black suit, his sparse grey hair plastered about his small square face. He paid an extraordinarily generous fee to his man of business, yet Spiverson would sooner risk an inflammation of the lungs than part with a few shillings to take a hackney.

The marquis cupped his hands about the coffee cup, rose from the table and strolled to the fireplace, leaving only bones as witness to the once present haunch of sirloin on his plate. He controlled the urge to inform his butler to send Spiverson away when he arrived. Although such caprice from a wealthy master would not be blinked at, the marquis had no desire to emulate his late father, who, with a snap of his fingers, blithely canceled appointments, leaving his house at sixes and sevens while he was off to inspect a new hunter or drink with one of his cronies. The marquis had returned order to the house, and he had no intention of allowing himself to slip into indolence at the sacrifice of his responsibilities. This once, though, he was sorely tempted, for his head ached from too much revelry the previous evening. The rest of his body was none too pleased either, for following a not altogether steady walk from White's to Melissande's apartment on Pemberley Street at two o'clock in the morning, he had roused his sleeping mistress and turned her bed into a shambles before pulling on his clothes and staggering into the dismal cold dawn back to Berkeley Square.

He supposed, the strong coffee engendering a certain objectivity in his thinking, that such orgies of excess could be viewed as an opiate, a not altogether satisfactory manner of burying unpleasant memories, but, perhaps, still better than nothing at all. It really was a pity that one could not learn wisdom, maturity and temperance without causing oneself exquisite distress in the process.

He turned from his post near the fireplace at the sound of his butler's catlike footsteps outside the breakfast room door. It was oddly comforting to him that he was so familiar with his surroundings. He could even hear Mrs. Gerville's wheezing breathing before she got within ten feet of a closed room he was occupying. It was at times like this, attuned to every sound in the house in which he had reached manhood, that he was most aware of his aloneness. None of his friends or family knew what his short marriage had meant to him, and he, of a certainty, had not loosed his tongue on the subject. If they believed his abrupt departure to Italy after his wife's death had masked a broken heart, he in no way sought to disabuse them of their opinions.

His butler's cat's feet drew to a halt and a muffled tap sounded against the door. The marquis consulted his watch. Damn, Spiverson was early. "Come in, Rabbell," he called as he placed his empty coffee cup onto the table.

"Your grace," Rabbell bowed, pausing in his speech to perform this courtesy.

The marquis sighed. "You may tell Spiverson that I shall join him shortly in the library."

"It is not Spiverson, your grace," Rabbell said, his smooth cheeks breaking into a special smile reserved only for the marquis. "The Earl of March, your grace."

"St. Clair! Good lord, man, whatever sends you out on this dreary morning!" Lord Cavander moved swiftly forward to clasp the earl's hand in a hearty shake.

"You might well ask, Jason," the earl replied, moving to the warm fireplace. "For that matter, my friend, I expected to be informed by Rabbell that his grace was not as yet receiving visitors."

The marquis grimaced. " 'Tis my man of business that has me up and about at this ungodly hour. Come, Julien, join me in a cup of coffee."

"It is your Spanish blend, I trust." The marquis nodded

and poured each of them a brimming cup, then seated himself opposite his friend.

"How did you find Italy, Jason?"

"Too warm for my tastes, if you would know the truth. One cannot fault the beauty of Florence, and yet, you know, I could not escape the feeling that I was somehow treading on an overripe fruit."

"You become fanciful, I think," the earl smiled. He crossed a gleaming hessian and sat back comfortably in his chair. Like all the marquis' friends, he knew that his extended trip was the result of his wife's death. He was loath to broach the subject directly.

"Always the gentleman, are you not, Julien?" The marquis' dark eyes rested with mocking humour on the earl's face.

"What would you have me say, Jason? That my ears have been filled with the most exotic and frivolous stories of your rakehell activities? That the Italian ladies heaved deep sighs of regret when you sailed from their sunny land?"

A slow, bitter smile held the marquis' features in frozen irony. He replied after a moment, his gaze fastened on the orange glowing embers in the fireplace. "I have an excellent notion of the drivel spouted from the gossips' mouths. If you would know the truth, my friend, I did indeed go to the devil himself. A most interesting experience, I assure you, and yet—" The marquis paused, his spoken thought left unfinished.

The earl said gently, "And yet, Jason, it was no balm for the soul."

The marquis' head snapped up, his lips twisting into a bleak grin. "Such philosophy! Enough of dissecting my character, Julien! My head aches from too much brandy and I have the most unpleasant notion that Spiverson will keep my nose in his damnable account books until the afternoon!"

"As you will," the earl said easily.

"Now you will tell me what you are doing in Berkeley Square. Surely your mission was not to pull me from the doldrums."

"You have me there, Jason. Actually, I was on my way to visit Tattersall's. I want to purchase a sporting phaeton for Kate, and unfortunately I must rise with the birds, if she is not to know what I am about. 'Tis a surprise for her, you see." The earl lost his negligent air and sat forward in his chair. "Congratulate me, Jason. Kate is pregnant."

"Fine news, indeed! But you may forget a toast for the moment, my addled brains would surely rebel." He pumped the earl's hand, a smile of understanding lighting his face. "So your Kate balks at being a lady of leisure, eh, Julien?"

The earl laughed aloud. "Yes, she even went so far as to inform me of the fact in the middle of our fencing lesson. I was giving her a fine trimming, or at least, endeavoring to do so, when Harry and that new friend of his came to visit. Which reminds me, Jason, what do you think of my new protégé? I saw to making him a member of White's yesterday."

"Protégé? Enlighten me, Julien."

"Monteith is his name. Harry Monteith. An interesting lad, I think. Certainly a good influence on Harry."

"Good God! You do not mean to tell me that you are responsible for that young whelp running free in the club! Hold a moment, Julien. The lad I'm thinking of is rather slight of build, has fair coloring and a damnably sharp tongue."

"Yes, that is a fairly accurate description," the earl said, frowning at this unexpected outburst. "You have more than simply met the lad, I gather."

"Met him! Hellfire, Julien, I was sorely tempted to beat the fellow to a pulp!"

"My, my, a mere stripling has upset the noble Marquis of Oberlon?"

"Noble!" the marquis snorted. "That arrogant puppy had the effrontery to tell me to my face that I was no gentleman, *merely* a nobleman!"

The earl frowned, confounded. "You say the lad is not yet dead?"

The marquis said frankly, "No, at least not at this moment, but I tell you, Julien, if he doesn't keep his tongue still in his head, he is not long for this world."

"Good lord! Since he has offended you, my friend, I begin to question my depth of perception. Tell me, did you not gravely push him in some way to retaliate in such a manner?"

"No, not in the least. As a matter of fact, I recall that my interference was brought forth by the most protective instincts. Monteith was playing faro with Sir Robert when I chanced to overhear that ass, Filey, blatantly draw the boy. Monteith rounded on him—" The marquis paused, memory forcing him to grin. "Damned fine job he did on Filey, I tell you! Said something to Filey about the pot calling the kettle black. Then, with all the aplomb in the world, he told Filey that he was mistaken in his metaphor—a *pot de chambre* was what he had intended to say! As you can well imagine,

81

Filey turned quite purple, then nasty. The villain was on the point of calling Monteith out, when, fool that I am, I stepped forward into the fray and drew Filey off. Instead of gratitude, Monteith turned on me. He made unflattering comparisons between me and Filey—called me a bully, a predator, and the like."

"Perhaps you wounded his pride, Jason. You remember when we were his age, if anyone dared to call our prowess and courage into question, however obliquely, it got our backs up fast!"

"No, 'twas not that," the marquis said slowly. He leaned forward and rested his elbows on his knees. "If I could think of some likely reason, I would believe that the lad hates me. His insults were deliberate and vicious. He was pushing me to violence, Julien, of that I am certain."

The earl was loath to credit such an analysis of a lad barely out of short coats. He arched an unbelieving brow. "There must be a seduced sister somewhere in the background. Monteith has no Italian relations, does he?"

The marquis succumbed to his friend's humour and smiled wryly. "I did wonder about that, so you may stop laughing at me, St. Clair. No, I cannot credit so glib an explanation. There was purpose and design to his attack." He shook his head and waved his hand in indifferent dismissal of Lord Harry Monteith. "No doubt I shall discover his reasons soon enough. Now, Julien, when is the future Earl of March to make his appearance into this world?"

"Late summer or early fall, so Kate obligingly informs me." The Earl glanced at his watch and rose. He said as he stretched out his hand, "I will leave you now to the mercy of your man of business. You know, do you not, Jason, that you are always welcome at Grosvenor Square?"

"Of a certainty I do. Who would not welcome such a *nobleman* as I to his establishment?"

9

"Come on, Miss Hetty, wake up! You'll never believe who just arrived on the doorstep!"

"Oh, Millie, no. It cannot yet be time to dress for luncheon," Hetty moaned, burrowing under the covers away from her maid's prodding hand.

"It is Sir John and Lady Louisa, Miss Hetty. Quite surprised Sir John was that you were not yet up and about."

Hetty assembled her champagne-clouded wits and forced her eyes open. "Good lord! You don't mean it, Millie! Jack and Louisa here?"

"Downstairs in the drawing room, miss, with Sir Archibald. You might well guess that he is fairly itching to be gone. You must hurry, else they will be left quite alone!"

Hetty groaned and swung her bare feet to the floor, wiggling her toes about for the warmth of her slippers. She looked up, suddenly apprehensive. "They did not arrive last evening, did they?"

"No, thank the good lord. 'Tis true luck that follows you, Miss Hetty. They arrived but a few minutes ago."

"Is Little John with them?"

"No, just their servants and mountains of luggage."

Hetty felt a momentary tug of disappointment, for she would have liked to see her small nephew. She looked in the mirror and grimaced. She pinched color into her pale cheeks and rubbed at her puffy eyes.

"Blink your eyes, Miss Hetty, 'twill make the puffiness go down," Millie said as she pulled a gown over Hetty's shift. "Hold still now, I've got to brush out your hair. You can't go downstairs until I've done something with this mess of curls!"

It was some more minutes before Millie stepped back and surveyed her mistress with a critical eye. "You'll do. But do blink your eyes, Miss Hetty. You still don't have the look of a young lady rising from a good night's sleep."

"With good reason," Hetty said, stifling a yawn. She rose and gave her gown a final tug. "Well, off I go. I wonder what in heaven's name Jack and Louisa are doing in London! And without any warning."

"Them that asks are them that finds out," Millie said.

Hetty skipped down the stairs, and mindful of Millie's advice, blinked her eyes all the way.

"Good morning, Miss Hetty," Grimpston hailed her. "Sir Archibald just retired to his study, miss. 'Tis just in time you are. I asked Mrs. Miller to bring tea and morning cakes to the drawing room, begging your pardon, miss."

"Excellent, Grimpston." Hetty gave the butler's hand a grateful squeeze and made her way quickly to the drawing room. "Jack, Louisa! How wonderful it is to see you, my dears!"

She took two quick steps into the room and found herself swooped up in a tight embrace. "Jack, you giant, you are breaking my ribs!" she cried in delight, her arms tight about her brother's neck.

"Hold off, my love," came Louisa's bright laugh, "I do not want Hetty crushed to death before I have even had a chance to say hello to her!"

"My little Hetty's made of stern stuff, Lou," Sir John said, but drew back, releasing Hetty. He studied her pale face and felt the months roll back to the past summer. Damn, she was still mourning Damien. He suppressed his own pain at the thought of his brother, and said with a wolfish grin, "Not trotting too hard, are you, Hetty?"

Hetty saw the darkening of concern in her brother's blue eyes. "No, my love," she said quickly, "I do not trot too hard. But you know, London is a racketty town! One must always struggle to get enough sleep. Now, let me go, for it has been an age since I have seen Louisa."

Hetty gathered the smaller Louisa into her arms and kissed her soundly on the cheek. "How very well you are looking, Louisa! I daresay that marriage with my brother here suits you."

"You may be right about that, my love," Lady Louisa replied. She took both Hetty's hands into hers and smiled happily. "You are the one who grows more lovely by the day, my dear Hetty. And that paleness Jack so heartily deplores is all the crack, you know. At least it used to be. Come, my love, let us sit down. You must tell me all the latest *on dits*."

Hetty sat down in a small bergere chair between Sir John and Lady Louisa. "Now, tell me, you two, whatever are you doing in London? And where is Little John?"

"Hold a rein on your tongue, Hetty," Sir John said, laughing. He turned and winked at his wife, then sat back in his chair, hands in his waistcoat pocket, and said smugly, "It just so happens that London is merely the first stop for Lou and me. Paris is our final destination."

"Paris! Louisa, I began to think you are no mortal woman. However did you manage to pull Jack from his cows and crops?"

Lady Louisa patted an errant wisp of shining chestnut hair back into its coif as she replied, her brown eyes twinkling, "I told him that Little John is quite able to run the estate now that he has reached the advanced age of five. You know, Hetty, your brother does occasionally show signs of reason."

"All right, Lou, enough of your fripperies! I'll have you know, Hetty, that I am a man who keeps to his word. Promised Lou a holiday before she got too fat to travel."

"Fat?" Hetty glanced quickly at her sister-in-law's trim figure.

Before she could seek enlightenment, Grimpston drew her attention. "Do forgive me, Miss Hetty, here is the tea and morning cakes."

"How kind of you, Grimpston. I assure you, Jack, Louisa, we are usually much more organized. I shall pour tea, Grimpston, thank you."

As Hetty handed her brother the plate of cakes, she said, "Now, you man who keeps his word, what do you mean that Louisa's getting fat? She's as slender as a reed!"

"Lord, Hetty, what an innocent you are! Eighteen now, ain't you?"

"Jack," Louisa chided, a blush tinting her cheeks. "Do not tease your sister. What the big bear refers to, my dear, is that I am breeding. It is only fair, he told me, that we have a second wedding trip before we have a second child."

"How marvelous!" Hetty sputtered over her teacup. " 'Tis great news! Why, I believe your baby will be born about at the same time as Kate St. Clair's." She bit her tongue at her impetuous speech, for Henrietta Rolland had never met the Earl and Countess of March. She hurried on, "Where do you stay in Paris? How long do you plan to be there?"

"Damn, but you've got a runaway tongue," Sir John interrupted.

"Did you hear that, Lou, our Hetty's making high and mighty friends. So you've been rubbing shoulders with the Countess of March, have you?"

Drat your tenacious mind, Jack, Hetty thought in vexation. "Well, not precisely," she temporized, "I just know of her, that is all."

"You must know, Hetty," Louisa said, "that Jack has known Julien St. Clair—the Earl of March—for quite a number of years. Neither of us has met his countess as of yet. I understand that she is a charming girl."

Hetty pictured Kate St. Clair in her tight black breeches with a foil in her hand. "Yes, that is what I have been told," she agreed readily.

"Enough of the Countess of March," Sir John said. "Tell us, Hetty, what have you been doing for these past months?"

Hetty silently breathed a prayer of thanks to Lady Melberry. She launched into a description of the soiree she had attended, embroidering upon the event sufficiently to lead Louisa and Jack to believe that she had been gaily flitting from one party to another. As she prattled on, she chanced to see her brother gaze meaningfully at his wife. She halted her monologue and asked quietly, "Did you believe that I was sitting about still mourning Damien?"

Louisa's hand flew to her mouth, and it was Sir John who replied, his voice gentle. "Do not deny us the right to be concerned about you, Hetty. We had thought you were not going out much since that Worthington woman left you months ago."

Louisa added hastily, "Pray do not think that we wish to pry into your affairs. We were simply—concerned, that is all."

"I assure you both that there is no reason to worry further about me. I do go to routs and parties and there are always kindly dowagers about to chaperone me. Now," she continued, closing this subject, "do tell me about what you think of Mavreen. Does she get along well with Little John and, of course, Nanny?"

Louisa replied, "Mavreen is a dear girl, is she not, Jack?" After her husband affirmed her opinion with a nod, she said, "Little John has quite taken her into his confidence. He has even shown her his rock collection! She is one reason why we have no second thoughts about leaving him for a while. Hardly a sad look he could muster when we took our leave of him."

"How kind you were to take her into your home. I prayed that she would work out well for you."

Sir John stretched out his long, muscular legs toward the

fireplace, and said with a frown darkening his brow, "There must be many such waifs as she, I fear. Many such men as her Uncle Bob were hailed as heroes, yet the government did naught for their widows and children. At least we have all done the right thing in this one instance."

Lady Louisa said, "She is such a bright, pretty girl, Hetty, as you know. When the time comes, we will see to it that she makes a suitable marriage. In the meanwhile, she will have the security of wages and a good home."

The frown disappeared from Sir John's brow and both wife and sister realized that his thoughts had strayed elsewhere. He gave a rueful crack of laughter, confirming their supposition. "My father never changes! Lord, Hetty, how do you ever manage the care of him?"

Hetty dimpled. "There is no care, Jack. The servants tell me that Sir Archibald's schedule is a flawless clock. Once, but last week, he had luncheon with one of his Tory cronies, and left the servants bewildered for the remainder of the afternoon! My only interference has been to give Cook the hint never, never to serve any dish to him that contains even the remotest suggestion of corn." At the puzzled frown on Louisa's face, she added with a grin, "You must know that the wretched Whigs are brewing all sorts of mischief with the Corn Laws. I do not think that I could endure another impassioned lecture on their collective perfidy, which, I assure you, would be the outcome!"

Sir John said seriously, "I would never, of course, even dream of talking politics with Father. Yet, being a farmer myself, I begin to see that there are flaws with our new Corn Laws. Not importing corn until our own English corn reaches eighty shillings a quarter—well it seems to me that our poorer people are going to have a hard time of it. Already the price of bread is out of reach for the poor wretches in the larger cities. Damien, I know, was beginning to grow quite concerned about the worsening conditions, particularly in Manchester. I can remember him saying that in not too many years there would be trouble there and demand for sweeping reforms." He sighed and shook his head. "I wonder if Father will ever admit to the fact that there are other points of view that merit consideration."

"You speak blasphemy, Jack!" Hetty swept her eyes heavenward for forgiveness. "Father was born a conservative Tory and he will die a conservative."

"Have you ever been to the House of Lords to hear him speak, Hetty?" Louisa asked.

"Oh, Louisa, I hear each of his speeches at least ten times before they ever make their way to those hallowed halls. Surely, that is enough!"

Louisa rose suddenly and shook out her modish traveling skirt of twilled grey muslin. Sir John, seated, was nearly of the height of his wife standing. She leaned over and kissed him lightly on the lips, then remarked in a teasing voice to Hetty, "You see, my dear, you must show affection to your oversized brother when he is seated. It quite saves one from being crushed or getting an ache in one's neck. Now, Jack, you have done your duty and chatted with the ladies sufficiently. Both Hetty and I excuse you, for I am certain that you are itching to visit your clubs. I will see that Planchard unpacks for you and lays out your evening clothes."

"Dismissed by a little slip of a girl who hardly reaches my chest. I ask you, Hetty," Sir John continued, rising from his chair, "should I box her ears for such an impertinence?"

"Nay, Jack, not when she's carrying another precious heir. Perhaps she will add inches—in height I mean—when she grows up." Hetty smiled down at her sister-in-law, who stood, hands on her hips, glaring at both of them.

"Both of you are impossible!" Louisa declared, stamping her small foot. "Off with you, Jack. I don't wish to see that insufferably grinning face of yours until dinner."

"She leads me about by the nose, Hetty," Sir John said in a mournful voice. He gave his sister a gentle pat on the cheek and strolled from the drawing room, humming a tune whose words were best left unspoken and unsung.

Hetty led her sister-in-law up to the blue guestroom to chat about styles, Little John and the new baby that nestled inside its mother's womb. It was finally Lady Louisa who changed the topics of conversation from her own concerns to Hetty's. She gazed pointedly at the hem of Hetty's gown, that was, unfortunately, several inches too short, and said, "You have grown taller since last I saw you, Hetty. I hope that your party gowns are sufficiently long to cover your ankles. Come, love, show me your wardrobe, for if you have need of something, I would like very much to go shopping this afternoon."

As Hetty could think of no polite way to keep Louisa from seeing the pitifully few dresses, she acquiesced, hoping that at the worst, her sister-in-law would think her guilty of bad taste.

Louisa made a rapid inspection. She was appalled by the outmoded gowns and wondered just exactly what Hetty wore to all the parties she attended. Because she knew Hetty's pride to be as great as Sir John's, she held her tongue, and silently determined to get Hetty to a dressmaker's that very afternoon under the guise of selecting several new gowns for herself. Unjustly, she blamed Sir Archibald for not providing Hetty sufficient funds to gown herself properly. Did he not realize that a young lady preparing to embark on her first full season was in need of gowns that did not positively shout that she was fresh from the country?

Hetty received Louisa's proposed shopping expedition in good humour, knowing full well that her sister-in-law was shocked by her meager wardrobe. Well, she could hardly tell Louisa that Lord Harry was excessively expensive to dress!

Hetty knew a moment of trepidation as they entered her father's carriage, bound for Madame Brigitte's. She could only hope that Lady Melberry and the other ladies she had met at the soiree would not be shopping. Upon their arrival at the select little shop on Bond Street, Hetty darted her eyes to every corner of the fashionable outer display salon in search of anyone who might recognize her. My luck is holding so far, she thought to herself. She then turned her attention to a very décolleté cerulean blue satin gown that would, Madame Brigitte assured her, transform her into a regal princess. "Yes, indeed," she fluttered, nodding her little bird's head vigorously, " 'tis just the thing for a young lady of your height."

"Allow me to make a present of it to you, my dear Hetty," Lady Louisa begged. "After all, I did not get you a birthday present."

Hetty acquiesced with good grace. If only Lord Harry would complete his *affaire* with the Marquis of Oberlon so that Henrietta Rolland could emerge into society as she really was. Only then could she wear the lovely gown.

Lady Louisa was artfully convinced by Madame Brigitte to purchase a morning dress of emerald green and a bonnet of similar color. "Actually," Lady Louisa confided to Hetty on their way back to Grosvenor Square, "I do not think that I shall show the gown to Jack. He has promised to buy me the latest fashions in Paris and I do not want to give him any excuse to go back upon his promise!"

When the ladies arrived at Sir Archibald's townhouse, they found Sir John in the drawing room, dressed in severe black

89

evening clothes, his cravat meticulously arranged by his perfectionist valet, Planchard. To Lady Louisa's fond eye, he presented a most handsome picture. Hetty appeared to agree with Lady Louisa's assessment, for she exclaimed, "Jack! What a handsome devil you are!"

He grinned engagingly from his noble height. "Damned good taste you've got, little sister. I suppose that I haven't a groat to my name with both of you gone for such a long time."

"Oh, pooh, Jack," Hetty said, "all you did was to purchase me a belated birthday present!" Hetty pulled up short and looked at him accusingly, for there was a certain smugness in the smile he presented. "Come clean, brother. You've been brewing some mischief!"

"Not exactly mischief," he temporized, then continued nonchalantly, brushing an invisible speck of something from his coat sleeve, "but it is provident that you have arrived home in time to make yourself beautiful."

"Beautiful? For what purpose?" Hetty demanded, suspicion heavy in her voice.

"If you must know, my dear, we will be having a guest for dinner this evening. Do not worry, for I have already spoken to Mrs. Miller. I believe, Lou, that you will be quite pleased."

"Jack, for heaven's sake, just who is coming to dinner?" his lady snapped, knowing well her husband's penchant for teasing.

"Jason is to be our guest."

Hetty frowned, for she knew no gentleman named Jason. To her surprise, Louisa flung herself into her husband's arms. "Why, 'tis marvelous, Jack! I vow it's been an age since we've seen him. Is he quite recovered from his tragedy?"

"I am not certain, Lou. You will have to judge for yourself." Sir John was aware of the irrepressible gleam of matchmaking in her eyes.

"Jason who?" Hetty demanded.

Sir John looked mildly surprised, then shook his head. "Of course, you would not have met him, Hetty. He has only just returned to London, and when I knew him before, you were still in the schoolroom. Jason is Lord Cavander, Marquis of Oberlon."

"Lord Cavander," Hetty repeated stupidly, hoping she had not heard him aright, yet knowing that she had. "How come you to know Lord Cavander?" she asked finally.

Louisa said, "Did you not know, Hetty, that Jason Cavan-

90

der and Jack were thick as thieves some years ago? They were both in the same class at Oxford."

Hetty shook her head. "Then Lord Cavander also knew Damien back then?"

"Of course," Sir John replied, taken aback at his sister's unusual reaction. "Not as well as I did, of course, for they were separated by some five years. I adjured him, you know, to keep an eye on Damien, whenever he was in London, after Lou and I married and left for Herefordshire."

Hetty felt a gush of anger course through her. Jason Cavander had to be the most vile, cold-blooded man imaginable—to profess friendship with Jack and at the same time push Damien to his death. She was trembling, her anger turning outward. That Jack could be so taken in! Words tumbled out. "How dare you, Jack! How dare you invite Lord Cavander here! I am mistress of this house, and you had no right to invite anyone without my leave!"

"Hetty!" Louisa gasped.

"Well, what is done is done," Hetty railed, disregarding the stunned faces in front of her. "Since you have invited that man to this house, he can not now be uninvited. But I tell you, Jack, I will have none of him! Do you hear?" She drew to an abrupt halt, realizing that her unbridled anger had led her to blunder. Sir John and Lady Louisa, mouths agape, stared at her. Sir John was the first to recover his tongue. "What the devil are you talking about, Hetty? How can you possibly become such a shrew over a man you've never met? Damnation, girl, this passes all bounds!"

"Now, Jack," Louisa tried to intercede, placing a restraining hand on her husband's sleeve.

Sir John's outburst had a calming effect on Hetty. She drew a deep, shaking breath and said in measured tones, "Do forgive my ranting, Jack, Louisa. You will, I pray, give Lord Cavander my apologies." She backed toward the drawing room door. "I am engaged already for the evening, and indeed, must go now and dress. I shall not be home until very late, so you need not wait up for me. I shall see both of you in the morning."

"But, Hetty," Louisa wailed as Hetty turned abruptly to flee from the room, "we are but just arrived! Surely, you could send word—"

"I am sorry, Louisa, truly I am, but I cannot. It is an engagement of . . . long standing." She saw the flushed anger on her brother's face, and before he could demand an explanation of her, she grabbed up her skirt and rushed from the room.

"Hellfire, this is ridiculous!" she heard him shout.

" 'Tis a fine kettle of fish," Millie said after Hetty told her the disastrous news. "Of course, you must leave, Miss Hetty. I cannot imagine that the marquis is a stupid man. He is certain to recognize you, or at least wonder about you. And, knowing you, you could not keep a civil tongue in your head where he is concerned." Millie's unruffled good sense, as always, calmed Hetty, and she stopped twisting her hands in her lap.

There came an urgent knock on the door, and both Hetty and Millie spun about.

"Hetty, Hetty, my dear," Louisa called. "Can I not speak to you for a moment?"

Hetty forced herself not to succumb to her sister-in-law's worried voice, and said sharply, "I am sorry, Louisa, but I must hurry. I must not be late. Please, Louisa," she added, a plea in her voice, "leave be. I shall see you in the morning."

Hetty heard her sister-in-law sigh deeply and could picture the troubled, confused look on her face. She did not move or again speak, and, at last, she heard Louisa's retreating footsteps down the corridor.

"I feel like a beast," Hetty said, and dropped her face into her hands.

"Feeling sorry for yourself isn't going to help, Miss Hetty." Millie's voice was severe. She stood before her mistress, arms akimbo, waiting for her to regain her composure. "If you do not leave soon, as you know you must, you will meet Lord Cavander on the doorstep!"

This prospect sent Hetty cannoning into action. In a short ten minutes, she was clutching her cloak about her shoulders and peering outside her bedroom door. It appeared that Jack and Louisa were either in their room or closeted, awaiting the marquis, in the drawing room. She slipped quietly to the servants' stairs and made her way quickly down to the side entrance, Millie following closely behind her. "You stay here," Millie said, "I shall fetch a hackney." Millie disappeared around the corner and Hetty huddled back against the servants' entrance until she heard the sound of carriage wheels drawing to a halt in front of the house.

"Psst! Come, Miss Hetty."

Hetty slipped from her hiding place and hurried around the corner to a waiting hackney. "Now, you take care, Miss

Hetty," Millie admonished, as she shut the door. "I will be waiting for you."

"Yes, yes, thank you, Millie." She drew a shaking breath and forced herself to sit back against the well-worn squabs. She had escaped, and none too soon.

Upon the arrival of the Marquis of Oberlon, Grimpston bowed lower than was his wont, indeed, lower than his stiff back normally allowed him to. He recognized the signal honour paid to Sir Archibald's house by the visit of such an exalted personage, and made haste to conduct his grace to the drawing room.

"His grace, the Marquis of Oberlon," he announced in a deep, rich voice. Both Sir John and Lady Louisa gave a guilty start, for he had been the focal point of their conversation.

Louisa recovered herself quickly. "Jason! How very marvelous to see you again!"

"You are as beautiful as ever, Louisa," the marquis murmured in her ear, as he swept her up in his arms. "When will you leave this oversized oaf and come away with me?"

Sir John looked benignly upon this scene, then stepped forward and clasped Lord Cavander's hand in a strong grasp. "Beautiful she may be, Jason, but you'd soon be at *point non plus!* It would look damned awkward, you know, prancing all over Europe with a pregnant lady in tow!"

"Good God!" the marquis exclaimed, holding Louisa back in the circle of his arms. He gave her a dazzling smile that revealed his strong white teeth. With his face deeply tanned from the harsh Italian sun, he looked so devastatingly handsome that Louisa thought Hetty must assuredly have lost her wits to have taken him into such strong dislike.

The marquis continued, "It would appear that I am to be surrounded by pregnant ladies. Kate St. Clair is also breeding. Julien told me of it just this morning."

"Yes, Hetty told us," Louisa said, and immediately bit her tongue.

"Hetty?" The marquis looked questioningly down at her, then over her head at Sir John.

"My little sister," Sir John said shortly. "Glass of sherry, Jason?"

"Don't mind if I do," the marquis said easily, giving no sign that he had even noticed anything out of the ordinary with his friend's behavior. "Come, Louisa, let us sit down. 'Tis only just that little John waits on you now."

Louisa gave a trill of laughter as the marquis solicitously assisted her to the settee. "You cannot call him *little* John anymore, Jason. You must know that our son also bears that noble appellation!"

The marquis made a suitable rejoinder about the swift passage of time. As he accepted a glass of sherry, he observed, "I begin to think that my presence this evening has disaccommodated you. Does no one live in this house when you are not here?"

As if to a cue on the theatre stage, the drawing room door opened and Sir Archibald entered, the habitual look of distraction on his face disappearing at the sight of the marquis.

"My boy, welcome to my home. How are your dear mother and sister?"

"Both are quite well, sir." The marquis pumped Sir Archibald's slender hand. "You recall, of course, that my sister, Alicia, married Henry Warton last summer."

Sir Archibald had no such memory of either the sister or the marriage, but he nodded in gentle agreement. He asked, "Warton . . . Sir Waldo Warton's son? Excellent . . . excellent. Good Tory family, the Wartons."

"Indeed, sir," the marquis affirmed gravely. As the marquis had never much concerned himself with politics, he wondered now with a sinking in his stomach if Sir Archibald would beleaguer the company with anecdotes about Tory victories. He reckoned without Louisa.

Artfully, over the first course at dinner, she maneuvered the conversation to the sights they should visit in Paris and the people that they would be meeting. The Bourbon Louis was discussed at length, but only in terms of the festivities offered by the French court at this time of year. By the main course of flaky fish in a rich wine sauce, the marquis found himself describing the wonders of Italy. In deference to the polite company, he dwelled upon the spectacular ruins and the warmth of the weather.

Sir John found himself much pleased with Sir Archibald, for his sire asked such sensible questions, with no political overtones, at least to Sir John's sensitive ears, that by the time Grimpston served apple tartlets topped with rich whipped cream, he was quite in charity with his father.

"I say," Sir Archibald said suddenly, "I thought something was not quite right. Where is dear Hetty?"

94

Louisa's eyes flew to her husband's face. Seeing no immediate help from that quarter, she said with as much nonchalance as she could muster, "Hetty was otherwise engaged this evening, sir. She regretted it most profoundly, yet was unable to cry off."

"Where did she go?" Sir Archibald pursued, sometimes as tenacious as his offspring.

"To . . . to Covent Garden," she replied, nearly choking on a bite of the apple tartlet.

"Odd," was the only reply Sir Archibald offered to this untruth.

As Louisa could think of nothing more to say, it was left to the marquis to make polite conversation until Grimpston appeared with the gentlemen's port.

Louisa made to rise, leaving the men to their time-honoured pastime. She was forestalled by her father-in-law. He eased himself gracefully out of his chair and smiled in a general sort of way at everyone at the table. "I hope you young people will excuse me. There are pressing matters of economics that the Prime Minister has asked me to look into. I mustn't shirk my duty, you know."

As the door closed behind Sir Archibald, Sir John said, grinning at his wife, "At least Jason understands Father's preoccupations, Lou. Is not your uncle, Lord Melberry, also a rabid Tory?"

"That he is, Jack, that he is. The whole business of politics, much to my uncle's disapprobation, quite sends me to sleep." He rose and offered his hand to Louisa. "I trust you agree, Jack, that we have no need to linger over port this evening? I find myself far more animated in Louisa's company than in yours, old fellow."

"He's a damned rake, Lou," Sir John said amiably. "I think I'll keep you hidden in the wilds of Herefordshire while the fellow's running loose in London."

"Don't regard him, Jason," Louisa said over her shoulder on her way to the drawing room. "He is merely jealous because he's been leg-shackled for many a long year now!"

It was on the tip of Sir John's tongue to say that the marquis had also known the matrimonial state, when he remembered the early death of his young wife. He quickly broke into fluent conversation about his estate in Herefordshire. This led to a heated discussion on the value of estate managers. While Sir John would not allow anyone but himself to manage his estate, the marquis praised the diligence and efficiency of Spiverson. At a lull in the discussion, the marquis sat back in his chair and remarked with a twisted grin, "You were always an abominable liar, Louisa. Covent Garden, indeed! Had you been in town but several more days, you would have heard that the play there is vulgar in the extreme and not fit for a young lady. I gather that Hetty is a young lady?"

"Oh," came Louisa's flustered reply.

Sir John tugged at his cravat, as if it were suddenly too tight. The look on his wife's face was reproachful, telling him all too clearly, he thought, that it was now his turn to respond to such thorny questions. Sir John's voice was half apologetic, half rueful, as he said, "You've always been too damned perceptive, Jason. If you must know the truth of the matter, Lou and I really do not know where Hetty went this evening."

A dark brow winged upward to the temple. "May I inquire as to the age of your sister, Jack?"

Damn the cravat anyway! It was much too tight, Sir John thought.

Louisa replied to the marquis' question, her voice tight with embarrassment, "She is eighteen, Jason."

The dark brow remained arched and questioning.

Sir John shot his wife a look that said clearly that it could now not be helped, and silently cursed Hetty for placing him in such an awkward position. He said slowly to the marquis, "It would appear, Jason, that my sister, for some reason unknown to either Louisa or me, holds you in strong dislike, which, I might add, leaves us both in a fog, for she does not even seem to know you."

"Good God," the marquis said, sitting forward in his chair. "It seems that my popularity lessens by the day." He thought briefly of young Harry Monteith. At least that young cub sought him out rather than fleeing from him like Henrietta Rolland. He looked meditative for a moment, not bothering to enlighten either Sir John or Lady Louisa as to the meaning of his cryptic comment.

Louisa said suddenly, "Jack, did not Hetty tell us that she had attended a soiree at Lady Melberry's?"

"Aye, that she did, Lou."

"Then perhaps I've found the answer. Jason, by any chance were you in attendance at your aunt's party, say sometime last week?"

96

"Yes," the marquis replied. "But what has that to say to anything, Louisa?"

"Don't you see—both of you—Jason must have inadvertently rubbed Hetty the wrong way, offered her an unintended insult, or something of the kind."

The marquis stroked his chin with long fingers. "It was a sad crush, you know, quite to my aunt's delight. Tell me, what does your sister look like, Jack?"

"Oh, she's quite a pretty little thing, I suppose. Really a bright chit, not one of your simpering misses."

Louisa interrupted her husband's altogether unsatisfactory description. "Come, Jack, you're not at all to the point! Actually, Jason, Hetty is the beauty in the family. She's not a 'little' thing at all, rather tall and slender. If you can imagine Jack the giant here as a female, blonde hair and all, you'll have Hetty."

The marquis cast about in his memory to place such a paragon, then shook his head. Suddenly he recalled someone mentioning a Miss Rolland and pointing toward a very nondescript female seated with a deaf old dowager. Yes, he remembered now stepping towards the lady, but she had turned her face pointedly away from him. At the time, he had thought her quite rude. He pictured a hideous alexandrine cap of the most putrid shade of green imaginable . . . and a gown of pea green, equally as revolting as the cap.

"She's a beauty, you say, Louisa?" he asked slowly, believing of a certainty that he must be mistaken as to the lady's identity.

"Yes, Jason. Did you meet her at Lady Melberry's?"

"No," he repiled positively, dismissing the pea green cap and gown. " 'Tis a mystery we have then. The young lady has taken me into dislike, yet I cannot recall having ever made her acquaintance. Such a beauty as you describe—rest assured that I would have remembered her."

"Enough of Hetty," Sir John said, as Grimpston appeared in the drawing room with tea. "Don't, I pray, Jason, concern yourself about the chit. Maybe it is that dandy cravat you wear that has offended her!"

"If that is the case, Jack, then perhaps you should introduce her to the honourable 'Tulip' Adderstone. Why, the fellow cannot even turn his head, his points are so high!"

While the occupants of Sir Archibald's townhouse were discussing in high good humour the vagaries of fashion, the mention of "Tulip" Adderstone's shirt points having paved the way, Hetty was in the midst of wiping the remains of cold chicken from her lips and fingers.

" 'Tis a coil, Pottson," she said with a sigh. "Lord, I can only hope that Louisa does not wish to take me to Almack's or some other exalted place before she and my brother leave for Paris."

Pottson removed the tray to the sideboard, remarking gloomily, "Bound to meet lord Cavander, particularly at Almack's. 'Twas a narrow escape you had tonight, Miss Hetty, too narrow for the warmth of my blood!"

"You are always one to cheer me up, aren't you, my dear Pottson! Well, just never you mind, for at least now I am warned and will contrive in a much less dramatic manner to escape further attempts to bring me to the notice of Society and Jason Cavander."

A sudden rap on the outer door brought Hetty springing to her feet. "Good God, whoever can that be! Quickly, Pottson, you must answer." Hetty sped to the narrow hallway that separated the small drawing room from Lord Harry's bedchamber.

"Good evening, Pottson," she heard Scuddy's boyish voice. "I've come to see Lord Harry. Is he about?"

Hetty reached a quick decision and called out in Lord Harry's deeper voice, "Hello, Scuddy. Do come in, old boy! I am dressing and shall be with you shortly. Fetch Mr. Scuddimore a glass of sherry, Pottson."

As she stood in front of her mirror arranging her cravat into The Pavillion, an elegant yet uncomplicated series of folds inspired by the Regent's residence in Brighton, various schemes on how she would spend the evening with Scuddy flitted through her mind. Suddenly, an idea burgeoned in her head, an idea so daring and outrageous that she refused to examine its less desirable offshoots. Was Lord Cavander not otherwise occupied for the evening? Aye, indeed he was, she thought with a gleam in her eyes. She had observed cynically over the past months that gentlemen were far more possessive toward their mistresses than toward their wives. What better way to push the marquis to fury than to poach upon his preserves? She glanced up at the clock above the mantelpiece. Only shortly after nine o'clock. Ample time, indeed more than enough time, she thought, knowing that Sir John and Lady Louisa loved to entertain. She resolutely banished a seed of guilt at using her brother so purposefully to further her own ends. After all, was not Lord Cavander playing a far more perfidious game than was she, posing as the friend of a man whose brother he had killed?

As she shrugged into her coat, she thought of Melissande. Indeed, an unforgettable name and an equally unforgettable woman. Hetty had seen Melissande only upon two brief occasions, neither of which had provided her with many clues as to the lady's character. If Melissande happened to be faithful to her protector, then Hetty—or rather Lord Harry—would be in for a resounding set down! Ah, do not doubt Lord Harry's eloquence, she told the slender image in her mirror.

Although Mr. Scuddimore frowned slightly at the mention of visiting someone in Pemberley Street, he could think of no reason not to accompany Lord Harry, and thus climbed into a hackney alongside his friend.

"I say, Lord Harry," Mr. Scuddimore said finally, barely able to make out a face in the dim coachlight, "who does live on Pemberley Street? If it is your high flyer, I really don't think it is at all the thing that I tag along." His protest was a halfhearted one, for he realized that Sir Harry would willingly give a guinea to be in his place.

"You need not worry, Scuddy, 'tis not my high flyer we are visiting this evening. She is only a very lovely woman whose acquaintance I seek to make. Be at your ease."

The hackney creaked and swayed upon turning into Pemberley Street. Hetty perused the line of small, elegant townhouses that lined the brick pavement, and dug the head of her malacca cane into the roof of the hackney when she spotted the small Queen Anne residence. The jarvey obligingly drew to a halt and Hetty alighted, a smile of anticipation on her lips. "Come, Scuddy," she said over her shoulder, after tossing the cabby the requisite shillings. "I promise you an interesting evening." Had Mr. Scuddimore realized that this charming house was owned and maintained by the Marquis of Oberlon, Hetty with all her persuasions would not have been able to extricate him from the relative safety of the hackney. Unaware of this fact, he stepped gingerly down, resplendent in a waistcoat of red cabbage roses, and walked up the steps beside Lord Harry.

Since Melissande was not expecting Lord Cavander this evening, particularly after his excesses in her bed the night before, she was attired *en négligée*, a frothy confection of green silk and gauze that revealed more than covered her voluptuous charms. A slender red vellum book lay in her lap, and as her eyes traveled down the page, a frown of boredom

99

crossed her forehead. Really, she was thinking, the heroine is such a stupid, simpering little miss! Must she fall into a swoon at the end of every scene? Lord, what would the young maiden have done if Lord Cavander visited her as he had Melissande the previous night? Melissande grunted. The stupid chit would have probably screamed her head off and removed herself to a convent! But still, she thought, torn somewhere between envy and cynicism, the dashing hero appeared to cherish the heroine all the more for her frailty and feminine weakness. In a moment of pique, she flicked her finger against the thin volume and sent it spinning to the carpet. She was not at all certain that she had any desire to be so cherished, but still it might be nice to be offered the choice.

She rose from the settee and stretched lazily. Her apartment was beautifully furnished, and she had, after all, most of what she desired. When Jenny, her maid, tapped on the small drawing room door, her lips were pursed in deep concentration, her uppermost thought being how she could bring the marquis around to the idea that she would look most charming driving her own phaeton and pair in the park.

"There are two gentlemen here to see you, madam," Jenny announced, a touch of surprise to her soft voice. "His grace is not with them," she added by way of explanation.

"How very peculiar," Melissande murmured, consulting the mirror over the mantelpiece. Boredom slipped from her shoulders and she felt a tingle of excitement. Someone to visit her besides Lord Cavander! "Well, Jenny, just don't stand there, do show the gentlemen in!"

Since there was no butler in Melissande's small household, Jenny performed this duty. "Lord Harry Monteith and Mr. Thayerton Scuddimore, madam."

Melissande's first thought upon the entrance of the gentlemen was that the infantry had just invaded her house. Why, they were but boys! She frowned ever so slightly before advancing toward her guests.

Hetty was aware of Melissande's initial response, but was not at all surprised or discomfited by it. She and Scuddy perforce presented a far less prepossessing image than the older, more experienced Marquis of Oberlon. Well, I can but try, she thought. She halted in her tracks and stood poised in rapt wonder, causing Mr. Scuddimore to bump into her.

"You are much more beautiful that I ever imagined," she breathed reverently. Then, as if gathering her scattered wits, she coughed in mild embarrassment. "Do forgive our in-

100

trusion, ma'am, but both Mr. Scuddimore and I have worshiped you for many weeks now, always from afar. To be allowed to see you, to be in your divine presence but a moment—it is all a man could desire!"

Melissande wondered fleetingly if she had just stepped into the pages of her discarded novel. Though she had thought the hero rather silly in his high-flown phrases to the fragile heroine, she wondered if she had not been too abrupt in forming her opinion. She gave the young gentleman a dazzling smile and said with a tinkling laugh, "Fie on you, sir, such flattery! You are—"

"Lord Monteith, ma'am, Lord Harry Monteith," Hetty supplied quickly. "And this is my friend, Mr. Scuddimore." Hetty stepped forward, as if propelled by a powerful unknown force, and reverently clasped Melissande's white hand. She planted a moth-light kiss on her palm. "It is beauty such as yours, ma'am, that launched the ships to Troy!"

Melissande quirked an arched brow, and Hetty rushed on, "No, it is too little to compare you to Helen. You are Aphrodite emerged from the ancient myths to cleanse the jaded palates of Englishmen!"

Although such names as Helen and Aphrodite meant very little to Melissande, she was, nonetheless, able to deduce from Lord Monteith's passionate tone that he was paying her high tribute indeed. None of the gentlemen she had ever known had compared her to an ancient myth! She smiled an enticing woman's smile, and with an effort, turned her attention briefly to the plump gentleman—were those indeed cabbage roses!—at Lord Monteith's elbow. "You are Mr. Scuddimore," she said only, one glance at his flushed countenance assuring her that dazzling compliments to her beauty would not be forthcoming from his quarter.

"Yes, ma'am, but you may call me Scuddy. Everyone does, you see."

"Unusual," she said. "Gentlemen, do sit down. Jenny, sherry, if you please."

Melissande turned willingly back to Lord Harry, and was taken aback to see him gazing with a frown on his fair forehead about the small drawing room.

"My lord?" she asked. She felt a twinge of disappointment that he had not continued in his praise of her person.

Hetty turned readily back to Melissande. She had seen the novel lying upon the carpet and had made out its title—a dripping, maudlin romance! Emboldened by this discovery,

101

she said, her voice deep and husky, "Oh, my dear ma'am, do forgive my wandering wits! It is just that your apartment—lovely though it may be—does not adequately reflect the loveliness of the person in its midst. 'Tis a palace you require, beautiful lady, with silken drapes and mirrors to cast your image to every corner!"

Hetty knew a moment of trepidation. Had she carried her praise to a ridiculous point? To her delight, Melissande sighed and seated herself in a graceful, languishing pose, and patted the chair beside her. Hetty cast a quick glance at Mr. Scuddimore, saw that his eyes were glazed in bewilderment, and said under her breath, "Come, Scuddy, the lady has invited us to be seated."

"Nice house you have, ma'am," Mr. Scuddimore said lamely, much of Lord Harry's high-flying prose having floated gently over his head.

"Thank you, Mr. Scuddimore," Melissande said, her attention already turned back to the charming Lord Harry. "Ah, your sherry, my lord! I will join you, I think."

Hetty accepted the crystal goblet, her eyes never leaving Melissande's face. "A toast to your eternal beauty, Aphrodite." She allowed the goblet to tremble ever so slightly in her hand, then raised it to her lips and sipped the amber liquid. She lowered the glass and gazed soulfully into the deep rich sherry. Her voice was intense with adoration. "But look at the depths of the color, ma'am, it glistens and glimmers with the lights of your hair. I beg you will forgive and understand my poor mutterings, dear Melissande," she continued, audaciously using the lady's name, "but these moments in your exquisite presence turn my very thoughts into water. I am but a lowly slave, and as such, I beg you will forgive my ineptness."

Such pearls, such beautifully flowing words—hardly inept, Melissande thought. She hastened to reassure her slave. "Nay, my lord, your words gratify me to the extreme. 'Tis not often, I must tell you, that I am the recipient of such exquisitely forthright comment."

It was fortunate that Hetty was not in the midst of sipping her sherry, for she would most assuredly have choked. So, my dear marquis, she thought gleefully, you do not cozen your mistress with charming flattery! A mistake, your grace; and now a woman will show you the way to your mistress's heart.

"Beauty must always inspire truth, Melissande. Your face

102

is the eternal food for gods, the gentleness of your person is the inspiration of the poets!"

Melissande was on the verge of placing herself in the slippers of the frail, weak heroine. For a brief moment, she even felt as though she could swoon in the most helpless fashion if this worshipful youth continued in his blatant attentions. She controlled these fancies, and said, "Do tell me, Lord Monteith, you said you have viewed me from afar. Where, sir, was that? You see," she added on a small sigh, "I am not often out in company nowadays."

"Ah, but that is infamous! To hide Aphrodite from the adoring eyes of the world. Dear ma'am, I cannot believe such a thing."

Melissande lowered her vivid green eyes demurely and fingered the silken folds of her négligée. "His grace, the Marquis of Oberlon, does not particularly care for the entertainment one enjoys at the theatre or say, Vauxhall Gardens."

"The Marquis of Oberlon!" Several drops of sherry splashed on Mr. Scuddimore's red cabbage roses. He sputtered to regain his breath, his eyes darting reproachfully toward Lord Harry.

Hetty interposed smoothly, "Did I not tell you that our gracious hostess is a close . . . acquaintance of Lord Cavander, Scuddy? Well, no matter." She chose to ignore the two bright spots of color on Mr. Scuddimore's cheeks, and turned back to Melissande with a look of puzzled inquiry on her face. "How very odd, to be sure! Why, Mr. Scuddimore and I often see his grace at White's and, of course, riding in the park. But that, indeed, is not any of my affair! Do forgive me, Melissande. You asked where we had drunk in your ethereal beauty . . . 'twas not above two weeks ago, at Drury Lane." Pleased with herself for sowing seeds of discontent, Hetty willingly turned the topic. From the corner of her eye, she saw that Mr. Scuddimore wore a hunted look. Well, she would deal with his recriminations later.

Hetty was surprised when Melissande said suddenly, a warm glow in her eyes, "I remember now remarking upon your fair countenance, my lord. Were you not seated in the pit, looking up at my box?"

"Yes, 'twas so. I am honoured that you deign to recall my presence, for there were so many gentlemen vying to catch your eye." Hetty decided that it was time for her and Mr. Scuddimore to take their leave. She managed a guilty start,

103

her eyes flying to the clock beside her chair. With a charming blend of ruefulness and contriteness, she murmured, "It was wrong of me to seek you out, Melissande, very wrong of me, yet I could not help myself. Cupid's arrow has found its way to my breast. Certainly, his grace would not be overly gratified were he to discover that one of your many admirers had the audacity to visit you unattended . . ." Hetty let her voice trail off in meaningful silence.

Melissande was much touched, more by Lord Monteith's declared admiration of her person than by his concern over the marquis. She gazed at him under her lashes. He was much too young for her, admittedly, yet he was so much like the hero from her novel. She was far too experienced to believe that she would ever live under his protection, but she could see no harm in a light flirtation. She thought speculatively about Lord Cavander. Perhaps just such a flirtation with a gentleman some years his junior would make him realize her value. Maybe, she thought dreamily, he would purchase her the phaeton and pair.

"I do not wish you to concern yourself about Lord Cavander. As to never visiting me again, I vow that it is not at all what I would wish. You have committed no impertinence, my lord." She rose and laid her hand lightly on Hetty's sleeve.

Hetty surged to her feet and clasped Melissande's hand in her own.

"What is your direction, my lord, so that I may send word to you . . . when the opportunity presents itself? I do love to ride in the park," she added with a small sigh.

"Your wish must always be my command, dear Melissande."

Once Lord Harry's direction was written down in a thin white book, Hetty clasped Melissande's hand once again and brought it to her lips. "*Au revoir, my goddess,*" she said.

No sooner had the front door closed behind them than Mr. Scuddimore exploded, "Damn, but you've taken leave of your senses, Lord Harry! That *lady* is under the protection of the Marquis of Oberlon! Not the thing, not the thing at all! Why, when Sir Harry told me of your argument with the marquis at White's—" Mr. Scuddimore drew to a sudden halt, his brain having finally leaped to an obvious conclusion. "You are doing this on purpose," he said with heavy accusation, wagging his finger. "Thought all that flattery praising the lady's eyebrows was flummery! You want to provoke the marquis!"

Hetty set her jaw in a stubborn line and rounded on Mr. Scuddimore. Her voice was icy with hauteur. "How *unmanly* of you, Scuddy, to be all in a quake at the mere mention of the Marquis of Oberlon! If you have water in your veins rather than blood, I shall most gladly not include you in any further of my . . . adventures. If I choose to dally with his grace's mistress, it is my affair, and I shall not suffer any recriminations from you!"

"Now see here, Lord Harry," Mr. Scuddimore sputtered, taken aback by this new side of his friend. "I ain't unmanly. It's just that I, unlike you it seems, wish to reach my thirtieth birthday! Powerful man, the marquis, powerful and ruthless. Not one to cross, that's for sure! Ask anyone, he's one of the best swordsmen in England!"

"Keep your tongue in your mouth, Scuddy! I told you it is my affair. Now, old fellow, I think I shall shortly need a showy mare to escort the fair Melissande to the park. You will oblige me?"

Mr. Scuddimore drew up, mouth agape. He nodded his head from habit.

"Excellent! My thanks, Scuddy, I would far rather spend my blunt on an exquisite riding habit for Melissande, rather than a horse. Now, let me see, I think an emerald green velvet, with a dashing plumed hat, of course, would be just the thing to set off her beauty. Well, don't stand there, Scuddy, it grows late, and I, for one, have much to do tomorrow!"

10

Sir John looked a thundercloud as he gesticulated with his fork to his sister at the breakfast table. "Just where the devil were you, miss? Damnation, Hetty, 'tis bad enough that Lord Cavander knew you did not wish to be in the same house with him! But that you would stay out until all hours, then sneak in the servants' entrance passes all bounds!"

Sir John was in quite a taking, and Hetty knew there was very little she could tell him that would not exacerbate his anger. A ghost of a smile flitted over her lips. She certainly could not tell him that she had enjoyed a comfortable prose with Lord Cavander's mistress!

Lady Louisa sent a placating look at her furious spouse and said in a more gentle voice to Hetty, " 'Twas most awkward, my love. And if you must know, I but made the situation worse. You see, when Jason Cavander asked me where you were, I replied that you were at Covent Garden."

Hetty could not control her shout of laughter. "Good God, Louisa! What a marvelous whisker! No lady of any breeding would attend Covent Garden this week!"

"I begin to wonder if you have any breeding," Sir John said irritably. "And you, Lou, don't sidetrack the issue. Come, miss, where were you last night?"

Well, a lie it must be, Hetty thought as she gazed at her brother's implacable face. "If you must be such a grouch, Jack, I will tell you. I was not at Covent Garden, but rather at Vauxhall Gardens. Lou at least had the *Garden* part correct!"

Lady Louisa giggled, and the throbbing muscle in Sir John's jaw ceased its furious pounding. "Lord, but you're a madcap, Hetty! You need a sound thrashing, my girl! I pity the poor mortal man who has the taming of you."

Order was on the verge of being restored when Hetty unwisely retorted, "You men! Why must you always think that if a woman shows any spirit at all she is to be *tamed!* I had hoped that being married to Louisa would have given you more wit!"

"Hetty!" Lady Louisa wailed.

"Oh pooh, Louisa, don't be such a coward! Jack is all bluff, gruff platitudes! And you, my dear brother, you may be a domestic tyrant in Herefordshire, but here you have no authority. In short, dear Jack, I shall do exactly as I please, and with no interference from you!"

Sir John's fork clattered to his plate, sending scrambled eggs plopping to the tablecloth. Before Hetty could draw another breath, he jerked her from her chair, clasped her about the waist and lifted her above his head. He shook her until her teeth rattled.

"Jack, please, you must not—" Lady Louisa groaned.

But Hetty was not the least bit afraid of Sir John's whirlwind attack. As he swung her above his head, she remembered times long ago when her giant of a brother would gleefully toss her about. "Oh, Jack," she said between gasps of laughter, "you are such a bully! I do love you so."

"Damnation, Hetty, you do have a way of drawing a fellow's cork," he said gruffly. He lowered her feet to the carpet and drew her against his broad chest.

Hetty snuggled her face against his shoulder and said, her voice breaking, "How I wish Damien were here. God, I miss him so." She burst into tears.

Sir John's eyes met his wife's above Hetty's head. She nodded silently and slipped quietly from the breakfast room.

He gently stroked her soft fair curls, momentarily bereft of speech. It was several moments before he said softly, "I know, Hetty, I know. Damien was a part of me also."

Hetty raised her tear-streaked face. "Do forgive me, Jack, for being so selfish. Of course you feel his death as strongly as I." She pulled herself suddenly from his arms and whirled about, pounding her fist upon the table. "It is so beastly unfair!" Her cry of anger helped her to get a hold on herself. She drew a deep breath. "I have distressed you enough, my dear. Please, Jack, do not worry about me. I go along quite well, really."

Sir John sighed and patted her on the shoulder. "I suppose you do, Hetty. It is just that Sir Archibald takes no notice of you."

Hetty gave him a lopsided smile. "Father is Father, Jack, and will never change. I am quite used to his ways, and, indeed, wish him to be no other way. He does not interfere with my activities, you know."

"Does that mean that you still refuse to tell me why you did not wish to see Jason Cavander?"

For one long instant, Hetty wanted to pour out the truth to her brother, to tell him that Jason Cavander was no friend. She thought of the letter, safely locked in her dresser drawer, Elizabeth's heart-rending farewell to Damien. She shook her head, her tongue still. No, revenge was hers—and Lord Harry's. She realized that were she to tell him, and were he to believe her, the outcome could be disastrous. Jack was all the family she cared about, Sir Archibald being of little influence in her life. Were he to die in a duel, she would be alone. As would Louisa, little John and the small unborn infant in Louisa's womb. Yet, she could not bring herself to lie outright to her brother. There was a soft plea in her voice as she said, "Please do not demand that I give you an answer, Jack. Suffice it to say that I loathe the Marquis of Oberlon. My reasons must remain my own."

Sir John, his little sister's defender, rapped sharply, "He has offered you no insult, has he, Hetty?"

"No, my dear, you may rest *easy* on that. He has in no way offended Henrietta Rolland."

There was relief in Sir John's voice, though he said stoutly, " 'Twould be unthinkable in any case. Jason Cavander is a man of honour. Of a certainty he has a Corinthian's tastes and habits, but there is naught to shock one in that."

Thinking to bring this uncomfortable interview to a close, Hetty smiled brightly at her brother and asked, "What plans have you for today, Jack?"

Sir John dismissed Lord Cavander momentarily from his thoughts and said, "Louisa wishes to visit Richmond, a picnic, you know, and a visit to the maze. And tonight, there is a masked ball at Ranleagh House. Lou told me she wants to recapture some of her wild youth before turning stout and matronly. You will join us, will you not, Hetty?"

A masked ball. She could act herself, without fear of discovery. "I should love it above all things, Jack. Let me discover what Louisa plans to wear before you steal her for the rest of the day!"

As Hetty skipped from the breakfast room, it occurred to Sir John that he had also asked Jason Cavander if he planned to be in attendance at Ranleagh House this evening. His grace's reply had been quick, a wicked smile on his face. "I had planned to, Jack. Melissande would much enjoy such sport, you know. Your sister will be there, will she not?" Sir John had nodded, hopeful that Hetty would agree.

He thought meditatively that if Jason were to come close to Hetty, she might discover he was not a bad sort after all. Since it was a masked ball, she could easily escape his attentions, if she really disliked him. As he strolled to Sir Archibald's library to bid his sire a good morning, he grinned, wondering just how the devil his very experienced friend was going to storm Hetty's defenses.

While Sir John and Lady Louisa explored the maze at Richmond, Lord Harry trained his eyes on the circular targets set at twenty paces from the marking line at Manton's and stroked the trigger. A shout went up from Sir Harry.

"Bravo, Lord Harry, yet another bull's-eye! At twenty paces, too!"

Mr. Franks, a bluff, merry attendant at Manton's, added his praise. "An excellent marksman, ye be, my lord. Now, Sir Harry, ye see the way his lordship caresses the trigger, his eyes never leaving the target. Ye mustn't be in a hurry, Sir Harry, no sir, never be in a hurry."

Sir Harry grunted, not particularly desiring a comparison between his and Lord Harry's skill. "Well, I for one have had enough practice for one day. What say you, Lord Harry, I am off to Gentleman Jackson's. You've never joined me, you know. Let us see if you're as fine in the ring with your fists as you are at caressing triggers!"

Hetty handed the pistol to Mr. Franks before replying, "Harry, I've told you countless times that you could dash me down in but a moment in the ring! No, I thank you, but I've no taste or ability to embroil myself in a mill. Besides, I have my fencing lesson in but an hour with Signore Bertioli."

Mollified by Lord Harry's frank admission of his superior skill at boxing, Sir Harry said only, "Does the Italian think you've improved?"

A frown puckered Lord Harry's brow. "Yes, he is forever giving me encouragement, but I confess I believe his sense of diplomacy is stronger than his honesty." Hetty did not add that Signore Bertioli had ceased several weeks ago to concern himself about her lack of endurance. All their time together was spent in practicing his master's techniques—delicate feints, subtle flicks of the wrist that could catch an opponent off guard.

"Well, it ain't a matter of life or death, old boy," Sir Harry

109

said bracingly, clapping Lord Harry on the shoulder. A queer gleam shone an instant in Lord Harry's blue eyes, then disappeared.

Sir Harry said uncomfortably, "Here, Lord Harry, you ain't thinking of a duel, are you?" He thought of the Marquis of Oberlon and the outlandish story he had heard just this morning from Mr. Scuddimore's lips of their visit to Melissande's house the previous evening. He blanched.

"Of course not, Harry," Hetty said lightly. She turned quickly from his inquiring gaze and allowed an assistant to help her into her greatcoat. With the knowledge that Jack and Louisa were leaving on the morrow, she said over her shoulder, "Why do you and Scuddy not come to my lodgings tomorrow evening? I promise you a substantial dinner, an excellent claret and a sound thrashing at cards."

"Sorry, old boy, but I've other plans for tomorrow night."

"I gather the fair Isabella Bentworth plays no part in them."

"As a matter of fact, she doesn't. But it's none of your affair, Lord Harry!" Hetty grinned, but said nothing. "Blast, I almost forgot," Sir Harry said suddenly. "My sister, Kate St. Clair, wants both of us to come to dinner tonight."

Hetty shook her head regretfully. "Do give her my regret, Harry, but 'tis off to a masked ball at Ranleagh House for me."

"Now, which one of you charming ladies is my Louisa?"

"My dear John, why 'tis obvious," Sir Archibald informed his son seriously. "Hetty is a half a head taller than Louisa."

Sir John grinned in amusement at his sire's literal reply. "Right you are, Father. The short, plump one it is!"

"John, you're abominable," Hetty laughed, her blue eyes twinkling from behind the slits in her red mask.

"He will get his comeuppance, Hetty, for I intend to dance him into the ground this evening! You know these oversized men, no endurance."

Endurance, indeed, Hetty thought with a wince, her arm still aching from the hour she had spent with Signore Bertioli.

"Well, come on, my midget and my amazon, let us be off for our evening of dissipation. Father, have a pleasant evening."

Sir Archibald nodded. "I shall, my boy."

110

"I believe he's off to Lord Melberry's house," Hetty said softly to her brother as they swept out of the drawing room.

"The subject being a hapless Whig, no doubt," Sir John whispered back as they walked past Grimpston into the cold night.

Once they settled into the Rolland carriage, Sir John disposing his long legs diagonally across from his wife and Hetty, conversation turned to the complexities of the maze at Richmond.

"They've added more rows to the maze since we were there last," Lady Louisa said. "Poor Jack, he was so certain that he would have us out in a thrice."

Sir John stoutly defended himself, and Hetty, only half listening to their banter, thought about the evening ahead of her. Although Jack, in that big brother way of his, had demanded that Hetty stay close to him, parroting nonsense about there being too much license granted at a masked ball, she had no intention of doing so. The red mask gave her anonymity, and she had no intention of jeopardizing it by remaining near to Sir John, whose deep voice would be recognizable to even a slight acquaintance. She had every intention of thoroughly enjoying herself, and that meant keeping the dowdy Miss Henrietta Rolland as well as Lord Harry well in the shadows.

Her excitement mounted as the carriage pulled off the main road onto a long, circular graveled drive in front of Ranleagh House. It was a mammoth three-story building that sprawled atop a slight hill. Scores of lighted candles sparkled from every window, making it appear more a huge diamond, aglow against the backdrop of the black night. A seemingly endless line of carriages lined the drive, and it was with some difficulty that John coachman maneuvered around them to deposit Sir John, Louisa and Hetty at the front stone steps.

"Impressive, eh?" Sir John said blandly.

"You are so unromantic, Jack," Louisa chided at his prosaic turn of phrase. "Hetty, does it not look like a great fairy castle?"

Hetty nodded. "One would think that all of London is in attendance."

They were met just inside the front doors by a deeply bowing butler and three footmen, who deftly removed their cloaks. The laughter coming from the great ballroom down the corridor mixed with the strains of a fast German waltz made Hetty's eyes glow with anticipation. "Come, Jack,

Louisa, do not tarry so," she said over her shoulder as she moved swiftly after the butler.

She paused for a moment at the entrance of the grand ballroom, taking in the imaginative decorations. Yards upon yards of red and white satin had been gathered at the ceiling and dipped down like countless sultan's tents over the heads of the guests. Huge urns filled with every imaginable flower graced each corner, their sweet scent filling the room. There must not be a bloom left in the Ranleagh greenhouse, Hetty thought, turning her attention to the magnificently arrayed guests. She laughed aloud her excitement as a gallant Robin Hood clad in forest green bowed low in front of her and offered his arm. Without a moment's hesitation, she turned from Sir John and Lady Louisa, smiling at her brother over her shoulder, and whirled away with her partner into the throng of guests.

Sir John raised his hand to remonstrate.

"Nay, Jack, do not be a clucking mother hen. Let her enjoy herself. No harm can come to her here, and, you must admit, it has been too long a time since Hetty has showed such pleasure." She clasped her husband's hand. "Now, my lord, let us begin your test of endurance!"

No sooner had Hetty's Robin Hood left her side than she found herself locked in the arms of an English knight. After several more waltzes and a score of country dances, Hetty's feet felt as though she had danced with every gentleman in the room. Notwithstanding, she gladly accepted the hand of a Greek God, who, upon being gaily asked by Hetty if he were not Zeus, replied in a husky voice that he would much rather be called Bacchus.

At the end of another lively country dance, Hetty was shocked to hear her partner, a rather paunchy gentleman dressed as Louis XIV, say between heaving breaths that it was near to midnight.

"Surely you mistake, your majesty," she said, her voice light and teasing. "Why the evening has but begun."

"The time has flown by in your exquisite company, my Scarlet Queen," he said. Hetty heard a strange, husky sound in his voice and felt a stab of alarm. She looked pointedly at his face and thought his eyes overly bright behind the white satin mask. Don't be such a goose, she chided herself, the poor fellow has simply imbibed too much punch. She smiled engagingly. "I must leave your majesty now, for there are so many of your subjects awaiting the pleasure of your company." She thought her parting line rather witty and was utterly chagrined when the gentleman did not release her hand. "A king has but to command, my Scarlet Queen, and his wishes are fulfilled. You are heated, my dear. May I suggest a stroll on the balcony?"

Hetty forgot further attempts at wit and fell back on common sense. She did not at all care for his possessive manner or for his none-too-subtle suggestion.

"A masquerade this may be, sir, but it gives you no proprietal rights! Now, if you would excuse me, I am returning to my brother."

Her initial alarm turned to anger when the gentleman lifted his other hand and laid it gently against her cheek. "Nay, my little innocent, I do not wish you to leave me as yet. I have watched you dally quite outrageously with many gentlemen this evening. I must confess that I am now desirous of enjoying your charms myself. As to your having a brother—I confess that I am in doubt about that."

"Why you insufferable bore! Dally indeed! Unhand me this minute, sir, else I shall cause you bodily harm!"

"Bodily harm," the gentleman scoffed. "Come now, my pretty, no need to play the coy wench with me."

"I believe the lady tired of your company, your majesty," came a cold drawling voice from behind Hetty. She whirled about to see a tall man in a black domino and mask standing close behind her.

Louis XIV turned glittering eyes to the intruder, was unable to determine the gentleman's identity, and growled, "Away with you, sir! You may enjoy the lady's charms after I am done with her."

"I am curious to know what lies beneath that white peruke," the black domino continued in the same cold drawling voice. "No doubt it covers an empty and foolish head. Leave go of the lady now, else I shall personally tip you over the balcony into the lovely fish pond just below."

Louis XIV's hand loosened slightly on Hetty's wrist, and in his moment of uncertainty, she wrenched her hand away and moved back toward the black domino. Her anger with the man was now turning to amusement and she gave a light trilling laugh. "And I, sir, will personally assist him! Do leave off, your majesty. Doubtless you will find a lady who has imbibed enough punch to find your advances not at all repulsive."

Louis XIV realized that he must relinquish his pretentions.

He growled at the black domino, "You shall pay for your interference, sir." As his threat was an empty one, the black domino did not bother to reply.

Hetty watched silently as her erstwhile partner turned drunkenly and disappeared into the crowd.

She turned and smiled up into the face of her rescuer. "Your sense of timing is flawless, sir. Of course, I would have dispatched that fellow quite handily," she added quickly, not at all liking her role as the damsel in distress.

"I do not doubt that for an instant, ma'am," he replied promptly, laughter deep in his throat. "Do tell me, what sort of bodily harm did you have in mind for our leering Louis XIV?"

So he had overheard her threat, had he! She believed he was making sport of her and drew up to her full height. "Had you not interfered, sir," she snapped, "you would have observed my methods."

"Ah? You fascinate me, ma'am. What rough and ready methods were you about to employ . . . if not for my interference?"

There was something vaguely familiar in the black domino's voice, in his tone, and teasing deep laughter that stirred just out of reach in her memory. Suddenly, she wasn't quite certain that her rescuer was any less dangerous than the drunken Louis XIV. She sensed that he was pushing her to be outrageous. Behind the anonymity of her mask and domino, she willingly obliged him. "Why, I would have kicked him just below his yellow waistcoat! And now, sir, that you have amused yourself at my expense, I shall leave you to search out some helpless maiden."

She saw his dark eyes flash suddenly, but his deep voice still held laughter as he said in a mocking voice, "What an unusual young lady you are. Do you wish to leave my company because I interfered or is it because you fear that my intentions may be as low as those of our departed Louis XIV?"

"Of course I am not afraid of you," she snapped, "nor of any other foppish gentleman in this room!" She saw a mocking gleam of triumph light his eyes and realized that she had just given him the upper hand. He said quickly, "Excellent! I dearly love to waltz. Surely you would not refuse to dance with the poor mortal who mistakenly thought to be chivalrous?"

"You, sir, are totally unscrupulous! Very well, lead on!"

114

Hetty placed her hand in the crook of the black domino's arm and allowed him to lead her onto the dance floor.

He slipped his hand lightly down about her waist and drew her into the circle of his arms. She responded readily to his lead and soon found herself being whirled in large, sweeping circles about the room. He quickened their pace suddenly, and she laughed aloud in breathless excitement, tightening her hold on the black domino's shoulder.

He lowered his head slightly and whispered in her ear, "A token of affection, my dear? Or is it that you fear I shall drop you?"

"Do not try to flirt with me, I beg you," she said severely. "I am enjoying myself far too much to be bothered about such nonsense! Now, sir, please heed your steps, for you very nearly stepped on my toe!"

He threw back his head and laughed aloud, his strong white teeth flashing in startling contrast to his black mask.

"There, you see, making love is such a bore, particularly when one is dancing!"

Although he responded by tightening his hand ever so slightly about her waist, Hetty chose to ignore it. When the music came to a halt, she could not prevent the *moue* of disappointment that tugged down the corners of her mouth.

"You are an excellent dancer, sir," she said, gazing up at the black domino with frank candor. She saw him raise his hand in some sort of signal to the musicians. In but an instant, another waltz was struck up.

"What a complete hand you are!" she laughed in admiration, and without any thought as to the complexities of propriety, slipped her arm upon his shoulder.

It was several breathless moments before the black domino slowed their pace. He looked down into the upturned smiling face and said meditatively, "Your Louis XIV was a stupid fellow indeed to believe you experienced in dalliance. Rather, I would say that you are a young lady enjoying her first ball."

Although his observation was entirely accurate, she bridled at the thought that this fact was so obvious. "First of all, my dear sir," she said coldly, "I would much prefer that you not refer to that ridiculous knave as *my* Louis! And as to my experience in dalliance, do not think me a young chit just because I have no desire to set up a flirt with you!"

"Ah, so the little cat has claws! I wonder if you would be so outspoken were we to remove your mask."

"My mask stays right where it is, sir," she retorted sharply, and managed to tred upon his toe. At his wince of pain, she mocked softly, "If not claws, the cat does have feet—or is it paws? Now, sir, I believe the waltz is about to end. Even you, I am persuaded, would not demand a third dance."

He said nothing, but whirled her about in a wide circle. When he came to a halt, he landed adroitly upon her foot.

She jumped and cried out more in surprise than in pain.

"Do forgive my clumsiness, my dear," he said smoothly. "Now, before you scratch my face, I shall return you to your brother."

Insults forgotten, Hetty quickly backed away from the black domino and asked in a tight voice, "You know my brother?"

"Of a certainty I do, Miss Rolland."

Hetty felt a rush of anger toward Jack. What was he doing anyway—telling all his friends that his little sister was in the scarlet domino and mask, and in need of partners? She said in a voice trembling with annoyance, "I bid you good evening, sir." She turned abruptly and slipped into a throng of guests.

She heard the black domino calling her name. She ignored his call, looking now only to find Jack and give him a scathing set down. Drat him! Her enjoyment of her first ball was paling rapidly. The black domino knew who she was; others might know also. Her voice could not be that different from the dowdy Miss Henrietta Rolland's voice or, for that matter, Lord Harry's.

A high, trilling laugh drew her up short at the perimeter of a boisterously gay group of gentlemen. In their midst stood Melissande, her lustrous red hair piled high upon her head and a daring expanse of white bosom provocatively revealed by the extreme décolleté of her green velvet gown. Hetty felt her heart starting to pump in a most erratic fashion. If Melissande was here, then Lord Cavander's presence was assured. She scanned the knot of gentlemen but did not believe him among them.

She wanted nothing more than to leave the ball at that very instant. She walked toward the edge of the crowded ballroom, hoping to position herself where she would see Jack and Louisa. She slipped behind a huge potted fern to avoid an amorous-looking fellow, too deep in his cups, she thought, not to make a scene were she to refuse to dance with him.

116

She curled her lips. Lord Harry would not have to put up with such nonsense!

She suddenly saw Jack, leaning negligently against a curtained wall, in laughing conversation with another man. She stepped forward, then froze in her tracks. It was the black domino.

She ducked quickly behind the potted fern again. She simply could not approach Jack while that man was there. For that matter, she couldn't very well hide behind this ridiculous plant for the rest of the evening. What she needed was a very good excuse to remove herself from the ballroom. Her young lady's repertoire was not a very impressive one, and she fell back upon a ploy that seemed instinctive. She leaned down and gave a vicious tug on her domino, but the velvet was too strong for her fingers. She raised it to her mouth and bit into the hem with her white teeth. She felt it obligingly rip, and without thought to the beauty of the garment, pulled it away in a jagged circular tear. There, she thought with satisfaction, that should keep me from the dance floor for the remainder of the evening! She soon found Louisa conversing with Lady Ranleagh herself, and slipped quietly beside her.

"Oh, Hetty, my love," Louisa greeted her. "You have not been formally introduced to Lady Ranleagh. Lucille, my sister-in-law, Henrietta."

Hetty mumbled automatic civilities to the purple gowned lady, then tugged on Louisa's sleeve. "Louisa, I have quite ruined my domino."

"My dear child," Lady Ranleagh interposed, leaning over to inspect the gapping tear. "One would think that you were partnered by a clumsy elephant! Such a pity."

As Hetty had hoped, Lady Ranleagh directed her to a large dressing room at the top of the stairs, where, she was informed, Lady Ranleagh's maid, Celeste, would mend her costume. Louisa prepared to accompany her, but Hetty, having no wish for Louisa to see her dally away the rest of the evening, laid a restraining hand on her arm. "No, Louisa, I shall be fine. A stupid accident and 'tis all my fault. I would not spoil your fun."

She had nearly made good her escape when she heard Jack's deep, booming voice behind her. "Hetty, hold a moment! Where are you off to, little sister?"

She turned reluctantly, fearing to see the black domino with her brother. To her relief, Jack was alone. "I have torn my domino," she said, "and must see to repairs."

117

" 'Tis probably just as well," he grinned, taking off his mask and rubbing his cheek. "You have enthralled so many young bucks already, I fear the ladies will scratch your eyes out."

"That's utterly ridiculous!" she cried. "I was but enjoying myself, Jack."

"I say, Hetty, are you all right?" Sir John asked suddenly, stepping forward.

"Do not be a ninny, brother," she said more sharply than she intended.

"Well, 'tis the bell of the ball you are, Hetty, no mistaking that."

Hetty dismissed his observation with a shrug of her shoulders. She turned and set her foot upon the wide staircase. "Oh, Jack," she said, "who is that gentleman you were talking to in the black domino and black mask?"

Jack gave a bark of laughter and gazed at her, a deep twinkle in his blue eyes. "I believe you must have enjoyed the fellow's company, Hetty. Did you not waltz with him twice?"

"He was a rude, arrogant fop!" she said irritably. Even to her own ears, she heard a lamentable lack of conviction in her words.

"Well, Hetty, I did put a word in the fellow's ear—you know, to stay clear of you, but he is always one to tempt the fates."

"Drat you, Jack! Who is he?"

Sir John paused a moment, taking in every detail of his sister's flushed face, from the narrowing of her eyes behind the mask to the thin line of her pursed lips. He lifted a fair eyebrow and said blandly, "None other than your arch enemy, Hetty, the Marquis of Oberlon." He turned about and waved to her impishly over his shoulder. His booming laughter rang in her ears.

Hetty clutched at the banister, her heart thumping erratically against her ribs. No wonder his voice had sounded so familiar to her! She forced herself to draw a deep breath. Obviously, his grace had not recognized her. If he had, everything would have been lost.

"Had you continued to dance with me, my dear Miss Rolland, I am persuaded your domino would not now be in tatters."

Hetty whirled about and very nearly tripped on her skirt at the sound of that lazy drawl. The marquis stood but a few feet away from her.

118

"You!" she hissed between clenched teeth, and without another word or backward glance, gathered up her skirts and fled up the stairs.

"An arrogant and rude man, I grant you, Miss Rolland—but a fop?" Rich, deep humour sounded in his voice, and without looking at him, she sensed there was a wide, mocking grin on his face.

Lord Harry spent the better part of ten minutes cursing Henrietta Rolland for her witless behavior. She meekly accepted her counterpart's strictures, for she knew well enough that she had blundered with the Marquis of Oberlon.

Lord Harry rose and morosely kicked a log in the fireplace with the toe of his boot, sending crackling embers up toward the flue.

A knock sounded on the door, yet Lord Harry did not look up until Pottson tugged on her sleeve.

"Look at this, Miss Hetty. 'Tis a message from a lady. The lass would not tell me the lady's name."

Henrietta Rolland's folly was promptly forgotten as Hetty raised the soft pink envelope to her nostrils and inhaled the heavy musk scent. "This is from no lady, Pottson," she said with a grin. She ripped the envelope open and drew forth a single sheet of pink paper, covered with a flowery script. Her eyes widened and she gave a shout of glee.

"What goes, Miss Hetty?"

"My dear Pottson, you must forgive me for not telling you, but I did not wish to hear your clucking. I paid a visit to Lord Cavander's mistress—as Lord Harry, of course. Her name is Melissande, and she is no lady, I assure you. She most coquettishly informs me that she is free this afternoon for a ride in the park."

"Lord Cavander's mistress! Gawd, Miss Harry—I mean Miss Hetty—you can't be meaning to set up a flirt with his mistress! Why, if he finds out, he'll be after your blood!"

"Precisely, Pottson. Now, if you will excuse me, I am off to purchase a green velvet riding habit for my lady and secure a docile mare from Mr. Scuddimore."

It was a properly unassuming, yet charming young gentleman who strolled into Madame Cartier's fashionable boutique and purchased a riding habit and matching bonnet at an outrageous price. Mr. Scuddimore proved a bit more difficult, but after much wheedling and coaxing, Hetty secured a bay mare named Coquette—a most appropriate name, Hetty

119

thought. At promptly five o'clock in the afternoon, Hetty secured Coquette at the railing outside Melissande's townhouse.

Melissande was a vision to behold when she glided into the small drawing room where Lord Harry sat drinking a glass of sherry.

"Naughty, naughty boy!" she exclaimed delightedly, no hint of reproach in her voice. "However did you know my exact measurements! I vow I would have chosen no other riding habit myself!"

The green velvet riding habit was high cut, and fit snugly below her voluptuous breasts. Row upon row of frothy white lace sprung from the green to touch her chin. An arched black plume swept in a high circle, framing the thick auburn ringlets about her face. Although Melissande had felt a brief moment of uncertainty about accepting such a personal offering, she had managed to effectively squelch it. After all, Lord Monteith was a charming boy, no more, and if she wished to spend a small part of her time with him—well, there could be no harm in that. If the marquis were to find out—she drew up a moment with this rather daunting thought, then shrugged her shoulders. Perhaps he would take her less for granted.

Now, as she pirouetted in front of the raptly admiring young Lord Harry, she applauded her decision. The marquis never extolled her beauty in such glowing terms. Nor, she thought, forgetting momentarily the ruby necklace he had bestowed upon her after his return from Italy, had he ever bought her such an exquisite riding habit.

"I shall be the most envied man in the park today, Melissande. A winged Pegasus you should ride—'tis the only mount to equal your dazzling beauty. You must forgive the gentle mare I have secured for you."

Although Melissande could not imagine a sidesaddle perched atop a horse with wings, she made no comment.

Melissande was not a particularly competent equestrienne, and Hetty was thankful that the gentle Coquette was docile to the point of being lazy. She led Melissande carefully through the London traffic and into the park. Few pedestrians were present, for the winter wind was sharp, and the air so chilly that Hetty could see her breath.

But phaetons, horses and carriages were in abundance. Hetty felt her heart jump into her throat as a gentleman astride a huge black stallion cantered toward them. It was not the marquis. She had wondered just what she would do were they to meet Lord Cavander in the park, had ruminated over possible scenes, then finally banished it from her mind. She wanted very much to finally confront him. She was prepared, she knew, with a limitless array of insults.

They cantered past a closed carriage, and Hetty was delighted to see Lady Melberry's face pressed against the closed window, her eyes fastened in surprise on the magnificent Melissande. Hetty raised her hand in polite salute, suppressing the smile on her lips. Even if Lady Melberry were not a gossip, Hetty thought, even the most sainted of persons would have difficulty keeping such a juicy tidbit to themselves.

"You are not cold, my beautiful Melissande?" Hetty asked, remembering that she must not let Lord Cavander's mistress doubt Lord Harry's romantic passion.

Melissande was chilly, but she had no intention of allowing her ride to be curtailed. She was very much enjoying the effect she was creating by being in Lord Harry's company. She shook her head, allowing the arching plume to brush against her rosy cheeks.

By the time they had cantered nearly the full perimeter of the park, their presence had been duly noted by at least a half a dozen very interested ladies and gentlemen. Hetty slowed her horse as a phaeton with a gentleman riding alongside pulled onto the green. She glanced sideways at the driver and drew abruptly to a halt, handily catching Coquette's bridle in her fingers. She looked into the smiling face of the Countess of March. She felt nothing but pleasure at the encounter until she realized that the gentleman on the black stallion was the earl.

"My lady"—Hetty bowed in her saddle—"I see that you have taken to more mild forms of exercise."

Kate gave a trill of laughter at the gentleman's unfortunate choice of words and gazed sideways at her husband. She was surprised and confused at the sudden set look on his face, that tightening of his jaw that was in evidence only during their more colorful arguments.

"Lord Harry, how delightful to see you again! Such a pity that you were otherwise engaged last evening. Harry was quite full of your praises, you know. Hitting the target from twenty feet at Manton's is no small feat, I understand."

"You are too kind, my lady," Hetty replied smoothly, fully aware of the earl's narrowed eyes upon her.

Kate ignored this civility and continued with a wry smile. "So you applaud my husband's insistence on this mild form

121

of exercise. 'Tis a present, you know. Between us, my lord, I believe the earl thought I might go dashing about, *ventre à terre*, on my stallion if he did not present me with this more sedate means of enjoyment."

Hetty smiled at this sally and looked squarely into the earl's set countenance. "My lord," she acknowledged politely, "it is an exquisite phaeton. I, myself, admired it at Tattersall's."

"Indeed." The earl's voice was chilly and his grey eyes rested a meaningful instant upon Melissande, who was growing decidedly restive at not being the center of the conversation.

Kate misunderstood her husband's unusual reaction, and made haste to make amends. "Do forgive me, Lord Harry, but I have not made the acquaintance of the lady."

There was scarce a tremor in Hetty's voice as she said calmly, "Melissande Challicr, allow me to present the Earl and Countess of March."

Kate gave a friendly smile and nodded. Melissande said with a toss of her plumed hat, "Most honoured, my lord, my lady."

Hetty guided her horse away from the phaeton. "I fear we shall all grow icicles if we converse much longer. I pray you will enjoy yourself, my lady, only do not, I beg you, overturn the phaeton!"

"You need have no concern on that score, Lord Montieth! Not with Julien's hand within inches of the reins!" She waved her hand as Lord Harry and Melissande cantered down the green.

Kate turned to her still scowling husband. "I find young Lord Monteith to be such a charming lad. Now, Julien, do come off your highropes. I admit to my rudeness, though it was unintentional! Miss Challier is a most beautiful woman, though, I think, not exactly in Lord Montieth's style. 'Tis amusing how opposites attract, do you not agree? Why, one has but to realize my beauty, wit and grace to understand why you are such a perfect husband for me!"

The corners of the earl's mouth tugged upward at his wife's sally, yet inwardly he was seething. He said heavily, "My love, I am not on my highropes, as you colorfully phrase it, because of any supposed rudeness on your part. And, as usual, you are quite correct, the lady is not at all in Lord Monteith's style."

"And just whose style is appropriate to the lady?" Kate's

122

voice held an impish, bantering tone, yet her eyes were watchful.

"If you must be so inquisitive, my love, that was no lady! You have just been your most charming to Jason Cavander's mistress."

Kate blinked rapidly at this information and then whistled. "Oh dear! But Julien, if she is Jason's mistress, whatever is she doing with Lord Monteith? Surely it is not at all the thing!"

"No, Kate, it is not at all proper," he said slowly, his eyes following the retreating figure of Lord Harry. He remembered his conversation with Jason but a few days before. What a fool he had been to so blithely discount his friend's story about Lord Monteith's blatant provocation! God, when Jason found out, as most certainly he would, about Lord Monteith openly flaunting Melissande with all society to see, the young man might very well find himself thrashed to an inch of his life. Just as the marquis had done, the earl wondered at the young man's motives for such outrageous behavior. Did he wish to be thrashed to an inch of his life, or perhaps have a foil run through his gullet? He decided that it would be better that he himself tell Jason Cavander. Perhaps he could temper Jason's explosive black rage.

"Julien, whatever are you plotting, love?"

He turned to see Kate's eyes gazing questioningly upon his face. She knew him far too well for him to dissemble. Thus, he spent the next hour relating to her all that he knew about this strange imbroglio.

At the end of his recital, Kate was silent for several moments.

"What are you thinking, Kate?" he asked finally.

"I think," she replied in a quiet voice, "that Lord Monteith is far too intelligent to embark upon such a course as you describe without an excellent motive. He's an unusual boy, Julien. I would hate to see him cut down so young by Jason Cavander. Yet, you feel that he is purposefully pushing Jason until there is no choice but retaliation. Is there nothing you can do, Julien?"

The earl said frankly, "Probably not much. But I will speak to Jason on the morrow. Perhaps between us we can ferret out just what it is that is driving the lad to such fatal extremes."

11

Pottson was busily engaged in adding a dash more garlic to a steaming mutton dish upon Hetty's return from her ride in the park with Melissande. She sniffed the concoction and was persuaded to taste a spoonful. " 'Tis delicious, Pottson, much too good for Sir Harry and Mr. Scuddimore. Undoubtedly, the spices will make Scuddy sneeze."

The dinner was destined, however, not to be sampled by either Sir Harry or Mr. Scuddimore, for no sooner had Hetty repaired to Lord Harry's bedchamber to change into formal evening attire, than a loud knock came upon the front door.

"Go ahead and take your bath, Miss Hetty," Pottson called toward the bedroom. "I'll see who disturbs us." He grumbled under his breath, out of Miss Hetty's hearing, " 'Tis probably Mr. Scuddimore . . . can't keep his hours straight worth a tinker's damn."

He wiped his hands upon his voluminous apron and unlatched the door. "Millie! Good lord, woman, whatever are you doing here?"

"Step aside, Pottson, 'tis Miss Hetty I must see, and now!"

Pottson quickly did as he was bid, for only the most dire of emergencies would bring Miss Hetty's maid here, to Lord Harry's lodgings. "She's in her bedchamber, Millie."

Millie nodded curtly. She did not bother to remove her cloak and bonnet, but sped down the narrow corridor.

"Heavens, Millie," Hetty exclaimed at the unusual sight of her maid in Lord Harry's room. "You nearly startled me out of my skin!" She quickly pulled a robe about her shoulders. "Pray do not tell me that Sir John and Lady Louisa have returned! Have they decided not to continue to Paris?"

Millie shook her head, shuddering inwardly at such a thought. Lord, had Miss Hetty's brother and wife remained in London much longer, the cat would have jumped willy-nilly out of the bag.

"Well, do not keep me on tenterhooks!"

" 'Tis your father, Miss Hetty. He's up and done it again. Lady Melberry has invited you to another party and Sir Archibald accepted on your behalf. He wanted to see you, Miss Hetty, but I told him you were resting. You must know that I had to tell him that you would be delighted to go, so as to keep him from suspecting that you were not at home."

Hetty fastened the large towel securely under her arms and looked ruefully at her maid. "You have done quite right, Millie. Drat Sir Archibald anyway! More than likely he did not even recall that I asked him to consult me before he accepted any more invitations!" She drummed her fingertips along the back of a chair, deep in thought, then turned suddenly. "We must hurry. Quickly, Millie, fetch a pen and writing paper from Pottson. There is just enough time for him to pay a visit to Sir Harry and Mr. Scuddimore and cancel our evening together."

A scant two hours later, Miss Henrietta Rolland, the dowdy specimen who had made her début but a week before, made her way into Sir Archibald's carriage, pressing the green alexandrine cap against the top of her head to keep it from being whipped away by the harsh evening wind. As before, she did not balance the spectacles on her nose until she prepared to sound the knocker at the Melberry townhouse.

She quickly scanned the assorted ladies and gentlemen clustered in small groups in the drawing room. Her sense of wariness eased, for nowhere did she see Lord Cavander's tall frame. Miss Henrietta Rolland wished to avoid his grace to the same extent that Lord Harry Monteith wished to be thrown into his presence. She said all that was polite to Lady Melberry and quickly made good her escape to a far corner of the drawing room, there to observe, and hopefully, not to be observed by any of the other guests. Her gaze soon fell upon a lovely, dark-haired girl who was seated demurely beside her mama, looking for all the world as if she would yawn loudly from boredom at any moment. Hetty's mouth curved up at the corners. She was certain the vision of loveliness was none other than Miss Isabella Bentworth, Sir Harry Brandon's *amour*. Lord Harry had met the young lady only briefly, and had exchanged only superficial civilities. Perhaps Miss Henrietta Rolland could make Miss Isabella's acquaintance. She had a lively curiosity to speak to the young lady who had captured Sir Harry's devotion, though not as yet, it seemed, his proposal of a marital lifetime together.

As Hetty drew closer to Miss Bentworth, she began to believe that Sir Harry must have rust in his brainbox. She was indeed a beautiful girl, her deep brown eyes doe soft and

125

with that melting quality that made gentlemen wish to do nothing more than languish at her feet. Her black hair, shining like a glossy raven's wing, was swept high atop her head, with myriad small curls framing her ivory face. Thoughts of matchmaking could not help but intrude. She managed to quell the momentary nagging feeling that she was being a pushy, interfering female.

Hetty was at the point of gaining Miss Bentworth's wandering attention when she was drawn up suddenly by the grating voice of Miss Maude Langley.

"My *dear* Miss Rolland," the young lady gushed in a way that set Hetty's teeth on edge, "how very delightful to see you again! Do forgive me for not calling upon you, but I was invited to so many balls and routs that I scarce had time to purchase new gowns!"

Miss Maude must needs be seen speaking to me, Hetty thought wryly, because I am the most homely female here. She took a deep breath and turned, her only ambition at the moment to rid herself of the unwelcome Miss Maude. "I most readily forgive you, *dear* Miss Langley," Hetty replied, raising her voice and forcing her vowels to be irritatingly nasal in quality. "And where is your beautiful sister? Surely, the gentlemen would demand her presence before long."

Miss Maude sniffed audibly and became less friendly. "Oh, Caroline is probably off in some corner flirting outrageously. Mama quite despairs that Caroline's unladylike behavior will drive away the more serious of eligible gentlemen."

"Indeed? I cannot believe that you are correct, Miss Langley. Gentlemen adore lively, beautiful girls. She will probably have half a score of marriage proposals before the season has even begun!"

Miss Maude decided that Henrietta Rolland was as impertinent as she was homely. She looked down her long thin nose, taking in every aspect of the pea green gown that hung shapelessly on Miss Rolland's shoulders, and gave a tittering, tight little laugh. "You, certainly, Miss Rolland, need not concern yourself about being so importuned."

Hetty choked back a laugh, squinted at Miss Maude and said nastily, "Perhaps you can bear me company during the season, Miss Langley. We can together animadvert upon the imagined shortcomings of all the beautiful girls as we sit along the ballroom walls watching them dance."

Miss Maude drew an audible breath, her eyes glittering in

anger. "Impertinent little twit," Hetty heard her mutter as she flounced away in high dudgeon.

"Such an insufferable girl!" Hetty turned about to see Miss Isabella Bentworth at her elbow. "She quite cuts up one's pleasure with her boorish, jealous observations."

"Not if one knows how to properly insult her," Hetty replied with a wry smile. "Do forgive me, but I am Henrietta Rolland. I was anxious to be rid of the depressing Miss Maude so that I could make your acquaintance. You are quite the most beautiful girl in the room, you know."

Miss Isabella Bentworth's eyes widened at such uncalled for adulation, then she smiled. At least Miss Rolland was not a spiteful cat like Miss Langley! "And I am Isabella Bentworth, Miss Rolland. I have not met you before, I think. Are you new in town?"

"Somewhat," Hetty said obscurely. "But I have seen you, Miss Bentworth, and with a most handsome young gentleman."

Miss Isabella raised an inquiring eyebrow, yet she felt her heart begin to flutter in a most alarming manner. "A gentleman, Miss Rolland?"

"Yes. He is tall and fair complexioned. Most dashing and handsome I thought him."

Miss Isabella's cheeks turned suddenly warm and she looked quickly down at the toes of her blue satin slippers so as not to betray her feelings. "You speak of Sir Harry Brandon," she said softly.

Hetty was not deaf to the tinge of forlornness in Miss Bentworth's voice. She knew that she should not make a judgment of character on such short notice, yet she could not help being drawn to Miss Bentworth. She said carefully, "Yes, I have heard of Sir Harry. He is considered a most eligible bachelor, is he not?"

"I suppose so," came the still forlorn answer.

So Miss Bentworth does return Harry's affection, Hetty thought, giving Sir Harry a mental kick. "You hold him in some regard, I gather," Hetty said, knowing she stated no startling insight.

Miss Isabella caressed her chin with slender fingertips, eyed the sympathetic Miss Rolland, and said in a spate of confidence, "Oh, yes, Miss Rolland, but you see, I am in such a coil! Dear Mama wishes to see me wed by the end of the season, for I have three sisters who await their turns, and Harry

127

blanches at the thought! He is all of twenty-four, yet he believes himself too young."

Hetty felt no sympathy whatsoever for the three unknown sisters and wondered fleetingly if her own mother, were she alive, would have pushed her to wed at the end of her first season as Isabella's Mama was doing. She asked, "Does your mama have anyone in particular in mind, other than Sir Harry Brandon?"

Miss Bentworth shuddered delicately. "Alas, she does, Miss Rolland. Sir William Filey has been most particular in his attentions of late. Of course, he is quite rich and toadies up to Mama in the most disgusting fashion! He is most polished in his manners, yet there is something about him . . . I am not certain that he is what he seems."

"Well, he is almost old enough to be your father," Hetty exclaimed in contempt. "Surely, your mama could not believe that such a match would prosper." Hetty thought Miss Isabella most astute in gaining Sir William's measure. Lord, but she could tell her some very good reasons why indeed she was wise to wonder about Sir William! Hetty found her thoughts turning to the unfortunate Elizabeth. Did Sir William have an affinity for young débutantes?

Miss Bentworth said, "It is true, Miss Rolland, he is too old for me. But if Sir Harry does not wish to wed me, I fear that I shall have no other choice in the matter. My mama is quite strong-willed, you know. And there are my sisters," she added on a sigh.

"Nonsense," Hetty said sharply. "Everyone has choices, Miss Bentworth. It takes but a little resolution!"

Miss Bentworth thought privately that the homely Miss Rolland could well afford to state her mind, for she could not imagine any gentleman importuning *her* to wed. How could Miss Rolland possibly understand?

Hetty misunderstood Miss Bentworth's silence, and began to believe her a spiritless chit. She knew she should not be meddling, but someone had to do something about these two! "As I said, Miss Bentworth, it takes but a little resolution . . . and a sound strategy! Listen and tell me what you think."

Miss Bentworth obligingly bent her dark head close to the pea green cap. Hetty became so engrossed in weaving her plot and in gaining Miss Bentworth's agreement, that she was unaware of Lord Cavander's arrival. Thus, when the sound of his deep rich voice came to her ears, not ten feet away from

128

her, she jumped, the remainder of her cajoling words dead on her tongue.

Miss Bentworth was too involved in Miss Rolland's daring plan to notice anything amiss. When Hetty grabbed her arm and pulled her into a corner, she believed merely that Miss Rolland had no wish to be overheard. It was some five minutes later, when the orchestra struck up a lively country dance and two gentlemen were purposefully approaching her to secure the dance, that Miss Bentworth agreed. "You are certain that Lord Monteith will agree, Miss Rolland?" she asked yet again.

"Very certain," Hetty said firmly. "He will call upon you tomorrow, Miss Bentworth. Remember, you mustn't breathe a word of this to anyone!"

"Oh yes, Miss Rolland, I promise. You may trust me." She waved a conspiratorial hand to Hetty and took her place in the set. Whatever the outcome of Miss Rolland's plan, she looked forward, in any case, to furthering her acquaintanceship with Lord Monteith. Perhaps he would influence Sir Harry where she had failed.

Hetty slipped even further into the corner, Miss Bentworth and her trial with Sir Harry for the moment forgotten, her eyes upon Lord Cavander. He was laughing easily with Miss Caroline Langley. She glanced at a clock, saw that it was just after ten o'clock and realized with a sinking in the pit of her stomach that it would be quite rude for her to depart so early in the evening. She thought about developing a sudden, painful headache. Yes, that just might do it. So busy was she in planning her migraine that a light touch on her sleeve made her whirl about in consternation and stumble with embarrassing awkwardness into a table.

"Did I frighten you, Miss Rolland?" Lord Cavander asked in a silky mocking voice. He was readily prepared to tease the spirited, outspoken young lady whose company the previous evening at the Ranleaghs' masquerade ball he had found most stimulating, when she whipped about and his horrified eyes took in the hideous green cap, the squinting eyes behind wire spectacles and the most ill-fitting gown he had ever seen in his life.

"You are Miss Henrietta Rolland?" he asked awkwardly, praying that this daunting vision gaping stupidly at him was some errant relative of Lady Melberry.

Hetty, after her initial shock, was well aware of the effect of her appearance upon him. Without thought, she snapped

129

haughtily, "Of course I am Henrietta Rolland, sir. Unfortunately or fortunately, depending upon one's perceptions, I am not acquainted with you!"

She instantly regretted her unruly tongue, for the marquis was staring at her, his dark eyes puzzled and one black brow lifted in inquiring confusion.

"I believe we danced together at the Ranleaghs' masquerade ball last evening, Miss Rolland," he managed to say at last. "My aunt, Lady Melberry, pointed you out to me but a few moments ago."

"Did we, sir?" she asked coldly. "I do not seem to recall you."

"Perhaps I have made a mistake," he said slowly, knowing full well that he had not. Somehow, the wretched specimen before him simply did not appear to be what he thought she must be . . . her parts did not fit themselves logically together. That is, he thought, striving to make sense of the situation, everything fits, but her voice and words. The coldness, the quickness of wit, the arrogance . . . decidedly something was quite wrong.

Hetty saw the myriad emotions flashing over Lord Cavander's face and knew that she must cease taunting him. He had found the masked Miss Henrietta Rolland to be most entertaining the previous evening. She must become all that that Miss Rolland was not. She placed a firm clamp on her tongue, squinted and simpered.

"Oh, la, sir, you have found me out! Pray do not think Jack too naughty for telling you that I had taken you into a strong dislike." She tittered at the incredulous look on the marquis' face, silently begged her brother's pardon, and simpered on in the most vulgar manner, "Indeed, sir, or rather *your grace*," she amended coquettishly, "you are so very popular with the ladies, I believed my little joke the only way to dance with you. Surely such a spanking handsome fellow as yourself does not mind a little deception."

Hetty was already congratulating herself on giving Lord Cavander a strong disgust of her, when the tight, angry look again blended into puzzlement.

The marquis was certainly angry. He was ready to throttle Jack for making him appear the fool, and most desirous of removing himself as far away as possible from Jack's wretchedly vulgar ape leader of a sister. But there was a nagging doubt in the back of his mind. Those damned parts again—something still did not fit properly. Though his lips

130

were curled in contempt, he inquired with tolerable calm, "How curious, Miss Rolland, that you seem so terribly in need of spectacles now. Yet, I recall last evening that you got along quite well without them. Indeed, one would think that you had the vision of an eagle."

Hetty produced a grating, high-pitched giggle. "Fie on you, your grace! 'Tis impossible to wear spectacles and a mask at the same time. Such a smart gentleman you are, I vow my heart is still fluttering—"

She got no further, for the marquis was so put off by her display of vulgarity that he no longer cared about the parts fitting properly together. The look he gave her was so very cold and contemptuous that had he not spoken, she might not have been able to control her tongue.

"Congratulate your brother on his joke, ma'am. If you will excuse me, I wish to enjoy some fresh evening air."

Hetty could not prevent the deep chuckle that burst from her throat. To her consternation, the marquis stopped in his tracks, stood quietly for a moment, then continued on his way.

Well, you arrogant devil, she thought as the marquis was charmingly waylaid by Miss Caroline Langley, Miss Henrietta Rolland need no longer be concerned about your unwanted attentions. She had routed him quite successfully. She wondered idly just how long it would be before Lord Cavander discovered Lord Harry's underhanded poaching with his mistress. To doubly ensure his wrath, it seemed not at all a bad idea to escort the willing Melissande once again to the park. Hopefully, Melissande would not yet try to seduce Lord Harry into her bed. That, Hetty thought with a crooked grin, would prove most interesting!

For Lord Harry Monteith to pay the promised morning call to Miss Isabella Bentworth required a great deal of hurried activity and exquisite timing. Under no circumstances could Sir Archibald's luncheon be even a second past the noon hour, and Hetty's presence at his table was nearly as requisite as the hour itself.

Lord Harry sat with Miss Isabella in the company of her mama, a tall, beak-nosed lady, who tried at each juncture to determine the exact degree of affluence among Lord Monteith's relations. Hetty smoothly parried Lady Bentworth's none too subtle questions. She saw that Isabella was in an agony of embarrassment and prayed devoutly for Sir Harry's

131

sake that Isabella would not in the indeterminate future assume any of her mama's proclivities. All in all the visit achieved its purpose and Hetty had few doubts that Sir Harry would be out of reason cross, and, hopefully, jealous, at Lord Harry's sudden attentions toward his beloved.

Quite satisfied with her morning's work, Hetty took her leave of Isabella and her mama and rushed back to Thompson Street to change into a gown.

It lacked but a minute to noon when Hetty slipped into her seat at the dining table, her gown slightly askew and one slipper loose on her foot.

There was no newspaper in Sir Archibald's hands, and he greeted his daughter brightly. "My dear Henrietta, how very charming you are looking, my child."

While Hetty gazed at him in some surprise, he turned to Mrs. Miller. "Serve the soup now, if you please. Then leave us, for Henrietta and I have much to discuss."

Hetty's eyes flew to Mrs. Miller's face, to seek enlightenment. The housekeeper gave an infinitesimal shrug and went about ladling the soup. Hetty felt a nervous knot begin to grow in her stomach. Up until now, Sir Archibald had always stood as an unmovable rock amid the uncertainties that surrounded her. Had he somehow discovered that his daughter was not always what she appeared to him? She forced herself to sip at her soup, and waited.

Upon Mrs. Miller's departure from the dining room, Sir Archibald said with great good humour, "Well, my dear child, I must tell you that I visited a moment with Lady Melberry last evening, after you had left her party."

Oh, God, Hetty thought, paling, she has told him about the pea green gown and the spectacles!

"She told me, Henrietta, that you were quite the popular one! Not dancing and all that falderall, but rather intimate conversations, one after the other."

I have been granted yet another reprieve, Hetty thought, taking a shaking breath. She felt a touch of amusement, for obviously the good Lady Melberry had found herself in a situation which required diplomatic untruths.

"I think that Lady Melberry exaggerates, Father," she said finally.

"Now, my dear child, I applaud your natural modesty, but facts are facts."

Whatever was he talking about? struggled Hetty, trying to remember just which facts he could be talking about.

Sir Archibald leaned over and took her hand into his. "Do you like the Marquis of Oberlon, my dear? Lady Melberry thought that you quite encouraged his grace in his attentions."

Hetty dropped her spoon, sending asparagus soup over the edge of the bowl onto the tablecloth. "The Marquis of Oberlon!" she cried, seized suddenly in the grip of unreality. "My dear father, I do assure you that I did not in any way encourage his grace, as you put it! Why, I barely spoke to his grace! He is not at all the kind of gentleman I admire."

To Hetty's chagrin, Sir Archibald merely smiled at her indulgently. "A coy little miss you are, Henrietta, just like your dear mother. Why, I remember that she swore up and down to her parents that she did not care for me at all! Protested in that ridiculous manner until the day we were married!"

I have sorely wronged you, Mother, Hetty thought, remembering Lady Beatrice as a rather cold, constantly complaining parent. You were far more perceptive than I had ever imagined.

Sir Archibald continued serenely, " 'Twould not be such a bad alliance at all. Cavander is, after all, a Tory, even though he does not often appear in the House of Lords. There is John too. He and Cavander have been friends since they were up at Oxford together. No, my dear child, if you wish the marquis for a husband, I shall throw no rub in your way." He pursed his lips a moment, caressing his chin in thought. "Ah, I've got it, my dear. I shall call upon the marquis, perhaps invite him to dinner. Give him the hint, you know, that I'll not oppose his suit."

"Father, I pray you not to refine so upon Lady Melberry's words. His grace has no interest in me whatsoever, I assure you. Why, the only reason he spoke to me at all was because . . . he and Jack are friends! He was merely being kind. Father, believe me, I have no wish to further my acquaintance with Lord Cavander."

Hetty had always been rather proud of her stubborn streak, as Damien had called it. But now she found herself silently cursing it, for her tenaciousness of mind derived from Sir Archibald. She knew well enough that once his mind had grasped a certain course of action, there was no budging him. Indeed, it would be less of a herculean effort to change the flow of the river Thames. She looked up, realizing that he had not even attended to her words.

Sir Archibald fixed Hetty with a patriarchal, benign smile.

133

"You are such a good child, Henrietta. Trust me, my dear, to do what is best for you. Now, let us finish our luncheon, for I must meet with Lord Bedford, whom we have elected to whip Sir Edwin Barrington into shape for the upcoming election."

"Which election, Father?" Anything, Hetty thought, to divert her father's thoughts.

"The borough at Little Simpson. Up to this time, the wretched farmers have not listened to reason. But Sir Edwin is a popular man, though he does not know a thing about political necessities."

Hetty pursued doggedly, "But if Sir Edwin is not a politician, Father, why do you want him?"

Sir Archibald grinned indulgently at this errant bit of nonsense from his naive daughter. "Don't worry your head about it, child. Sir Edwin will do well enough."

Hetty thought fleetingly of Damien's desire to channel himself into the political arena. She wondered if he would have had an honoured Tory member whip him into shape. Or would Sir Archibald have been his mentor?

Sir Archibald spoke no further of the Marquis of Oberlon and Hetty sent a plea heavenward that once her sire got involved in his political activities in the afternoon, he would forget his intentions.

She excused herself shortly from the dining room, giving her father a hurried hug, and slipped out of the house to make her way to Lord Harry's lodgings. She forced herself to be lighter of heart, for, even if Sir Archibald happened to approach Lord Cavander, she was fairly certain that he had taken Henrietta Rolland into such dislike that he would never accept such an invitation to dine.

As she slipped into breeches, frilled shirt and hessians, she quickly reviewed her schedule for the remainder of the day. First she would be meeting Sir Harry at Manton's. Now that would be a most interesting experience. Lord Harry would start the worm of jealousy gnawing in Sir Harry's breast. With any luck at all, that should make Sir Harry realize that Isabella was ripe for the plucking in more than one orchard.

Oh yes, Hetty thought as she bade Pottson a good afternoon, he must take a note to Melissande, inquiring if the fair lady would deign to ride again in the park with Lord Monteith.

At the thought of how she would be spending her evening, she grimaced in distaste. Impossible to extricate herself from going with Harry and Scuddy to that wretched cockfight.

Still, it was with a light step that Hetty strolled to meet Sir Harry at Manton's, her face down against the winter wind.

As for the marquis, he neither felt light of step nor light of heart. Indeed, he was frozen with cold deadly anger as he listened to the Earl of March.

"So, Julien, I am now fast bidding to become a laughing-stock of London, am I not?" His voice sounded so very calm that no one save his closest friends would have realized that his grace was at all perturbed.

"Most likely," the earl replied.

"Now you will believe me that the young whelp wishes death by my hands?"

The earl paused an instant, seemingly intent upon removing a fleck of dust from his coat sleeve. "Indeed, my friend," he said finally, "I must agree that young Monteith wishes something. Whether it is death at your hands—well, I must believe that that is a bit extreme."

There was no response from the marquis. The earl sat forward in his chair. "You know, Jason, Kate immediately agreed with our conclusions that there is something driving the boy to behave in such an outrageous manner. You are certain that you have never before heard his name, that you can think of no insult ever made to him . . . anything, Jason?"

"Damn it, no! We've asked ourselves these questions, even before this latest exploit! I tell you, I know nothing about Monteith save that I intend to beat him to a bloody pulp!"

The earl decided upon another tack. "Tell me, Jason, do you care so much about Melissande? I recall only the other day your telling me that you were rapidly becoming bored with her."

"I am not a fool, Julien," the marquis said quietly. "It hardly matters what I think of her now. She is, after all, still under my protection." He rose and strolled to the fireplace, his dark eyes resting a moment on the glowing coals. He turned to face the earl, digging his hands into his breeches pockets. "It is now a question of honour, Julien. Surely you see that I cannot ignore this insult."

The earl sighed and nodded slowly. "No, of course you cannot ignore it. And yet—"

"And yet, you do not want to see me kill the boy," the marquis finished, gazing searchingly at the earl.

The earl grinned ruefully. "Pray do not think that I am becoming lost to all sense of honour, Jason. Yet again, I must concur with Kate's perceptions. There is something deuced unusual about Monteith, as if he were a complex puzzle whose pieces simply did not fit together. I ask only that you do not act rashly. Surely, if the lad continues in his outrageous behavior, you will have no choice but to call him out."

"Strange that you say Monteith is like a puzzle whose pieces do not fit together."

"I thought it apt, Jason. Why?"

" 'Tis really of no importance." The marquis shrugged. "Damnation but this is an impossible situation! Were it a toad like Filey, I would feel not the slightest hesitation. But hellfire, Julien, as you say, Monteith is just a green boy. The difference in our ages, in our experience . . . why, I would look little less than a murderer were I to call him out."

"That is certainly true," the earl replied calmly. "I think though, that if you remain, shall we say, impervious to the boy's taunts, it is he who will call you out. Think on it, Jason. Now, I must be off. George informed me on my way out that Kate was preparing to direct the carpenters in the refurbishing of the nursery wing. If I know her, she will be climbing about the rafters with them!" The earl rose and clasped his friend's hand.

"I shall take your advice until I can do naught else, Julien. Give my love to Kate."

The earl turned at the door of the drawing room and gave the marquis a lazy grin. "Are you certain, Jason, that one of your succulent beauties in Italy was not distantly related to any Monteith?"

"Bedamned to you, St. Clair!"

After the Earl of March had taken his leave, Lord Cavander, in a fit of excess energy, departed to Gentleman Jackson's boxing salon, where his hapless opponent in the ring took on the features of a fair, blue-eyed youth.

12

"You what?" Sir Harry Brandon dropped his pistol into its case and turned in stunned surprise to Lord Harry.

"You really should be more careful with your guns, Harry. Thank God it was not loaded. You might have shot your toe off."

"Dammit, Lord Harry," Sir Harry sputtered, his face growing alarmingly red, " 'tis bad enough that you must needs add Lord Cavander's mistress to your string of fillies!"

"But Harry, I find Miss Isabella Bentworth a most charming girl. You must realize that both Mavreen and Melissande are redheads. Isabella has the most beautiful black hair—silky like a raven's wing."

Sir Harry ground his teeth. "I will not have it, Lord Harry. Isabella is pure and innocent, and not a young lady who will succumb to your light flirtations!"

"Do not mistake my intentions, Harry. I do not intend a light flirtation with the lady, if that is your concern. After sitting with her an hour this morning, I was filled with the more tender emotions."

"But—" Sir Harry's voice trailed off into shocked silence. He leaned over and very carefully fastened the clasp on his gun case. As he straightened, he said heavily, "Then you are thinking of marriage, Lord Harry?"

"Perhaps."

"You are younger than I!"

Hetty replied with insouciance, "Neither of us are in the infantry, old fellow. If you wish to admire the fair Isabella from afar until you have reached the exalted age of thirty, in keeping with what you believe to be your brother-in-law's dictums, then you had better relinquish her right now. Do you not know that that fortune-making mama of hers is fair to forcing Isabella to wed Filey by the end of the season? Really, Harry, as a gentleman, I cannot allow that lecherous old satyr to warm her bed!"

"Yes, of course I knew that. But that old harridan cannot force Isabella to wed Filey." Sir Harry knew that he sounded halfhearted in his protest. He had thought about Filey's attentions toward Isabella, but had refused to believe that marriage could ever be the outcome.

Hetty allowed a look of incredulity to pucker her brow. "I begin to think that you have more rust in your bandbox than Scuddy! Young ladies have not the choices you impute to them, even though it suits you to think differently."

Sir Harry blanched at the contemptuous irony in his friend's voice. He asked quietly, "You really believe that Isabella will be sold to that old lecher, Filey?"

"Do not forget, Harry, that Filey is titled and as rich as a golden ball. It would take a gentleman of similar qualifications and much persuasion to convince Isabella's mama differently. The old eagle was appraising me most openly this morning. Her questions were impertinent to the extreme. I think I found favor in her mercenary eyes, but not as yet as much favor as you have." Hetty paused a moment, then added lightly, "But I daresay that I shall bring her around. After all, old boy, it isn't as though I were cutting *you* out. You've left the field wide open, you know."

Sir Harry suddenly turned on her and growled pugnaciously, "I don't think I like it too much that you are seeing Isabella. You're a damned rakehell, Lord Harry, and I'll not let you break the poor girl's heart."

"But Harry," Hetty said reasonably, "I told you that I felt very tender and protective toward Isabella. It is not *I* who will break her heart."

"Damn you for a meddler!" Sir Harry flung from the shooting range into the large outer parlour at Manton's.

Hetty grinned at his stiff back and followed him slowly, not displeased with his reaction. If only she could enlist the help of the Earl of March. A few well-chosen words from that powerful peer would put the icing on the cake. She sighed, knowing such a conversation with Harry's brother-in-law was out of the question. Still, I have done quite well enough, she told herself stoutly. She left Manton's whistling.

Her complacency grew when, upon returning to Lord Harry's lodgings, she found awaiting her another flowery note from Melissande, begging Lord Monteith's charming company for another ride in the park. Sir Harry's problems slipped from her mind as, not long thereafter, she cantered through the London traffic to Melissande's apartment, leading the docile Coquette. She found herself shivering with a kind of frightening anticipation. Surely Lord Cavander must have

138

found out about her meeting with Melissande the day before. She knew that no gentleman could in honour support such an insult. It cannot be much longer now, she told herself with more bluff confidence than she felt.

Melissande stood arrayed in the green velvet riding habit Lord Monteith had presented to her the day before, peeking through the curtains onto the street in front of her apartment. She realized that she had, in all honesty, accepted yet another invitation to ride with the young Lord Monteith because she was indulging in a fit of pique. Not that she minded all the languishing phrases that seemed to flow in an endless stream from the young gentleman's lips. Yet, Lord Cavander seemed not even to be aware of her minor transgressions, for after that altogether delightful evening spent at the Ranleaghs' masquerade, he had not come to call, had not even sent her a note.

Lord Monteith suddenly came into view astride his bay mare, leading her mare, Coquette. She pulled quickly back from the window and schooled her features into a welcoming smile. Perhaps his grace would come visiting while she was out with Lord Monteith. She shrugged an elegant shoulder. Well, if he did come, Jenny could simply inform him that Melissande was otherwise occupied.

"My dear sir!" she greeted Lord Monteith demurely. "How kind of you to escort me again today."

As Hetty was becoming, perforce, adept at her constantly shifting roles, she managed to greet Melissande with a soulful sigh and an undisguised look of admiration. "You have but to command me, my fair Melissande." She proffered a flourishing bow. "It is, of course, my good fortune that finds you unoccupied. 'Tis a shame though to find you so much alone."

There was a sudden gleam of petulant anger in Melissande's green eyes, and Hetty knew that she had scored a telling point. If naught else, Melissande would take Lord Cavander to task for being lax in his attentions. She realized that a mistress, dependent upon her protector for all her needs, would never mention another gentleman's name in the master's presence. But, she thought confidently, there were many others who would relish filling Lord Cavander's ears with tales of his mistress and another gentleman. Hetty was somewhat disappointed when Melissande's gleam of anger changed to a sad yet brave demeanor. She sighed softly. "Yes, 'tis so what you say, my lord. But now that *you* are with me, there can be naught else on my mind!"

Hetty suddenly gulped down a sinking thought. Had Lord Cavander relinquished the beautiful Melissande? Lord, if that were so, Lord Harry's antics were not only needlessly expensive but also pointless.

But as Hetty had no evidence that such a break had occurred between the marquis and his mistress, she was careful to maintain the depressingly romantic chatter that Melissande appeared so much to admire. If references to Aphrodite were not to be heard, no matter, for Helen of Troy provided ample new food for flattery. She pressed Melissande to ride two turns about the park, ensuring again that the usual habitués had an excellent view of Lord Monteith in the company of Lord Cavander's mistress.

By the time Hetty returned to Lord Harry's lodgings to change for dinner and the inevitable cockfight, she wanted nothing more than to sink chin deep in a hot bath. She could still sniff faint whiffs of Melissande's heavy perfume.

Shortly after eight o'clock she repaired to Mr. Scuddimore's lodgings on Queen Street, hopeful that the wretched cockfight would not last very long.

A closed carriage, the eagle and raven crest barely visible on its paneled doors, drew to a jolting halt on Thompson Street. A cloaked gentleman flung open the doors and alighted before the driver scarce had time to quiet the steaming horses.

"Walk the horses about, Silken. I shall not be above thirty minutes within," the gentleman said tersely over his shoulder.

"Aye, your grace."

The Marquis of Oberlon took the front steps two at a time, his features so coldly set with anger that his dark eyes appeared black sockets in the dim light. He pounded his fist upon the closed oak door.

Pottson, who was enjoying a warm mugger of ale, contemplating a quiet, uneventful evening by himself, jumped in his chair at the sudden loud knocking, spilling some of the frothy liquid to the carpet. His eyes flew to the clock over the mantelpiece. It was scarcely after nine o'clock. It could not be Miss Hetty, that was for certain. He set down his ale and hurried to the door.

"Who is there?" he called, wondering fleetingly if it was the constable come to collect some unpaid debt of Lord Harry's.

140

"Open the door, damn you! Be quick about it man, else I shall kick it in!"

Pottson fumbled with the latch, suddenly sweating with premonition. He pulled vigorously on the knob. He could pratically hear another curse forming on the visitor's tongue. No sooner had he unfastened the latch than the door burst open and a large, black-cloaked man strode past him into the room.

Lord Cavander took in every empty corner of the small, cozy drawing room in an instant. He whirled about to the small, plump man who stood, mouth agape, in the open doorway.

His voice was tense with suppressed fury as he rapped out, "I presume you are Monteith's man. Fetch the young puppy this instant, for I would have speech with him."

The most dire of Pottson's forebodings were fulfilled. He knew without being told that he was face to face with the Marquis of Oberlon. Miss Hetty had succeeded.

He licked his tongue over his suddenly dry mouth and stammered, "I—I am sorry, your grace, but Lord Harry is not here."

"Your grace, huh? So, my good man, you know who I am."

"Aye, your grace. You must believe me, Lord Harry will not be back for hours."

"You will not mind if I doubt your word!" Lord Cavander turned abruptly from the trembling Pottson down the small corridor to Lord Harry's bedchamber.

It struck Pottson forcibly in the few moments he stood alone in the drawing room that making all sorts of plans and plots in no way came close to the dreadful reality he now faced. Obviously, his grace must have discovered that his mistress had flaunted herself with Lord Harry and was now in the blackest of rages. Gawd, Pottson thought, his legs beginning to tremble beneath him, the marquis is fit to kill!

He searched about frantically in his mind for some way of protecting Miss Hetty. Of all evenings when she might return early, it was this evening. "That disgusting cockfight," she had said grimly, "I pray only that I do not heave all over the birds!"

Pottson looked up helplessly as the marquis strode back into the room. "What in God's name is this?" he shouted, waving Miss Hetty's gown in front of Potttson's horrified eyes.

It's all over now, Pottson thought, not without a feeling of relief. How stupid of him not to have hung up her gown! What an ironic way for all of Miss Hetty's plans to come to an end. She would most assuredly want to skin him alive. "It's a dress, your grace," he said inconsequentially.

"You mutton-headed fool, do you think me blind? To be more specific, 'tis a lady's gown! It is obvious that your master is a dissolute young rakehell! Because I am a gentleman, I did not search through the closet—no doubt if I had, I would have found a trembling naked young maiden awaiting Monteith's return!"

Pottson thought the world had suddenly taken a faulty turn. He shook his head stupidly.

"You protect him, do you, my good fool! You may now tell me where I can find the perfidious young puppy, else I shall break your neck!" The marquis flung down the gown and walked purposefully toward Pottson.

"I do not know where Lord Harry is this evening," Pottson lied bravely, drawing himself up to his full diminutive height.

Lord Cavander looked fully for the first time into the ashen-hued countenance of the terrified valet. Damn, the little man had pluck! He reined in his black rage and forced himself to survey the situation rationally. It would not solve a thing were he to throttle the hapless valet. That the man was loyal to his master, he could not help but admire.

Perhaps it was just as well that he did not find Monteith at home, for he admitted to himself, the consequences of his anger might have produced very unpleasant results. He had no desire to depart from England unless it was by his own volition.

"Very well," he said finally. "You may tell your master that the Marquis of Oberlon is desirous of seeing him. If Monteith is not a coward, I shall expect him at White's to-morrow evening. There, you may tell him, he will apologize to me, in full company." The marquis paused a moment, then added with deadly preciseness, "If he does not choose to make full apology, or if his bravado extends only to the bedroom, you may expect me to call again. Is that clear?"

Pottson nodded mutely. "I shall tell him, your grace." He had an almost undeniable urge to tell the marquis the truth. Yet, even though Miss Hetty was only a female, she seemed to have a man's courage and sense of honour. He could not bring himself to serve her such a turn. He stood in miserable

142

silence as the marquis swept past him and slammed the door behind him.

Pottson walked slowly over to Miss Hetty's discarded gown and automatically picked it up, smoothing out the wrinkles. The marquis had held the answer to Lord Monteith in his hands, yet had not realized the truth. She had fashioned herself too fine a reputation as a wild, dissolute young gentleman.

Pottson walked slowly into Lord Harry's bedchamber and hung up her gown in the closet. He looked about the room. Had the marquis not been so angry, he would have noticed the ribbons and hairbrushes scattered about on the dressing table.

Pottson walked back into the drawing room, his shoulders hunched forward. The marquis' words burned into his mind. There would be no backing out now.

Signore Bertioli faced the sweating, heavily panting Lord Monteith. He placed his foil carefully into its velvet case and handed the young gentleman a white lawn handkerchief to mop his brow.

"You fight with the calm desperation of a man who knows the test of his courage to be near," Signore Bertioli said softly. "The *vendetta* draws to a close, my lord?"

Hetty did not immediately reply, for she felt as though her lungs would burst with the effort. Signore Bertioli gently removed the foil from her unresisting hand and waited patiently for her to speak.

"Yes, Signore," Hetty said at last. "As you say, the *vendetta* draws itself to a close." She read concern in the Italian's dark eyes. "Do not fear for the outcome, Signore, I beg of you. All will be resolved with pistols, not foils."

Signore Bertioli frowned. "Then why have you pushed yourself to learn the tricks of the masters, my young lord?"

Hetty managed a rueful grin. "They say, Signore, if a man goes into battle with but one weapon and a prayer on his lips, he is a fool. In all truth, I would have much preferred foils, yet despite your excellent instruction, I must face the fact that I have not the endurance nor yet the skill to dispatch my opponent."

Signore Bertioli wanted very much to know the name of Lord Monteith's enemy, yet he knew that such an inquiry would be impertinent. He asked instead, "Your opponent, my lord, he is much skilled with the foil?"

"Yes, so I have heard. And he has ten more years experience than I have."

"Does he not also have ten years more experience with a pistol?"

"My skill with a pistol cannot be questioned, Signore. If you have a biblical turn of mind, you could liken me to the small David. The tiny ball from my pistol will bring down my Goliath. The pistol levels all our differences. Now, Signore, I must leave you. 'Twill be a most interesting evening and I have no wish to be late."

Hetty shrugged into her greatcoat and drew on black leather gloves. "Signore," she said, turning, "I thank you. That I have been a disappointment to you, I own to regret. If I do not see you again . . . well, you will know that the young lion had no more than a great roar. Goodbye, Signore."

"Goodbye, my lord," the Italian said softly as the door closed behind Lord Monteith.

Hetty gazed with vividly glittering eyes about the vast gaming salon at White's, noting that fewer gentlemen than usual lounged about the gaming tables. She registered surprise until she remembered the races at Newmarket. Many of the *ton* were drawn away to wager their guineas in the company of the Regent.

She turned to a footman who stood at her elbow balancing a silver tray that held an array of liquor. "Have you yet seen Sir Harry Brandon?"

"Yes, my lord. He is, I believe, at the faro table."

"And the Marquis of Oberlon. Has he yet arrived?"

"I have not as yet seen his grace, my lord."

Hetty nodded and turned to make her way to the far corner of the room to the faro tables, her footsteps sure, her back ramrod straight. She did not allow herself to question the strong grip of purpose that held her calm in her resolve.

She saw Sir Harry lounging in one of the Louis XV chairs, observing the game's progress.

Sir Harry was feeling altogether out of sorts. He already had imbibed too much brandy, and his bowels were fiery warm. If only he could erase Isabella's pale, pensive face from his mind. He had not meant to take her to task over receiving Lord Harry during their speedily arranged ride in the park in the afternoon, yet when she had spoken in such glowing terms of Lord Monteith, he had been unable to help him-

144

self. She had said to him in a tight little voice, "I would liefer marry him than Sir William Filey," and he had retorted in a fit of unhappy jealousy, "Be my guest, madam! You appear to have some sort of fascination for rakehells!"

He gulped down another swig of brandy, then gazed morosely into the amber liquid.

"I am glad you are come tonight, Harry."

Sir Harry looked up into the face of Lord Harry and grunted. "You said it was urgent that I come to White's this evening. What is it—you wish to announce your marriage to Isabella?"

Hetty managed a crooked grin. "No, 'tis naught to do with Isabella, though there is much I could tell you on that score, would you but listen."

Sir Harry gave a sarcastic hurrumph and downed the rest of his brandy.

"I would ask that you do not become any more foxed, Harry. I have need of your services this evening . . . and your clear head."

Sir Harry looked up quickly. "What's afoot, Lord Harry? You sound damned serious." Lord Harry turned suddenly, his attention riveted toward the doorway.

He followed Lord Harry's gaze and hastily placed his brandy glass on the table. In the doorway stood the Marquis of Oberlon and Harry's brother-in-law, the Earl of March. He felt Lord Harry stiffen beside him.

"Come, Harry, you must not fail me." Hetty's eyes sent an urgent plea. "I can count upon you, can I not, Harry?"

"Of course you can," Harry sputtered, rising quickly to stand next to Lord Harry. "Dammit, tell me what is going on!" Even from across the room, he sensed a tension, a cold seriousness from the earl and the marquis.

He felt something was very much amiss, yet when he saw the tight closed look on Lord Harry's face, he choked down further questions. As they drew closer, he saw his brother-in-law's cool grey eyes alight upon him, first in surprise, then in angry speculation. He would have liked to stop dead in his tracks, yet his feet moved forward.

"So you have come."

Harry heard the marquis speak directly to Lord Harry, his words so very simple, yet Harry felt the icy edge of unspoken words linger in the air.

"Yes, I am come," Lord Harry replied coldly. "I have many failings, your grace, but I submit that cowardice and

145

arrogant cruelty are not among them. Perhaps your grace would care to elaborate upon these most interesting flaws of character."

Sir Harry was too stunned by his friend's blatant insult to do more than gaze at him openmouthed.

Strangely enough, at least in Sir Harry's eyes, the Marquis of Oberlon did not so much as flick an eyelid at Lord Harry's outrageous remark. Indeed, his dark eyes seemed to gleam all the brighter.

Actually, Jason Cavander felt an oddly mixed sense of anticipation. He had sensed that young Monteith would not apologize to him, and hoped at the very least to push the young gentleman into explaining his obvious hatred for him. He raised a haughty black brow and drawled with a lazy sneer on his lips, "You have but to provide me with suitable circumstances and I would be most willing to explain cowardice and cruelty to you, Monteith. Without a frame of reference, though, I fear I am unable to the task. If you wish to pursue flaws of character, perhaps you can readily enlighten me upon the seduction of other men's women. Methinks I see a young Sir William Filey in the making."

Damn, Hetty thought furiously to herself, he has turned my own arguments against me! She tried to prevent the dull red flush from creeping over her cheeks, but failed.

"How very interesting that you mention Sir William, your grace." She smoothed an invisible wrinkle from her sleeve, then continued with deep sarcasm, "I thought him the most vile of creatures when I first came to London, yet, I found readily enough that I was quite mistaken. Vile though he may be, he wears his villainy openly and does not slither about like a snake, hiding his dishonour under his belly!"

"Your insults wander about in too many different directions, Monteith. They have no substance, and no ring of truth to them. Are you too cowardly to speak your mind? If so, you may simply apologize to me and I shall gladly be rid of your irritating presence."

He spoke calmly and indifferently, as if she were naught but a troublesome boy. Frustration and anger mounted in her and she spoke harshly. "I would as lief apologize to that monster, Bonaparte! You spoke of my seducing other men's women—I do not think the fair Melissande quite thought of herself as belonging to a *man*. Indeed, she was so eager for my embraces, that, if I did not know of her close proximity

146

to your grace, I would have thought she had been marooned alone for many a long month!"

"God, Lord Harry—!"

"Shut up, Harry!" Hetty growled over her shoulder, her eyes never leaving Lord Cavander's face.

She thought she had succeeded, for rage was building in his eyes, tightening his lips into a thin line. She stood proudly, stiff and erect, waiting for him to strike her.

She felt as though someone suddenly whipped her feet from beneath her when the Earl of March threw back his head and laughed heartily.

Lord Cavander unclenched his fisted hand. He blinked rapidly several times and turned to the earl's laughing face. "What the devil!" he ejaculated.

The earl, amusement still lingering in his deep voice, said more to Hetty than to the marquis, "You pick the wrong barb, my boy. Cavander here has been so plagued by women that he must needs flee from them! As for his mistresses, it has been said that their sighs of pleasure can be heard from two rooms away! Now, Monteith, may I suggest that you either tell Lord Cavander why you find him so abhorrent or simply apologize for your many unprovoked insults and be done with this nonsense!"

"Yes, do, my lad," the marquis added, his temper restored. He was thankful that Julien had turned the world back in the right direction. "Come, Monteith, I hesitate to kick a bothersome puppy!"

"Lord Harry, please, leave go!" Sir Harry pleaded in her ear.

Hetty gritted her teeth against a wave of sheer impotence, and it was not until she tasted her own blood that she realized that she had bitten her lower lip. She could think of no more insults, no more sarcastic taunts. She had vowed so long ago not to tell the marquis the reason for her hatred until he lay bleeding away his miserable life at her feet. She could see all the months of her careful charade as a gentleman crumbling into failure in front of the condescendingly tolerant marquis and earl. It was her lack of years that made her look ridiculous. For an instant, she pictured herself as the marquis must see her—an arrogant, foolish young boy. They could afford to be amused, these proud gentlemen. She was naught to them but a bothersome puppy, just as Lord Cavander had drawled to her in his most bored manner.

Had Lord Cavander thought Damien just as insignificant?

147

So unimportant, in fact, as to dispatch him out of the country with no self-recrimination? Only dimly did she hear Lord Cavander give a crack of rude laughter, and mockingly observe to the earl, "Come, Julien, the farce is ended! I need no apology from a young whelp who is scarce breeched, and who now appears to have lost his tongue!"

Suddenly Hetty felt a surge of hatred that coursed through every fiber of her body. A footman passed near to her bearing a tray of glasses filled with sparkling champagne. Instinctively she grasped the slender stem of a glass and held it in front of her, as if readying for a toast. She heard her own voice spilling out words with surprising calmness.

"That I have afforded you such entertainment, your grace, leaves me most gratified. You find my insults nonsensical. Perhaps 'tis true, for I have not your years of studied cruelty. Where my words have failed, oh most noble lord, perhaps this will not!" She dashed the sparkling champagne into Lord Cavander's face.

She heard a moan of helpless distress from Sir Harry, and saw from the corner of her eye small knots of whispering, shocked gentlemen who had observed this short violent drama; yet her attention did not waver from the marquis.

She watched him pull a white pocket handkerchief with a deft, graceful movement, and slowly mop the champagne from his face. In a voice so quiet that she had to lean forward to hear, Lord Cavander said, "You give me now no choice, Monteith. Do you wish to fight in the middle of White's, or can your mad rush to dispatch yourself to hell wait until the morrow?"

"A night to anticipate your demise will give me great pleasure."

"Very well," he replied in a flat, emotionless voice. "Julien, will you act for me?"

"Yes, if it must be, Jason," the earl said quietly.

Sir Harry felt his brother-in-law's grey eyes resting almost pityingly upon him. And even as Lord Harry turned, he knew that he had no choice but to second his friend. His *yes* was a croak.

The Earl of March stepped forward and laid his hand on his brother-in-law's sleeve. He said formally, "It is my duty as a second to seek reconciliation."

At the silent set faces of Lord Monteith and Lord Cavander, he continued with a sigh, "As you will. Tomorrow morn-

148

ing at eight o'clock at the north end of Hyde Park. Harry, come with me now, we must make arrangements."

"Such a fool you are, Monteith," Lord Cavander said in a pensive, almost sad voice. He turned abruptly on his heel and strode from the gaming salon.

Hetty was left standing alone, the empty champagne glass still held tightly in her hand. Whispering gentlemen began to disperse back to the gaming tables. She thought she saw a footman speaking behind a white-gloved hand to one of his peers. Slowly and with deliberation, she strode to the footman and placed the champagne glass down upon his tray. She wondered fleetingly if her own face was as pale as the footman's. She drew a deep breath and walked from the gaming salon, not looking back.

Strangely, Pottson said not a word when Hetty, an hour later, tried with as much calm as she could muster to relate to him what had happened.

"We both knew this night had to come, Pottson, for there was, after all, no other reason for Lord Harry's existence. On the morrow, Damien will be revenged."

Pottson raised weary troubled eyes to Miss Hetty's young, innocent face. "Aye," he murmured softly, "Master Damien will be revenged, or you, Miss Hetty, will follow him to the grave and it will all have been for naught."

She felt a sudden chill touch her heart and shivered despite the warmth of the small parlour. "Pray do not seal my fate so quickly. A man's chest is a much larger target than the wafers at Manton's." She paused a moment and looked about her. Odd how this small apartment seemed more her home than Sir Archibald's townhouse.

"When we return tomorrow morning, Pottson, we must decide what is to be done with Lord Harry Monteith. And, more importantly, my friend, we must discuss your future. If you have a liking for Herefordshire, my brother, Sir John, would, I am certain, be most willing to engage Damien's valet."

Pottson merely grunted an unintelligible reply, and Hetty, mindful of being refreshed on the morrow, rose and walked slowly into Lord Harry's bedchamber to change into a gown.

As was his habit, Pottson accompanied Miss Hetty back to her father's townhouse. As they drew up to the servants' entrance, where Millie stood waiting, Hetty said, "I shall see you at seven o'clock, Pottson. When it is over, we shall enjoy a hearty breakfast and bid Lord Harry a fond adieu."

Her bracing words, quietly spoken, seemed to fall on deaf ears. Pottson looked at her searchingly for a moment, then lowered his eyes, turned and disappeared into the night.

"Whatever is wrong with him?" Millie demanded once they were in Hetty's bedroom. "Acts like he's got a maggot in his ear."

"Pottson is merely out of sorts, Millie," Hetty replied lightly, avoiding her maid's eyes. She had no intention of telling Millie of tomorrow's adventure.

Once nightgowned, the pomade brushed out of her fair curls, Hetty bid Millie an affectionate goodnight. With single purpose, she carried her candle to her writing desk and prepared herself to perform a task for which she had no liking, but a task that had to be done. She smoothed out a piece of plain white paper, dipped the quill into the ink pot and began painfully to form phrases in her mind. "My dearest father," she wrote, pausing to chew on the quill handle before continuing. "When you read this letter, you will know that you will never see me again. I pray that you will find forgiveness in your heart for the inevitable scandal that my death will cause. I have tried to act in accordance with principles that carry the highest honour, and although my failure must leave you in the forefront to deal with the unpleasant aftermath, I beg that you will try to understand my motives. . . ."

The single candle had gutted in its socket before Hetty laid down her pen and rubbed her cramped fingers. Her explanation had covered five long pages, and although she feared much repetition, she had no wish to reread her work. Wearily, she stood and stretched. She saw with a shock that it was past midnight.

Hurriedly, she drew forth more paper, took quill in hand, and wrote much in the same style to John and Louisa as she had to her father.

She thought as she sealed both letters into their envelopes that if she were not to leave the dueling field alive, John would perforce have to seek redress from the marquis. John's friend . . . the man who was responsible for both his brother's and sister's deaths.

She flung away from the writing table and paced back and forth across the width of her room until the chill drove her to her bed. She sank beneath the heavy covers and stared into the darkness, her eyelids refusing to close. How strange it is, she thought, that death has happened so very close to me, yet I cannot really imagine it coming to me.

When word of Damien's death had reached her, she had felt as though a part of her had died with him. Yet, she still breathed, still felt the sun upon her face, still heartily enjoyed her father's political vagaries. Even though the past months had moved with unremitting purpose to this point, the possibility of her own death had always seemed only a vague specter, the meaning of death lying only with Damien and in the final revenge she sought from his murderer.

She thought again of Sir John, his open, bluff good nature, his sincere friendship with the Marquis of Oberlon. Perhaps she should have told him of the marquis, of Damien, of Melissa. She turned a stiff shoulder to the thought. It was *her* revenge, a debt she owed to Damien. She realized with sudden insight that her single-minded goal had hurled her back into life. How very different she was now from the Hetty who had moved through her days and nights after Damien's death like a vague shadow, allowing nothing to touch her.

If she emerged the victor on the morrow, she would again lose part of herself—the proud, outspoken Lord Harry, the brash counterpart of Henrietta Rolland. A small twisted smile turned up the corners of her mouth. Which Henrietta Rolland? Parts of her seemed to be strewn all about London, each with a different function, each unwhole, wanting. How strange it was too, that Lord Cavander had known each of her parts. The Henrietta Rolland who had attended the masked ball did not care for this thought.

As the clock chimed one o'clock in the morning, Hetty resolutely refused to think further of *that* Henrietta Rolland, and, thwacking her pillow, buried her face in its softness and forced her eyelids shut. She had but five hours until Millie would awaken her. She finally fell asleep wondering if Millie suspected that something other than an early ride in the park with Mr. Scuddimore was the purpose for arising at such an ungodly hour.

When the Marquis of Oberlon unceremoniously slammed out of White's, his many-caped greatcoat flung carelessly over his shoulders, he was in the grip of such unreasoning anger that he covered the entire length of Bond Street before he was aware of the frigid night wind cutting unhampered through his elegant evening clothes. He drew to a halt and

151

fastened his greatcoat securely about him, and jerked on the fur gloves that had hung precariously out of his pocket.

It was perhaps the feel of the sticky dried champagne on his face and the still damp touch of his cravat against his neck that finally brought forth the reasonable man. Having a glass of champagne dashed into one's face was certainly not a pleasant experience, yet it had proved to be as effective an insult in 1816, a year when dueling was considered most unfashionable, as a slap with a glove or a few well-chosen words had been to his father's contemporaries in the bygone days when dueling was an honoured activity that cut many a gentleman's life short. The marquis remembered his bewigged grandfather, a full-lipped, lecherous old gentleman who, had he not broken his neck cramming his horse over a fence, would very likely have been felled by a ball from a pistol the very next day by a one-time crony whom he had negligently insulted. As it was, the one-time crony had sniffed copiously at his grandfather's funeral and the marquis' father had sarcastically muttered to his small son that he did not know if the man's sniffing was from grief or from being cheated out of putting a bullet through his grandfather's heart.

Lord Cavander paused a moment, realizing that his wayward thoughts had carried his feet into Millsom Street, altogether in the opposite direction from Berkeley Square. He turned and began to retrace his steps. How very ridiculous it was, he thought anew, to be forced to fight a duel with a young gentleman whose very existence had been unknown to him but a month before. There was but one man whom Lord Cavander had ever wanted to call out. Even so, his father's sincere disgust at the waste resulting from duels had stilled his fury, if not his contempt for Sir William Filey. He found himself wondering, even now, what he would have done if he had been able to prove conclusively Filey's loathsome conduct in the affair. Damn Filey anyway! And damn Elizabeth! Filey had cared too much for his own skin to ever openly taunt the marquis. As for Elizabeth, he knew that toward the end she had hated him as much as she had Filey. He shut his mind against further unpleasant memories. Elizabeth was dead and long buried, her hatred and bitter unhappiness locked away with her forever.

The marquis ascended the steps to his townhouse and raised his hand to the knocker, only to have Rabbell open the door. "Good evening, your grace," the butler said carefully, his eyes avoiding his master's face. "The Earl of March awaits you in the study, your grace."

"Ah, so my faithful second comes to give me encouragement." Lord Cavander felt no hesitance in speaking aloud of the duel, for Rabbell's unnatural mannerisms told him clearly enough that every servant was undoubtedly aware in the most minute detail of the evening's fiasco. Sometime, he thought, as his butler helped to divest him of his greatcoat and gloves, I must force him to tell me how the servants' infallible grapevine can be so damnably efficient.

He walked thoughtfully to his study. "Well, Julien," he said, upon opening the door, " 'tis a fine night's work. Have you come to ring a peal over me?" Lord Cavander disliked the sarcastic irony in his tone, yet was unable to prevent it. The earl was lounging next to the large Italian marble fireplace, looking as lost in his thoughts as Lord Cavander had earlier. "It is I who should be in a brown study, St. Clair, not you."

The earl pushed his shoulders from the mantelpiece and walked to the marquis. "You have been long coming back, Jason. Actually, when you came in, I was plotting the possibility of trussing Monteith up in a sack and having my captain sail away with him to the West Indies!"

"I daresay the young gentleman would rule the islands within a month! Either through persuasion or by dispatching all the current leaders in duels." He chuckled at his own humour. "It's hellishly cold, Julien, would you care for a sherry?"

The earl nodded and there was companionable silence until both gentlemen, glasses in hand, seated themselves near to the crackling fire. After a moment, the earl said reluctantly, "As much as I dislike it, Jason, I must of course inquire as to your preference of weapons, as Monteith was the challenger."

"Need you really ask, Julien?" he said. "A pistol is far too deadly a weapon, and you must know that despite all the young puppy has said and done, I have no wish to kill him. He cannot be all that experienced with the foil, and I hope to contrive a quick and clean prick through his arm. That ought to cool his murderous instincts, at least for a month."

There was an undisguised flash of relief in the earl's grey eyes. " 'Tis what I hoped you would say, Jason. I might tell you too that Harry informed me that Monteith is a crack shot. I would have feared the outcome had you chosen pistols."

"You unman me, Julien," the marquis observed wryly. In a

153

quieter tone, he asked, "How is poor Harry taking all this? Judging from his openmouthed expression, I gather he did not know what Monteith intended this evening."

"The boy is obviously torn in two directions. Of course, his honour forbids him to refuse to second his friend. I left him with Kate; she has always had a way of soothing him."

The earl rose and placed his empty glass on the sideboard. "I must off now, Jason. 'Tis past midnight and you must be clear and steady on the morrow. I shall be here—with my carriage—before eight o'clock."

"Your carriage, my friend? You terrify me. I had hoped to ride from the park all in one piece!"

The earl merely smiled slightly, refusing to be drawn. Actually, it was Kate who insisted on the carriage, and he could not dispute her reasoning. It is always better to be well prepared for any eventuality, she had said, her green eyes darkened with concern. The earl said casually as the marquis walked with him from the study, "What do you intend to do about Melissande now, Jason?"

Lord Cavander shrugged and replied indifferently, "Her apartment has three more months on its lease. She may stay until then. With her beauty and figure, I have no doubt that she will attach another well-breeched gentleman long before that time." He added, a hint of amused incredulity in his voice, "Did you know that Monteith gave her a riding habit?"

"Lord, the boy was awake on every suit!" The earl turned to his friend and clasped his hand. Mindful of Rabbell standing near, he said softly, "You have acted quite rightly in this wretched business. Until tomorrow, Jason."

13

It was a blistering cold overcast morning, and the heavily wooded north end of the park boasted little else this time of year but hard-frozen ground and naked-branched trees. There were no onlookers, not only because of the earliness of the hour but also because the carriage tracks and walking paths clustered more to the south, like spokes in a wheel circling the Grand Strut.

The dull thudding of horses' hooves and the crunching of carriage wheels were the only sound to break the monotony of the gently rustling branches, and the chirping of the more hearty sparrows.

Sir Harry Brandon stole a sideways glance at Lord Harry. He shifted uneasily in the saddle at the sight of his friend's set face. His usually sparkling eyes were narrowed in deep concentration and his lips were drawn in a bloodless thin line. Lord Harry had said not a word to him, save to beg a mount from his meager stable for Pottson. Wordlessly, Harry had obliged, but the precious time this detour had cost put the hour much too close to eight o'clock for his peace of mind. But Lord Harry seemed oblivious of the hour, leaving Harry to wonder if he was aware of the nicety of the gentleman's code that forbade a duel if either of the opponents arrived after the appointed time.

Sir Harry was forced to conclude that Lord Harry knew exactly what he was about, for it lacked two minutes to the hour when their small cavalcade broke into the clearing. Not twenty feet away stood the Earl of March's town carriage.

As they dismounted and tethered their mounts, Hetty turned to Sir Harry and said in a heartening voice, "I hope you did not fear that we would be late, old boy. One always makes an entrance after all the guests have arrived."

Sir Harry could find no witty rejoinder for this admirable display of *sang froid*, and managed only a strangled, "Quite."

As Harry fidgeted with his horse's bridle, Hetty said gently, "Should you not meet with the Earl of March, Harry? The weapons, you know."

155

"Aye," Harry replied, falling back on his sister's Scottish word for the affirmative. When he was beyond earshot, Hetty turned to Pottson, who stood in grim silence, his hands wringing into the folds of his coat.

"Do not fail me, Pottson. Whatever happens must occur without any interference from you. Give me your promise."

At the valet's numb silence, Hetty grabbed his arm, her voice a grating whisper. "Your promise, Pottson!"

"Master Damien would never wish for this, Miss Hetty. Gawd, he would never—"

"Damn you! 'Tis far too late for maudlin scenes! Do you swear to keep a still tongue in your mouth?"

"Yes, Miss Hetty," he said finally, looking squarely into her fierce blue eyes, "I swear."

"Good. I wish you to remain here." Hetty turned on her heel, her boots crunching loudly into the frozen earth, and without a backward glance, strode toward the small circle formed by the three gentlemen.

She knew that concentration was born of calmness, and had, for the past two hours, mentally raised the dueling pistol in her hand, turned her body sideways so as to present the smallest possible target, aimed carefully and tenderly stroked the trigger. Over and over she had played through each minute movement until her mind finally settled with single thought to its one purpose. There was now no room for fear or self-doubt to slip in uninvited.

Her stride was a confident swagger, her hands still inside their warm gloves, steady and dry.

She glanced only cursorily at the Earl of March, her eyes narrowing haughtily upon the marquis.

"I bid you good morning, your grace . . . my lord. I do not wish my mare to become restive. Shall we begin?"

Admirable, the marquis thought reluctantly, the boy shows courage beyond his years. But his voice belied his thoughts as he said with a mocking drawl, "By all means, Monteith. I would not wish you to be late for your visit to the surgeon."

Hetty's eyes crackled dangerously. " 'Tis not a surgeon that will attend to you, your grace."

The earl interposed sharply, "Do you have wish to inspect your foil, Lord Monteith?" He opened the long narrow case and carefully lifted out a glittering silver rapier.

Hetty looked stupidly down at the foil. Damnation, what a ludicrous mistake Harry had made! He, of all people, knew that she preferred the pistol! She turned to him, her jaw working with frustration and anger. Her voice was as hard as the frozen earth. "What is this, Harry? You know it is the pistol I choose. Explain yourself!"

Sir Harry's eyes widened in disbelief at his friend's incredible words. He shook his head back and forth in confusion. "But Lord Harry, I know you prefer pistols, but there was naught I could say in the matter."

Lord Cavander observed this interchange initially with as much confusion as Sir Harry now evinced. How could Monteith ever have assumed that the choice of weapons would be his?

The Earl of March intervened smoothly. "As the challenger, Monteith, you have no choice in the selection of weapons. Lord Cavander has decided upon foils."

Sir Harry added desperately, "Do you not recall, Lord Harry? It was you who dashed the champagne in his grace's face!"

The marquis said dryly, "It would appear that Lord Monteith fences well only with words. I will accept your explanation, lad, as well as your apology, if you choose now to sincerely give it."

Hetty's secure mental fortress had shattered into myriad unrelated thoughts, uppermost among them the ridiculous phrase she had spoken to Signore Bertioli the afternoon before—"a young lion with only a roar . . . we shall soon know if I am only a young lion with a roar."

She looked blindly at the three faces staring at her, and saw only contempt, for she was not looking at them but back into herself. She remembered her blithely spoken words, again to Signore Bertioli, that a man who goes into battle with but one weapon and a prayer is a fool.

"You have but to explain and apologize," the marquis' words sounded in her mind. He invited her to crawl away with a sincere apology, in shame and dishonour.

She saw Damien, lying lifeless on the bloody battlefield of Waterloo, crying out for vengeance. Her mind fastened upon his image, and in that instant, her thoughts wove themselves together again.

She said with cold flippancy, shrugging her shoulders with sublime indifference, "Foils, your grace? It makes no difference to me how you wish to die."

She picked up a gleaming rapier from the case and tested its weight in her hand. It was light, steady and exquisitely forged.

The marquis frowned at Monteith's baiting words, not in renewed anger, but in perplexity. He was not a blind man, and the stunned shock on the lad's face, then the empty coursing of fear that had left his eyes glazed, made the marquis suddenly wonder fancifully if he was not playing the part of the villain in some sort of cheap melodrama at Drury Lane, a villain who seemed, strangely, to have the upper hand over the hero.

"Jason."

He shook his head, clearing away these extraneous thoughts, and took his foil from the earl's outstretched hand.

"Take care, my friend," the earl said.

The marquis only nodded, wondering if Julien meant him to take care of himself or to take care of young Monteith. He found, foolishly enough, that he had to hand the foil back while he stripped off his greatcoat and gloves.

"Damn, but it is cold," Hetty said inconsequentially, as she unbuttoned her waistcoat.

"Lord Harry—" Harry began.

"Yes?"

"I—I will keep your greatcoat warm," Harry murmured unhappily.

Stripped to her loose, frilled white shirt, breeches and hessians, Hetty slashed her foil through the air several times, testing its flexibility, then moved forward to where the marquis stood, his side presented to her.

She flexed her knees, leaning slightly forward, and placed her left hand lightly upon her hip. She slashed the foil again in a wide arc and stood ready for the earl's command.

"*En garde!*" The earl's words rang out harshly in the silent wood.

The marquis began to move gracefully toward her, his blade carefully poised, his eyes intent upon her face. His foil suddenly flashed out wide to her right side, testing for the quickness of her reaction.

Hetty caught his blade handily, parrying his thrust easily, and skipped lightly to bring her weight down on her left foot. He drew back, his foil making small circles, readying like a viper, Hetty thought, to strike again. She sensed his easy control, his practiced mastery, the silver blade appearing to her like an extension of his arm and his will. Thus it was with Signore Bertioli. Give me your skill, Signore, she prayed silently, then with a quick sidestep, lunged forward. The edge of her foil rang against tempered steel and slid nearly halfway up the marquis' blade, until with a powerful flick of his wrist, he parried the strike. The force of his parry sent stabs of pain up her arm.

The marquis was mildly surprised at the quickness of her lunge, but felt the loosening of her foil when he disengaged with brutal strength. The lad had quickness, but not the strength and endurance to last for any length of time against him. He needed only to engage the boy in a continuous flurry, giving him no time to rest, and, above all, rigidly control the encounter so that he could not slip through the marquis' guard. He drew a wide path of control in front of him, discouraging further sudden attacks, but engaging with pounding force. He saw the uncertainty and frustration growing on the boy's face, and held stoutly to his strategy.

Hetty tried to save her strength, and drew back and began to stalk him, lightly on her toes, dancing in a circular direction opposite from his. He drew toward her to force a flurry, and in that instant, she lunged forward.

He evaded her attack handily, giving ground to her. She followed, her blade dancing in the silent air in the brief seconds between clashes. Then she felt the power of him, unchecked for an instant, driving her back. She saw his powerful thigh muscles bulging in his knit breeches, and felt her own legs begin to tremble.

Beads of perspiration formed on her forehead, and she quickly dashed her hand across her eyes. Her breath was coming heavily now, and she knew she had to retreat at least a moment from his raging foil.

She took three light jumping steps backward, disengaging her blade from his, letting her lungs gulp in the precious air. But he was on her in an instant, his lunge curiously shallow, yet clashing against her blade with such force that her fingers nearly crumpled on their grip. She met his eyes in that moment, saw that they were calm and coolly calculating, and felt a quiver of anger at her own weakness. With more anger than skill, she stepped into the onslaught of his foil with a furious lunge. The blades crackled together and he bore his hand upward, pulling her forward until the foils were locked at their base. She hated her own raspy breathing, for he was but inches from her face and could hear her weakening. Damn, but there was not even a drop of perspiration on his forehead!

With a cry of frustration, Hetty jerked back, almost losing her balance. Her free hand clutched wildly at the empty air, in a frantic attempt to keep from falling. Even as she regained her balance, she was aware that the marquis could have been upon her in a second. Yet, he stood silently back, the look on his face curiously dispassionate.

159

"Damn you," she growled between heaving breaths.

The marquis readied himself for a wild lunge, his eyes, this time, resting coolly upon her right arm. The lad was fighting bravely and with some skill. But he was tiring visibly. It was time to bring the duel to an honorable end.

Hetty wanted to leap upon him, to tear the foil from his hand. It was the severe, rapped out words of Signore Bertioli spoken on a long ago afternoon, that held her back. "Young lord, he who loses his head will most certainly lose his heart! And not, young sir, to a lady!" She had laughed heartily, digested his words and proceeded to feint with such subtle skill that for the only time during his tutelage, she had nearly managed to break through his guard.

She became aware of the calm yet expectant stance of the marquis. *He expects me to lunge wildly*, she realized with a start. *Very well, let him think it to be so!*

She clumsily lurched forward, her foil extended its full length, its tip aimed for his heart.

The marquis saw his opportunity, for she had forfeited her guard. He swiftly parried her blade to one side and lunged at her upper arm. In that instant, Hetty executed the Italian master's most difficult trick: she drew back her blade, jumped quickly to the side, deflecting his blade from her arm, and lunged with all her strength toward his shoulder.

From instinct born of long practice, the marquis whirled about, slid his foil under hers and threw her off balance. But he could not temper the force of his lunge, and with sickening ease, he felt the tip of his blade slice into her side.

Hetty jerked her head up, startled that she had failed. She felt the jab of a tiny prick in her side, then a strange cold sensation, as if a slap of frigid air had hit her skin. The marquis stood frozen in front of her, his face a shocked mask.

She saw that his foil was covered from its tip to almost a quarter of its length in bright red. *It is blood, my blood*, she thought inconsequentially, but she felt no pain.

She heard the Earl of March command loudly, "Hold Monteith! Lord Cavander has drawn blood. It is over!"

Over! No, nothing was over! Did they expect her to crawl away in dishonour because of a slight prick in her side? She cried out suddenly, her voice strong and clear, "Damn you, Cavander! I have just begun with you! *En garde!*" She felt strong, confident, as if her body no longer existed—only her mind and her arm, the foil its extension.

The marquis shot a helpless glance at the earl. He had time for naught else, for Hetty lunged at him with the fury of

160

demons from hell. He leapt back, parrying the thrust. He saw the glazed look of purpose in the lad's eyes and knew that his mind had closed itself to any pain. The lad would bleed to death before he realized how badly he was wounded. The small circle of blood that stained the loose white shirt was spreading rapidly, flattening the material against the wound.

He called out over the hissing of the blades, "Monteith, draw in! Look at your side!"

He might as well have spoken to the wind, for though Hetty heard his words, her mind refused to allow her to understand their significance. She heard herself laugh aloud, a strong triumphant laugh. She pressed him, her blade cutting so swiftly through the air that he backed away and to the side to diminish the force of her thrusts.

Her attack was unmeasured, wild. There was no timing or skill in the frantic lunges. The boy's mind keeps him from seeing the truth of the matter, the marquis thought with growing concern. If he did not quickly bring the duel to a halt, the boy would die. He knew Monteith to be beyond understanding, and he swallowed back further words of warning.

For the next several minutes, the marquis gave ground, parrying thrust after wild thrust, his movements wholly defensive. The boy was tiring, his attack so clumsy and ill-timed that the marquis could have easily slipped through his guard. Yet, he held back. He was waiting for the instant when he could catch Monteith's foil high near his hand and rip it from his fingers. He watched, parried, his eyes alert, waiting for the perfect moment.

He is weakening and falling back, Hetty's mind told her. Press him, press him harder!

The marquis made a mistake. For the instant his eyes returned to the matted, now huge circle of blood that had spread upward toward the boy's chest, he broke his concentration.

Hetty whipped her foil under his, and the suddenness of the impact, at the same instant as his attention wavered, jerked his blade from his fingers and sent it flying to the ground.

What a damned fool you are, he observed to himself dispassionately. He felt the pressure of the boy's blade against his chest.

You have won, you have won! Hetty's mind cried triumphantly. She stood poised forward, her weight on her right leg, her foil extended its full length, the tip against her enemy's heart. Why does he not say something? Why does he not plead for his life? The glazed shock that had held her in sway loosed its grip on her vision, and she stared at him. He stood quietly before her and she could see no fear in his fathomless dark eyes.

The Earl of March forced himself to hold his place. "For God's sake, Jason, jerk away his foil!"

The marquis made no sign that he had even heard the earl's words. He could not be certain why he made no move. There was something in the boy's eyes that held him.

Hetty felt the powerful, single purpose of her mind begin to fall away from her, and in that instant, she saw herself as she used to be. She saw Henrietta Rolland before she discovered the marquis' hand in her brother's death. She had been hollow with grief, hollow with the touch of death. Still, death had not claimed her, and she had savored the full consciousness of life, even in those months when she felt most alone. It had seemed so simple to her to plan the marquis' execution, his death a just retribution, a full payment for the grief he had brought to her. Yet, he stood before her now—proud, arrogant—but alive, just as she was alive. She realized that she had used the idea of his death to assuage her own grief. But to run her foil through his heart, to rob him of life, to actually bring about another human being's death, was beyond her. Her single-minded hatred, her pact of vengeance crumbled.

She gasped aloud, jerked back the foil from his chest, and, clasping it in both hands, plunged it into the frozen ground with all her remaining strength. She jerked her fingers away from it as if it were evil.

She had thrust it deep enough so that the handle swung back and forth, its gentle hissing sounding softly in the silence.

"I cannot kill you! Damien, forgive me, I cannot do it!" Her cry was filled with the deep pain of her spirit and the growing agony in her body. She looked into his face, the face she had hated even in her dreams. His face grew distorted, twisting into a mask of death—Damien's face. "I cannot kill him," she sobbed, wrenching cries tearing from her throat. Her body was taking her over now, closing off any control from her mind. A searing pain tore through her side and she doubled over, clutching her arms about her. She felt hot stickiness on her hands and looked down in dumb surprise at her blood-covered fingers. She looked wildly about her, but

162

saw only blurred images. She heard loud voices, yet they came to her ears as unintelligible sounds. Her knees buckled beneath her and she fell heavily to the frozen earth, her head striking an outjutting rock. Blackness flooded her.

14

The marquis was at her prone figure in an instant, his hands tearing at the blood-soaked shirt. He had to stop the bleeding. Damn, but he wasn't going to be Monteith's murderer! He acted on instinct, not allowing himself to think about the incredible scene in which he had just played a part. He ripped open the shirt and tugged at the buckskin breeches to bare the wound. It was not bare skin that met his eyes, but a tight-fitting muslin wrap hemmed with blue ribbon. He had torn it apart before the significance of the garment hit him. Though side, ribs and belly were covered with blood, the gentle inward curving to a slender waist, the soft smoothness of the white skin jarred his benumbed mind into the undeniable truth.

Lord Harry Monteith was a girl!

"Jason, how badly is he wounded?"

In that instant, the marquis made a decision and acted on it without further consideration. He jerked the shirt back over her side and simultaneously answered the earl.

"It is bad, Julien. Quickly, give me your handkerchief. Harry, your neckcloth. We must stop the bleeding."

"Mi— Lord Harry! Dear God, Lord Harry!" The marquis glanced up at the frantic countenance of the valet. God, the man had nearly given all away! He looked Pottson straight in the eye and said firmly, "*Lord Harry* will be all right. I promise you."

"Aye, your grace," Pottson said quietly. He saw the silent warning in the marquis' eyes. Come what may, he knew the matter was out of his hands.

The marquis used his body as a shield as he pressed the wadded handkerchief against the wound. "Now your neckcloth, Harry." Gently, he slipped the wide band of material under her back and knotted it over the pad.

He spoke forcibly to the earl, even as he lifted her easily into his arms. "Julien, I require your carriage. I very nearly killed the boy and now I intend to take care of him." He turned to the valet. "You will accompany me to Thurston Hall."

"Now, see here, your grace!" Sir Harry stepped forward, uncertain of what he should do.

"Hold, Harry," the earl said quietly. He looked searchingly into his friend's eyes, then said evenly, "Lord Cavander will do what is best, Harry. You may depend upon his word."

As Pottson threw the heavy greatcoat over Hetty's unconscious form, the earl asked, "Thurston Hall, Jason? 'Tis an hour and a half to reach."

"I know," the marquis replied carefully, not meeting the earl's questioning eyes. "It makes no matter. Once the bleeding is stopped, it makes no difference whether Monteith is abed in London or at Thurston Hall. It is better for the lad to be out of London."

The set of Sir Harry's mouth was mulish and only the iron grip of his brother-in-law's hand prevented him from demanding just the devil why it was better for Lord Harry to be out of London.

"You will keep us informed of his progress, Jason?"

"You may depend upon it, Julien. Now, we must be off. I would cover as many miles as possible before the lad regains consciousness."

"But a doctor! Lord Harry needs a doctor!" Sir Harry cried as he and the earl trailed after the marquis.

Lord Cavander turned as he stepped into the carriage. "A doctor can do naught that I cannot do, Harry. I suffered a like wound several years back and I assure you that I will provide him the best care." He mounted the carriage steps, mindful of the light burden in his arms. "Julien, see to Monteith's horse, will you?"

"Do not concern yourself further," the earl said. He took Sir Harry's arm and drew him away.

"You, what is your name?" Lord Cavander called to Pottson.

"Pottson, your grace," he replied and moved quickly to the door of the carriage.

Lord Cavander lowered his voice, for he had no wish that even Silken hear his words. "Now, Pottson, what is the young lady's name, if you please?"

Pottson stared vacantly at his unconscious mistress pressed close to the marquis' chest. His promise to her rang clear in his mind, yet, he knew at the same time that all had changed.

"Well, man? Do you not see that I must know everything now if we are to pull through this mess without a scandal that would rock all of London?"

"She is Miss Henrietta Rolland, your grace," Pottson whispered finally.

Damnation! Sir Archibald's daughter . . . Jack's little sister! He pulled himself together. "It is good that you told me, Pottson. Now, ride with Silken. I must have time to think!"

Dear God, it was not enough that he had dueled with just any young girl . . . no, it must needs be the daughter of a well-known Tory and the sister of one of his best friends! He shouted out the window, "Spring 'em, Silken! If they're blown, we'll change them at Smithfield!"

Silken took his master at his word, and Lord Cavander clutched Hetty tighter to his chest to keep her steady as the carriage lurched and swayed over the cobblestones.

He gently pulled back the greatcoat that covered her and carefully eased up her shirt. The wadded handkerchief was near to soaked with blood. He placed his fingers atop the wound and pressed down. He tried to cradle her as best he could with his free hand, and drew the greatcoat over her.

He stared down into her pale, still face. Henrietta was the beauty of the family, Louisa had said. His eyes followed the slender column of her neck to the firm smooth chin, a stubborn chin, he thought inconsequentially. He looked closely at the high cheekbones, the straight proud nose, the thick fair lashes lying in wet spikes on her cheeks. How strange that looking down at her now, everything made sense; the myriad parts he had thought about so fancifully now fit perfectly together. She had Jack's blond hair. Curling ringlets were working themselves loose from the black ribbon at her neck, and the thick pomade no longer held the curls back from her forehead.

I think you were born a fool and will most certainly leave this world an equal fool, he told himself, shaking his head at his blindness.

It was often said that the clothes made the man. He was now inclined to believe, rather, that one saw what one expected to see. Lord Monteith dressed as a gentleman, talked like a gentleman and partook in all the gentleman's sports. Everyone had accepted him as such. Now, gazing down at her undeniably feminine face, he was forced to admit with rueful admiration that she had pulled the wool over everyone's eyes. Even Melissande!

Why had she hated him so much as to force a duel upon him? Why Jack's sister, in particular? It made no sense to him. He could bring Pottson into the carriage with him and demand the reason. Yet, somehow, he wanted to hear from her own lips why she had planned and executed this outrageous charade. He realized too, his hand covered with her blood, that his most pressing concern was not to discover her motives, but rather to save her life.

The miles slid by and he began to grow concerned that she did not regain consciousness. Minutes ago, they had bowled past the signpost for Helderton, a small village not many miles from the halfway point to Smithfield. He gazed down at her again and saw for the first time a dark purplish bruise forming over her temple. She must have struck her head when she fell. He quickly laid his hand over her breast to feel for her heartbeat. It was, he thought, rapid but steady. A blow on the head could keep her from regaining consciousness. He prayed silently that it was not serious.

He found himself wondering if he was not a coward. Had he hidden her identity from the others to protect his own reputation as a renowned Corinthian? Was he, in fact, endangering her life to keep himself from being a laughingstock?

He did not relish casting himself into such an undesirable mold. His opponent was a female; more than that, she was Miss Henrietta Rolland. Surely, she would approve his actions, for was he not saving not only her but also Sir Archibald from certain social ruin?

He looked up as the carriage drew to a halt in the yard of the Red Rose Inn, in the center of Smithfield.

Silken's small, pointed face soon appeared at the carriage window. " 'Tis winded the cattle are, your grace."

"Change 'em, quickly, Silken." As soon as Silken had bustled away to search out the ostler, Pottson scratched lightly on the carriage door to gain the marquis' attention.

"Beggin' your pardon, your grace," he said carefully, not wanting to displease the marquis, yet knowing that his words were of importance.

"Yes, Pottson? Get on with it, man!"

"Miss Hetty wrote two letters, your grace. One to Sir Archibald and the other to Sir John. If something happened to Miss Hetty, I was to give the letters to her maid. You see, your grace, Miss Hetty always has luncheon with Sir Archibald at precisely twelve o'clock. If she's not there, he'll miss her." Pottson had hoped that his words would flow forth more fluently. He was relieved to see understanding flood the marquis' face but an instant after pondering his speech.

Pottson opened his mouth to continue, but the marquis waved an impatient hand. "Quiet, man, I must think." He soon hit upon what he thought was an excellent solution. In a

167

precise voice, he said, "Heed well, Pottson. You were quite right to tell me. You will procure a hack from the ostler and return to London immediately. Tell Miss Rolland's maid—"

"Millie, your grace."

"Yes, Millie. Tell her to inform Sir Archibald that Miss Rolland has been invited by my sister, Lady Alicia Warton, to spend several days with her at Thurston Hall. She will then accompany you to Thurston Hall—by this evening if possible, Pottson. I shall attend to my sister. Do you understand?"

"Yes, your grace. Lady Alicia Warton."

"You may ask my butler, Rabbell, in Berkeley Square, the directions to Thurston Hall. Here," the marquis said, reaching into his waistcoat pocket, "are several quineas. 'Twill be sufficient, I believe. You must pull it off correctly, Pottson, there is much at stake."

"Aye, your grace, I know. 'Twas a mad scheme, your grace, but once Miss Hetty had the bit between her teeth, there was no stopping her."

The marquis gentled his voice. "You need say no more, my good man. Go now, there is no time to lose."

The marquis thought about Sir Archibald and his general vague perceptions of his family, and decided that his plan was likely to work. Moreover, Sir Archibald would not question an invitation from Lady Alicia Warton. He must remember to write to his sister this very evening, and warn her not to appear in London.

The marquis lifted Hetty's shirt again and saw with dismay that his hand was covered with her blood. If anything, the bleeding had increased. He shouted to Silken to bring him several very clean napkins from the inn.

Gently, he laid her on the opposite seat and unfastened the soaked handkerchief.

He winced at the raw wound, remembering all too clearly the unbearable pain he had borne when he had accidently been run through the shoulder by a school friend, George Pulmondy. Strange, he thought, that he remembered George's name, for he had not seen him for years.

He did not let Silken spring the horses until he had fashioned a new bandage from the clean napkins and settled Hetty again against his chest.

He found himself impatiently gazing out the carriage window for familiar landmarks that would tell him they were drawing close to Thurston Hall. He had never greatly cared for the rambling mansion with its forty bedrooms and ghostly draped ballroom, yet when he saw the entrance to the park,

168

lined with naked-branched lime trees, he thought it a welcome sight. He breathed an audible sigh of relief when the carriage drew to a jolting halt in front of the great pillared front entrance.

Silken jumped nimbly down from the box and jerked open the carriage door. "Can I help your grace with the young gentleman?"

"No, Silken, I can manage," the marquis replied and gently carried the still unconscious Hetty up the deep-inlaid marble steps. He had thought initially that he would enlist the aid of his housekeeper to minister to Miss Rolland, but he had realized that Silken would spread the story of the duel and the "young gentleman's" presence at Thurston Hall. If his servants were to find out that the young gentleman was in reality a young lady, the fat would be in the fire. He had also dismissed the idea of asking one of his male staff to help him care for her. Even if he could trust him to keep quiet about the affair, she was, nevertheless, a young lady, and he wanted to shield her as much as possible from her inevitable embarrassment.

That left only himself, a prospect he did not relish.

Silken reached the great oak front doors a few steps ahead of the marquis and soundly thwacked the knocker. Croft, the butler at Thurston Hall since before the marquis' birth, inched the door open and peered out into the grey winter morning.

"Open the door, damn you, Croft!" The marquis eyed his butler's bloodshot orbs and the hooked nose that grew more bulbous and red-veined as the years passed. His irritation grew as Croft, striving desperately for dignity, weaved about noticeably in the doorway.

"Your grace," Croft managed, his words slurred together despite his efforts.

"Foxed again, you blighted specimen! Get out of my sight before I lock you in my wine cellar and throw away the key!"

"Your grace," Croft tried again, unable to fathom why the marquis should arrive at such an hour at Thurston Hall, and who the devil that boy was lolling in his master's arms.

The marquis gave an unintelligible growl and turned back to Silken. "Shake up the servants, Silken. I need hot water, clean strips of linen—very clean, mind you—basilicum powder and laudanum." He whirled about to his glassy-eyed butler. "You, Croft, go dip your head in a bucket of cold water! You're next to useless as you are now!"

"Don't forget that laudanum," the marquis shouted after Silken, who had already scurried down the long entrance hall toward the kitchen. He could count on Cook to have hoarded a supply of laudanum, particularly when there had not been enough to ease his pain when his shoulder had lain raw and open.

He unceremoniously kicked open the door to the huge master bedchamber at the top of the winding staircase. He was so intent upon his burden that he nearly tripped over a lion-claw leg of a large gold brocade sofa, a remnant of his father's delight in the Egyptian influence that had swept the country some years earlier.

He cursed fluently, more from habit than from his bruised shin, but did not break his stride toward the four-postered, canopied bed.

He balanced her on the crook of one arm and swept back the heavy goosedown spread. Gently, he eased her down upon her back and lifted off the greatcoat. To his relief, the napkins were not soaked through with blood.

He had just finished baring her side when Silken, accompanied by two stout footmen, entered the room carrying a bucket of hot water and rolls of white linen.

He moved quickly to shield her body from the footmen's inquisitive eyes.

"That will be all," he said tersely, and waved his hand in dismissal. If his servants thought it odd that he would not seek their help with the young gentleman, well, so be it.

He was thankful that she was still unconscious, for it required more than gentle scrubbing to cleanse away the dried blood from about the wound. Carefully, he pressed his fingers against her side, probing the area. His hand shook. But one more inch inward and he would have run through a vital organ.

He sprinkled basilicum powder liberally over her side and bandaged her as best he could. He straightened and gazed down at her. If I am to have the care of you, Miss Rolland, he observed to her still figure, 'tis time you were out of your clothes and into a nightshirt.

He fetched a long white linen nightshirt, exquisitely hemmed by his great-aunt Agnes, and with gentle efficiency stripped off her bloodied shirt. He tugged carefully at the laces on the chemise and snipped the straps with a pair of scissors. Once released from the tight garment, her breasts swelled into soft roundness. He found himself wanting to smooth away the sharp lines that the tight laces had cut into

170

her breasts. He frowned at himself for his momentary lapse and whipped his hand away from her. You're being damned ridiculous, he chided himself, the doctor is not to feel such things for his patient. Besides, she's a virgin and hates the ground you walk on!

He moved quickly to pull off her hessians, stockings, and finally her breeches. Wise of her not to wear tight knitted pantaloons, he thought fleetingly, holding the loose buckskins in his hands. Though her legs were long and slender and her hips rather boyish, anything but the loosest of breeches would surely have given her away. He found himself comparing her slender beauty to Melissande's ripe charms, and made haste to slip the nightshirt over her head and pull it gently under her hips. He smoothed the cover over her, bringing it just short of her chin.

After building up the fire, he pulled a large leather chair close to the bedside, sat himself down and prepared to wait. He looked up at the ormolu clock on the night table and saw with a start that it was but eleven o'clock in the morning. It was hard to believe that in three hours he had nearly lost his life, discovered that his opponent was a woman and had decided to take sole charge of her care. He made a steeple with his fingers and tapped the tips thoughtfully together. What the devil was she going to do when she woke up and found the man she hated taking care of her?

Hetty lay some minutes in half consciousness before her eyelids slowly opened. In those few precious moments before her mind communicated to her that all was not well with her body, she gazed about her, her thoughts clear and alert. She saw herself, foil in hand, jumping suddenly forward, catching his blade at its base. She felt the shattering impact as his foil whirled from his hand to the ground and she stood unsteadily in front of him, the deadly tip of her blade against his chest. She gave a small cry, remembering how she would not be his executioner.

"Welcome back to the world of your fellow *man*," came a deep, oddly familiar voice from just beside her. She turned her head ever so slightly to search out the source and her gaze fell upon the Marquis of Oberlon. He was standing over her, his dark eyes resting intently upon her face.

"You!" she whispered. Though she did not understand why she should be with him, she felt suddenly awash with anger. "God, I must be dead and in hell . . . since you are here." Without warning, further rational thought slipped away from her and plunged her into breathless pain.

"I will not always allow you the last insult, Miss Rolland."
She heard the words, yet her mind refused to let her fathom
their meaning. Her eyes were clouding and in but an instant
the man next to her blurred into a vague shadowy form.

"No!" she cried, striving to maintain a hold. She flung out
her hand to ward off the pain that was consuming her. She
felt strong fingers close over her hand.

The searing pain in her side mounted, and she writhed,
first arching her back, then twisting sideways, to lessen the
white-hot jabbing in her side.

Someone was lifting her, tilting her head back. There was a
man's voice speaking quiet, meaningless sounds to her. Her
mouth was being forced open, and she felt herself choking on
bitter-tasting liquid. She struggled against the intruder who
was holding her so firmly, mindlessly flailing her hands
against his chest and arms. The arms went suddenly about
her shoulders, pressing her firmly onto her back and holding
her there so that her body could not move against the pain.
She tried to draw her knees up to somehow ease the ferocious
burning that was ripping through her side. But there was a
weight on her legs and there was naught she could do but
dwell within herself, within the pain.

Suddenly, the agony grew less intense, like a leashed monster pulling its fangs out of her flesh. She felt the wet of her
own tears upon her face and realized that the hopeless rasping sobs were coming from her own throat. Gradually, the
man's face above her took on shape, his words now distinct.
She heard her own name sounding over and over in her ears.

"I am not Lord Harry Monteith, you know," she whispered, something deep within her demanding that this point
be undeniably clarified. Was it a chuckle she heard?

"I know that you are not, Hetty," the deep voice reassured
gently. "I know the pain is unbearable. The laudanum will
ease it. Soon you will sleep."

As the laudanum began to dull the pain in her side, she
felt a dull pounding against the side of her head. She tried to
focus on this new pain, but the effects of the laudanum
pulled her into sleep.

The marquis gently replaced the covers over her and
straightened. He dipped a strip of linen into the basin of cool
water atop the commode and lightly bathed her face. The
deep purple bruise above her temple was now ugly and swollen.

She whimpered softly. He froze above her. He had hoped
that the large dose of laudanum he had forced down her

172

throat would hold her in a healing sleep. She quieted again and he drew a breath of relief and lightly stepped away from her bedside.

He found himself staring back at her, his eyes searching her pale face. It was such a young face, and vulnerable, with all the lines and expressions of Lord Monteith's hatred and anger smoothed away. Vulnerable bedamned, he swore suddenly. He saw again the naked gleam of purpose in her eyes when she had lunged at him again and again, until, through his own blundering, the tip of her foil pricked at his chest. He had in that moment felt her hatred, then her indecision. He felt the hair prickle on the back of his neck, uncertain now if he would have been able to wrench the foil from her hands.

He turned away from the bed and strode to the long windows that overlooked the west lawn. The morning was grey and eerily silent. Even the peacocks that habitually strutted through the rose arbors, squawking loudly as they displayed their colorful plumage, were nowhere to be seen. As he stared out, her face rose in his mind, drained of color and laden with fear. They were to duel with foils, not with pistols as she had so obviously anticipated. Yet her hatred of him had been so powerful that she had overcome her fear. He found himself caught again in the mystery of her hatred. He racked his memory for a plausible answer, but found none. Jack had acted toward him as he had always done, with open, bluff friendship.

He looked back at the bed. What kind of a woman was she anyway? Woman, he scoffed to himself, girl, more like it. Had not Jack said she had just turned eighteen? He had fought a duel with an eighteen-year-old girl. The thought was ludicrous! He had rarely in his twenty-eight years known a female who could even bring herself to discuss pistols and foils, much less known one who displayed such proficiency in this masculine domain. He admitted to a grudging respect for her courage, yet, at the same time, he looked forward to the moment when he could face her as man to woman and scathingly put her in her rightful place.

He strode to his writing desk, unwilling to continue this train of thought. He had to write Alicia and ensure that he need not have any worry from that quarter. Although he was fairly certain that his dashing, very feminine sister was carrying her child-swollen belly in the privacy of Sir Henry's Devonshire estate, he intended to make doubly sure that she remained there. Unwittingly, he found himself thinking of

173

Miss Henrietta Rolland in feminine ruffles and laces, her belly stretched with child. You're a stupid ass, he grunted to himself. He would have liked to bury away this discomfiting thought, a lunatic thought considering the circumstances, but he saw her as the spirited excited girl in scarlet domino and mask whirling about in his arms at the Ranleaghs' masquerade ball. Had that young lady been the real Henrietta Rolland? Or, like that ghastly, vulgar girl dressed in the pea green gown and ugly spectacles at Lady Melberry's soiree, had she simply been playacting another role? He was forced to admit yet again to respect for her talents, even though he knew with chilling certainty that her sole motivation for all her different roles had been her hatred for him. At least now he knew that he had a young lady on his hands, one perhaps with many talents, and one, certainly, who hated him enough to seek his death. And he was, after all, a man with many years' experience and maturity. Damn, but he was going to give her the raking down of her life! After that, he was not quite certain exactly what he was going to do with her.

He quickly set himself to the task of writing to Alicia and then to Rabbell to cancel all of his appointments in London for the remainder of the week. Having finished, he rose and rang the bell cord for luncheon and went to his dressing room to change his clothes.

After consuming a large plate of ham slices and crunchy warm bread, he returned to his vigil by her bedside. He allowed his mind to wander back to the various encounters he had engaged in with her. Whenever he caught himself either frowning or smiling at one particular memory, he gazed over at her quiet figure. He was surprised to realize that the afternoon had melted away, and a frown settled upon his brow. She was sleeping overlong and he grew concerned. Perhaps he should fetch a doctor and damn the consequences.

The downstairs clock chimed six deep, resounding strokes. He saw her eyelashes flutter open. There was no awareness in her eyes this time, and as she stared unseeing at him, a low, aching moan came from deep in her throat. In a jerking motion, she brought her hand up to press against the swollen bruise on her temple, then with another gasp of pain, she dropped her hand and hugged her side.

He laid a damp strip of linen on her forehead, for he could not risk more laudanum so soon. He hoped, without much optimism, that it would relieve the pain in her head. He lowered himself gently down beside her. He pulled her arms away from her side, fearful that her frantic clutching would cause the wound to start bleeding again. She fought against him with surprising strength, but he tightened his grip until she lay still, moaning helplessly.

"Hetty," he said softly. "You must lay quietly. Can you understand me?"

She gave no sign of understanding. His arms began to ache with holding her down. At last, he was no longer able to stand her pain and measured a lesser dose of laudanum into a glass of water and forced it through her lips. She choked on the fluid and doubled forward in a paroxysm of coughing. He pulled her against his chest and held her close until the racking shudders subsided. He began to rock her gently, until finally, he felt the tension in her slender body gradually ease.

The laudanum was beginning to blunt the jagged edges of Hetty's pain. She was seized by a sudden sense of urgency. *"Millie! Millie, where are you? What is the time? Oh, please hurry. Father will wonder, I mustn't let him suspect. Millie!"*

Millie did not come, but there was someone else near to her. A low, soothing voice. *"Signore Bertioli . . . the vendetta. I have failed. You must help me, Signore, please you must teach me. I was a fool, Signore. I went into battle with naught but a prayer and a foil."*

A light, a soft shimmering light was shining in her eyes. A dark face was staring at her, dark eyes, deep and fathomless. *"Oh my God, Damien! Please forgive me, I could not do it, Damien, I could not kill him!"*

Dry hot fire consumed her body. She was burning, waves of scalding heat swelling her tongue. There was suffocating material swathing her, tightening about her throat, yet she had not the strength to pull it away. She ripped at the material about her neck. Fingers were closing over hers, pulling them away from her throat. There was a sudden lightness of her body, then the touch of warm air caressing her skin. Her fingers clawed at the mounting waves of drenching heat. The dark eyes were again close to her face. *"Hot, I am so very hot. Please, stop the heat."*

A cool wet cloth glided over her face, like a light summer's rain upon a sun-baked earth. Cooling drops of liquid rolled down her face onto her neck, soothing and burning, cutting a trail of prickly cold in their wake. The damp coolness floated over her shoulders and breasts, down to her belly, quenching and unbearable heat that burned her legs. She was being slowly lifted, the strange cooling liquid cleansing away the ghastly burning from her back. The flames of heat in her

175

body surged with new intensity as the damp soaked in and disappeared into her burning skin. Again and again, the soothing liquid settled onto her skin, lapped up by the heat. The burning was dying, as embers doused over and over until they steamed away the last of their existence, hissing and spurting small streams of orange flame until at last they lay cold and lifeless.

Was that a woman's voice sounding softly near to her? *"Louisa, Louisa, is that you? You have come to curse me. There were so many lies, Louisa. I cannot bear that Jack must now risk his life because I have failed. Please do not hate me, Louisa. It was all lies . . . I lived naught but lies."*

"Miss Hetty. Oh God, Miss Hetty!"

"Thank God you have come, Millie. Yes, 'tis you, I know 'tis you. Quickly, Millie, you must help me to rise. Father's schedule, you know. I cannot seem to rise. Help me, Millie. Help me!"

There was a strange, wrenching sob, then a deep voice sounding next to her face. The cold rim of a glass touched her dry lips and she opened her mouth, greedily gulping down bitter liquid. Her body felt suddenly light, or was it her mind, floating above her, scornful of the weakness that held her a prisoner. The shuddering sobs were from the helpless weak body, not from her.

"Why is it suddenly so very cold? Millie, if you please, light the fire, 'tis frigid in my room. Millie, where are you? Pottson, please help me. My greatcoat, Pottson, how can I go about in the winter without my greatcoat?"

A chattering, clicking noise sounded in her ears. She could not hold her jaw still. She was weighted down, mounds of greatcoats piled over her, yet she was naked to bitter winter winds. She tried to draw her body up, but the heavy greatcoats held her prisoner. They grew frigid with cold, weighing her down so that she was motionless beneath them.

Suddenly, there was movement next to her and dizzying warmth touched every part of her frigid body. She breathed in the warmth, pressing her face against the yielding, warm flesh. She clutched at the warmth, burrowing her body so tightly that she felt one with it, fearful at any second that it would fade away from her and she would once again feel the bitter coldness. She felt gentle hands slowly caressing up and down her back, enfolding her, and she nestled close as would a small babe in its mother's arms.

She thought she felt warm breath upon her hair, and softly blurred sounds touching her hearing. Her teeth stopped their uncontrolled chattering, her legs quieted their trembling. Deep shadows closed over her mind and gently, she fell into a silent, warm sleep.

Vaguely, she became aware that her face and body were being gently touched with a damp cloth. She tried to turn away from it, unwilling to relinquish the peacefulness of sleep. There was a feather-light probing at her side, and she cried out at the intruder's touch. Then it was gone. With a soft sigh, she drifted back into a deep sleep.

Hetty awoke suddenly and blinked away the last scattered remnants of the laudanum. She felt only a moment of confusion at the unfamiliar room, for memory stirred, and even before her eyes fell upon the marquis seated in a large chair near to the bed, a newspaper in his hands, her mind flashed over the duel and his presence with her before she had fallen unconscious. As though he felt her eyes upon him, he looked up and she saw a smile of relief light his face.

He spoke as he rose to come to her. "Now you really are joined again to your fellow humans. How do you feel, Hetty?"

Feel? How should she feel? Should she be feeling less pain in her side or should she feel relief or anger that she had not killed him? She felt lightheaded and uncertain at the moment how she should respond to him. She said only, "I am with you. Where am I?"

"You are at my home just south of London—Thurston Hall. After I discovered Lord Harry Monteith was not what he purported to be, I thought it wise to bring you here."

But she was no longer listening to him. She cast an anxious glance at the lengthening shadows of the afternoon sun. "I must go now. Father will worry, he will find out!" She tried to rise. A stab of throbbing pain shot through her side and she fell back against the pillow with a gasp. She felt his hands upon her shoulders, holding her down.

"Quiet, Hetty," he said sternly. "You are causing yourself needless pain. If you will but listen to me, you will realize that the world is not quite as you left it."

What did he mean, the world was not quite as she had left it? "How long have I been here?" she thought to ask, still panting from the pain in her side.

" 'Tis three days since our . . . duel." She was staring at him incredulously and he gentled his voice. "Do you remember nothing?"

Three days! Father, dear God, Father . . . whatever could he be thinking? She closed her eyes tightly and forced her thoughts to untangle themselves. She felt his hands leave her shoulders, but still did not open her eyes. Carefully, slowly, as if she were afraid of further betrayal by her body, she let her fingers gently trail down to her side. She felt the bulky strips of linen binding about her waist, and remembered with sickening clarity the dizzying pain and the huge pool of blood like splayed red fingers pressing her shirt against her body. She opened her eyes slowly and glanced curiously at her hand. She realized that she was not attired in her own nightgown, for the material did not fasten at her wrist, but rather flopped over the ends of her fingertips.

She turned her head slightly, carefully avoiding any sudden movement, and regarded the marquis' face above her. She remembered for a brief instant the raging fever, then the damp cool cloth that had, over and over, traversed the length of her body, soothing away the burning. She trembled at the memory of the bitter frigid cold that had invaded her body, freezing her from within. The soothing, yielding warmth . . . it had been him. He had held her against him, pressed her against the length of his body.

"Is this your nightshirt?" she asked foolishly. She refused to let herself be consumed with embarrassment, and thus uttered the first words that popped into her mind.

He answered her matter of factly, for he sensed her embarrassment. "You should thank my great Aunt Agnes, for it is her tenacious needlework that has kept you clothed. Yes, it is my nightshirt."

Lord Harry would not have asked, yet Henrietta Rolland could not help herself. "Where is the doctor? And Millie? I know that I heard her voice. Has . . . has she taken care of me?"

"Hold a moment, Hetty. You wonder about many things. I shall answer all of your questions, but first, it has been three days since you've eaten. Are you hungry?"

She realized suddenly that she could quite easily devour anything that called itself food, and nodded weakly.

"Good. I've had all sorts of invalidish dishes prepared daily in hopes that you would come about."

As she only regarded him warily, he turned and tugged on the bell cord. He had scarce time to turn back to his patient before there sounded a soft knock on the bedchamber door. As had become his habit during the past three days, he walked swiftly to the door, to shield her from the view of his servants. She looked so much like a young girl that he could not imagine anyone else seeing her any differently.

178

Croft stood owl-eyed and quite sober, alert to receive his master's orders. The marquis grinned, realizing the dignified image was a result of the stern raking-down he had given his habitually tipsy butler. No doubt Croft would be back to the wine cellar the moment the marquis left Thurston Hall. He rapped out his orders and shut the door.

He turned and walked back to Hetty. He thought she looked rather flushed, and in that instant dreaded the onset of another fever. As he reached out his hand automatically to touch her forehead, she jerked away, her face now scarlet.

"Good God!" he said, drawing back. He had forgotten for the moment that although he knew her slender body almost as thoroughly as was possible, she, on the other hand, was unaccustomed to his intimacy. As he did not have time to soothe her maidenly sensibilities, he said sternly, "I merely want to see if you've developed another fever. Don't be missish, for I have no intention of assaulting a helpless virgin!"

"I am not helpless," she choked. She tried to inch away toward the center of the large bed, but another sharp pain in her side held her rigid. She closed her eyes tightly and silently allowed his hand to rest upon her forehead.

Her skin was cool to the touch. In a wayward attempt to bring her attention back, he said lightly, "Well, at least you do not deny being a virgin! At last we are in agreement about something."

"You would not speak to me so if I were Lord Harry," she uttered in a strangled voice, feeling more and more at a disadvantage with this talk of virgins and such. How very different her reaction had been when such comments were bandied about by Lord Harry and his friends!

"Given Lord Harry's reputation as a rakehell, no, you are quite right, such topics as virginity are not at all to the point. Come now, Hetty—"

"Miss Rolland," she snapped, knowing of a certainty that she was to the point this time.

He looked faintly amused. "Het—Miss Rolland, I believe that I know you well enough to dispense with such formality."

"You have taken care of me, have you not? There is no doctor."

"Yes, of course I took care of you," he replied shortly. He regarded her flushed countenance with some asperity. "Remember, my girl, I engaged in a duel with Lord Harry. Lord Harry you must remain if we are to pull through this mess without a scandal that would rock London. I've really done quite well by you, you know."

He suddenly wished that he had kept his mouth shut. Her eyes darkened and narrowed, and her hand balled into a fist. He realized belatedly that she'd had so much to adjust to that her hatred of him had been momentarily forgotten. He wondered with amused irony whether feeding her was wise. The moment she gained back some strength, she would be at his throat.

"Ah, your luncheon has arrived," he said bracingly. He walked away from her before she could speak to answer the rap on the door.

Hetty eyed the steaming bowl of soup and fresh warm bread longingly. She tried to struggle to a sitting position, only to fall back, biting her lower lip, as the wound in her side took exception to her intention.

"Dammit, Hetty, how many times must I tell you to keep still!" He frowned at her, saw how very near to tears of pain she was, and felt the boorish oaf. "You must allow me to assist you."

She found that her body was too weak for any resistance, and felt so dizzy with hunger that she could think of no useful retort. She lay wretchedly limp as he gently slipped one arm behind her shoulders and the other under her legs. He carefully eased her to more of a sitting position and fluffed the pillows behind her head.

"There, my lady, you are now ready to dine."

He pulled out the wooden legs of the bed tray and set it across her lap.

"I do hope it isn't corn soup," Hetty said, eyeing the steaming liquid vaguely.

"Corn soup! Why the devil not?"

"Father's a Tory, you know."

He decided it wasn't worthwhile to further analyze this bit of information, and sat himself on the bed beside her. He picked up the spoon and stirred the hot soup.

To have him feeding her was simply too much. "I will feed myself," she gritted.

"As you will," he replied aimiably, and handed her the spoon.

Hetty found to her chagrin that her fingers refused to do anything more than curl weakly about the handle. She slid her thumb closer to the bowl of the spoon and dipped it into the soup. Her hand was trembling visibly, and before the spoon reached her open mouth, her thumb lost its leverage and she grimaced as the hot liquid splashed onto her nightshirt.

"Damn, but you're stubborn," he said and pulled her fingers unresisting from the spoon. "Now, lie back, open your mouth, and stop trying to prove how invincible you are."

Hetty bristled, but hunger overcame the power of his provocation, and she opened her mouth.

The bowl was empty and the fresh bread rested comfortably in her stomach and still she felt her mouth watering greedily.

He stood and removed the tray. As if he read her longing, he said gently, "No, my dear, any more and you will make yourself sick. You may have some more solid food this evening with me."

She turned her face away from him and he saw her fingers bunching at the cover.

"Are you in pain?"

She shook her head, then suddenly turned to face him and whispered, "I wish to have Millie, if you please, your grace."

He said cynically, "Really, Hetty, it is I who have looked after you for the past three days. You have no need of Millie. Come, what is it you want?"

He watched in confusion as color crept over her pale cheeks. "I—I—oh, do let me be alone with my maid!"

Understanding dawned suddenly upon him, and although he felt a tremor of amusement tugging at the corners of his mouth, he said only, "Very well. But attend me, Hetty. Millie will have only fifteen minutes with you. I cannot allow any gossip to start among the servants."

Hetty was perfectly prepared to agree to any stipulations he might impose, and so nodded her head vigorously.

He strode to the door, turned and said over his shoulder, "I shall return when the fifteen minutes are up. Then, Hetty, we must talk."

It seemed an age before Millie's large, spare figure appeared in the doorway, and Hetty wondered sourly if the marquis had been giving her all sorts of orders.

"Oh, Miss Hetty! My poor little lamb!"

"For God's sake, Millie, I am not a poor lamb—though, I suppose I have been shamefully fleeced!"

But a poor lamb she was destined to be at least for the next fifteen minutes, for Millie cosseted her and clucked over her like a mother hen finally returned to her lost chick.

Hetty's more basic needs having been attended to, she nervously eyed the clock and exclaimed, "Drat, Millie, we have but a few minutes before that dreadful man returns."

"His grace is hardly a dreadful man, Miss Hetty," Millie said with unwanted candor. " 'Tis a tangled state of affairs he's saved you from, and," she added, clinching the matter in her own mind, "he's taken care of you better than any doctor! Not, of course, that I approve of an unmarried man being so intimately familiar with a young girl."

Hetty colored to the roots of her hair. "Millie," she said desperately, seeing the look of speculation on her maid's face, "will you not brush my hair? I fear it is dreadfully tangled."

"Aye, that it is, Miss Hetty." She grinned hugely. "I daresay that is the only care his grace did not render you."

Hetty decided to let this exasperating observation pass. As Millie brushed out her hair, she gathered together all the questions she felt were the most urgent. She had not intended it, but the first inquiry that popped into her mind and out of her mouth was the innocuous, "What have you been doing the past three days, Millie?"

"Naught of anything, Miss Hetty," Millie replied calmly, rolling an errant curl about her finger. "His grace said I needed a holiday after all the wild doings you put me through. Of course, Sir Archibald believes that I am attending you here during your visit with the marquis' sister."

Hetty pulled away and said angrily, "Please don't tell me how the *dear* marquis has arranged simply everything! How can you forget that he is a vile, cruel—"

"Arrogant is next on your list of compliments, is it not, Miss Rolland?"

Hetty whipped her head up to see the marquis standing in the doorway. "Yes," she cried, "then devil!" She quickly regretted her display of anger, for she felt a sharp stab of pain in her side. She wanted to cry, but at the same time had no intention whatsoever of doing so. She bit at her lower lip and glared at him with undisguised anger.

The marquis was not at all discomfited and said calmly to Millie, "The fifteen minutes are gone. You can see your mistress again—perhaps later this evening when it is likely that she will prefer your services again to mine."

"Yes, your grace."

Hetty watched as Millie curtsied to such an obsequious depth that she would have liked to kick her.

"And now, Hetty," the marquis said after Millie had closed herself out of the bedchamber, "we have, I believe, much to talk about. I find Miss Rolland as viciously insulting as the

182

indomitable Lord Harry. Would you now care to inform me exactly why I am a vile, cruel and arrogant—"

"Devil!" she shot out.

"Ah yes, devil," he repeated softly and seated himself negligently into the large chair beside the bed.

Hetty suddenly felt ridiculously tongue-tied. How very differently she had planned her confrontation with him! It should have been him lying wounded and at *her* mercy. Somehow the words she had carefully prepared and rehearsed over the past five months did not at all fit her plan gone awry.

At her continued silence, the marquis said pensively, "You know, Hetty, while you were in a high fever, you were delirious. You ranted of many things. You thought, for instance, that I was your brother, Damien, and screamed at me that you could not do it . . . that you could not kill me."

"So you admit your guilt!" she gasped.

"Guilt? What guilt? I admit nothing, but merely relate to you what you said." He tapped his fingers together. "You seem to think that I was or am involved in some way with Damien. Come, Hetty, you've never been at a loss for words in any guise I've known you!"

"You killed Damien!" she cried, the words hurtling from her mouth.

He dropped his fingers from their thoughtful pose and sat forward, staring at her incredulously. "What arrant nonsense is this! If my memory does not fault me, your brother was killed at Waterloo."

"Yes, he was killed at Waterloo. At the last moment before the battle, he was assigned to lead a cavalry charge that meant certain death! You are his murderer for having placed him there!"

She fell back, gasping as a sudden jab of pain ripped through her side. As the waves of pain did not subside, she hugged her arms about her waist and gritted her teeth. To her shame, she felt tears swimming in her eyes and tightly closed her eyelids, furious at herself for her weakness.

When she felt his hand upon her forehead, she had not the strength to draw away.

"Here, drink this, Hetty, 'twill make you feel better."

She wanted desperately to knock away his hand and yell "no" at him, but when she opened her mouth, she felt the cool rim of a glass touching her lips. When she tried to turn her face away, he clasped her head in the crook of his arm and held her firm until she drained all the bitter-tasting liquid.

It was several minutes before the laudanum began to take effect and dull the pain. She concentrated all her energies on not moaning aloud. She was only vaguely aware that he was clasping her limp fingers in his hand. At a particularly sharp wave of pain, she realized that she was clutching his hand, in some way seeking comfort from him. She heard him say something to her about sleep, and when the laudanum dulled her mind and her body, she willingly obliged.

When she again awoke, it was night. She turned her head carefully and saw that the marquis was standing against the mantelpiece, staring down into the crackling embers, a thoughtful expression on his face.

She queried her body, received no painful reply, at least for the moment, and slowly began to pull herself back up in a sitting position.

Her clumsy movement caught his eye, and a tentative smile touched his lips as he strode quickly to her.

She held herself in stiff silence as he put his arms about her and eased her up. He straightened over her. "If you promise not to rip up at me, I shall feed you."

Her voice was decidedly waspish. "I daresay that you, your grace, have already enjoyed a huge evening meal."

"True." He added in a plaintive tone, "I do believe that you should show me more consideration, Hetty. I changed your nightshirt, you know. The soup you spilled was quite sticky."

She choked on her embarrassment and regarded him with loathing. She wished she could slap that confounded wolfish grin from his face.

It was near to midnight before Hetty had finished another ration of soup, and Millie had left after her fifteen minutes' allotment.

The marquis firmly closed the door and walked to the bedside. He eyed her intently. "The fact of the matter is, Hetty," he began as if in midthought, "that you did not kill me when I most stupidly gave you the upper hand. You either doubted my imagined guilt over your brother's death or you had not the stomach for murder."

He waved his hand to keep her silent. "No, attend me a moment longer. I gather that you must have some sort of proof, some sort of evidence that made you believe me guilty and arrange for your elaborate charade as Lord Harry. Now, without any female hysterics, I want you to tell me clearly and concisely exactly what the devil makes you believe I killed your brother."

"Female hysterics!" she cried, then drew up short, realizing that the words bursting to come forth were indeed laced with heavy emotion. "Very well," she said flatly, holding herself in firm rein, "we shall see how well you can lie, Lord Cavander! I trust you do still remember your wife—Elizabeth Springville."

His eyes darkened and his jaw tightened perceptibly at the mention of his wife's name. "What has all this to do with Elizabeth?" he demanded coldly.

"How can I be concise and clear if you must needs interrupt me?"

It was his turn to keep a tight control on his temper, and he said only, "Continue."

"You've a short memory, your grace, so I will refresh it. Not such a long time ago, you, Sir William Filey and my brother, Damien, were all enamored with a beautiful young lady named Elizabeth Springville. Evidently your respective assaults to win her favor led you to lay a wager at White's—a large wager, I understand—to see which of you would succeed in winning her."

Hetty paused a moment and regarded him. Grim lines were etching about his mouth.

"Although I am shocked that Damien could engage in such despicable behavior, and indeed cannot excuse him for that, what followed bears witness to your true nature. You are correct in one thing, your grace, I do have proof of your treachery. Pottson was Damien's batman. It was he who found a letter from Elizabeth to my brother. The letter damns you, your grace! You will have to tell me the details of your villainous plot, but I will tell you what I know. Elizabeth chose Damien. Then you, your grace, getting wind of your defeat, used your influence with the ministry—through Lord Melberry no doubt—to have Damien quickly removed from England to be sent on a series of dangerous missions that, you hoped, would lead to his death. It is my belief, your grace, that Elizabeth gave herself to Damien as a proof of her love. When she discovered she was pregnant with Damien's child, she had no choice but to wed her lover's murderer.

"Perhaps the reason she died in childbed, your grace, was that she loathed you so greatly, particularly after hearing of Damien's death, that she had no further wish to live. There is much on your conscience, if you have one, for even Damien's child did not survive!"

The marquis stared at her long and hard. When he finally spoke, his voice was level, though Hetty sensed an undercurrent of cold anger lacing his words. "You are telling me that you engaged in your suicidal charade all on the basis of a letter written from Elizabeth to your brother?"

"Yes, 'twas enough!"

"You are a fool, Hetty, a damned, irresponsible, stupid little fool! Now you will attend to me, my girl! When you are recovered I shall want to see this infamous letter of yours. In the meanwhile, allow me to disabuse you of your romantic, ridiculously idealized reading of the entire sordid affair! Despite what you believe of me, I am a man of some scruples. Were I not, I would not have kept quiet about the true facts, and none of this need ever have happened."

A deep shadow crossed his brow, but his voice remained cold and hard. "On several points, you are correct. The three of us, Filey, your brother and I, were foolishly enamored with Elizabeth Springville. Obviously, you have heard that she was an exquisite girl, renowned and fêted from the instant of her coming out. Foolishly too, one evening when all of us were deep in our cups, Filey suggested the wager—to add spice to the chase, he said. Although the next day both Damien and I regretted our action, it could not be undone. Elizabeth was graced, I can tell you! Like a woman with all the wiles of Cleopatra, she gave each of us encouragement in turn, yet never declared her preference. Although you may not choose to believe me, after several weeks of this sport, my supposed affection for the young lady began to wane. I began to believe her vain, cold and quite calculating in her actions."

He seemed to struggle with himself for a moment, as if loath to put into words distasteful memory. "No," he said more to himself, "I must tell you the full of it."

He gazed at Hetty and drew an audible breath. "I shall never forget coming to White's one afternoon to be told that Damien had left suddenly for the continent. I thought somewhat ruefully at the time that he, like I, had grown tired of Elizabeth's capriciousness. Filey seemed vastly amused by what he termed *Captain Rolland's defection* and taunted me to declare him the winner of the bet. Although, as I said, I was no longer much interested in the lady, I did not believe that he had succeeded in winning her favor. That, along with his taunting, made me tell him to go to the devil. Not long thereafter, I began to revise my opinion, for Elizabeth appeared to be in his company more than in any other's.

"You can imagine my shock several weeks later when Elizabeth, hooded and masked, arrived at my townhouse near to midnight one evening. I will not sully your ears with the particulars of that memorable night, save that Elizabeth did not leave until near to dawn the following morning. Nor will I attempt to justify my actions that night. I have repeatedly cursed myself for my galling stupidity. Suffice it to say that Elizabeth, before her most innocent and artful seduction of an experienced Corinthian, ensured that I had consumed a half a bottle of brandy.

"Three weeks later, I was tearfully informed by a hysterical Elizabeth that she was pregnant. Fool that I was, I accepted her word unblinkingly, and unhesitatingly offered her marriage. We were married by special license three days later, then removed immediately to one of my northern estates near to Harrowsgate."

Hetty could contain herself no longer. "You rant at me about romanticizing the entire affair, your grace! Yet you have been weaving the most outrageous of Banberry tales! Damn you, you must have been the one to send Damien from England. There is no one else!"

She expected explosive anger from him. Before she could goad him further, he said softly, his lips twisted ironically, "I will tell you, Hetty, I would have offered your brother half my estates had he but returned to take Elizabeth off my hands."

"God, that's a bloody lie! She was pregnant with Damien's child! They loved each other, he would gladly have wed her!"

"You have looked too long into only one side of the mirror. Elizabeth was not pregnant with your brother's child. 'Twas Filey's seed that grew in her womb."

She gasped aloud at his outlandish accusation.

"I have no reason to lie to you, Hetty," he said wearily.

"No!" Hetty cried. "Elizabeth could not have—the letter, I read her letter to Damien! She loved him, I tell you! Filey, indeed!"

"It is entirely possible that if your brother had remained in England, it would have been he who would have led the pregnant Elizabeth to the altar. But no, Hetty, she did not love him. Elizabeth loved no one but herself. No, please do not interrupt me. I have no desire to speak of this private human tragedy, much less remember it, but I see that you will never believe me otherwise."

He was silent a moment, remembering the ugly scenes, the

187

growing hatred. For an instant, he was sorely tempted to tell Hetty to believe what she liked and to go to the devil. Yet, there was so much pain and confusion in her fine eyes, and only he held the key to the maze of distorted truths.

"Elizabeth's father, Colonel Nathan Springville, was a stern taskmaster, a ruthless martinet whose word was undisputed law in his family. I tell you this to help you understand why she acted as she did. She hated her father and wished only for escape, but her escape had to be through lawful marriage, else he would have consigned her to perdition. I cannot prove it, else I would have killed Filey with my bare hands, but it is my belief that he seduced her, then instead of offering her marriage, offered her a *carte blanche*. Damien was gone. She had no one to turn to save myself. Perhaps you are right; perhaps she and Damien were lovers and she would have preferred marriage to him rather than to me. Perhaps she felt some affection for your brother and her letter was a plea for his forgiveness. I can only speculate, as can you."

"Yes, your grace, I can also speculate," Hetty burst in. "You paint the picture of a vain, unscrupulous woman, a woman who cared for no one save herself. But there is the letter, your grace, a letter that damns you. And there is Pottson. He told me of Damien's unhappiness, not, of course, that Damien ever confided the cause to his batman; but Damien was affected, your grace, and deeply saddened."

The fire was dying in the grate and the night shadows deepened between them. The marquis turned away, not answering her, and with mechanical movements lighted several candles and placed them near to the bed. He turned then, still silent, and added new logs to the fire. He kicked up the embers with the heel of his boot and watched the flames dance into life, then fall back upon themselves.

He walked back toward Hetty, and she saw naked pain in his eyes. But an instant later, he had drawn a mask over his feelings and faced her with an impassive countenance. She felt a small seed of doubt begin to grow within her. When he spoke again, his voice was curiously flat and emotionless, as if he were reciting an impersonal story.

"As I said, after I married Elizabeth, we removed to Harrowsgate. By the time we reached Blanchley Manor, we were scarce speaking to each other, nor did I ever again touch her. After but a month of marriage, her belly was round with child. I pressed her to tell me the truth of the matter, but she only laughed at me and hurled half-veiled taunts until I could bear the sight of her no longer. I had no desire to return to

London and instead visited some cousins in Scotland until I knew that her time was near.

"Upon my return to Blanchley Manor, her hatred of me was as heavy as her huge belly. The night the child was born, she had consumed a great deal of wine at dinner. I remember to this day thinking that her angel's face had become cold and hard, as if mirroring her true character. How she laughed at me that evening, for she knew that I would not divorce her, that I would accept her child as my own." He could still picture her taunting him: "Ah, so you do not care for your fine, beautiful wife!" He remembered how she had bared her swollen breasts and mocked, "See all the milk I have! What a fine bouncing child I shall present to you, your grace!" He drew a breath and got a grip on himself.

He continued with an effort, as though the words were wrenched out of him. "There is more ugliness, of course, but suffice it to say that my fury grew to such heights that finally I grasped her shoulders and shook her. She tore away, all the while laughing at me. In her drunken state, she tripped and fell heavily over a chair. The fall brought on her labour, and it was I who delivered my wife of another man's child. It was a little girl and she lived but a few minutes. Her mother lay in a half-drunken stupor, uncaring."

He paused a moment, then added in a voice devoid of emotion, "Elizabeth did not die in childbed, as I have allowed everyone to believe." He pictured again in his mind for perhaps the hundredth time what must have happened from his frightened groom's account. Elizabeth had ordered his curricle without his knowledge, his half-wild bay stallion harnessed between the shafts. She had whipped the animal about his head until in a spate of fury the stallion had kicked out the flooring of the curricle and sent Elizabeth hurtling down a steep incline. He said to Hetty, "She died in a curricle accident about two weeks after the birth of her child. That is all, Hetty, there is no more that I can tell you. It is, of course, up to you if you wish to believe me."

He turned and walked away from her. As he had spoken, she had felt almost as if she had been there, standing near to him and Elizabeth as they wreaked their anger on each other. She had seen the bitter pain lighting his eyes, had sensed his unwillingness even now to unbury his painful ghosts. But the letter, she always came back to the letter. The letter and Damien's unhappiness, as described by Pottson.

She lay staring into the dark shadows about the room, trying to make some sense of her thoughts. Deep within her she knew that he had spoken the truth. She also realized that she wanted to believe him.

She thought of her life as Lord Harry, of the decision to make herself into a gentleman. Lord Harry had given her life meaning and focus. The sharp pain in her side was preferable to the wrenching doubts that now coursed through her. Had Lord Harry's existence been for naught? She felt hollow as she forced herself to ask, "You said that Elizabeth would never tell you who fathered the child. Yet you believe that it was Filey."

He turned to face her and saw that she was no longer hurling him a challenge, but rather a plea to understand. "Yes, that is true. I told you that if I had been certain, I would have killed him. The babe carried his general features, very fair with a thatch of reddish hair. There was no resemblance whatsoever in the babe's features to Damien. There is nothing more I can tell you, Hetty."

"No, there is nothing more. I believe you have told me everything," she said quietly. She felt a surge of relief well up within her; she was awash with it until suddenly the terrible import of her false assumptions laid her bare. She struggled up on her elbows and whispered despairingly, "God, I have been like Don Quixote, fencing with windmills, searching for vengeance, when I had naught to do but ask for the truth! You were my *vendetta*. May God forgive me, what if I had killed you!"

She stared at him wildly.

"Hetty, no, you must not—" He shook his head to stem her destructive flow of words.

"I gloried in my own vain pretensions and closed my eyes and mind, searching only to affirm your guilt." Her voice broke. "I shall never forgive myself for my blindness."

She turned her face away from him, muffling her broken sobs into the pillow.

He strode to her and gathered her in his arms, rocking her gently against his chest. She offered him no resistance, but he sensed her struggling with herself against the tears. He stroked the soft curls atop her head and waited quietly for her to regain control. He found himself smiling as her sobs dissolved into hiccups. He shifted her in his arms so that he could see her face.

"Come, Hetty," he chided softly as she tried to burrow her face into the open neck of his white shirt, "Lord Harry would stare me straight in the eye and call me some sort of offensive name." As she did not raise her face at his sally, he tried another track. "Lord Harry is also a most honourable young gentleman, albeit somewhat misguided. His courage and strength of principle are admirable, and since you, my dear Hetty, are Lord Harry, I would that you would desist from this display of guilty tears. Surely Lord Harry would very quickly find another bone to pick with me."

Hetty raised her face, unable to ignore this provocation. She was aware of his eyes, dark and tender upon her face. She sniffed loudly, then blurted in a clear, accusing voice, "You have seen me naked!"

He instantly repressed several inappropriate, highly spicy retorts and an accompanying grin that would have been totally inexcusable. He mustered indifference into his voice, hoping not only to soothe her but also to depress the odd, twisting desire he felt in his loins. "One does not shirk one's duty, Hetty. Surely you would have cared for me had there been no other choice."

She was rather struck by this unusual perspective on the matter, and flushed at the thought of ministering in like manner to him. Her thoughts were so clearly written on her face that he was obliged to laugh in spite of himself. "Next time we duel, I shall contrive to be the one who is wounded."

She shuddered involuntarily. "You know it is odd. I much enjoyed my fencing lessons with Signore Bertioli. Yet—"

He tightened his hold on her shoulders and finished her unspoken thought. "And yet, there is no sport, no dashing romance in slicing up a man, or a woman, as the case may be."

"You would not like to kill Sir William Filey?"

There was a sudden, dangerous gleam in his dark eyes. "Yes, I have wanted to for a very long time, but my hands are tied. After Elizabeth's death, I returned briefly to London and confronted him. Sir William is many things, but he is not stupid. He knows me to be his better with foils and pistols. Thus, he denied any involvement with Elizabeth and sullenly swallowed my insults."

She moved slightly against his chest to relieve the sudden sharp pulling in her side. He became very much aware of her womanness at that moment, of her soft breasts brushing against him.

" 'Tis time for you to rest, Hetty," he said hurriedly, and removed himself as quickly as possible from contact with her body.

191

"Yes, I suppose you are right," she said, and snuggled down under the covers.

"Jason."

He whirled about at the sound of his name upon her lips.

"I—I am truly sorry for all the . . . inconvenience I have caused you."

"It is over now, Hetty, over and done with. Shall we haul out our Shakespeare and say that all's well that ends well?"

"You are most kind," she said softly and closed her eyes.

The marquis blinked several times at this unusual compliment. He had been called many things in his twenty-eight years, but never *kind* in that particular way. He blew out the candles and prepared himself for bed.

15

"Who are you writing to?" Hetty asked, struggling up on her elbows and blinking the sleep from her eyes.

His pen poised in midair, the marquis paused at his task and smiled across the room at Hetty's tousled figure. "Good morning, Hetty. 'Tis nearly noon. You've become a sluga-bed!"

She stretched lazily, relishing the absence of pain in her side, and returned his smile. The previous evening seemed eons ago.

"If you will know, Miss Inquisitive, I am writing a charming letter to Sir Archibald."

"What?" she gasped.

"My dear, Lady Alicia Warton is an excellent hostess, though she sincerely apologizes for not informing Sir Archi-bald sooner of the delightful visit she is having with his daughter. She is, at the moment, endeavoring to create and recount the various activities you have enjoyed since your ar-rival at Thurston Hall."

"You are the most complete hand, your grace!"

"I much prefer that you call me Jason."

Hetty shifted uncomfortably and dropped her eyes to the velvet green cover. "Lady Alicia is your only sister?"

Adroitly done, he thought. "Yes, and fortunately for us, she is pregnant and thus unlikely to venture this time of year into London. Now, let me order your breakfast and finish this letter. Pottson must leave shortly to deliver it."

She looked at him wonderingly. "Is there nothing you've forgotten?"

"No, at least I do not think so. I have also just finished writing my daily note to the Earl of March on Lord Harry's progress."

Hetty lay back quietly and thoughtfully chewed on her lower lip as the marquis finished the letter to her father. "When is Henrietta Rolland going home?"

"In about three days, I expect. Lady Alicia has begged your father, very prettily, I might add, to allow you to extend your visit to a full week."

"Oh," she said and lapsed again into thoughtful silence.

The marquis, having finished his sister's letter, sealed the envelope and rose.

"Do you believe that Sir William Filey could have had the influence to have Damien sent out of the country?" Hetty asked, speaking aloud her thought.

He rubbed his hand over his jaw. "I do not know, Hetty. We still have a mystery on our hands. Does Lord Harry feel that he still has more work to do?"

Hetty suddenly thought of Lord Harry challenging Sir William to a duel and shuddered. She splayed her hands in front of her.

He misinterpreted her gesture. "Thank God you are ready to send that imperious young gentleman back to the wilds of Scotland! 'Twas a foolish and dangerous game you played, Hetty. Now, at least, you may again don your skirts and leave me to do the hunting."

She eyed him with dangerous calm. "Ah, let me understand. You mean that it is time for the *real* gentleman to search out the truth! The lady will return to her proper place, simpering and serving tea!"

The marquis was annoyed, for he considered his offer most fitting and chivalrous. "Naturally you will return where you belong. I said nothing of simpering and serving tea. 'Tis altogether ridiculous, my girl, to think of your donning breeches again."

"Go to the devil!"

"What did you say?"

"I said to go to the devil," she repeated, stressing each word. She saw a muscle twitch in his jaw, and throwing back her head defiantly, said in a hard voice, "If I wish to remain Lord Harry and don my breeches, 'tis none of your affair, your grace! You have absolutely no authority over me, and I shall do exactly as I please!"

Hetty watched, fascinated, as the marquis drummed his long fingers along the top of the large chair near her bed. She did not raise her eyes to his, as she was certain they spoke volumes. When he finally spoke his thoughts, Hetty heard a distinctly unpleasant tone enter his voice.

"Don't push me, Hetty. Do you really think, you foolish chit, that I would ever again receive Lord Harry in polite society? You are ranting stupid nonsense and I will not have it!"

"You will not have it!" she cried, her eyes flashing daggers. "You conceited, arrogant——"

"Must you always catalogue all my defects of character?" he snapped. He shoved the chair from his path and strode to the bedside. He sat down and clasped her shoulders in an iron grip, ignoring the bright anger in her blue eyes. "Now you will listen to me, Henrietta. I have quite a lot to say about your future actions! Don't forget so conveniently that it was you who chose to embroil me in your insane scheme that could have made us both social outcasts! I'm still doing my damnedest to save us from your ruse. You will do exactly as I tell you, else I shall have to employ other means to ensure your cooperation."

The marquis, who had scarcely ever had to issue such a resounding command, much less had his orders gainsaid, rocked back in astonishment when Hetty stared him straight in the eye and scoffed, "I pray you to save your paltry threats for your servants! I begin to find you quite a bore, your grace. You will do precisely as I wish you to, else I shall announce to the world that the Marquis of Oberlon, that most famous Corinthian, fought a duel with a girl. I shudder to think what would happen to your esteemed consequence!"

He glared at her speechless, his fingers fairly itching to wrap themselves about her slender throat. Suddenly he drew up short. All that he admired about her—her courage and her tenacious will—would not be bowed by any threats from him. He realized that the last thing he wanted to do was to wring her neck, or to see her docilely submit to his wishes. It struck him that what he wanted now was a far cry from further angry insults or orders. His hands loosed their iron grip and it was with an effort that he kept his fingers from caressing her. He could very nearly taste the softness of her lips when he saw that she was staring at him, her eyes widened in confusion.

"Damnation!" He hurled away from her and strode from the room without looking back.

16

Hetty gritted her teeth and held herself in stiff silence. The marquis forced himself to calm matter-of-factness, carefully snipping away the dressing from her side. The wound had closed nicely and the flesh surrounding it was a healthy pink. She had grown thinner, he thought, as he gently bathed her side with warm soapy water. With great deference to her modesty, he had slipped the nightshirt only midway up her chest and the sheet down to the middle of her belly. She trembled as the soft washcloth touched her skin.

His hand paused momentarily in the hollow of her belly. He spoke his thought aloud. "Your father will think that Lady Alicia starved you. You must force yourself to eat more, Hetty. We've but a day to fatten you up."

He felt a tightening of her muscles beneath his hand, and gingerly moved to another spot. In but a few more minutes, he had dried her with a fluffy towel and was reaching for the basilicum powder.

"You have healed quite nicely," he said briefly, liberally sprinkling her side. He looked up, expecting to see her face flushed with embarrassment. He was taken off his guard to see her staring at him, wide-eyed, with a kind of stunned expression on her face. He warily averted his gaze, thinking that whatever was going through her head could not bode well for him. He straightened quickly and began to unwind strips of linen to wrap about her waist. After gently laying a soft pad of linen over her side, he said, without again looking at her face, "You must not lie so stiffly, for I have to slip the linen under your back."

Rather to his surprise, she released the stiff hold she had on her body, and she was soft and yielding to his hands as he slipped the linen beneath her waist. It was damned unnerving, and he felt beads of perspiration break out on his forehead. He felt a clumsy oaf, thinking that his bumbling movements must be hurting her. But she made no sound, nor did she again stiffen under his hands, even when he pulled the cover lower down her belly. He knew his hands were shaking, and strove to get a grip on himself. She was in his house, indeed in his bed, and every shred of his honour demanded that he not in any way take advantage of her.

"There," he said inconsequentially, " 'tis done." He gently pulled the nightshirt back down and rose from her bedside, still avoiding her face. "You will be a bit sore for another week, but Millie will be able to see to you quite sufficiently after you're home. Now, if you can force yourself, I should like you to eat something more substantial than chicken soup."

"Thank you, your grace," she said in a strangely calm, flat voice.

Her show of sudden formality baffled him. He merely nodded and left the bedchamber.

Hetty lay very still, her eyes fixed upon the closed bed-chamber door. He will be much relieved to have me off his hands, she thought. I have done naught but fight and argue with him, goad him almost beyond endurance. She felt a large tear squeeze out of the corner of her eye. With sudden loathing for herself, she raised her fingers and dashed it away. I am naught but myself, she told herself angrily. I shall never be a helpless, fragile female, regardless of what he would admire. And it does not matter anyway, for he already knows me for what I am.

She thought of the touch of his hands on her body and trembled as a slight, delicious wave of pleasure coursed through her. She turned her face against the pillow and let the soft cover soak up the salty tears. No, I will not cry like a female watering pot, she told herself angrily. She jerked away the pillow and heaved it to the foot of the bed.

She stared grimly into the darkness and forced her thinking resolutely to the still unsolved mystery. Someone had forced Damien to leave England; and that same person, still maddeningly unknown, had sent him to his death at Waterloo. Lord Harry still had much to do.

The following morning, dressed as Lord Harry and leaning heavily upon Lord Cavander's arm, Hetty bade a silent fare-well to Thurston Hall, a mansion she was quite certain she could come to admire, if the opportunity were offered to her.

As she expected, Sir Archibald's carriage was standing in front of the gothic-pillared entrance, with both Millie and Pottson standing by the open door. She pulled her greatcoat more closely about her shoulders to ward off the onslaught of winter wind. Of course, she had to leave Thurston Hall as Lord Harry—for the servants' sake—the marquis had said evenly. She did not relish the prospect of changing back into women's clothes, even with Millie's assistance, in a moving carriage.

He did not even allow me the three days, she thought, a trifle miffed. She gazed covertly at Lord Cavander's set profile, wondering if perhaps he would have admired her more if she had had the sensibility to have at least one relapse.

She realized the marquis was speaking to her and turned up her pale face to meet his.

"I cannot, of course, accompany you, Hetty. Millie and Pottson have my instructions. You will be well taken care of. I shall call upon you in a couple of days to see how you are faring."

"Yes, I understand, your grace," she said flatly. She was very much aware at that moment of the hard line of his jaw and felt an absurd desire to touch his face.

As he assisted her into the carriage, his hand resting a moment on her back, she stole a final look at his face. He had already turned away to give Pottson further instructions. She stiffened, angry that he was giving *her* servants orders.

"Take care, Lord Monteith," the marquis said, and closed the door to the carriage. He turned and walked back up the steps.

"Silken," he shouted, "have the carriage ready in half an hour. We are going back to London."

Tired and somewhat depressed, Hetty arrived dressed modestly in a woman's gown at the stroke of noon. Thinking that her father would demand all sorts of details of her visit to Thurston Hall, she had carefully invented several parties and outings. She was rather unnerved when her sire, after greating her with a negligent kiss on the cheek, asked only, "Was the marquis in residence during your visit?"

"He put in an occasional appearance, Father," she replied and quickly lowered her head. She did not see the speculative look that lit Sir Archibald's face.

After luncheon, Hetty excused herself and trailed wearily up to her bedchamber. She flopped down upon her bed and stared up at the ceiling. She thought of Lord Cavander's autocratic command that she was never again to appear as Lord Harry. She hunched a stubborn shoulder, for Lord Harry, it seemed to her, had a far better chance of discovering if Sir William Filey had indeed been responsible for Damien's death. And she could not turn her back upon poor Isabella's

198

plight. The thought of Sir William even being near Isabella made her grow pale with anger. My motives are of the highest order, she told herself stoutly, and if the marquis wants to despise me, well, there is naught for it. Damn, why could gentlemen, the marquis in particular, not realize that they were not the sole guardians of honour and pride?

"You intend to do *what?*" Millie cried, the next afternoon, as Hetty evenly informed her of her intention to invite Sir Harry and Mr. Scuddimore to dinner at Lord Harry's lodgings.

"You heard me, Millie. If you do not choose to accompany me to Thompson Street, I shall just have to go alone."

"But the marquis—"

"To the devil with the marquis! I am your mistress, and he has no say whatsoever in whatever I choose to do!"

Short of tying her mistress to a chair, Millie found that she had no alternative but to escort her to Lord Harry's lodgings. When she tried to remonstrate with her young mistress, she received only cold, uncommunicative stares.

Pottson served only to strengthen Hetty's resolve. "The marquis, Miss Hetty," he wailed, "he gave me strict orders to pack away Lord Harry's belongings. He said that *he* was going to find out who was responsible for sending Master Damien away."

"He did, did he!" Hetty's voice rose. The nerve of him! And without so much as a "by your leave" from her! She gritted her teeth and said coldly, "Now, listen, Pottson, Millie, Lord Harry is still very much in existence, and it is I who will decide just when he will disappear from London. If you do not obey me, I swear that I will go directly to White's and yell the truth of this entire matter to the world!"

Millie glanced at Pottson and saw him give a defeated shrug. She guessed that, at the first opportunity, he would take himself to Lord Cavander's townhouse and fill his ears with Miss Hetty's obstinacy.

Although Hetty suspected that Pottson, after delivering her invitation to Sir Harry and Mr. Scuddimore, had paid a visit to the marquis, she did not challenge him, but rather stared at him coldly, making him feel the perfect traitor, she hoped.

As she vigorously pomaded down her blonde curls and drew them severely back at the nape of her neck, she found herself wondering just how Sir Harry and Scuddy were going to react upon seeing her. They would have many questions, of that she was certain. I shall just have to take them as they come, she decided, as she pulled on her breeches. She directed a grunt of disgust at the thin image in the mirror. If her breeches had been loose fitting before, now they positively hung. She heard a loud knocking on the outer door, and with a final defiant glance at her image, turned and strode from the room, hopeful that during her illness she had not lost her masculine swagger.

"Good God!" Sir Harry exclaimed, clasping her hand. "You've become a damned scarecrow! You still feeling pulled, old fellow?"

"Ho, Harry, it is only that I thought of you and became too ill to eat!" How strange it was that she had slipped back so easily into Lord Harry's role.

"Well, Scuddy here ain't the worse for wear. Ate like a man mountain, he did, in sympathy for you, at least that's what he kept telling me."

"Welcome, Scuddy," Hetty said warmly, turning. " 'Tis good to see you again."

"Well, we're surprised to see you, Lord Harry," Mr. Scuddimore said.

"Surprised? Did you believe I would curl up my toes and pass to the hereafter?"

"Certainly not," Mr. Scuddimore said, shocked.

Sir Harry continued in his stead. "What Scuddy means to say is that the Marquis of Oberlon informed Julien—my brother-in-law, the Earl of March, you know—that when you recovered from your wound you would be returning to Scotland. We're dashed glad, though, that you returned to say goodbye before going back to that barbaric place."

Hetty sternly repressed her anger at Lord Cavander's autocratic handling of her affairs. She said coolly, "I am not quite ready yet to say my farewells. It appears the marquis was a bit premature in his assumptions." She turned before either Sir Harry or Mr. Scuddimore could offer any comment and led the way to the table.

They were midway through the first course of a raised pheasant pie when Sir Harry asked her the inevitable question. "I say, Lord Harry, will you tell us now just why the devil you forced the marquis to fight a duel?"

Hetty paused a moment and lifted her wineglass to her lips before responding with a trace of hauteur in her voice, "I certainly have no intention of telling you the cause of our disagreement, 'twould not be honourable to do so. Suffice it to say that the marquis and I have amicably resolved our differences."

"Well, I'm glad you decided against killing his grace. It would have been a messy business," Sir Harry said frankly.

"You mistake, Harry, 'twas the other way around. It was the marquis who did me in and then like the true gentleman that he is, cared for me personally."

"Don't be a nodcock, Lord Harry," Sir Harry said with some disgust. "I was there, remember?"

"You deloped, Lord Harry," Mr. Scuddimore said simply.

"Deloped? Come, Scuddy, one delopes with a pistol. Our duel was with foils."

"Same thing, at least in principle," Sir Harry chimed in. "Damned brave thing to do. Like I've told Scuddy here countless times, you had the tip of your foil at Lord Cavander's throat—could have sliced him up right then!—but chose to do the honourable thing."

"You can't disagree, Lord Harry," Mr. Scuddimore said, "it is the marquis who professed your bravery and honour."

"The marquis?" Hetty asked, at sea.

"Button your trap, Scuddy—after all, they were *my* letters. Well, at least," he amended, "they were my brother-in-law's letters and 'twas I who read them. You see, Lord Harry, while you were on the mend at Thurston Hall, the marquis kept Julien informed of your progress and also how he had developed the greatest respect for you."

Hetty suddenly wished that she could be alone. She wasn't quite certain whether to curse the marquis for his interference or to thank him for forging an exquisite reputation for the departing Lord Harry. In any case, she had no desire to discuss further with Sir Harry or Mr. Scuddimore the duel or the marquis.

She turned to Sir Harry. "Now, enough of my affairs. Tell us, Harry, may Scuddy and I yet toast your impending wedding with the lovely Isabella?"

A deep scowl settled on Sir Harry's smooth brow.

"Proper mad, he is," Mr. Scuddimore offered by way of explanation.

"What has happened in my absence, Harry?"

A rather woebegone expression settled on Sir Harry's handsome face, and he muttered, "Damned if I know what the chit's about. Seems she ain't so adverse to Sir William Filey's suit anymore."

"Explain yourself."

" 'Tis just as I said," Sir Harry said petulantly. "That lecherous rakehell is making himself very agreeable to Isabella. Showers her with flowers and silly notes praising her eyebrows, even takes her riding in the park. He had the damned gall to approach me at White's, smirking all the while, to lay a wager on which of us would win the chit."

Hetty felt herself go cold. Did Sir William want to repeat with Isabella what he had done to Elizabeth? "Surely Isabella does not welcome his attentions. It must be her mother forcing her to be complaisant."

Harry did not reply, and stared down into his glass of sherry.

"Dammit, Harry, answer me! Have you proposed to Isabella, told her of your feelings? Has she turned you down?"

Sir Harry, roused, retorted in a blustery voice, "If you must know, she hasn't given me the chance! And I've told her time and again not to be taken in by that old roué's buttering ways."

It occurred to Hetty that Sir Harry was making a great mull of his courtship. "So what you're telling me is that when you're with Isabella, you spend all your time raking her down! How stupid of you, Harry. I would not have thought it of you!"

There was a sudden gleam of enlightenment in Mr. Scuddimore's eyes. "By jove, Lord Harry's in the right! A girl can't like to be preached to all the time. Bet when you leave, Sir William comes by and tells her that she's the light of his life. Deuced stupid, Harry, deuced stupid!"

Hetty saw angry lights leap into Sir Harry's blue eyes, and forced herself not to heap on more coals to an already smoldering fire. "Harry, heed me. There is much that I know about Sir William . . . things that you or Scuddy would scarce believe true. Suffice it to say that Sir William need not necessarily have marriage to Isabella in mind. He is most admiring of young virgins, Harry."

"Just what the devil do you mean by that, Lord Harry?" Sir Harry demanded, sudden doubt assailing him.

"Just what I said. The man is vile and he will do anything to achieve his ends. He is a man of much experience and Isabella knows nothing about the sordid world he habitates. She is innocent and pure. If you do not take action, she will be ruined. Even if it is marriage Sir William must offer, he will very quickly turn her life into a living hell."

"What if she won't have me?"

Hetty regarded him steadily for a long moment. "If you

care for her, Harry, then you must haul her off to Gretna Green. It would be an act of true chivalry."

Sir Harry nervously gulped down a full glass of sherry, then thwacked the glass so hard upon the table that its slender stem nearly cracked in half.

"I must think. Bedamned, I must think!" He rose unsteadily from the table, jerking at his cravat as if it were suddenly choking him.

"Lord Harry's got a point there," Mr. Scuddimore offered hopefully.

Sir Harry suddenly crashed his fist upon the table, having reached the most portentous decision of his life. "I'll do it! Lord Harry, if Isabella refuses me, will you help me? I cannot imagine that kidnapping a young lady can be so easily accomplished!"

Hetty realized that if she did not instantly offer her assistance, she would be the total hypocrite. Her lack of action would belie all her accusations about Sir William. She said calmly, "First, Harry, you must press your suit to Isabella. Be all that is romantic, mind you. If she refuses . . . well, of course I shall help you."

"I have more horses," Mr. Scuddimore offered quickly. "Horses are always helpful, you know."

Before Sir Harry could turn with impatient anger on his hapless friend, Hetty interposed hastily, "Indeed they are, Scuddy. Most generous of you."

She turned back to Sir Harry. "Send me a note here as to the outcome of your proposal to Isabella. If she refuses you, Harry," she continued bracingly, "I shall come by to see you at your lodgings and we shall make plans."

When at last she had seen them out, she leaned heavily against the closed door. She admitted to herself that she was weary; the wound in her side was aching dully. Her thoughts willingly settled upon the marquis, and she found herself wondering crookedly if it was possible for a gentleman to love a lady who was also a gentleman.

She gazed down a moment at her breeched, booted person. Lord Harry Monteith had granted her the greatest freedom, had allowed her adventures that no lady would ever experience. Yet, she thought, she felt now that Lord Harry was trapping her, holding her prisoner in a role that she no longer desired. The marquis had planned a gracious and honourable exodus for Lord Harry, yet she knew she had no choice but to thwart him, at the very least until Sir Harry and Isabella had come to a felicitous understanding, or, for that matter, had not.

She walked wearily into Lord Harry's bedchamber, wondering just precisely how one went about eloping to Gretna Green.

17

"Good morning, Grimpston. His grace is in the drawing room?"

"Yes, Miss Hetty. I offered him tea but he said he preferred to wait for you."

"If you please, fetch tea now, Grimpston." The moment the butler removed himself from the entrance hall to do her bidding, she rushed to the small gilt-edged mirror and peered uncertainly at her image. Her blonde curls were sparkling clean and brushed neatly into place. She supposed she looked well enough; the blue muslin gown, though a trifle short, did not at least resemble buckskin breeches. That in itself was an improvement over the last time he had seen her.

She opened the door to the drawing room quietly and was thus afforded a view of the marquis before he was aware of her presence. Bedamned but he was handsome, she sighed, the flavor of Lord Harry's speech in her thoughts. She did not realize it, but the marquis had dressed himself with rather more care than usual this morning, the powder blue coat of broadcloth having just yesterday arrived from Weston's, and his hessians polished to such a bright shine that he could see his reflection. He stood by the tall bow windows, his back to her, gazing out onto the square.

"Good morning, your grace," she said, finding that her voice did not hold quite the calm assurance she had hoped.

He turned quickly and for a long moment said nothing, but merely stared at her.

Unable to read his gaze, she wondered if perhaps her sandals were scuffed or the blue bow had come unfastened and was dangling in her face.

"Good God," he said slowly, whistling under his breath. "Louisa was really quite right."

"Right about what?" she asked uncomfortably, wondering what the devil her sister-in-law had said about her.

His dark eyes twinkled in amusement at her curiosity. "You must ask Louisa, Hetty. I do wonder, though, where your spectacles are. And do not let us forget that hideous pea green gown and cap. A most *lasting* effect."

He advanced upon her and lazily lifted her hand and kissed her fingers. "How are you feeling?"

"A little sore, that is all," she replied, appreciatively eyeing his exquisitely tied cravat.

"It is my own design. Lord Harry may disabuse himself of the notion of copying it!"

Slightly ruffled that he had guessed her thought, and at the same time aware that he still held her fingers in his strong grasp, she said defensively, "Lord Harry does quite nicely, I thank your grace. 'Tis the 'Mathematical' he aspires to." It did not occur to her to remove her fingers from his hand.

She found her hand her own in the next moment when Grimpston, bearing tea and morning cakes, loudly cleared his throat upon entering the drawing room.

"Oh, thank you, Grimpston," Hetty said in a rather high voice. "Please set the tray upon the table. I shall serve his grace."

"Yes, Miss Hetty," Grimpston replied in his gentle voice, carefully regarding the marquis from the corner of his eye as he deposited the tray in its appointed place. He liked what he saw, and with the unquestioned freedom allowed to an old retainer, caught Hetty's eyes and nodded his approval.

Hetty flushed and began to study the faded pattern in the aubusson carpet until Grimpston left the drawing room.

"It would appear that your butler finds me unexceptionable," the marquis said blandly. "Would you not like to ask me to be seated, Hetty?"

I am behaving like an idiot schoolgirl in the throes of her first infatuation, she chided herself, and managed to say much in her old way, "Of course you may be seated! But I have no intention of holding a chair for you, your grace. Do you care for sugar in your tea?"

"No, only cream. I will pour it this time, but I trust that you will not forget in the future the way I like it."

Her eyes flew to his face, but he looked so very impassive that she believed she must have misintentioned his words.

After sipping his tea, the marquis asked quietly, "How did you find Harry and Mr. Scuddimore last night?"

"They were much pleased to see me," she replied without thinking. "Oh, how very odious you are! *Not,* of course, that I would not have *told* you that Lord Harry was entertaining last night."

"I quite understand, but a little prodding never hurts. Pottson was understandably concerned and practically begged

206

me to 'break you to the bit,' I believe was his colorful allusion."

"Drat him!" Hetty scowled. "I *knew* that he would take it upon himself to interfere! As to *your* breaking me to the bit ... well, I shall give him a sound raking down for that!"

"I would that you would not," the marquis said with a wry grin. "After all, it is what I asked of him—to keep an eye on you—and you must know that he would obey me since he will most likely be in my employ for many years to come."

She was on the point of remonstrating with him about his high-handed ordering about of her servant's future, when she chanced to see an amused gleam in his eyes, and, suddenly rather uncomfortable, turned the subject.

"I find it odd, your grace, that you were so very adamant in sending Lord Harry back to Scotland on the one hand and praising him to London society on the other. I find your actions difficult to fathom."

"Do you really, Hetty?" he asked gently.

She had meant to take him to task for his peremptory assumption that Lord Harry would not show his face again, but she found the tone of his voice most disturbing. She lowered her eyes to her teacup.

"I am not at all like Melissande!" she blurted out suddenly.

"True," he replied calmly. "Melissande is really quite voluptuous. I might also add that she rapidly becomes a dead bore! But, of course, you, I am persuaded, are already much aware of that fact."

She sighed inwardly, well aware that she, unlike Melissande, was most unvoluptuous. The sharp point of an unseen knife turned in her breast at the thought of his making love to that exquisite piece of womanhood. She realized that he expected an answer from her and forced a light voice. "She is rather silly, I expect, but so very beautiful."

"I would like to know what the devil you said to her to make her pine so for Lord Harry."

"Men are sometimes stupid, I think," she said, her tongue outracing her mind. "That is," she hastily amended, "women like Melissande need to be nourished on the most outlandish flattery. It makes them quite malleable, you know."

"I see," he said carefully. "Just how did you proceed?"

"I likened her first of all to Aphrodite, being fairly certain that she would have heard of that lovely goddess. When images of Aphrodite began to pale, I cast her first as the romantic Helen, the most beautiful woman in the world, then threw in a dash of Daphne with handsome Apollo in hot pursuit. I must admit though," she added with great honesty, "that I did buy her a riding habit. That, I think, was the clincher!"

He threw back his head and laughed heartily. "You should have kept the habit for Miss Henrietta Rolland, 'twould have suited her fair coloring most admirably."

"Oh no," Hetty protested, not seeing the twinkle in his eyes, "the habit would have been far too large for me and too short. Melissande lacks inches, you know."

"She lacks inches only in height, my dear Hetty, not, I assure you, anywhere else!" He was heartened at the dull red flush that spread over her cheeks. Since Hetty was not so easily embarrassed, he thought perhaps her blush was the result of a more private sentiment. "I was only teasing you, Hetty. Now, let us down to business. 'Tis impossible that you haven't been scheming these past two days."

Oh well, Hetty thought, this is at least safe ground. She hesitated only a moment before recounting to him Sir Harry Brandon's difficulties. He listened to her without interruption, his dark eyes never leaving her face. "So, you see," she finished after some minutes, "depending upon Isabella's answer to Harry, Lord Harry may very well find himself in the thick of another outlandish situation. Do you believe, your grace, that Sir William would dare to offer Isabella a *carte blanche?*"

"Jason," he corrected her absently, his thoughts elsewhere.

"Jason, if you will," she said, then fell into silence, watching him.

"You have done rightly, Hetty," he said finally, "in telling me, that is," he added at the look of surprise on her face. "Would Lord Harry be much insulted if I took some direct action at this point? I think Gretna Green a most extreme measure."

"What would you do?" She was rather piqued, for she felt her solution, albeit somewhat improper, at least expedient.

"Don't be stupid, Hetty," he said, not mincing matters. "First of all, I have no intention of allowing you to race off to Scotland with those ridiculous children. I told you that Sir William holds me in healthy fear. In no less respect would he hold the Earl of March, when and if Julien decided to embroil himself in the matter. Will you allow me to see to the affair . . . in my own way, without Lord Harry's colorful interference?"

Hetty shot him a roguish look. "I think that Lord Harry would much enjoy putting Sir William's nose out of joint. To have to forego such excitement is asking a lot of him, your gr— Jason."

"Hetty!" His voice held a distinctive menacing quality and his eyes darkened.

She said blandly, "I suppose that 'tis only fair that you be given *your* chance. Lord Harry, shall, of course, closely attend to your progress and decide in due course if he will be needed."

"Your confidence in my abilities is most gratifying! I shall return later this afternoon. You will have your note from Harry by then?"

"Yes, as I said, he means to try his luck this morning. If Isabella turns him down, I will begin to think she has butterflies in her head." She was suddenly flustered, for had Elizabeth not succumbed to Sir William's blandishments? And she, after all, had been the marquis' wife. "I—I am sorry, Jason, I should not have said—"

He waved his hand in dismissal of her apology. " 'Tis an episode best forgotten. Now, to other matters. I would see your brother's letter now, if you would fetch it to me."

Hetty nodded and whisked herself out of the drawing room. She was back in a trice, clutching the folded square of paper tightly in her hand.

"Humm," was all that he said after his third reading of Elizabeth's missive.

"Well, what is your opinion?" Hetty demanded, finding his noncommittal grunt hardly sufficient.

He said slowly, "It would seem to me that regardless of Elizabeth's true feelings in the matter, Damien was sufficiently involved with her to make his keeping of her letter understandable. The manner in which she tied my name to her predicament is rather ambiguous, yet, Hetty, I now understand how you drew such a conclusion."

"But it was inexcusable!" she burst out. "I shall never forgive myself for serving you such a false turn!"

"Calm yourself, my dear. Our contretemps is in the past, and you can hardly accuse me of holding you any grudge."

She felt strangled with his nobility. "I would much rather that you shouted and ranted about, 'twould make me feel less low."

"I should infinitely prefer other pastimes to shouting and ranting." He grinned at her in a decidedly sensuous, intimate manner as if, she thought, suddenly mortified, he was looking right through her clothes. Unconsciously, her hand stole over her breasts in a tentative protective gesture.

The grin vanished from his face as suddenly as it had appeared, and he rose and took a quick turn about the drawing room. She watched him apprehensively, wondering what he was now thinking. He turned back to her abruptly.

"Your other evidence is conversations Pottson related to you . . . conversations with Damien?"

"Yes, and, of course, the fact that Damien was, at the last moment, ordered to lead that cavalry charge."

He shook his head. "I simply cannot imagine that Sir William has that kind of connection in the ministry to direct Damien's orders like that."

"Then who, for God's sake, sent Damien out of the country with such speed? Who could have directed his activities with such a close hand?"

"That is precisely what I intend to find out, Hetty. Now, my dear, I shall take my leave of you. To erase all doubt in our minds respecting Sir William's involvement with Damien, I shall search out his lordship this afternoon. I wish to converse with him, in private, about his entanglement with Harry's Isabella."

"You swear that you will keep me informed?" Hetty asked, rising.

"You may depend upon it. The last thing I want is to have Lord Harry doubting my prowess and rushing in like Saint George!"

Her eyes gleamed with indignation, but before she could word a protest, he clasped her hands in his and gazed at her so intently that his meaning could not be misconstrued.

He said softly, squeezing her fingers, "Believe me, little one, I wish to conclude this business as quickly as possible. Then, Henrietta, I will speak to you of other matters."

"Oh," she said inconsequentially.

He released her hands and turned to the door.

"Jason," she called after him. "Do take care, else Lord Harry must needs come rescue you."

He cocked a black brow and was gone.

Toward the middle of the afternoon, the Marquis of Oberlon sauntered into the gaming salon of White's, his eyes on the alert for the florid person of Sir William. He had scarce time to begin his search when his attention was caught by a loud commotion and the rising of angry voices. Intrigued, he walked unobtrusively toward a far corner of the salon, where a small knot of gentlemen formed a wide circle.

He drew up short at the sound of Sir William Filey's voice.

"Go lick your wounds in private, Brandon! If you are not enough of a man to hold the lady's affections, then go back to the infantry where you belong! Don't come whining to me about it being all my fault."

Damnation and hellfire, the marquis cursed silently. He could readily have strangled Harry Brandon for interfering in his plans. He moved quickly forward, edging his way through the circle of gentlemen.

Sir Harry Brandon stood facing Sir William, his hands balled into fists and his face aflame with anger.

"You lecherous old rake," Sir Harry shouted. "Isabella is not for the likes of you! You have pulled the wool over her eyes with your cozening ways! I demand satisfaction, do you hear?"

It struck the marquis that Harry was emulating Lord Harry's violent example and endeavoring to force a duel. He stepped quickly forward and grabbed Sir Harry's arm. Before Sir William could respond to Harry's challenge, he said smoothly, "Hold, Harry. Though I would never gainsay your justification, I must confess that my grievance with Sir William predates your own. I am sorry, old boy, but surely you must bow to my prior claims."

"Prior claims! What the devil, your grace!" Sir Harry sputtered, taken aback.

Sir William sneered, but the marquis saw from the corner of his eye that he had backed away a step.

"Yes, Harry, prior claims. As a gentleman, I of course cannot disclose to you just what is entailed. Further," the marquis continued blandly, "I believe that your argument with Sir William is a trifle premature. Allow me, I beg, to hold a brief discussion with Sir William. It is my belief that he will wish wholeheartedly to offer you an apology for his impertinence in this affair."

"Apology!" Sir William shouted, his face suffused with angry color. "If this young puppy cannot keep the silly wench in line—"

"Do shut up, Filey," the marquis said quietly, bending a menacing eye. "Well, Harry, will you give way to my request?"

Sir Harry stood uncertainly, wondering what the devil he should do. Isabella's cold refusal of his proposal had left him in such a fury that he wanted nothing more than to blow Sir William's brains out. That he had not followed Lord Harry's advice and had, indeed, taken Isabella to task for her flirtatious, coming ways, rendered him all the angrier. Well, he would show her that he was more the man than was Sir William!

"Harry?"

Sir Harry pulled himself away from his thoughts to meet the marquis' questioning eyes. "Very well," he muttered finally, "but only if he will be mine when your grace is done with him!"

"You shall have him or an apology, Harry. Does that suit you?"

"Aye," Sir Harry replied. He bowed curtly to the marquis and strode away, leaving a group of very interested gentlemen in his wake.

The marquis gazed about him, his brows raised inquiringly. "If you would now excuse us, Sir William and I must needs converse together." He smiled sweetly at Sir William and said gently, "Come, Filey."

Sir William deplored this sudden turn of events, yet realized that if he were to refuse the marquis, he would be hard pressed to stave off ridicule. He nodded coldly and followed the marquis from the room.

"I believe we can be assured of privacy here," the marquis said, drawing to a halt in a darkened corner of the vast reading room.

"You've no quarrel with me," Sir William began. "I cannot help it if Brandon forces a fight."

The marquis said with dangerous calm, "My quarrel with you is of long standing, Filey."

"I had naught to do with Elizabeth and you cannot prove otherwise, your grace," Sir William countered, his thinking sharpened by fear.

"No, as you say, I cannot prove otherwise. Yet," the marquis continued pensively, "when I see you playing the same game once again, I cannot help but grow perturbed. With Elizabeth though, you enjoyed much more sport. After all, both I and Damien Rolland were involved. And that, Filey, has led me to wonder exactly how you managed to have Rolland removed from England with such exquisite timing."

"Rolland! Your grace pulls the girth in the wrong direction! How could I have known what Rolland was about?"

The marquis said evenly, "You must admit that it was a curious coincidence. Elizabeth veered from both of us, toward Damien. Then suddenly he is gone and the field is once again yours."

"And yours, also, your grace!"

"Yes, but I know that I had nothing to do with his leaving.

212

Whereas you, Filey, are an unspeakable cur and would stoop at nothing to gain your ends. Now I ask you again, what do you know of Damien Rolland?"

Sir William shrugged uncertainly. He would have liked very much to tell the arrogant marquis to go to the devil, but he knew that such a gesture would very probably cost him his life. In a sulky voice, he said, "Maybe Rolland realized that Elizabeth would make a very poor wife for an aspiring politician. Damn, I tell you, I know nothing about it!"

He saw that the marquis was staring at him, an arrested expression in his eyes. Filey could not figure out for the life of him just why the marquis should be so interested in Damien Rolland. Ancient history, that was, and Rolland, by all accounts, was killed last June at Waterloo.

"Aspiring politician, you say?" the marquis asked.

Sir William was held a moment by surprise, before he said impatiently, "Something like that. Mentioned it when he was deep in his cups one evening. I gathered he did not want it bruited about."

The marquis looked decidedly thoughtful for several moments. Then he said abruptly, "Very well, Filey, I will believe you—but only in that matter! Now you will listen to me carefully. As I said, I grow perturbed that you play a new game with Isabella Bentworth and Harry Brandon."

" 'Tis not a game, as you phrase it, your grace," Sir William growled. "I intend to marry the chit."

"So she carries a more appetizing dowry than did poor Elizabeth, does she? No, do not bother to mouth your protestations, Filey. I grow quite bored with your presence. I will tell you this only once. You will never again speak to Isabella and will proffer a very gentlemanly apology to Harry Brandon before the day is over. If you fail to comply with either of my . . . requests, I make you this promise: your dissolute son, whom I understand is following quite closely in your footsteps, will find himself the head of the family before the end of the week. Do I make myself clear?"

Hatred and fear blended into an indistinct blur in Sir William's mind. His cravat felt suddenly too tight and there was a curious knot forming in the pit of his stomach.

"Do I make myself clear, Filey?"

He raised his eyes to meet the marquis' implacable gaze. His long-nurtured sense of self-preservation rose to the forefront. He nodded slowly.

"Excellent. I fancied that we could arrive at an amicable solution." The marquis turned, then said over his shoulder,

"Incidently, I am quite certain that the Earl of March will be at White's this evening. He will, of course, be very interested in your actions." Without waiting for Sir William to reply, he strode away, leaving his defeated adversary to roundly curse a hapless footman.

The marquis arrived at Sir Archibald's townhouse within the hour, his mind greatly relieved on one score and cruelly confused on the other. He did not disbelieve Sir William in his recounting of Damien's political ambitions. Sir William, had, he was certain, thought it most unimportant, and thus blurted it out without a moment's hesitation. Indeed, the marquis wondered, as he pounded the knocker, *was* it important? Surely Sir Archibald must have known if Damien had wished to follow in his footsteps. As painful as the subject must be to Sir Archibald, it had to be broached.

"Your grace!"

"Good afternoon, Grimpston. I trust Miss Henrietta is home?"

"I shall ascertain, your grace."

"Jason!"

The marquis looked up to see a distraught Hetty speeding down the staircase toward him. "Quickly," she cried, unmindful of Grimpston's presence, "we must do something! I've just received a message from Harry! He means to take matters into his own hands!"

The marquis clasped her hands and gave them a warning squeeze. "We will discuss it in the drawing room, Hetty. Grimpston, some brandy, if you please!"

"Yes, your grace," Grimpston said, his eyes riveted on his young mistress.

"Yes, please go fetch it," Hetty seconded. She got a hold upon herself and said in a calmer voice, "Please come to the drawing room, your grace."

"Good girl," the marquis whispered in her ear.

No sooner had Hetty snapped the drawing room door closed, than she whirled about. "Jason, the most terrible thing has happened! Harry wrote me—that is, Lord Harry—a letter! Said he intended to resolve the matter just as Lord Harry had done! Jason, I know what he intends! My God, Filey might kill him! We must do something!"

"I have."

"Oh my God, 'tis all my fault," Hetty cried, ignoring his words. "If I—that is, Lord Harry—had not insisted upon such bravado, such arrogant behavior, I am persuaded that such a thing would never have occurred to Harry. That is, it might have occurred to him, but he would have sought counsel from the Earl of March. Only Lord Harry can talk him out of this! I must go, don't you see, I must!"

"No, you must not."

" 'Tis easy for you to be so calm, for he is not *your* friend! Don't you understand, Jason, only Lord Harry can put a stop to this!"

"I suspect that there are others just as persuasive as Lord Harry."

She stamped her foot in impatience. "I have no more time to indulge in useless arguments with you! I don't care what you may think of me, but Lord Harry must come forth again. I am sorry, Jason, but it is something I cannot ignore. It is my duty."

"But I am not arguing with you, Hetty. Now will you be seated and calm yourself?"

She shot him a look of acute disgust. "I am quite calm, I will have you know," she said, squaring her shoulders. "Now, your grace, if you will excuse me."

"I will not excuse you. Sit!"

"Go to the devil!"

The marquis sighed. "You have already consigned me to that rather warm climate, and, despite your repetition, I have no intention of complying. Now, before I have to tie you down, come here and listen to me!"

Hetty glared at him, her look decidedly mutinous. "Very well, but only for five minutes." She flounced down, positioning herself on the edge of her chair.

"Did you not promise to give me a chance in this affair?"

"Yes, of course, but—"

"You doubt my abilities so much, Hetty?"

"No, 'tis not that! Everything has changed! It is now not a question of fleeing to Gretna Green!"

"No, it is not a question of Gretna Green. Indeed, it is no longer a question of anything."

"No longer—! What the devil do you mean?"

The marquis grinned. "My dear, if you would but adopt the habit of listening to me, you would save yourself a lot of wasted energy. As it happens, I was present at White's when Harry was in the midst of flinging his gauntlet in Filey's face, so to speak. I, of course, put a stop to it. As a matter of fact, Filey will be apologizing to Harry this evening at White's. Further, he will never again speak to Isabella, so you can put your mind to rest. And Lord Harry Monteith."

215

"You put a stop to it?" Hetty faltered, beginning to feel the perfect fool.

"Would you not have expected me to?" the marquis asked gently.

"Yes, of a certainty, but—"

"It is most impertinent of you to doubt my word, Henrietta. Now, please sit back, I would not wish you to fall off your chair."

"It—it is *all* settled?"

"Do not sound so disappointed, my dear. Lord Harry cannot be expected to right every wrong. We other poor mortals do occasionally succeed, you know."

"Of course I am not disappointed!" She gave a half laugh. "It seems that I am always flying out at you. I do thank you, Jason."

"You are most welcome, Hetty. Now, I have something of a more serious nature to tell you."

"Yes?" she asked, her attention fully focused upon his face.

"While I was chatting with Filey, I accused him of knowing what happened to Damien. He swore that he knew nothing, and I believe him. But there was something he said, Hetty, something that meant nothing to him, so he blurted it out in an attempt to appease me. He said that Damien had talked about 'political ambitions' one evening when he was rather foxed. Filey evidently taunted him about Elizabeth making a very poor wife for a politician."

Hetty frowned, then shook her head. "Jack said something about Damien's feelings on the growing poverty in the industrial cities. He said Damien likened the people's lives to bondage and slavery, and that it could but grow worse. But Jack said nothing about Damien wishing to take an active role in political life. I'm afraid that I really don't see the importance of Filey's statement, Jason."

"Hetty, don't you see? Only someone highly connected in the ministry could have had Damien sent so quickly and permanently from England. Only someone very powerful in the government could have put him at the lead of that cavalry charge."

Hetty nodded slowly, her mind working furiously. "Yes, perhaps someone who did not agree with his politics. Perhaps even a group of men who feared he might succeed and displace them." She pulled up short, exclaiming, "But this is ridiculous! It's all speculation! I cannot credit such a motive!"

"There are some men, powerful men, whose very lives are consumed by their political beliefs. Do not forget our English

216

history, Hetty, 'tis filled with powerful men struggling to govern the country as they wished. It's a bloody history."

Hetty rose, her hands pressed against her temples. "Even so, Jason, it is 1816, and the vicious struggles for power are over. And even if it could be true today, who could have done such a thing? Who could have even known what Damien believed and feared him for it?"

"I did."

Both Hetty and the marquis whirled about, openmouthed, to see Sir Archibald standing quietly in the doorway.

"Father!" Hetty cried, running to his side. "Father, no! It cannot be true. Surely you did not understand our conversation!"

Sir Archibald gazed fondly down at his daughter and fought down the stab of pain he felt whenever he thought of his second son. "You must forgive me," he said, his eyes searching out the marquis, "for overhearing your discussion, but I was coming to greet you, my boy."

He sighed deeply and laid his hand upon Hetty's shoulder. "I did not realize, my child, that you had even discovered that there was more to Damien's leaving England than a simple reassignment. I had hoped to spare you further pain. Now I see that you and the marquis have become embroiled in the affair. You must understand, my child, there was no other choice. You see, Damien had become a traitor to his country."

Hetty stared in shocked silence at her father.

The marquis said, "Surely, sir, that cannot be so!"

Sir Archibald sighed again and shook his silver head. "Alas, it is all too true. I never told either you, Hetty, or Jack, for I did not want you to think less of your brother."

Hetty gazed at her father, a gentle man, yet a man impassioned by political fervor, a man whose life was dedicated to directing English affairs as he envisioned them.

"Please, Father," she pleaded, her hand upon his sleeve, "you said that Damien was a traitor. I cannot believe it."

"Sir, if you would prefer that I leave," the marquis quietly interposed. He was torn, for he did not want to leave Hetty alone; yet, Sir Archibald might consider this a private family affair.

Sir Archibald peered at the marquis and a gentle smile played about his mouth. "No, indeed, my boy, 'tis only fitting that you stay. I have intended you all along as the husband for Henrietta, and since soon you will be one of the family, it is your right."

Hetty appeared deaf to her father's words. Her voice cut through the momentary silence. "Father, please, you must tell me why you did such a thing. How could you ever believe Damien a traitor?"

"Very well, my child," Sir Archibald said finally. "You must be brave, for you will be as shocked as I when you learn of your brother's actions. I trust when I am done, you will understand why I had to take such drastic steps."

As Hetty and the marquis said not a word, Sir Archibald moved wearily to a large winged chair near to the fireplace and sat himself down. He stared a moment into the glowing flames before continuing in a surprisingly strong and forceful voice. "You had not yet come to London, Henrietta. For some reason that I did not at first comprehend, Damien asked for and received an extended leave from his military duties. I believed at first that he had finally decided to find himself a wife and settle down. I was disabused of that notion when your brother informed me that he intended to run as the Whig candidate from a borough in Somerset, under the patronage of that infamous, thieving Lord Grayson. I was, of course, appalled that my own son would desire to join in the political fray against me, and I reprimanded him sharply. He told me that Tories, Whigs, they were all one and the same to him, and that he sought only justice for Englishmen. His notion of securing justice, Henrietta, was to join forces with the baser element of the Whig contingent to incite the rabble in Manchester and Leeds to riot. You will not wish to credit this, my child, but he then called me a mindless old fool. Accused me, he did, of trying to hold England back from her rightful destiny, the destruction of the aristocracy that would elevate the common man to political equality with his betters! His subsequent words were even more fanatical and traitorous, and I will not sully your ears with his raving insults. I finally became convinced that my blood—my son—was one of that lot bent upon destroying the very fabric of England!

"So you see, my child, I had no honourable choice left to me but to use my influence with Lord Melberry in the ministry to have your brother removed immediately from England."

Hetty said in a peculiarly quiet voice, "You are telling me, Father, that because Damien held radical political views, you had him ordered from England? You arranged that he be engaged in dangerous missions in Spain and Portugal? You arranged that his orders be changed so at the last moment he led a suicidal cavalry charge at Waterloo?"

218

Sir Archibald gazed at his daughter with some surprise. "You make it sound as if I dismissed your brother out of some fanciful whimsy of my own fabrication. You question my actions in this affair?"

The marquis interposed quietly, "What then was your role, sir, in Damien's activities?"

Sir Archibald's voice suddenly became stern, a strange glint of inflexibility in his narrowed eyes. "Damien was a traitor to every honourable belief that I had instilled in him from his youth. He had shown himself a radical bent upon the destruction of all that any decent Englishman holds dear! You can quite imagine that Lord Melberry and indeed many of the gentlemen in the ministry were appalled when I told them of my own son's subversive activities. It was my request that Damien be forced to serve his country, to shed his blood, if need be, so that he would in some measure lift the dishonour from our house. I gave no direct order for him to lead that cavalry charge. I later learned that an overzealous general in whose charge Damien had been placed dispatched him to the battleground. You must know that I grieved at your brother's death. But he died as a hero of his country. The world will never know that without my actions, your brother would have heaped shame and dishonour upon all those who cared for him."

By God, the marquis thought, gazing at Sir Archibald, he is quite mad in his saneness. He suspected that his uncle, Lord Melberry, was as deeply involved in arranging Damien's activities as was Sir Archibald. He gazed past Sir Archibald to Hetty. Her face was pale and drawn with shock, her eyes unseeing. He shook himself into action.

"Sir," he addressed Sir Archibald, "you will understand, of course, that your words have caused Henrietta great surprise and distress. Needless to say, that since I am to become her husband, you can rely implicitly upon my discretion in this matter. If you would not mind, I think it best that you leave her with me alone for a time, so that she may recover from her shock."

"An unusual request; my boy, but no harm in it, I suppose, since you will become her husband." Satisfied, he rose with surprising grace for a man of his years, smiled down at his daughter in his gentle way, then turned and stretched out his hand to the marquis. "I accept you into my family, my boy. I told Henrietta all along that you would make her the perfect husband. Such a dear child she is—always obeys her father's wishes!" He patted Hetty's stiff shoulder and let himself out of the drawing room.

The marquis gazed worriedly at Hetty, wondering just what the devil he could say to her.

"You should not have told Father such a whisker, Jason. You will not, of course, be held to it." Her voice was dull, emotionless, and he knew that she was trying to grasp upon anything that would lessen her pain.

He strode over to her and sat down beside her, clasping her limp hands in his. "Hetty. Hetty, my love, I wish to be held to my offer."

"You would be better to leave, Jason, 'tis a home of tragedy, of needless death, all because of Sir Archibald's blind honour! I have no intention of ever holding you to any statement you may have made."

His black brows met over his eyes and his hands tightened over her fingers.

"Poor Jason," she said in a soft, singsong voice. "I've done naught but unearth old wounds and create new ones for you. How strange it is that you, whom I believed to be a vicious cruel devil, are the innocent one."

She felt strong arms enclose her, and for an instant held herself stiff and unyielding. The tears that were not far from the surface welled up and she collapsed against his chest. He held her until the hoarse sobs became rasping hiccups.

He pulled a handkerchief from his waistcoat pocket and pressed it into her hand. She clutched at him, burrowing against his shoulder. Finally she raised a tear-streaked face, her voice pitifully forlorn between the hiccups. "Whatever shall I do? I cannot remain in the same house with my father. Of a certainty, Lord Harry cannot challenge Sir Archibald to a duel."

The marquis took the handkerchief from her unresisting fingers and efficiently mopped her face. "Of course, my love, I realize that you cannot wish to remain in this house. I want you to come with me, Hetty, for we can be wed as soon as I can procure a special license."

To his consternation, Hetty flung out of his arms, her eyes bright with unshed tears. "I told you, your grace, that you will not be held to your nonsensical offer of marriage! I will have none of your pity, do you hear?" She stood before him, rigidly aloof. "I would now, your grace, that you leave and contrive to forget all that has passed here today."

The marquis rose and clasped her arms, forcing her to face him. "Don't be a goose-cap, Henrietta! You must have rust in your upper works to ever think that I would take a wife from pity! Hetty, can you not understand that I care very much for you?"

She appeared deaf to his final words. "Take a wife from pity!" she gasped. "You have told me yourself that you felt no love for Elizabeth! Yet, you offered *her* marriage!"

" 'Twas not at all the same thing, as you very well know," he retorted, resisting the urge to shake her. "Hetty"—he gentled his voice—"you must know how I feel. Indeed, it required a great deal of character to prevent me from declaring myself while you were at Thurston Hall! Stop being at cross-purposes with me, it serves no cause."

She regarded him coldly, in stony silence.

He continued softly, "You cannot make me believe that you do not care for me, Hetty. I have gotten to know you quite well, you know."

"Please, don't!" she cried, whirling away from him. "I do not wish to be reminded of . . . that!"

"Reminded of what, Hetty? Reminded of the fact that while you were in my care, you came to trust me? To desire me as I do you?"

Her face flushed scarlet, and he realized that a misguided sense of honour was holding her away from him. He saw that she was beginning to tremble. He would have preferred to get her away from this house, from her father this very moment. But he knew Hetty. She would very likely tell him to go to the devil if he became the least bit autocratic, even if it was for her own good. Yet, he hated to leave her to deal alone with her grief and shock. She had turned away from him, presenting a board-stiff back.

"Hetty," he said gently. She did not turn, so he continued addressing her back. "I do not want you to believe that I shall continue pressing you. I have told you how I feel, and I would that you think about my words. I will leave you now and if it would not disaccommodate you, I should like to return for dinner. Perhaps then we can more rationally discuss what we are to do."

"Very well," she said dully. He had the impression that she was not actually agreeing with him, merely acquiescing at the moment so that she could be alone.

"Until this evening, then, Hetty," he said. She did not again face him and since he could think of nothing else to say, he simply turned and strode from the drawing room.

Rabbell entered the library, his face set into deep lines of perturbation. "Your grace," he ventured.

The marquis pulled his attention from a sheaf of papers that, in all truth, he had been reading in a most cursory manner. "Yes, Rabbell?"

"It seems, your grace," his butler continued carefully, "that an odd person has arrived—knocked at the front door, he did—urgently demanding to see your grace. He informed me, your grace, that 'twas a matter of the gravest importance, concerning a Miss Rolland."

"What?" The marquis bounded to his feet. "Don't just stand there, man, show the fellow in!"

But a moment later, the marquis was facing a pale, out-of-breath Pottson. "What the devil, Pottson!" he ejaculated, striding forward.

"She's up and skuttled the pike, your grace!"

"She's what?"

"Loped off! Gone without a word, your grace! Millie's fit to be green with worry, begged me she did, to come to you, seeing as how you'd know what to do."

The marquis felt suddenly quite cold. Damn, but he was a fool for ever leaving her alone! He rallied and managed to address Pottson calmly. "Why does Millie believe that Miss Rolland has run away, Pottson? It has been but three hours since I left her." Even as he spoke, the marquis found himself gazing toward the windows. Night was falling fast.

"She told me, your grace, that Miss Hetty was acting odd-like, not saying a word, merely staring off when there was nothing to look at. Millie leaves her for only five minutes and when she comes back, Miss Hetty's gone. Nobody as even saw her leave, your grace."

"I see," the marquis replied, for want of anything better to say. "You have done rightly to come to me, Pottson," he said finally. As concisely and quickly as possible, the marquis placed Pottson in possession of the afternoon's events.

"Gawd!" Pottson said comprehensively, then whistled softly to himself. "Master Damien's own father!"

"Indeed, Pottson. Of course, I can rely on your discretion in this matter. Now, we must try to determine where she would have gone."

"Miss Hetty adored her brother, if your grace knows what I mean," Pottson said after but an instant, his words making perfect sense to him. The marquis, however, did not glean Pottson's meaning.

"What the devil does that have to do with the point?"

"Sussex, your grace. It is Sir Archibald's country home, Belshire Manor, I believe is the name, near to Atelsfield. 'Tis where Master Damien is buried."

"I have underestimated your good sense, Pottson. It seems likely to me that you are right." He continued more to himself than to Pottson. "We needn't worry about Sir Archibald, I don't think. If he misses her at all, he will merely believe that she accompanied me to Thurston Hall."

He clasped Pottson's hand and shook it. "Have no more worry. I will leave within the hour."

18

The marquis sat on the edge of a ditch and raised his voice to the heavens, his curses fluent and loud, despite the fact that he was quite alone. A curricle wheel was still spinning just beside his elbow, and his horses were stamping and whinnying in confusion and uncertainty. He pulled himself to his feet and soothed his horses as best he could, all the while searching out the scurrilous, half-hidden rock that had so arranged itself just beyond the turnpike entrance past Hatfield that it had ripped a curricle wheel cleanly from its axle and sent both the curricle and the marquis off into the ditch. He wondered humourlessly if the elements were conspiring to script a farcical play with him as the bumbling, ill-fated hero.

It did not help matters when the bay hack he was forced to hire in Hatfield proceeded to throw a shoe not many miles beyond where his broken curricle still lay at odd angles in the ditch. Leading his horse some five miles to the village of Davondale did nothing to improve his temper, and it was only after three mugs of strong local ale that he was finally able to review the day's events with a modicum of good humour. The marquis was slightly totty-headed when he finally made his way up the old winding staircase of the Greystone Inn to fall in between the none too clean sheets of a rather rickety, too-short bed. He found that he could not long nurture his sense of ill-use, for images of Hetty, perhaps courting the same types of minor disasters that had befallen him, made his stomach gnaw with worry. The shrill, off-key cuckoo chirped one o'clock in the morning before he was finally able to squelch his more dire imaginings and make peace with the lumpy bed.

The following morning, after an indigestible breakfast of watery porridge, he strode out of the inn and gazed grimly at both the slope-shouldered mare placed in his keeping and the grey sky. He had no doubt that before the day was out, he would be drenched to the skin. Damn, he thought irritably, if I catch a chill from this ridiculous escapade, I shall force Henrietta to wait upon me hand and foot!

It was not until midafternoon of the following day that the

marquis drew up his panting horse in front of a set of rusty iron gates just off the main road from Briardon and read the deeply etched sign, BELSHIRE MANOR. He was so certain that Hetty had reached her birthplace before him, for whatever else she was, she was unquestionably a girl of redoubtable ingenuity, that he began to picture their meeting. He could not believe that she would really be surprised to see him. Just let her try to turn me off again, he thought with autocratic determination, and I shall give her the raking down of her life!

He led his horse through the creaking iron gates and found himself facing a three-story pink brick structure, dating, he suspected, from the Stuarts, set amid a small park. The grounds, though not precisely neglected, showed only superficial signs of care. There was a general air of a long absentee master about the manor, and, he thought, of a less than sterling staff in attendance. He drew up his horse in front of deep-set flagstone steps and cast about for a stableboy. He quickly disabused himself of any such luxury, and tethered the mare to a bedraggled yew bush.

It was some minutes before his loud knock was answered by a gaunt-featured, bent old man wearing a shiny black suit with oddly pinned down lapels that reminded him forcibly of the garb his agent, Spiverson, habitually wore. Prim lips were drawn tightly into a line of suspicion as the old man looked him up and down. As if I were some sort of peddler, the marquis thought irritably, not realizing that in his dusty, travel-stained clothes, he could hardly fit anyone's idea of a peer of the realm.

"I have come to see your mistress," he said without preamble. "Tell Miss Henrietta that the Marquis of Oberlon requests her presence immediately."

Even though Dawley had rusticated for over twenty years, he still knew well the voice of Quality, and the line of suspicion became one of perturbation. Miss Henrietta! He did not believe that he could have overlooked her presence in the manor! But he doubted an instant, for his grace sounded so very positive.

"Begging your pardon, your grace," he said nervously, stepping aside for the marquis to enter, "but Miss Hetty has not been in residence for close to seven months now. It's in London she be, your grace, with Sir Archibald."

The marquis frowned. He did not doubt that the man was telling him the truth, yet it simply did not seem possible that he could have arrived here before Hetty. He grew suddenly cold. He, himself, had suffered several mishaps. He pulled himself from such unpleasant speculation and said, "It is likely that she will arrive shortly from London. I trust it will not disaccommodate you if I remain for the night."

Dawley thought that the marquis' presence would very much set Mrs. Dawley on her ear, but of course he did not relate this observation to his grace. He bowed low, silently praying that Mrs. Dawley had something beside the pig's cheek to serve the marquis for dinner.

The pig's cheek did not grace the marquis' table, but rather several slices of overly salted ham, unearthed from the larder by a frantic Mrs. Dawley. At least the port is passable, he thought in passing, as he stretched his feet toward the warm fire set in the parlour. He drummed his fingers together with rhythmic precision, trying to trace what would logically have been Hetty's movements from the moment she fled from London, but found himself almost immediately stymied, for he could not really be certain if she had traveled by horse, on a coach, as a female or as Lord Harry. He felt extraordinarily helpless, a state of mind he hardly relished.

He rose and absently kicked a crackling log with the toe of one dusty, mud-caked boot. Where the hell was she anyway? He had even delayed his journey until the morning, thus giving her many hours to reach her destination before him. At the moment, he seemed to have very little choice but to remain at Belshire Manor until noon on the morrow. If Hetty did not arrive by then . . . well, either she had been delayed, or had never intended to come here in the first place. He thought of Jack and Louisa and their home in Herefordshire. Perhaps the very fact that they were in Paris would induce Hetty there, for she could be alone.

But he did not find Hetty at Sir John's home in Herefordshire, and it was an extraordinarily weary and worried man who reined in yet another hired hack at the front steps of Thurston Hall, six days after his frenetic search had begun. There had been no main road or village that he had passed without inquiry, and, now, he admitted, he simply had no more ideas. He had not the energy to continue back to his townhouse in London. Deep within him, he knew in any case that there would be no news of Hetty awaiting him were he to return.

He mounted the steps, and without bothering to sound the knocker, pushed open the great front doors. As the afternoon was grey and overcast, the entrance hall seemed chill and dim, both the weather and his home reflecting, he thought with a depressed grunt, his own gloomy state of mind.

It was with sudden tight-lipped anger that he greeted the obviously tipsy Croft, who was weaving his way toward him, consternation paling his flushed face at the unexpected sight of his master.

"Your grace!"

"Damn you, Croft, get belowstairs immediately! I do not wish to see that bulbous nose of yours again until you've sobered up from drinking my port! I should sack you right now, 'tis no more than you deserve!"

"But your grace—" Croft tried to lower his voice to a more dignified pitch, but the marquis interrupted him brusquely.

"Out of my sight, Croft, I've no patience left for you!" He turned on his heel and headed for the quiet of the library. "Send a footman with sherry," he ordered over his shoulder.

He did not see Croft wave his hand jerkily at his back. He flung open the library door, kicked it closed with the heel of his boot and strode directly to the fireplace. It did not occur to him to wonder why such a brightly blazing fire was burning in the grate, and he splayed his hands toward the warmth.

" 'Tis about time you have returned home, Jason! After five days, I must tell you that the servants had seriously begun to doubt my word!"

He spun about so quickly that he had to grab the edge of the mantelpiece to retain his balance. For a long moment, he stared at Hetty, not one word taking form in his mind.

She stood quietly, her hands resting on the back of a chair. She was dressed in a modish yellow jonquil gown, her blonde curls tied charmingly with a yellow velvet ribbon. A small smile played about her lips.

"Hetty!" he exclaimed uncertainly, taking a jerky step toward her.

"Of course, it is I, Jason," she said demurely. "You have sorely used me, your grace. I was believing myself a cast-off woman."

"God, Hetty, I've been frantic with worry!"

The huskiness in his voice sent a delicious quiver down her back. She took a hesitating step forward, her arms open. He covered the distance between them in three long strides and pulled her roughly to his chest, burying his face in her hair. He tightened his hold about her back, as if fearful that she would slip away from him.

"I am truly sorry, Jason," she whispered, raising her head

from his shoulder to gaze into his dark eyes. "Pottson told me where you had gone. Lord Harry thought for a while to set out after you, but I decided it ridiculous for both of us to be riding the roads of England. Please forgive me for being so foolish."

He thought fleetingly to inquire just how the devil she had spoken to Pottson, but his nearness to her lips was disconcerting.

"Do you forgive me, Jason?" she asked, at the same time lifting her chin and pursing her lips for her first kiss.

As his mouth closed over hers, feather light, he felt her hands tighten on his shoulders and her breathing quicken. It was some moments before he drew back and gazed deep into her eyes. There was a dark, dreamy quality in their depths that he had never before seen. Tenderly, he kissed the tip of her nose, her chin, the soft curls at her temples. The weariness and concern that he had worn like a heavy mantle slipped from him, and he gave a shout of pure joy.

He hugged her again tightly to his chest. She lifted her face and said in a husky voice, "I had no idea that one could feel so very . . . urgent."

" 'Tis a feeling I would give you often," he murmured, kissing her ear.

Hetty looked at him, suddenly sober, and before her mind could censor her unruly tongue, she blurted out, "Jason, you must not needs marry me. I could not bear to think that I had . . . trapped you like Elizabeth."

"If you ever again compare yourself to Elizabeth, I shall throttle you," he said harshly, giving her a slight shake.

"But what of Caroline Langley?"

"Caroline *who?*"

All her doubts resolved, Hetty smiled happily. For the first time, she noticed the tired lines about his eyes and his travel-stained clothes. "Think no more of Caroline, Jason. You must be woefully hungry and in want of a hot bath. Shall I ring for Croft?"

The marquis snorted. "That damned butler of mine! He knows he's a time-honoured fixture, damn his eyes! I came quite close to kicking him out of the house on his bulbous nose just now!"

Hetty gave a trill of laughter and kissed him lightly on the cheek. "Actually, when dear Croft wasn't foxed, he treated me in the most suspicious manner! I swear he thinks me one of your mistresses!"

228

"Curse his impertinence! I shall quickly disabuse him of such a notion."

"But when I arrived at Thurston Hall five days ago," Hetty interposed with an impish smile, "after a short, quite uneventful journey of my own, it was Croft's weighty opinion that secured my entrance!"

"That reminds me, Hetty, when did you see Pottson? He came to me, you know, panting that you had 'skuttled the pike,' I believe were his exact words. It was he actually, who sent me to Belshire Manor."

"I—I fear that I did not behave wisely," Hetty whispered, turning her face into his shoulder. "I was so confused and upset, and I kept thinking that you had only offered for me out of pity. In truth, I packed my portmanteau and secured a stage ticket to Sussex. 'Twas early the next day that I realized there was nothing for me at Belshire Manor. I could not bring myself to return to Sir Archibald's house, so I paid a final visit to Lord Harry's lodgings and sent Pottson with a note to my father explaining that I had accepted an invitation from Lady Alicia to again visit Thurston Hall. Pottson thought it a rather neat idea, though he could not stop bemoaning the fact that it was he who had sent you to the far reaches of England."

"I looked for you in Herefordshire, too," the marquis said. "There is much you have to make up to me for, my dear."

"Perhaps I shall find a suitable way, your grace."

"Without any assistance from Lord Harry? As much as I like the boy, I cannot but hope that he has fulfilled all his obligations."

"Yes, I suppose so," she said. He heard reluctance in her voice and kept his eyes fastened upon her face.

She smiled ruefully. "It is just that Lord Harry was so very free! Ladies are not allowed to shoot at Manton's, you know. And as to visiting Lady Buxtell's most interesting establishment, I fear that Henrietta Rolland—"

"Henrietta Cavander."

"Yes, most certainly Henrietta Cavander—she, in any case, would hardly be welcome there!"

"Very true, my love, but one must make sacrifices. I, myself, must give up the voluptuous Melissande!"

"I had forgotten about *her*. Still, I would prefer that you did, Jason, that is if you do not mind overly much."

"Silly goose. Poor Melissande, she is losing both Lord Cavander and Lord Harry."

Hetty giggled. "Lord Harry did not care for her above half, let me tell you!"

He said blandly, "Of course, Lord Harry was unable to partake of her most winning charms."

"Odious man!"

He closed her mouth with a light kiss, then drew back and said soberly, "I do not wish that you ever feel anything but free, Hetty. I will tell you what: there is no reason I can think of why we could not set up our own version of Manton's, here at Thurston Hall. You have been bragging much about your prowess with pistols, my girl, but you have yet to test your skill against a master's!"

"Master!" she scoffed. "We shall see, your grace. As for foils, well, I think that I would much rather dispatch that sport with Lord Harry back to Scotland!"

"Agreed! Now, little one, I must leave you for a time and try to scrub off the dirt of our English roads. Then I wish to secure your agreement upon a wedding date, before you have time to fob me off with more nonsensical excuses."

"It must be a monstrous large wedding! A spectacle as befits your esteemed station."

"Of a certainty. I wish all the *ton* to see my beautiful bride—without any spectacles or pea green caps."

Her eyes dropped suddenly from his face.

"Does Lord Harry still admire the arrangement of my cravat?" he asked, teasing, yet alert to the change in her mood.

Hetty drew a deep breath, willing the words to come from her mouth. "What of Sir Archibald, Jason? I know what you must think of his actions. Yet, he is still my father. I would that he be present, as is proper."

"You are right, of course, Hetty," the marquis replied calmly. "That you can, in a way, forgive him, is most admirable."

"You are wrong. I will never forgive him, yet there is nothing I can do to change him or alter the past. He is as he is, Jason. But there is Jack," she continued with her next thought. "I would that we not tell Jack what he did." She felt tears stinging at her eyes, and resolutely gulped them away.

"Would it serve any purpose?"

"Nay, Jason, 'twould serve no purpose at all. It would come as a great shock to him, and he could not understand what I have learned to accept."

There came a light scratch on the library door. "Damn," the marquis muttered under his breath. Reluctantly he drew away from Hetty.

230

"Your grace! Miss Rolland!" Croft stood in the doorway, his bulbous nose like a red beacon in the candlelight, a tray balancing a bottle of champagne and glasses held firmly in his hands.

"Why you incorrigible jackanapes!" the marquis ejaculated.

Hetty held his arm and said in a laughing voice, "How very thoughtful of you, Croft! Do you not think, your grace, that it would be most proper for us to have a toast—among the *three* of us?"

Croft beamed at Hetty, choosing to ignore the dour cast to his master's countenance.

" 'Tis a wonderful event!" he proclaimed pompously and hastened to pour the bubbling contents into the glasses.

"To the Marquis and Marchionness of Oberlon!" Croft said grandly, and without further ado, emptied the glass in one long drink.

"Thank you for your thoughtfulness, Croft," the marquis said ironically. He sipped at his own champagne, then said, "Take the bottle with my compliments, and get out! If I require your presence, allow me to take the initiative and ring the bell!"

Unruffled, Croft bowed low, hastily picked up the tray, and weaved his way happily out of the library.

"He is an original, that you must admit!" Hetty gurgled, holding her sides.

"Well, if you will contrive to control your mirth, my love, I would propose a toast to another original!"

Solemnly, he clicked his glass to hers.

"To Lord Harry!"